Element Princess

Element Princess

Book One: The Commence

Jenaia Williams

Copyright © 2013 by Jenaia Williams.

Library of Congress Control Number:		2013910480
ISBN:	Hardcover	978-1-4836-5272-6
	Softcover	978-1-4836-5271-9
	Ebook	978-1-4836-5273-3

All rights reserved. No part of this book may be reproduced or transmitted in any form or by any means, electronic or mechanical, including photocopying, recording, or by any information storage and retrieval system, without permission in writing from the copyright owner.

This is a work of fiction. Names, characters, places and incidents either are the product of the author's imagination or are used fictitiously, and any resemblance to any actual persons, living or dead, events, or locales is entirely coincidental.

This book was printed in the United States of America.

Rev. date: 08/20/2013

To order additional copies of this book, contact:
Xlibris LLC
1-888-795-4274
www.Xlibris.com
Orders@Xlibris.com
128886

Contents

Introduction 9
Glossary 11

Story 1: We are a Fierce Flame and Mounting Water 13
Story 2: The Flame has a Heart 31
Story 3: You and me together 56
Story 4: Green ambition 79
Story 5: Talent comes in many sizes 98
Story 6: I'm simply brightening your night 118
Story 7: Found Elements 135
Story 8: Darkness always has a past 151
Story 9: The Chilling training 170
Story 10: Such a windy situation 190
Story 11: The howls of friendship 208
Story 12: Ties never die 228
Story 13: What I knew then and what I know now 250
Story 14: Should have known better 271
Story 15: The Flame of equation 288

Appreciations

First, I would love to thank my friend, Joshua Martin, for being with me through this lengthy journey since day one.

To my illustrator, Jet Kimchrea, for being totally awesome!

To my mother and grandmother for all of their love.

To Heather Ricket, for staying up until two in the morning helping me edit.

To Apiffany White, for helping with more editing (you'll get your white-haired beauty soon!)

To Meghan (Koko) Jones, for the little FB surprise you gave me. Love you!

And most importantly, for my followers, who continued to hear my rants about a book they expected not to read ... until now.

Introduction

In the heart of a leisurely town, Sazuma Kagami and her twin sister, Mary, enter a journey of action, adventure, and paths along the way. The spirit being, Kenta Shiroyama, searches for beings called Element Princesses. Element princesses are human girls who were given godly abilities. The seven princesses possess the seven elements; fire, water, earth, wind, ice, light, and darkness.

Kenta searches along with his close friend, Ayano Matsumoto, who was the first princess found. Ayano is the princess of darkness and death. Kenta's job is to find the princesses to stop the underworld group called the Demon Docks.

The objective of Demon Docks is to control and enslave all the species within the world, claim the earth as his own and rise up his demonic comrades from the depths of hell. The Demon Docks are a group of demons who take over one-third of the underworld. The remaining space is controlled by the Vampire Demon Lord Kouta Vulturine and The High Lords Lucifer and Hades.

The Dock's consist of demon bats, ogres, dragons, and even foot soldiers; sons and daughters of powerful demons like Lucifer and Hades. The Dock's are led by the High Lord Derek Southbound. He also has princesses of his own, but he also has princes. There are five princesses who control the feelings of emotion, time travel, shape shifter, body possessor and the power of explosion. One prince can cancel other supernatural abilities while the other is completely powerless. These groups of seven powerful demons are known as Demonic Princesses/Princes.

Along with their friends; Stella, Hiroko, Reiko, and Yumiko, Sazuma and Mary will come to face their enemies, their powers, unknown enemies and allies, and even each other. Join them as our heroes undergo mysterious encounters, new found powers, and even possible interests.

But, building this star team and welcoming the changes within themselves is far more difficult than the princesses realize.

Glossary

Adriane Ward—The third seat in the Vampire Demon clan
Aiko Tanaka—The second seat in the Vampire Demon clan
Akira Suzuki—Wolf Demon
Aurora Weatherly—Spirit Being
Ayano Matsumoto—Darkness and Death Princess
Bonnie Evergreen—The fourth seat in the Vampire Demon clan
Casella Southbound—Nicknamed 'the Dark Panther'. Is Derek's older half-sister
Chikara Yamada—One of the Demonic Princesses, has the ability to sense the emotions of her opponent, Daisuke The Element Angel of Healing
Damon Sasaki—Spirit Being, nicknamed 'The Silver Haired Menace'
David Takahashi—A male sorcerer in the Demon Docks army
Demon Docks—An underworld organization ran by Derek Southbound. This organization resides on Kyushu Island and contains millions of members
Demonic Princes—Men who possess a special ability and have a high rank in Derek's army
Demonic Princesses—Women that possess a special ability and have a high rank in Derek's army
Derek Southbound—Leader of the Demon Docks. Married to Diamond
Destiny—The middle child of the Three Death Daughters and is a Demonic Princess. She has the ability to possess the bodies of her victims
Diamond—The youngest of the Three Death Daughters and is a Demonic Princess. She has the ability to focus on a certain object/objects and explode them with a thought or physical motion. Married to Derek
Element Angels—Angels of the Heavens that specialize in one of the seven elements the princesses wield
Element Princesses—Girls/women who possess Godly abilities and can control one of the seven elements: fire, water, earth, wind, ice, light or darkness
Emiko Yamada—Demonic Princess, has the ability to control time and space
Eric Takahashi—A male sorcerer in the Demon Docks army

Hades—Demon Lord
Haley—Kenta's first crush
Haru—The Element Angel of Fire
Hiroko Faraway—A past princess that died in battle
Hiroko Kotani—Wind Princess
Jared—One of Yumiko's older brothers
Jeremy—Another one of Yumiko's older brothers
Jezebel—The Element Angel of Wind
Joseph Booming—Hiroko's stepfather
Jun—One of the Past Angels, is a member of the Demon Docks army
Kaito—One of the Past Angels, is a member of the Demon Docks army
Kenta Shiroyama—Spirit Being that brought the Element Princesses together
Kotare—Hiroko's mother
Kouta Vulturine—The Vampire Demon Lord
Lavida—The eldest of the Three Death Daughters and is a Demonic Princess. Has the ability to shape shift into any animal and control animals as well
Linda Kagami—Sazuma and Mary's mother
Lucifer—Father of the Three Death Daughters
Mary Kagami—Water Princess
Mayu—The Demon Queen, married to Lucifer and is a member of the Demon Docks army
Nao Nakamura—Demonic Prince, has no supernatural abilities. Nicknamed 'The Powerless Demon'
Past Angels—Angels of Heaven who went to the dark side: Either they made a deal with Hades and/or Lucifer or mass amounts of demon blood mixed in their system
Reiko Takashima—Ice Princess
Ryosuke Devider—The Gate Keeper of Hell
Riku Nakamura—Demonic Prince, has the ability to cancel out other supernatural powers. Is nicknamed 'The Canceller'
Saki—The Mother Angel of Heaven, deals with the supernatural world as a whole
Sazuma Kagami—Fire Princess
Spirit Beings—Warriors of the Heavens who carry out missions for the Mother Angel
Stella Jayberry—Earth Princess
Tammy Matsumoto—Ayano's caretaker before Kenta's appearance
Three Death Daughters—The daughters of Lucifer: Lavida, Destiny and Diamond
Yumiko Honozoro—Light Princess

Story 1

We are a *Fierce* Flame and *Mounting* Water

In the late afternoon, as the sun collided with the horizon, the mansion on Kyushu Island darkened measurably, now hiding with the increasing shadows. Its black walls were merging with the darkness of the approaching night.

Derek Southbound smiled as he looked outside of his enlarged throne room window. Its mahogany frame mixed in with the outside light, hiding it from view. Derek loved this part of the day. Dusk, is what humans called it. The sun would set and hide the features of his throne room. Its beige walls would dim as the sun faded. The stone stairs that circled his throne would become shining silver to a dull gray. The paintings hanging on his wall with straight gold frame would combine with the shadows, hiding its beauty from view.

Even if everything hid, Derek still loved dusk.

Standing in front of him were his servants of the castle. Well, some of them, at least. Three women wearing short black-and-white Victorian dresses stood shoulder to shoulder at the bottom of Derek's throne stairs. Their hands locked behind their backs. Their blonde, red, and brunette hair hung high in ponytails. Their eyes faced the setting sun.

"What a beautiful night there will be." Derek spoke longingly, as if dusk didn't happen every day. The maids agreed. Of course they did. They agreed with everything he said. If Derek told them to battle to the death for a pencil, they would do it and die happily, too. Loyal, yes. Annoying at times, definitely.

"We should have some fun tonight." Derek stood to his feet. His black leather boots clicked as he made his way down his stairs and approached the blonde. Her body was already shaking, urging him to touch her in any way. The redhead and brunette watched in envy.

Derek elegantly grabbed the blonde's hand and brought his lips to her wrist, where her vein throbbed ideally. She was motionless. Her cheeks burned red and her eyes stared lovingly. This was too easy. Then again, he wasn't complaining. Derek moved his soft lips from her wrist, up her exposed arm, lingered between the juncture of her shoulder and her neck then pressed his lips on her neck artery. He could pretty much feel the thing pumping blood as he licked there, unable to hold himself any longer. "There, there," he cooed. The blonde shivered as his warm breath tingled her nerves. "That's a good girl." He licked the maid's neck again but this time, he sunk his venomous fangs deep, drawing as much blood as he could capture.

She gasped at first but then let her leader continue to suck her blood. Derek took his sweet time, gently taking the woman's blood and fusing it with his own. Her blood tasted of tangy citrus. He gulped more, taking more than he needed, but leaving enough so she would live. Personally, Derek preferred sweet and cherry blood, like the blood of his most valued Demonic Princess. But, this woman would have to do.

Again, he wasn't complaining.

After less than a minute, he pulled away and wiped his mouth, spreading a thin crimson line across his silk black sleeve. He would have used his tongue to pick up the excess blood, but this wasn't a flavor he wanted more of. This bite was just a snack. The real meal would come shortly. He grinned at the thought of devouring the cherry blood he craved. He closed his eyes in ecstasy for brief moments, then opened his eyes and faced the girls.

"You three may leave." The maid's bowed, then scurried out of the room. As Derek walked back to his throne, he looked over by the large window that revealed the seashore outside. Its usual crystal waters now shined lavender and navy blue. The evening approached furthermore. Sitting on the platform by the window was none other than his most important puzzle piece. The carrier of the blood he desired.

Derek licked his lips and turned around, preparing to sit in his gold throne, but he didn't sit. He merely watched the woman-*his woman*-stare out the window, showing him no mind. "You seem curious about our next move. Are you wondering what's up ahead?"

Diamond didn't say a word. She wasn't much of a talker. A mysterious aura always hovered over her, but that's what Derek liked the most. It wasn't just her blood that he liked, it was everything else. Her hair was always straight, no split ends. Her curvy body swayed as she walked. Her clothes were mostly black, skin tight (her choice of clothing, by the way) and she was so independent. Usually, independence was an insult to Derek. It showed that the demon didn't want anything to do with him. But when it came to women, Derek loved the strong, tall, skinny, and lovely type. Diamond was that woman indeed.

Derek casually sat in his throne. One black-jeaned leg swung over the other. One hand rested in a fist under his chin while the other draped over the armrest. His eyes zoomed in on Diamond's black T-shirt covered back. Knowing his eyes were on her, Diamond peered over her shoulder.

Derek patted his thigh. "Don't you want to sit on Daddy's lap?"

As an answer, Diamond turned back to the window, ignoring him completely. It was so hot when she ignored him. But seriously, he wanted her blood. No jokes about that. Her blood was addicting and he would do anything to have it. He would pin her down and bite any place where her skin was exposed. Having her was essential.

"Come now Diamond. Why are you being so mean?" He asked in a pout. If he was resulting to role play, then he sure as hell needed some blood. A demonic High Lord didn't beg. She should have been lucky she meant more to him than anything. Well, maybe her blood was more important, but it was still a part of her.

"Why can't we make a move yet?" she asked. Her lusty voice swayed into his ear.

Derek groaned, as if she had whispered seductively into his ear. "We will make our move in time. By claiming this island, we have done more than enough to build our army and wait for the Heavenly Beings to move out. Now, all we do is wait." All hint of need exited his body. Derek was now in leader mode, informing his queen of the plan.

Diamond stood with a sigh. She didn't even straighten her black miniskirt that now exposed the bottoms of her black lacy panties. "We always wait," she grumbled as she exited the room, leaving one of the wooden entrance doors open. Now left alone, Derek looked out of the window. The sun disappeared into the horizon. Derek was enveloped in darkness, darkness he liked at times. Dusk was over and he had missed it dealing with the blonde and trying to get Diamond's blood. Oh well, it would come tomorrow, he supposed. But that would have to wait till tomorrow. Right now, Derek stood and exited his dimmed room. He had a neck to suck.

Twenty years later

"Rise and shine!" Mary Kagami said as she threw the window shades open in her and her sister's room; letting in the bright sunlight of the upcoming morning. Sazuma Kagami, the sluggish and indolent twin, squinted one of her black eyes open, then covered her body with her chestnut sheets.

Mary grinned. Sazuma did that every morning. It wouldn't help her in the past and it wouldn't help her today. "Come on now. It's time for school. Get up."

"I don't want to." Sazuma mumbled. She curled herself into a little ball. A small snore escaped Sazuma not even a minute later.

Mary's eye twitched. A sigh of annoyance escaped her. Day after day of being nice and waking her up with a smile, Mary had had enough. "Didn't I tell you to get your ass out of this bed! I don't care if you're tired from doing homework all night. You're getting up and that's final!" The younger Kagami twin grabbed the sheets and threw them off of the bed.

Sazuma's shocked expression was exposed. Her body was flinching. "Yes, ma'am," she answered in shock. Mary had gone so far as to cuss several times during the year. Mary wasn't a curser and she never resorted to violence. But every time Mary had come to cussing, Sazuma would scoot back to her little corner and whimper. Mary was daunting when she was pissed.

"Good. Breakfast is downstairs." Mary skipped out of the room.

Sazuma murmured, "And, I thought I was the bad one in the family." Compared to Mary, Sazuma *was* the bad one. She was the loner, the rebel, the mole who loved to sit around with the window shades closed on a sunny day, but, most importantly, she was the misunderstood. She had her past to thank for that.

But, flashbacks of the past would have to be thrown away right now. Sazuma had a boring Monday to have.

About thirty minutes later, Sazuma and Mary ate breakfast, were dressed and headed to school. Their school, Lane Way High School, was the main high school in this tedious town. It stood five stories tall with a campus of three football fields. There were many clubs to be a part of, but the twins weren't interested in participating.

At least Sazuma wasn't. She hated team spirit and why would she sign up to hang around people she already didn't like? Mary though, why she hadn't signed up, Sazuma didn't know.

Everyone loved Mary. She was kind, caring, helpful, smart, dependable, blah blah blah. Most people couldn't believe that they were related, much less twins. Still, Mary would succeed in any club she signed up for. It must have been one of those, "I want to protect my sister as much as possible," kinds of things. Because of Sazuma's past, Mary had been on the offensive of people and their actions toward her. She'd been like that for three years.

To Sazuma, she couldn't have asked for a better sister.

They walked to school with the nice placid breeze. Summer was ending but the sun still shined, now rising and bright. Not even a single cloud maneuvered in the sky. Sazuma observed the area. On the outskirts of the town, the oak trees stood tall but their green and brown leaves fell one after the other, slowly hiding the green grass. In the distance, the small brick buildings stood with the town's citizens looking through the large display windows. As you headed further in, roads parted, leading to schools, stores, malls and other places.

Sazuma liked where she lived, but this town, Kayta Plains, was just so boring. It would have been different if there was something to do, but nope.

What? Were stores supposed to fill her exploring desires? Sazuma was an adventurer. She wanted somewhere new to travel. She wanted something valuable to search for. Heck, it would have been nice if someone out of this world popped into her life. Was that too much to ask?

Sazuma sighed again. Lately, that was the only thing she'd been doing. "Sazuma? What's wrong?" Mary, who usually walked several steps in front of her, now stood on her left side; further from the road that currently had no cars. There weren't many early birds in this town.

"I can't stand this weather," she answered her sister groggily. The steamy shower this morning didn't wake her like it usually did. Oh well. Maybe the cheerful voices of her friends would wake her up. "All of this sunshine and fresh wind and all this—"

"You're such a bummer." Mary smiled. Mary was always smiling. What the hell was there to smile about? Sazuma never understood. Then again, she probably wouldn't smile even if she did understand.

"Good morning!" Hiroko shouted happily as she ran up to her friends from behind.

Hiroko Kotani. Blonde hair. Blue eyes. Now she was the *real* happy girl. The girl had the life. Big house, uncaring parents, no curfew, and the most upbeat personality. They weren't friends on day one, but they'd grown to appreciate each other.

"Hey." The Kagami twins acknowledged the blonde and continued on. Hiroko lived in one of the rich communities of the town, which was about a five-minute walk from the Kagami house. But Hiroko slept late all day, every day, so it wasn't a surprise she caught up to them, now of all times.

The conversation to school was the same as always; Hiroko having dreams of flying. If you asked her which superpower she wanted, she would say, "I wish to fly." Her favorite super hero was *Iron Man*. Not only because he had cool gadgets, but because . . . he could fly. Recently though, Hiroko had claimed to have dreams of flying more vividly and she would wake up feeling winded. Her hair would be in a mass mess instead of in a neat ponytail when she woke up. Sazuma called it a fun dream, causing the massive bed head, but whatever.

Spoiling Hiroko's hope entered you into a world of hateful stares and constant silent treatments. So instead of ruining her mood, Sazuma listened in on Hiroko's dream. Mary listened with curiosity, of course.

They entered the iron school gates minutes later, then ran into class; having five minutes to spare. Students filled the hallways with echoes of chatter and body heat. Why they couldn't just go in the classrooms and clear the halls, Sazuma didn't know.

As they entered their class, Classroom 3R7 (third floor, seventh room), one of their other friends welcomed them inside. "Late as always."

Stella Jayberry, a shy redhead with the smarts and wisdom of an adult. Stella had skipped tenth grade and entered the junior class at age fifteen. She was nothing like the usual rowdy, reckless, and stubborn children of high school. Sazuma and several others became her friends instantly.

They entered the classroom. "Late, but we're still here," Sazuma yawned.

"How are you?" Mary asked. It was her usual morning question. It was either, "How are you", "How did you sleep," or, "Anything interesting happen last night". Mary meant well, but she needed to stop caring for others. It was a nice trait to have, but kindness could easily be used against you. Sazuma had learned that lesson the hard way.

"I'm better than I was yesterday," Stella answered. "The rainy weather was depressing me but I'm all right now." Stella was never a fan of rain. She was a reasonably charming and joyful girl. It was no wonder she didn't like it.

"Good," Mary said, taking her seat behind Stella, who sat in the front seat on the second row closest to the three white framed windows on her left side. "Hey, how about this," Hiroko said, "How about a party at my house this Saturday. We can spend the day together then sleepover at night. That's a total party!"

She considered that a party? "We can't party every weekend, Hiroko." Sazuma slouched in her desk chair by Mary. She sat directly in front of window number one. There were no blinds to hide the sun from her vision, but she had a nice view of the town business buildings in the distance.

Hiroko stuck her tongue out. The girl always wanted to *party*. Just the previous Saturday, they had spent the night at Hiroko's house, playing video games, eating any food they could find, telling ghost stories, playing Ouija board—by the way, the girl might have a demon in her house—and staying up till six in the morning talking. Sazuma couldn't do that again. Never again.

Minutes later, the teacher walked into the room, clapping her hands as if they were elementary students. No one paid her any mind until she told them to settle down. Only the obedient students listened. Others simply continued. Sazuma sighed of irritability. This was how class started. This was Monday.

As time continued to go by, in the distance of Lane Way High, two beings of the supernatural world stood on the rooftop of a skyscraper and kept their eyes on the high school that their target was located in.

Shoulder length black hair flowed in the summer wind, which was oddly chilled for summer air. The spiritual being, Kenta Shiroyama, bent down and stared in the distance. His hands hung over his dark jeans. His burgundy shirt flowed, matching the rhythm of his hair. His mind blanked out. All he could do, all he wanted to do, was watch the school.

His ally, Ayano Matsumoto, stood behind him. Her knees, hidden behind long boots that reached just above those said knees, graced upon his back. The two didn't mind the touch. Her long hair, a mix between black and silver, matched the rhythm of Kenta's hair and clothes. Her gray shirt was too tight on her slender body to even join the dance. Her golden staff was in hand, resting close by her side. Her gray tattered cloak hung behind her shoulders, its hood hanging just below the back of her head.

Ayano focused on Kenta. Kenta focused on the school. Ayano looked up, landing her eyes on the school, as well. Her vision zoomed in, catching a glimpse of their target. Even in this distance, in this high place, she would see vividly. It was all thanks to her powers, she knew.

Their target, Sazuma Kagami, yawned in a slapdash fashion. She didn't have a care in the world. She was leaning her head in her awaiting hand and nodding off repeatedly. Ayano wasn't surprised. She had expected at least one of her fellow comrades to be carefree and lifeless. "That must be her."

"Yeah," Kenta breathed with no emotion in his tone. He wasn't excited. He wasn't shocked. Ayano would have thought her friend would have rejoiced. After so long of searching, they had finally found their target. He should have been a little more joyful.

Kenta shifted. His hand went from his knee to his pants pocket. He pulled out a sky blue sheet of paper. Ayano had seen that paper one too many times. She shifted to Kenta's right side and bent down, looking at the paper once again. Golden cursive was written on the sky blue document. Seven names were written on the list. One name was crossed off with a thick black line.

It was her name.

Beside the cursive names were descriptions of the people on the list. Beside Sazuma's name, lay *'Black hair, Black eyes, a heart of warning.'* Ayano detested these Heavenly beings with riddles at every turn. They could have just put a picture down with the name, but nooo, they had to make things utterly difficult. Still, this was the list the Mother Angel of Heaven had given them. Ayano only hoped this was the right person. There were people with the same name all over the world. It was hard enough finding one Sazuma Kagami. Finding over fifty people instead of the one they wanted . . . so many headaches.

"That's Sazuma Kagami. Her sister Mary might be in there too." Kenta's tone spiked up cheerfully. Now he was excited.

To Ayano's surprise, the second name on the list, Mary Kagami, Sazuma's younger twin, had gotten Kenta's interest. Beside her name, the description said, *'Black hair, Black eyes, a heart of love'*. Sazuma and Mary had the same face, literally. Why was she so important to him? He never met her, yet he always got excited when mentioning her. Had the Mother Angel said something to him that Ayano didn't know about?

"We can kill two birds with one stone," she said, ignoring Kenta's rise of glee.

"Let's not be hasty Ayano." Yeah, he was one to talk. "There could be a lot of Sazuma Kagami's here. We have to test her abilities and make sure we *do* have the right girl."

"Fine." Ayano turned her head. She would never grow old of Kenta's companionship or his orders. But when it came to these girls, she realized that following her orders might have been a little difficult.

Kenta stood, standing a full six-foot. Standing at five-foot-eleven, Ayano looked up at him, only a little bit. Their eyes, both burgundies, locked on. They nodded, dashing their separate ways; receiving an automatic message both of them understood.

At noon, lunch time, Sazuma, Mary, Stella, and Hiroko headed to the roof to eat. The roof was flat with smooth concrete and large iron bars with spikes on the tops. Eating up here was so much better than sharing a lunch room or eating in the classroom. Both places were filled with chatter the girls didn't want to hear. No one ever came up here, and the girls made sure no one followed them so they would follow their eating style.

Mentally, she thanked Stella once in a while. This was the fifteen-year olds idea after all.

Sazuma opened her white umbrella to hide herself from the sun she so much hated.

Meanwhile, Kenta stood on the top of a building right beside the school. Thanks to the stone platform that surrounded the building's top, he was able to hide from the girls he watched. "Stalked," Ayano would say at times like this. Kenta had stalked a lot of girls in search for his Element Princesses, people he would need in the future. He didn't mean to stalk them, and Kenta hadn't noticed until Ayano mentioned it, but this was necessary. He only hoped this wasn't a mistake like the times in the past.

Those girls he encountered didn't have to die.

It was his fault. His mistake. But as he watched these girls, he knew this was right. He knew this was Sazuma and Mary Kagami. Still, Kenta had doubts. Who could blame him? When lives were on the line, it was normal to have doubts.

Getting back on track, Kenta returned from his thoughts. His eyes moved around the group on the red and white checkerboard picnic sheet. There was a blonde with her long hair hung in a high ponytail. She was fair skinned with a gleaming smile. There was a redhead who stared at her blonde friend. Her focus was completely on her. To the redhead's left, there was Mary. Black hair, eyes a dazzling onyx and her focus was on her friend too.

Kenta didn't know why, but after seeing Mary's name on the paper, the urge to find her became strong. He wanted to find her, know her, befriend her ... he simply wanted to know everything about her. Where these feelings came from, Kenta didn't know. He suspected that finding Sazuma would find Mary, and these feelings were a spell Saki had placed on him. Whatever it was, he hoped it would dissipate. Feeling for a princess, or anyone, actually, was dangerous and could drastically affect both sides in the worst ways.

Nevertheless, why Mary? Why not Sazuma? She was the first name on the list. Shouldn't there be feelings for her as well? Maybe their fate was to meet, but not to fill Kenta needs. Could Mary do it? What if she didn't like him?

Why was he thinking about this now?

Back to focus, again, Kenta zoomed back on the teenage group. Beside Mary was her sister, of course, but she held a white umbrella. White reflected sunrays. Sazuma must have hated the sun. Smart idea, but did she really bring an umbrella to school every day for this reason?

"What's up with those names?" Ayano wondered, not really asking anyone in particular. "I never understood that. Why would a mother give her twin daughters a Japanese and English name?"

She was concerned about this now? This must have been a distraction, not wanting to start this mission. "Maybe their mother thought it would be interesting."

Ayano sighed, but Kenta knew she rolled her eyes as well. "Focus."

He licked his lips as he watched the girls and even leaned in to receive a clearer vision of them. "Let's test your abilities." Kenta said to himself. Thanks to the Mother Angel, Kenta gained several abilities to help determine if the girls were truly the princesses or not. Too bad Kenta had realized this after taking out their past mistakes.

He raised the palm of his hand to the sun and focused his attention onto Sazuma's sandwich. The girl hadn't even taken a bite. She was too busy shielding herself from the sun. Steadily, Kenta's ability awakened, manipulating the sun's light and darting it to her lunch. As the beam of sunlight zoomed, her sandwich started to heat up. Now, the test would begin.

Hiroko paused from eating her yogurt and she watched as Sazuma's sandwich started melting. It was kind of hard to notice bread, tomato slices, lettuce, and cheese melting together in a combination made for one to puke.

"What's wrong Hiroko?" Stella asked. She looked over and saw Sazuma's sandwich. The sandwich owner looked down. *Now*, she noticed. The moment Sazuma's eyes touched the lunch, it burst into flames. The girls jumped up in a panic. Stella ran around looking for a fire extinguisher—she was obviously the safety nut—while the other girls backed away.

"Sazuma!" Mary panicked.

"I didn't do anything. I don't know how it caught on fire!" said girl answered in the same tone. Kenta smiled. This was indeed Sazuma Kagami. Now it was time to test Mary's "abilities". Using his other ability of telekinesis, Kenta focused on the opened water bottle abandoned on the picnic sheet. His index finger swung to the left, tipping the bottle to the ground. The crystal water splashed and spread, but stopped on Kenta's command. Without the others noticing, Kenta brought the water midair and at eyelevel with Mary.

She jumped, threw her hands in the air and, suddenly, a wave of water flew out of her hands and landed on the fire. Everyone jumped and had their eyes wide. Stella, who approached the group without a fire extinguisher, froze in her steps. She had seen the incident as well.

Kenta nodded in approval, unable to hold back his grin of anticipation. "These are our girls. You take Mary while I take Sazuma. She'll be most troublesome."

"Fine," Ayano answered. She might have had irritation in her tone but Kenta knew she would complete the job without complaint. She wasn't usually this irritated, though. Maybe she was growing tired of raising her hope, excited of the fact that they found her fellow comrades, then ending up disappointed and saddened by the thought of having to kill the girls they wrongly brought into this supernatural world.

It had happened many times before. Ten years couldn't erase five years of deaths. The thought of having to do it again was saddening, but it had to be done.

With the snap of his fingers, a red and gold box appeared from thin air and landed in his hands. The box contained the orbs of the princess's elemental powers. The box was sacred and hadn't been touched in centuries. It was a true honor when the Mother Angel had given him the box. Now, it just seemed like the thing was a curse.

Delicately, he opened the box, revealing the six remaining orbs. Each one had a different symbol and shined a different color, ranging from red to ocean blue. He gave Ayano the blue orb, while Kenta kept the remaining orbs. She held the small object close to her, tucking it under her breasts.

Ayano went her separate path while Kenta kept his eyes on the girls. Watching them from afar was easy. Approaching them would be a very awkward moment.

"What was that?" Stella freaked as he remembered what just unfolded.

"I don't know, but let's keep this to ourselves, agreed?" Everyone nodded in agreement to answer Mary's question. Too disturbed to continue, the girls picked up their belongings, threw the sandwich and the sheet they used into the trash can, because there was no point in keeping a burnt up sheet, and went back to their class, leaving Kenta alone in the scene. He figured staying wasn't so bad, so he remained in his spot, hoping to learn more about his targets.

The final bell rang, ending the school day. Sazuma and her group allowed the other students to leave the school grounds first. This way, they would avert the traffic that was high school students. Going home was necessary, and to be allowed to leave was a blessing, but it wasn't worth being pushed and shoved by anxious teens.

Once most of the school cleared, the team headed out. They reached the school's gate and waved their goodbyes as Stella walked the other way from Sazuma's direction. She, Mary, and Hiroko traveled the same way, heading to their neighborhoods.

Hiroko led the way, automatically beginning her chatter of this, that, and the other. Sazuma never knew what she was talking about these days, however, she would not admit that. She didn't want silent treatments and hateful stares coming from her.

Speaking of stares, was it strange that she felt someone watching her all day, and even at this moment. Was it just her? Was she going crazy? Why was she asking herself these questions as if she was a British detective?

"Hey, I just noticed something." Hiroko said, while lightly skipping backwards. "Reiko didn't come to school today." Sazuma wasn't surprised. Reiko wasn't a fan of school so she dodged every chance she got. Plus, she hated Mondays. Then again, most people didn't like school and Mondays were tough days. If she could, Sazuma would skip, too. She only went because Mary bugged her to go and she didn't want to disappoint her mother. That was something Sazuma never wanted to do.

"She might have stayed home out of boredom again," Sazuma said, already knowing that was the answer. "God knows how lazy she is when it comes to school. Her parents don't even care anymore."

"Well whatever. I'll call her when I get home. Anyway, see you guys tomorrow." Hiroko waved, then ran inside her house at the edge of the block across the street from the twin's neighborhood. The place was huge, overall, with a green lawn; red tipped garden gnomes sat on her white painted porch. A rugged cement pathway welcomed visitors to the three porch stairs. The front door was painted cinnamon and the three-storied house had maple paneling. An eight-foot tall black pitch forked fence surrounded the entire structure. It had an electric system activated at night, Hiroko once informed.

The twins turned the corner and entered their neighborhood. Each house had tile roofs. Paneling covered the outside walls, its colors ranging in the rainbow. The girls' house was the last house on the left. The paneling was sky blue with white tile roofing.

Their mother was a true gardener so the front yard had multicolored flowers, growing green bushes and motion sensors that shined blue when turned on. The scorching summer hadn't affected the plants in the slightest.

The sun was setting. It still shined brightly, but it wasn't as high as it once was; thank God. The sisters stayed close together. Their neighborhood, Limely Lane, was a quiet little neighborhood with neighbors who acknowledged each other, but stuck to their business. Still, walking around alone with this silence raised a warning flag.

Sazuma couldn't beat off the feeling of being watched. In this community, you always felt that way. The quiet surroundings would cause anyone to be paranoid. Except, she had had this feeling all day; in class, on the roof at lunch-the melting sandwich and wave of water was still weird to her-and even now. It was like there was someone out there listening to her conversations, watching her as she now walked.

As the trees shading them wrestled with no wind to move them, Sazuma's suspicions had been confirmed. They were being watched.

Sazuma looked straight ahead, staring right at her neighbor's house. Her house was on the left. The eyes on her stared harshly. Her shoulders tensed. She watched Mary with her peripherals. She was in the same staring position as she was in. "Do you sense that?"

"Yeah," Mary answered. They had whispered, but somehow, Sazuma felt the unknown watcher had heard every word. The girls faced each other and gave a swift nod. Their minds were headed in the same direction.

They were running for it. Sazuma might have not been going far, but Mary could make it to the house and call 911 if Sazuma didn't return. The girl was good at running. Mary had been on the track team back in middle school and her skills never wavered. Sazuma on the other hand . . . let's just say she had trouble making it up the school's thirty-two stairs to the next floors. She might have been skinny, but she was no stairs fan.

They faced the front, staring at the neighbor's house again. Their house came into view. It stood tall on the left side of the cul-de-sac. The pulsating flowers stood straight and proud, waving off its vibrancy.

Now that they were close, all they had to do was run. No, not run, dash. They had to be a cheetah in order for this to work. Well, Mary was the cheetah. Sazuma was the little penguin in the back of the pack saying, "Wait for me!" Besides, they were two houses down from theirs. They could make it.

Even so, they were so out of here.

Without warning the other, the girls dashed out, entering the house their only focus. They did not even make it a house down. Something popped out of the canopies above and landed inches in front of them. No, not something, but someone. A woman, they realized. And, she was dazzling.

She was kneeling. Long black hair with a mix of silver curtained her face and torso. A gold staff brought back along with her hands. Her skin was caramel, a healthy glow illuminating her. Even though her face hadn't been seen, Sazuma couldn't help but gape. Already she looked so badass.

But when the woman looked up, Sazuma knew she not only looked badass, but she was indeed a fighter. Hard burgundy eyes slipped through her thick mass of hair, staring down at the girls. She straightened, standing inches taller than them. Sazuma doubted her thigh high-heeled boots had anything to do with it. A gray shirt hugged her chest, making her breasts seem larger. Sazuma wanted to lower her head in shame, but she was too shocked to turn away. Her eyes traveled down. The woman wore black-jeaned short shorts. Her hair hung loosely over and behind her shoulders. It was such a thick mass. Beauty radiated from her.

Behind her, a man jumped down, landing inches behind the woman. As he approached, he was scratching his black hair, eyes closed, and sighing. "You didn't have to scare them like that," his eyes opened. He was scolding his friend. She didn't seem too bothered by his actions. She merely looked at him, then rolled her eyes away.

Well, they knew each other. Awesome . . . but who were they and why had they appeared just now? Maybe these were her watchers. But, why would such handsome and beautiful people be following them, mere twin girls from Japan?

Sazuma focused on the man. He was at least an inch taller than the woman with a burgundy shirt and black jeans with matching boots. His skin was sun-kissed and he wore a maroon headband. Was he supposed to be cool or something? Was it a style trend Sazuma didn't give a crap about? Well, if she didn't give a crap about it, why was she asking herself this question? She really had to stop thinking.

The man released another sigh then faced the twins. His eyes matched the woman's. Were they related? Their genes must have been awesome if they were. Sazuma had never seen people with burgundy eyes. Plus, they were too gorgeous to be human. Yes, Sazuma believed in the supernatural world. She believed the Loch Ness monster existed. She believed vampires stalked people at night. And, she even believed that Sasquatch was in her backyard. So, if these guys weren't human, she would believe them in a heartbeat. *Here comes my adventure.*

"Who are you?" Mary asked. She always liked getting to the point. The twins stayed close together, touching shoulders.

All attention went to the man as he spoke, "My name is Kenta and this is Ayano." He pointed to the woman with his thumb. Those were nice names. It seemed to fit their appearances perfectly. But Sazuma hadn't heard names like that before. Were these two special? "We came for you two," Kenta said, his eyes holding them hostage.

"Us? What do you want?" Sazuma asked. Curiosity consumed her at a startling rate, but she loved this rush of wanting to learn more. It had happened so rarely. Nothing captured her interest. Now though, her need to learn popped up and expanded.

Slowly, as if teasing her, Kenta walked over and stood in front of the eldest Kagami. She remained still, but she was cautious. She still didn't know this guy well enough for close contact. Her vigilant onyx's stared him down-well, up, in this case.

He paused inches in front of her, leaving her enough space to know he wasn't going to do anything crazy. Their eyes locked. Maroon mixed with onyx. Damn, was he always this handsome? With his black hair playfully hanging over his headband, acting as a mist around his eyes, and that perfectly sloped nose along with those sharp cheek bones and those lush, seductive lips, Sazuma knew he was no human.

"We need you. Both of you," Kenta spoke agile. The last sentence, he had turned to Mary then back to Sazuma.

"Need us for what?" Sazuma tilted her head in mystification.

"We need you to stop acting like a human and enter a war that's been brewing for centuries." Ayano peered at her nails and shined them on her shirt.

Mary froze, "A war?" she asked with such shock, such disbelief. Mary was never a fighter, even though she had the skills to defend herself against kidnappers and horny teenagers. The girl hadn't even noticed Ayano had said *Acting like humans.* As if they'd been acting this whole time.

Kenta scratched his head, debating on what to say. "Ayano speaks true, but she didn't have to put it like that."

"What is going on here, Kenta?" Saying his name was different. Sazuma hadn't talked to boys much. And, the fact that she was saying a name she never heard before was indeed interesting to say.

"Well," he began, all nervousness diminished, "we have come before you to give you your place in our army. You are the princess of the flame, one of the seven soldiers needed for battle."

Army? Battle? War? Did she just enter a civil movie? What was this hocus pocus?

"You're nuts," Sazuma laughed without humor. She patted his broad shoulder. This dude was buff! "You're obsessing over a battle movie, aren't you? You want things to come to life and boom! Life worth living. That's awesome, but I don't want to play your game."

"Sazuma . . . I don't think they're playing." Mary stared with misunderstood wonder. She was contemplating on whether to believe them. Mary wasn't one to believe in the supernatural, but she could tell the difference between truth and a hoax.

Sazuma turned to Mary. "Come on now. You can't honestly believe them. Princess of the flame? It sounds like a movie title or something."

"No," Mary's confused expression turned into a modest smile. "I've heard stories about this. A scene, somewhat like this."

Great, story time, Sazuma stared. This was known as 'Mary's knowledge' moments. What did this girl not know?

"Over a hundred years ago, there was a spirit being who teamed up with a demon in search for seven girls who would one day save the world. The spirit being was in search of a team of women who could control the seven elements; fire, water, earth, wind, ice, light and darkness. Once the team was assembled, the spirit being along with the demon guided the girls to victory, winning their battle against their nemesis, the underworld group called the Demon Docks."

Sazuma paused. "A-And?" Was there a point to this knowledge moment?

Mary turned to her sister, as if she was stupid to not know the answer. "These girls were known as the Element Princesses. They saved the world from demonic influence and protected the universe. They were heroes to the Heavenly beings and the supernatural world."

"Great, someone knows the story. Can we move on?" Ayano had the attitude. Nice. Sazuma was going to like her.

Kenta turned to her, scolding again, then faced the twins once more. "You are correct Mary. The Element Princesses did once exist, but in time, they aged and died. Their orbs, spheres that held their power, escaped their bodies and flew back to Heaven, landing in a goddess's hands. That goddess became the Mother Angel of Heaven and she said the time of awakening had begun."

"Awakening? As in a new generation of princesses?"

Okay, not only was Sazuma perplexed, but she didn't know *what* the hell was going on. Mary was all excited about these "Element Princesses" and Kenta was staring down at her, as if enjoying her smile. Mary's smile might have brightened a whole room, but that didn't mean shit. Did this introduction come with a point?

"Can we get to the point?"

Thank you, Ayano! Sazuma knew she liked this girl.

"Of course," Kenta answered, never leaving his eyes from Mary. He snapped his fingers. Instantly, a red and gold box popped out of thin air and landed in his awaiting palms. The box was apple red with a sun golden top. Small diamonds hung from the top's four corners.

The twins came in closer, filling the distance between them and Kenta. He grinned. "These are the elemental orbs."

Mary was gaping. Sazuma was staring with bewilderment. Sure, she didn't know anything about these Element Princesses, but she knew for sure that these orbs were pretty. There were six orbs total, ranging in colors. But Sazuma focused on the red one. There was a gold outline of a flame. Inside of the orb, she could have sworn something was swirling inside. That same swirling movement resided in all of the orbs, except every color was different. But wait, why were there only six orbs? Weren't there seven elements? Was one princess already found?

Without warning, Kenta slammed the box, causing the girls to jump and stare at him. His expression, once settle and welcoming, was now stark. What had caused him to change so suddenly?

"Sorry, but I cannot allow you to continue further."

"Such a teaser," Ayano commented. Kenta overlooked her.

"Why not?" Mary asked, trying to remain calm. Seeing something so mythical must have raised her spirits. Taking away something so life changing for her caused her anger to rise. "Why would you come to us, inform us of your intentions and then leave us hanging? Is this some sick joke?"

"No Mary, but I cannot let you continue without receiving your total understanding and cooperation." He was so serious now. His welcoming side was gone, as if it had never been there.

"Then tell us what it is so we can sign up." Sazuma turned to Mary. She'd never been so determined to join anything. If this was a club, Mary would have joined instantly, Sazuma knew.

"I don't think you're understanding," Ayano finally stepped up. She'd been behind Kenta, watching as he talked to the girls and showed them the orbs. Now, her expression was stark too, her hands anchored on her curved hips.

"Accepting this gift isn't something you can come back from. Once you're given the orb, there's no going back. The human life you knew would be a distant memory to you. You will no longer be a human. As an Element Princess, you are claiming to be a supernatural being with unique abilities."

"Fine, let's do it." So resolute, Sazuma's sister was. Kenta's barren expression slowly faded.

"And, do you understand that you would have to kill to survive. You would have to sacrifice those you hold dear in order to live another day." Ayano was the first princess found, Sazuma realized then. As she spoke, Ayano proved her point, "You have no idea what the hell kind of world you're asking to enter."

Mary's shoulders, once squared with determination, slouched down as her head lowered. Ayano might have spoken true, but that wasn't a good enough reason to pull back now. The supernatural had already entered their lives. Human living was long gone.

Sazuma took this time to observe the area. The sun was setting. Shades of yellow, tangerine and plum filled the sky. The moon, which was a half phase, slowly raised as the sun set. She turned back to the conversation. Mary had turned to her. She was unsure. She wanted to make her next move, but she was unconfident. Mary never made her choices alone, and a choice like this most definitely was going to have Sazuma's input.

But was she ready to enter this world? This battle, as Kenta and Ayano had said. Mary was a defender. She'd been taking defensive lessons while Sazuma learned how to block thanks to her father; only because her father had been the one to violently attack her. They could manage. But could they handle what the supernatural world threw at them?

Sazuma looked at Kenta and Ayano. Ayano was still stark but Kenta observed her with confidence. He believed in them already. Ayano on the other hand . . . Sazuma might have liked her for getting to the point of things, but they might have had disagreements on the battlefield.

A battlefield she was willing to enter.

She turned to Mary once again. Her eyes still asked for approval. With a sure nod of her head, Mary smiled. And, as usual, it brightened up the area. The twins faced their watchers. "We agree," Mary announced.

"If, and only, if," Sazuma pointed to Kenta, "you act as our mentor and assist us when we need you."

Kenta grinned, "Of course." Ayano crossed her arms. At least her expression had softened.

All attention turned to the red and gold box in Kenta's hands. It was shaking now, rattling the orbs inside. Kenta placed his hand on the edge of the box, preparing to open, but stopping. His eyes touched the girls. "There's no going back after this."

They grinned, "We're well aware." They answered together.

In one swift motion, Kenta opened the box. The crimson and aquamarine orbs zapped out and shot themselves to Sazuma and Mary's breast bone. A wave of shock and pain coursed through Sazuma's veins. The force pushed her back, but she stood on her own, staring down and watching as the orb pushed through her shirt and merged into her skin.

Her heartbeat raced. Blood sped through her. Her brained pounded, causing an instant headache. Her nerve endings sizzled. Her breath escaped her lungs, but didn't come back in. As fast as it had morphed with her, a connection was made. The orb had locked inside of Sazuma's body. A contract had been made hadn't it? It was a contract she and Mary could not escape.

Then again, she wouldn't want to escape it even if she wanted to. Which she didn't.

Too exhausted from the sudden voltage, Sazuma and Mary dropped to the ground unconscious.

Kenta gently picked up Sazuma. Her head lolled into the crook of his neck. He stared down at her. Her small, yet lush, lips were parted and her eyelids hung loosely over her eyes. He turned to Ayano, who was picking up Mary. She had the same expression. He sighed with a grin. He'd never seen more beautiful young women.

"I hope we got this choice right this time." Ayano said. So much doubt shined through her tone. A ping poked Kenta's chest. A ping of guilt, he knew. There were so many mistakes in the past. He didn't want to end more lives.

He turned down to Sazuma again, observing her features closer. It was as if he had to know every pore on her skin. "I hope so too," he responded, never facing his comrade. Ayano was the first to make the move to the house. Kenta followed casually.

If this was another mistake, he felt that ending the lives of these girls would be the most painful. They attracted him already. Ending them would definitely kill him.

Story 2

The *Flame* has a *Heart*

Morning, a time of renewal and the promise to a new day.
At least, that's what Stella thought of mornings; it didn't matter what day it was.
There was always something to look forward to. It didn't matter if the same schedule welcomed her during the weekdays or if her friends had spoken the same conversations. Every day was different, even if the same schedules and conversations were said.
Stella Jayberry woke up in her sleeping bag and looked around the living room of her friend's apartment. Her attention traveled to the only window in the living room. It was large 3-Lite sliding windows with chocolate brown framing. The sun's light shined bright, its rays spreading through the sky, welcoming everyone to wake to a gleaming new day.
She stretched her arms up and rolled her head. Her usual sleep stiffness was subsided. After crawling out of her lavender sleeping bag, she turned to her right side and paused. There was a black sleeping bag folded up and placed beside the wheat colored couch near the far wall. A single white pillow rested on top of the folded bag.
With that, Stella knew her friend was gone for the day. She was at work, collecting what money she could get. Even though ramen, instant rice, Mac and cheese, and other quick foods was all they could afford, Stella never complained. She was blessed to have a meal every day, a roof over her head and a friend who assisted her every step of the way in her life.
God knew her life had been difficult. After crying for months on end, and going through a depression so strong she tried to commit suicide more times than she could count, Stella felt that she had hit rock bottom.
She had only been ten years old.
One bleak day, during a harsh thunderstorm, a wonderful event had happened; she was saved. A group of teens, drunk from the look of them, had come together and had pinned little Stella to the ground. They ripped at her

clothes, grabbed her arms, stuffed her mouth with one of their foul socks to shut her up and had nibbled her skin for seductive purposes.

Stella had run from an adoption agency that had been "trying" to help her. She had overheard the conversation from the head of the agency and another agency representative. They had been talking about her. "This child is too damaged to fix," the head of her adoption agency had said with regret. "She cannot be saved. I believe locking her up will allow her the experience she needs to-" Stella had dashed out of the building before hearing the whole story. Not only was the woman going to send her away, but she was going to allow others to lock her up; in juvenile most likely.

She hadn't even run long before the group of teens spotted her and dragged her to an abandoned shop outside of town.

She screamed, even with the sock in her mouth. She could taste the sweat of their feet. She could hear the giggles of the desperate drunks. There were no boundaries for them. They had touched her, licked her and continued to nibble. Her ten year old strength was nothing compared to their seventeen and eighteen exteriors. Deep down, she knew, hoped, this was it. If they killed her after raping her, then she could join her family. These boys might have used her body, but at least she would be free of their hold and the hold of other people disgustingly like them.

Just when all hope seemed lost for her, just when she was about to surrender her body to these low lives, one of the teens had grunted in pain and was shoved to the far wall, unconscious. There were five guys total. Four had been pushed out of the way and knocked out. The leader, the one currently straddling Stella's small waist, was grabbed by his nape. Spikes for nails dug into him, producing blood straightaway.

The teen grabbed the wrist of Stella's savior and grunted. "What the hell?" The next second, Stella's savior, a black-haired woman with a gray hood and shredded cape, had punched the guy's nose, throat and temple. She turned a 180 and threw the guy into the brick wall. He was out like a light.

"Disgusting," she slurred with distaste.

Stella was shaking. Moving was impossible. She could still feel the boy's teeth and hands observing and grabbing her. Her breathing hitched, but her eyes never left her savior. The savior's back faced her. The shredded cape had holes here and there with dirt marks near its ends.

Slowly, the woman turned to her. Stella's shaking only increased. When she faced her completely, the woman brought down her hood, exposing her red-rimmed maroon eyes . . . and the river of blood on the left side of her cheek.

Stella desperately tried to maneuver her hands to scoot her away but it was useless. They were limp, weak. Knowing what she was trying to do, the woman approached with her hands out in innocence. "Calm down kid.

Hyperthermia is around the corner for you." Was she shaking that badly? Well it was cold-December; if Stella remembered correctly-so it made sense.

Still, she couldn't just allow another stranger to put their hands on her, even if this woman did save her from drunken teens. The woman bent down and pushed massive strands of hair behind Stella's ears. She barely touched her, too afraid to do so maybe. "It's alright. I won't hurt you."

That's what the teens had said ... now look. She was on a freezing ground, her underwear the only clothes she had on. Her grip on consciousness was withering. Blissful darkness was calling her name. "Don't hurt me," Stella whimpered in absolute distress, "Please."

The woman nodded. "Don't worry, Stella. I'll take care of you." With that, she entered the darkness.

She had woken in this very apartment with a blanket over her body and a soft armrest as her pillow. Food had been prepared; chicken flavored ramen with a side of broccoli. But the woman was gone. Even though she wanted to search the place, Stella remained on the couch.

"How did she know my name?" was a question she asked herself frequently. She didn't remember meeting the woman. Maybe it was luck. Or, maybe she had been stalking her. Stella shook her head, not wanting to believe something so crazy. This was the only person who cared for her, who fed her, and kept her warm through it all. She was still shirtless, exposing her upper body, but she was covered. That's all that mattered.

The woman arrived through the front door an hour later. Stella had awoken around nine at night so the woman arrived at ten. The torrential rains glued to her, which was continuing their forceful dance outside of the single chocolate framed window.

Instead of having fear swim through her body like it should have, relief replaced it. She was glad the woman returned, even if she didn't know who she was. "Good, you're up." Her eyes turned to the empty bowls on the splintered coffee table. "And you've eaten. That's great."

Her cape was gone, exposing her tall, full form. She wore all black. Black short sleeved shirt-why was she wearing short sleeves in December?-black jeans and black boots reaching her knees. She squeezed a gold staff in her hand. Its sharp point poked the ground while the top end was circular with an extra bar piercing through it.

The woman rested the staff against the wall and leaned beside it, pressing herself on the framed windows. She was giving Stella the space she believed she needed. Right now, all Stella wanted was to know the woman's name.

"Don't worry. You're allowed to leave if you wish."

Why would Stella want to leave this place? She couldn't see anything. The moonlight was the only thing lighting the room, which didn't help for her to see the details of the place. All Stella knew was that there was another couch laid beneath the window the woman leaned on and the small kitchen to Stella's left with an island in the middle and cabinets enclosing the space. To her right, there was a small closet and another hall, probably leading to the bedrooms.

"C-C-Can . . ." Stella stopped. Without noticing, her hands were still shivering and she was still shaking. The wool blanket on her wasn't keeping her warm enough? The woman walked over, plopped beside Stella and wrapped her arms around her; blanket and all. She was drenched, but she was warm. So, so, warm. She was welcoming. She leaned her head on Stella, sharing her water and heat. Stella did not mind at all.

"Can you tell me your name?" Stella uttered out. She was surprised she could say the sentence clearly.

"Ayano," she answered lovingly, as if thanking Stella for not running away and for actually wanting to know what her name was.

"M-May I s-stay?" Asking was pointless, the ten year old thought, but she had to try. She had nowhere else to go.

"As long as you want," Ayano pulled her closer and even began to rock her. Instantaneously, Stella cried. She cried and cried, not even trying to stop her tears. She pressed her lips together, not allowing herself to whimper or shout in thanks. She simply allowed Ayano to rock her, warm her, and give her the affection she desperately needed.

Looking back, that had been the best day of her life. Five years had passed since then and Stella couldn't have been more grateful.

Ayano was such a giver. She read stories to her. She fed her what she wanted, except things that cost over seven dollars, so there was no steak or cow meat. But there was chicken. Lots and lots of chicken cooked in different ways. Stella's only drink was water or Kool-Aid. This was fine because Ayano made the best! She added more sugar than needed and would always stir the container as if she only had ten seconds to make the best drink in the world.

To Stella, it *was* the best.

But memories of the past and good times with Ayano would have to wait. Stella had school, and she did not intend to ruin her perfect attendance. Middle school had been ups and downs when it came to grades, but at high school, Stella had gotten it right. All A's and one B.

She despised Math class dearly.

Stella stood, folded her sleeping bag, placed it next to Ayano's, and headed to the shower. As she waited for the water to heat, which took a minute or two, she headed to the spare room down the hall, beside the bathroom and went to the closet on the left side. There were two closets, one for her and one for

Ayano. Ayano's wardrobe was black with a dash of reds, blues, and purples. Stella's, on the other hand, was full of color. She only wore black pants from time to time. Other than that, there was color everywhere.

After choosing her clothes for the day, which was her school uniform-a sailor uniform with short sleeves of auburn with a royal blue short skirt, bronze stitching and socks ranging from the ankles to the knees and black slip on sneakers—she headed into the bathroom, slipped into the shower and sighed in longing as the steamy hot water rained onto her awaiting skin.

Yes, this would be a good day.

Sazuma shot her eyes open. Her legs kicked in the air and her arms waved around. She sat up as her body flew back on the bed, her mattress bouncing at her activity. She slapped her hand on her chest on impulse. There was no pain. There was no object between her breasts. Whoa . . .

She quickly looked around. She was in her room. Khaki walls covered the space. Posters of Green Day and Evanescence covered Sazuma's side of the room while posters of concept art and even *Transformers* covered Mary's side. One cherry wood desk sat on the other side of the room, acting as the space between the two. A laptop sat on the table. It was turned off and the top was closed. The window near the desk, right in Sazuma's view, locked shut. The other window, on Mary's side on the left wall was also sealed shut.

There were two twin beds in this ten-foot-by-twelve foot bedroom. Sazuma's bed rested closer to the wooden door, which was closed by the way. Chestnut sheets covered her bed and her matching decretive blanket was pulled back. With another shove of her feet, Sazuma's blanket would have fallen to the floor.

She shifted on her bed to face Mary. She was sleeping. Her azure sheets were neat under her while Sazuma's sheets were wrinkled. Must have been from the jolt just a minute ago. Mary's blanket was also pulled back. One hand placed on her belly while the other lay on her side. Her head faced Sazuma. Mary was sleeping soundly. A light side grin was on her face, as if she was having a happy dream.

This was not a happy moment! This was downright weird. Sazuma could have sworn she'd felt her nerve endings sizzling. Her body was electrified. Her blood was rushing. Her heart was racing. There was an orb entering her body for crying out loud!

There would be no smiling.

She got up and stumbled to Mary's bed. A single cherry wood nightstand was between them. The distance might have been small, but getting to her was tougher than Sazuma thought. Her legs wobbled on contact with the wood floor. She dropped to her knees with a grunt, but stood and dragged herself onto her sister's bed.

She shook her sister until she woke up. Mary too woke with a jolt, reacting just as Sazuma had. But relief brewed. Sazuma knew Mary was alright. "Hey, you okay?" She had to make sure completely. Asking was better than searching her body. Sazuma was no-body—toucher.

"Yeah," Mary answered while grabbing her chest. Bewilderment shined her features. Maybe she was thinking the same thing Sazuma was. Had yesterday really happened?

"That wasn't a dream was it?" Mary asked.

Her and her sister's eyes locked. "I don't believe so."

Mary looked down. She grabbed her shirt. They were still wearing their uniforms, Sazuma realized. There was no dirt, but they were wrinkled. Even so, disbelief of yesterday's events still filled the air. They needed proof.

"How do we know it wasn't a dream?" Mary asked, going down the path of Sazuma's mind. It only took a second for an idea to pop in her head. She grabbed Mary's hand and dragged her into the bathroom beside their room. Their rushed footsteps pounded on the extended wood floors.

They entered the bathroom, closed the door and stood in front of the sink. They stared at their reflections in the 6"x6" mirror. Sazuma's braided hair was messy. Strands stood everywhere, exposing her bed head. Mary's straight hair was the same, except her eyes were bloodshot, showing she still needed sleep. She turned to Sazuma, who was still observing herself in the mirror.

She looked at her in wonder, "I don't think looking at ourselves will prove if yesterday happened."

"We're here to test something." Sazuma faced Mary. "Let's just see what happens alright? Nothing big, but we both need evidence that yesterday was not a dream."

Mary nodded in agreement. Sazuma only hoped this worked. If it didn't, she would track down Kenta and Ayano and demand answers. If she could find them, that is. They were a sneaky couple. Invisibility had been their friends. Sazuma was sure they could diligently hide again.

She turned the glass handle. Cold water rushed on the circular sink. The sisters faced each other again. "Every orb has a different element right?" More like a statement than a question. Still, Mary nodded. Sazuma continued, "Well I have a red orb and you have the blue one. That means we're fire and water." Sazuma felt stupid for not realizing this earlier. She was too busy being shocked over the fact that something was actually happening in her life.

"So this is an element test," Mary finished for her. The girls faced the sink again. Hesitant, Mary put her hands up and expanded her fingers. A minute later, nothing happened. "Am I supposed to say some kind of spell or something?"

It would have been nice if Kenta and Ayano had given them a manual. How exactly do you work element orbs? "I don't know. Just think about the water and see what happens." Easier said than done. Thinking only made you wander into memories and that got you nowhere. A manual would have been *damn* nice right about now.

Mary closed her eyes and took a deep breath. All of her attention on her surroundings was gone. Her shoulders sagged but her hands never moved. Sazuma's eyes widened when she saw water starting to lift up from the sink. It started as a small strand appearing from the still rushing water, but as it got higher, more water joined in.

"Oh my . . . Mary, Mary, look you're doing it!"

Mary shot her eyes open. Before she could look at her success, the water she controlled fell to the tile floor.

Now annoyed, Mary ughed. "You threw off my focus!"

"I just wanted to show you what you were doing. This is amazing." Sazuma pointed to the ground to point out what she was saying. However, as she did so, a blast of fire shot out of her finger and landed on the water. The entire floor steamed. Mary screamed with shock.

Not even a second later, Sazuma and Mary's mother dashed into the room. She swung the wood door open and peered inside, searching for her girls through the mist. Her room was down the hall, so of course she heard everything. Great. "What's going on here?" Her voice was groggy. A single pink curler hung in her face. The rest of them stuck to her brunette hair.

Past the steam, their mother could see dazed expressions and fuzzy hair. Mary glared Sazuma down. Sazuma was looking at her mother, smiling ear to ear. Sweetly, she said, "Nothing."

On Kyushu Island, Derek walked around his mansion, now going down a dark hall in search of the room housed by the woman he needed to see. To his right, enlarged windows glanced at the shoreline. The sun shined bright, lighting the windows with colors of the rainbow. The cobalt blue ocean, that's the color it was at this time in the morning, swung onto the shore. It washed out with pieces of sand as its daily gift.

He headed down the shadowed hall until he reached his destination. Only a large oak door stood in his way; blank as day. Casually, he grabbed the round golden knob and entered, without knocking. This was his house. For him to knock at all is a crime.

He opened up and kept the grin that was on his face. His eyes shined like rubies as he found the woman he desired to see. Sitting in a coffee colored chair was Chikara Yamada; the underworld ninja that possessed the power to sense people's emotions. She was one of his Demonic Princesses; female warriors he'd personally chosen to complete his personal assignments—and also chosen to defeat the Element Princesses if they were awakened.

Her younger sister Emiko, the girl that controlled time and space, was sitting in another coffee colored recliner on the other side of the room. They both faced a plasma screen TV hanging just above the entrance. Two queen-sized beds were beside each other with a single nightstand in the middle of them. Wood poles stuck out on both bed's four corners with translucent lavender curtains on Chikara's bed and pine green ones on Emiko's. To Derek, it fit their personalities perfectly.

The walls were thistle; a marble bathroom was on his left side. A single large window, matching the ones in the hallway was on Derek's right. Personally, Derek liked this room. But Derek's would always be better.

"Am I interrupting?"

"Never my lord." Chikara answered. Power radiated in her voice and through her pores. There were two maids in the room dressed in black and white Lolita. One was bent down and personally fed Chikara some purple grapes. The other was talking to Emiko. The maid actually had the nerve to sit down, chat with Emiko and eat grapes alongside her. That would have to change.

On his order, the maids scurried off, leaving them to their business. Derek approached Chikara. She was more powerful and wouldn't hesitate to get straight to business. Talking to Emiko would be a waste of time. She was a follower. She was no leader. She was no strategist. That's why Chikara was always the one he came to.

He stared down to her. She laid back with her feet up, one leg bent over the other. A bottle of champagne sat in one coaster while the other filled with damp grapes in a baggie. "My dear Chikara, how is life treating you?" She had just returned from a mission. She was ordered to get rid of several foot soldiers that infiltrated the mansion and stole from his weapons base. They had tried to run back to their leader, but Chikara had taken out the robbers and the organization. They had despised Derek and the Demon Docks.

They had to die.

The ninja smiled and batted her long black lashes over her luminous amethyst eyes. "Life is alright as long as the Element Princesses are out of the way and out of existence." She didn't hate the princesses merely because she was chosen to defeat them one day, but she hated them because she knew they would stop demonic plans of world domination. There were millions of Demon Docks members now.

Every single member wanted those princesses dead. But they'd been gone for a good century. They should have stayed down. "Well, that's what I came to talk to you about."

Chikara popped a grape in her mouth, not liking her lord's new attitude. "What is it?"

"Last night, Diamond and I were alerted of two element orb activations." Chikara's eyes widened. "Two princesses have been chosen. Kenta and Ayano are on the move." Derek had received the message from Lavida, one of his presence detectors, a shape shifter and animal possessor and also another Demonic Princess. If it wasn't for her, Derek would have known about the activation, oh, too late.

"How is that possible?!" Chikara pushed her recliner chair down with her feet, the rest locking back into the chair. Her unpainted nails dug into the arm rests. Her eyes, once shining with smugness were now red with fury.

"He must have found out that all of the girls on God's list were located in Japan. In either case, we need to find the other four before they do. I need you and Emiko's assistance."

"What do you want us to do?" No hesitation.

"I need Emiko to go into a certain town for me and see what's going on. She is already in human form and Kenta and Ayano have not seen her face before. She'll be our spy in plain sight."

Chikara looked over at her sister. Emiko was standing. Her long black hair hung over her shoulders and reached her waist. A long, sleeveless green dress covered her body. It was plain with no decorations. Her timid emeralds watched them. She clutched her hands near her chest and awaited a command. Yes, she was always like this.

"So what do you say Emiko? Do you want to do it?"

Emiko looked over to her sister and nodded. Of course, the girl said yes. Emiko did anything and everything Chikara asked. It was sad really, but this girl was also a Demonic Princess. Her time traveling abilities were useful. Derek wasn't stupid enough to let go of one so valuable.

Derek nodded in agreement. "Excellent! If you bring back one of the princesses, then I will personally make sure Hades gives you an advance in your powers." As if the girls weren't strong enough. Chikara smiled then stood to her feet. Her short black dress swayed as she headed to her maple wardrobe. Weapons wardrobe, Derek realized.

With that, Derek exited the room, leaving the job to his princesses. What would he do now? Well he would travel back to his room, where his precious Diamond was waiting for him. After chasing after her and pinning her down on his bed, Derek had sucked her blood until he was satisfied. In return, he allowed her to bite him, taking back what she had lost. Derek had more blood to give than lose anyway.

That night had been fun. And, it would continue today.

※

"Good morning." Hiroko smiled as she entered the classroom thirty minutes before the bell rang. That was extremely rare. Hiroko was the later tater.

Stella looked up from her book, grinning as a welcoming expression, "Morning."

"So last night," Hiroko started, excitement filling her tone, "I dreamed of something amazing. I dreamed that I was flying!" She threw her arms out as she stood in front of Stella's desk on the first row. "I had wings and everything. I was flying and naked and there were birds following me. It was like I *was* the air. It was remarkable!"

It wasn't a surprise Hiroko had dreamed like that. She was always too free and lively. But seriously, did she have to have the same dream every night?

"Flying and naked, huh?"

Hiroko paused, as if disbelieving her. Then, she smirked. "Is that all you heard?" she teased.

"No, but you didn't have to tell me that part." Stella looked down to read again. Once she found her place, her responsive mode was on autopilot.

"Whatever, so how's Ayano?"

"She came home late last night and left early this morning."

"Again, huh? Well tell her to stop doing what she's doing. I want to meet her. The way you describe her, it sounds like she's a nice person."

"She is," Stella smiled. Autopilot turned off, her concentration was gone, but she didn't face Hiroko again. "But if she stops what she's doing, then there won't be any money coming in. Plus, the sad part is, I don't see her much either."

"Good morning!" Reiko Takashima said as she entered the room in style. She wore her sleeveless light blue shirt, a black miniskirt and matching ankle high heels. Without a doubt, she needed to be reported for dress code, but no one was brave enough to mess with the seventeen year old. Even teachers were scared of her. It wasn't as if she was going to beat them up. Reiko sucked at fighting, but they were more afraid of her wealth status.

Reiko was the rich girl. She was nothing like Hiroko though. In fact, she was wealthier than Hiroko and most of the people in this school. Her father ran an international business in data and technology so he was getting money here, there, everywhere. So yeah, Reiko was spoiled but she wasn't a snot-nosed girl who waved her riches to the less fortunate. And, there were *a lot* of less fortunate.

"And just *where* were *you* yesterday?" Hiroko's fists pounded to her hips as her friend entered the room. Both girls were filled with such attitude and liveliness. At first meeting them, Stella thought that were related. Their facial structures looked so similar; the puppy dog eyes, the petite nose you could hold in between your fingers, the high cheek bones and the small but full lips. They could have been related. But in truth, the girls hadn't met each other until meeting Stella. They hit it off instantly.

Reiko answered while placing her black leather purse on the desk. "Oh, I had to watch my brother. My parents were out of town and he had a day off because of a rat infestation. He went back to school today and I'm here now. And you guys know I have to come back here in style." Reiko laughed.

"You're so hopeless." Hiroko sighed. Stella giggled. Hiroko was right though. One girl couldn't function without the other. She wondered how Hiroko made the whole day yesterday without going insane.

Reiko sat in her assigned seat, which was behind Sazuma near the window. The teacher wanted her as close to the board as possible, considering she was one of the failing students. But, thanks to her wealth status, Reiko chose to sit behind Sazuma. It was close to the board but far enough to text without being seen. That was the only genius plan Reiko ever had.

But just as quick as she sat down—because the girl always had to move—she stood from her desk and snatched Stella's book from her hands. She kept her finger on the page but flipped to the cover. Hiroko joined her.

"Hey," Hiroko said without a hint of scold, "you could have just asked her what she was reading."

"Hey, hey girl, if I want to know something, then I'll figure it out on my own. And why are you reading a vampire book?" Reiko shifted from Hiroko to Stella, "Because vampires and werewolves are interesting."

Reiko raised her eyebrow. "You scare me." She had no right to talk. Stella was scared of her sometimes. The girl knew everything about fashion, current styles and upcoming trends. The girl even knew how to style up a house's interior on a $100,000 budget. Style was good, but on Reiko's level, it was quite scary.

Students strolled into the classroom in groups of two or three, taking their seats and continuing their conversations. Most female students eyed Reiko as she stood. Some stared in envy, others in hatred. Reiko was beautiful. Her hair was black with many streaks of electric blue. Her eyes were hazel. They even seemed to shine if you stared long enough. But around her, Stella always felt cold. When going to Reiko's house for a study group—even though they didn't study; too busy talking—her house had been freezing and it was winter when she had visited. Stella knew Reiko had a heating and cooling system so that was no excuse. Reiko was just a chilling person.

Five minutes before the bell rang, Sazuma and Mary dashed into the classroom, pushing past students blocking the entrance. They didn't care that the blockers were glaring at them and calling them rude. Those senseless chattering teens deserved a pushing punishment.

Stella, Hiroko and Reiko applauded. "Wow that was quite impressive. Nice one." Reiko gave them a thumbs-up. While Reiko and Hiroko complimented their entrance, Stella noticed their wrinkled uniforms and random strands sticking out of Sazuma's braids and Mary's hair. They were obviously in a rush get to school. However, something told Stella that that wasn't the whole story.

The twins took their seats and threw their heads on their desks. Hiroko sat in her desk on Stella's left. Stella and Hiroko turned around to their friends, who were sitting directly behind them. "You guys sure got skill," Hiroko said to Sazuma's head.

"Give us a break will you," Sazuma grunted.

"No can do," the blonde said. She patted Sazuma's head. Her twin braids sat over her slouched shoulders. "Now you guys have no right to tell me I'm always in a rush to school. I can make fun of you now."

"I dare you . . ." Sazuma stared Hiroko down behind her bangs. Stella held back a giggle. She knew Hiroko would make fun of them from dawn till dusk. Hiroko always had a way of messing with people at the best of times.

"Alright class, let's begin." The teacher entered the room in a rush. Was everyone rushing this morning? The girls turned around and the students silenced. The school day had begun, and Stella loved it already.

Outside, Kenta stood on the rooftop of the building he had observed the girls on yesterday. Everything remained the same. No one was on the roof, and no one would ever be. The building was a good foot further than the school, so watching Sazuma's bored expression along with her friends was too easy. Good thing no one could see him. Humans couldn't see him. Spirit beings, which he was, could be shielded. Regular every day humans were oblivious to him. Psychics could see him though, which was a pain.

No going down memory lane, he told himself. Kenta brought back his focus. Sazuma looked as bored as ever. Tired, too. Kenta was there to see the girl's little experiment in the bathroom. He'd chuckled here and there but really lost it when their mother came into the room, wondering what her daughters were doing so early in the morning to be screaming.

Still, it was nice to see them curious about their new abilities.

It was even better knowing that this was indeed Sazuma and Mary Kagami.

Relief flooded him and Ayano last night. Knowing that they wouldn't have to kill them was a drastic relief. In the past, Kenta and Ayano had encountered Sazuma and Mary Kagami's nationwide. Worldwide, even. Unfortunately, instead of the orbs shooting out and entering the chosen one's bodies like what happened to the twins, the orbs willingly were pushed in, which caused immense pain. Even afterward, after gaining the abilities of the princess, the chosen girls wanted to give their orbs back. After encountering a demon or two, they gave up, screamed and pleaded to return to normal.

Sadly, there was no going back. They chose to enter this world. They were told they would never be humans again. They were told of the consequences of becoming a princess. They were told what their duty was. Still, the girls had said "Yes." They forced the orbs into their bodies and became supernatural beings.

But, the chosen ones wanted to throw the orbs away. They wanted to get their lives back and pretend this never happened; pretend that they never met Kenta and Ayano. Devastatingly, it wasn't that easy. Once entered into one's body, the orb acts as a life force in the carrier's body. That life force carries the ability to control the chosen element, yet, it also acts as the princess's lifeline. If the orb disappears, or if the power is overused drastically, the carrier would die.

The girls knew about this, too.

They had chosen death.

They didn't care that they were leaving their friends and family behind. The girls chosen had been teens who were unappreciated, teens who were unnoticed by others, or disrespected by their parents. When Kenta had asked for the orb back, the girls allowed him to take it.

Not every girl was willing. Some girls *were* actually loved by others. They had loving families who supported them and protected them. Those were the girls Kenta had to force down and wrench the orb from their bodies.

That had truly killed him. He loathed taking away daughter after daughter of families who did not need devastating influence. They could have lived happy lives with their little Sazuma. They could have watched as their amorous Mary graduated high school. Now though, those parents would never see their daughters becoming more than they were. Their time was forever gone, leaving room for them to continue through the spiritual world. Even now, the scars in Kenta's soul burned.

This was his duty. He was sent to find the Element Princesses and prepare them to defeat the Demon Docks. Was he brought back to life for this very reason? Kenta didn't know. All he knew now was that he needed to search for the remaining princesses. He knew Derek, the Demon Docks leader, had sensed the activation of the element orbs. It was his turn to move, his turn to strike.

And Kenta would be ready.

Footsteps sounded behind him. An ominous aura swayed in the wind.

Ayano had arrived.

She approached Kenta's right side, her staff in hand, her gaze turning to where Kenta was looking.

Right now, the students were standing up and moving their desks into groups. Sazuma's group was right by the window. The twins' back faced the window, the sun shining on them. The redhead and blonde girls from the roof yesterday were in front of them and a girl with black hair and icy blue streaks acted as the extra desk on Mary's left side.

Kenta's focus was on the redhead. She had orange-red hair and brown eyes. She was smiling, as if everything around her brightened her spirits. Her focus was on her friends as they spoke. Her head shifted in so many directions, Kenta would have thought she was dizzy by now.

Based on her looks, she seemed lively, fun, and full of life.

She looked like the next Element Princess.

"Kenta, do we have to involve her in this?" Ayano asked him painfully. He peered up at her. Her hood was over her head and the grip on her staff was tight. Her knuckles were white.

He knew the girl and Ayano knew one another. He knew this was painful for Ayano considering she only had one other female friend and hadn't seen her in years, but it couldn't be helped. "Her name is on the Mother Angel's list. She's already involved."

This morning, while the twins hurried to school, Kenta had perched himself on the tree hanging over their house, pulled out his sky blue paper and stared at it with shock. Sazuma and Mary's names were marked off with black ink. Kenta had never marked their names and the paper had been in his pocket the entire time, so Ayano hadn't touched it. This proved these were the girls he was looking for.

After getting out of his shock from the name cross out, Kenta looked at the next name. *Stella Jayberry. Red hair, Brown eyes, a heart of therapy.* Kenta knew Ayano was taking care of a girl with the same name and the same description. She'd taken care of the girl for over five years. Kenta had tried to hold back as much as he could. He'd even end up killing more girls with the same name. Now, his gut feeling was rising. He felt this was the Stella Jayberry they'd been searching for. No more holding back. No more waiting. No more death.

"I don't want her to go through all of this. She's been through enough. She lost her family when she was young and it's hard enough having her alone at home when I'm looking for the princesses with you. She can't become a princess." *"I refuse to let her be",* hung in the air, unsaid. Still, this needed to be done.

"She already is, Ayano. I can even test her powers."

"Please don't." Ayano lowered her head. Her tone was desperate, a plea.

Kenta rose from his kneeled position. They faced each other. She was frowning. Her lips were pressed together tightly and her shoulders were shaking. The thought of killing Stella would be painful for them both, he knew. But now that they knew the orbs would throw themselves to the princesses, there was still hope. Stella would be exposed to the supernatural world, but she wouldn't have to die.

"I'm sorry. I know this is hard and you don't want to look at what's right in front of you. But you have to. There's no way around it."

Ayano turned her head. Gently, Kenta placed his hand on her cheek, trying to make her face him again. Her face followed, but not her eyes. "Ayano," he came in closer. Her eyes closed painfully.

"Fine," she exhaled sharply, her mint breath fanning his face, "Show me what she can do."

She regretted the decision, but this was his chance to prove her power. It would bring the newcomer pain, Kenta knew, but it would prove to Ayano that this was the young girl they needed. "I can't right now. Her power has to be done at close range. But you will see just how much Stella will be able to handle herself."

Sazuma sighed as she watched her teacher talking and writing on the board. She had suggested the class work in groups to think of ideas for an upcoming physics project. Sazuma had paired up with her group, of course, the smart Mary, the creator Stella, the idealistic Hiroko, and the observer Reiko. Sazuma's job was the researcher. Together, they made A's on every assignment. Reiko didn't technically deserve it, but she helped with color schemes and the style. At least they passed with props.

Too bad the groups around the room couldn't think of ideas thanks to the teacher's inability to shut up. Currently, Mrs. Salter—most people loved to say her husband was Mr. Pepper; lame—was writing on the chalkboard while reading the textbook about wave movement. Not only did Sazuma, and most of the people in here, hate physics, but wave formation was the lamest of them all. There was a study of how waves moved back and forth. How was that fascinating?

It must have been fun for Mary because her complete focus was on the teacher. Then again, she could control water now. Maybe this was a learning experience for her. This *was* school. You *were* here to learn something.

Sazuma's eyes traveled from her listening sister to Stella. She was reading. The title this week was *Intertwined* by Gena Showalter. It was a vampires and werewolf book. Stella would talk about it and Mary would even join in. They were like members of a book club, and they were the only members. Mary loved vampires. Stella is a werewolf fanatic; she reads about werewolves, researches about werewolves, and even creates a scrapbook of them. Sazuma couldn't blame the girl. This was an obsession. Sazuma currently loved band groups. She understood the obsession.

From Stella, came Hiroko. She was sleeping. Out cold, was more like it. And was that drool sliding down the side of her mouth. Indeed, it was. Eww. But, she was smiling. It must have been one of her flying dreams again. She'd been having a lot of those lately. First, it was off and on during the month. Now, she had them every night. And, she commented on them the next day. It was a continuous cycle, yet, Sazuma didn't mind. At least she dreamed happy. Sazuma didn't have any dreams at all. Or, if she did, she forgot about them.

Lastly, there was Reiko. She was texting, hiding her phone the next second, then texting again when she got a message. Reiko didn't know that many people. Who was she talking to? Then again, she did go to parties late at night and met guys everywhere she went. She was a guy magnet and she loved it. She never overused her power, though. There were crazies out there. She was careful.

Still, was Sazuma the only one who had nothing to do? She was thinking to herself right now, but come on. She could have been reading—nah, she hated reading unless it was something she liked . . . nothing. She could be sleeping. Sleep sounded nice—nah, Mrs. Salter would notice and that's an instant detention. Her teachers didn't like her. She could be texting—heck nah; she didn't know anyone but the people she was grouped with. Well, she could text Yumiko, her friend in middle school, but interrupting her because she was bored wasn't right.

Was it?

Sazuma turned around, looking through the window and lighting her face. She hadn't realized how cold she was until the sunlight touched her face. Her eyes traveled the area. No one was around. There were no cars driving by or anything. It was always like this, but whatever. After checking out the scenery she already knew, and heating her face to the point of satisfaction, Sazuma turned back around and focused on the board.

But after looking back, rewinding her memories of a few seconds, she paused.

Wait a minute.

She looked back outside. Standing on the roof of a business building next door, a foot farther away from the school, on the roof, Kenta and Ayano stood firm, standing side by side and even waved at her with a grin.

"What the hell?!" she shouted. They hadn't arrived this morning or during the bathroom incident. Why the hell were they waving as if they'd been buddies for years? And, why the hell were they on the rooftop of a building in the first place? Were they watching—no—stalking her?

She stood in her seat and held her hands on the glass window. Kenta and Ayano disappeared completely beyond the building's roof before anyone could see what was going on. Yes, they were stalkers. Stalkers ran when their target spotted them. They were so going down when Sazuma got out of this place.

"Ms. Kagami," Sazuma looked over. Mrs. Salter glared at her with annoyance. Every student was staring her down in wonder, confusion, or entertainment.

Sazuma knew why they stared in confusion, though. Instead of speaking in Japanese, as Mrs. Salter usually did, she spoke in English, clear as day. Mrs. Salter knew Sazuma and her group spoke in English rather than Japanese—they were rebels that way—so she guessed speaking an American language would show a sense of authority. It didn't. "Why are you causing a scene in my class?"

It wasn't a scene. It was more like an outburst, but Sazuma kept that to herself. "Umm . . ."

"Never mind, step outside." In a split second, Sazuma glared back at her teacher. Was she supposed to answer while being kicked out of class? Smart.

Yes, she hated Mrs. Salter greatly.

Now clearly irritated, Sazuma grabbed her belongings and stomped into the hall, slamming the door behind her. She knew Mary would scold her later. Rude behavior was something Mary was trying to change in Sazuma. It had worked for a while but there was no point putting up a false face.

She leaned against her classroom wall with a sigh. She leaned her head back against the plaster wall. Halls surrounded her. Her classroom was on the edge of one of the four intersections leading to the remaining group of classes. The halls were filled with white tile floors and two rows of pitch black lockers. Surprisingly, some kids actually used the things. Sazuma was not one of those kids.

She trusted no one. She believed her belongings would be stolen, and she wouldn't even know where to start looking. She had enemies here. Not many, but enough to cause a crowd. Keeping her things with her was the best solution to her.

But, now that she had this power, she wouldn't have to carry her things. She could just get rid of her enemies then finally use the locker she sorta, kinda, always wanted to use. What was she going to do, though? Burn them? Sounded like a plan, but killing them wasn't the best way to take them out. She could use her fists, but burning them was so much quicker.

No, no, none of that now. Her conscious told her. Strangely, her mind was more logical than her mouth. That still didn't help her in the long run, though. Sazuma wasn't a big fan of thinking. That's one of the things she and Reiko had in common.

Sazuma giggled to herself. She and Reiko were idiots. Said with love, of course.

"Man, this is the seventeenth time this month," she said aloud, rewinding back to why she was out in the hall in the first place. Sazuma didn't like school, so what as the biggie? The biggie was her mother, Linda. Sazuma had promised to do her best in school and strive for A's and B's. Because middle school had been a tough time for her family—except her—she promised to try harder to impress her frail mother.

Linda was a strong, wise woman who had feared her own husband for over twenty years. That's how long they'd been married.

Now that her father was gone, her mother's terror had ended. She had gotten a job as a nurse at the hospital. She worked late nights, but the pay was good. Her mood had changed drastically for the better. She was jumping around, cooking breakfast and singing the occasional Disney song from the '90s.

Sure she had missed her husband, all wives did, Sazuma supposed, but still, it was better to say, "Life's great," than, "It's okay."

Was Sazuma upset about her father's death? Hell no. She hadn't shed a tear at his funeral. Her family had asked her "Won't you miss your father? There won't be a man around the house." Sazuma had responded, "Good. Men suck anyway." She was eleven when she had answered. The family members thought she was utterly rude and should have thought differently of her father.

To Sazuma, if they had been beaten, cussed at, pushed around, whipped with extension cords, had a broken leg thanks to a frying pan thrown at you, and nearly raped, then they would have agreed with her.

"Pssst..." Sazuma looked around. Flashbacks of her dire past retreated to the back shadows of her mind. There was no one around. The halls were silent. All she could hear was Mrs. Salter continuing her speech. So who...

"Pssst... Sazuma."

The teenager looked around. What *was* that? If it was some kind of sick joke, it was beyond not funny. Sazuma had a problem with surprises. Her father had snuck behind her so many times that slight movements behind her shoulders startled her. Kids here knew about her fidgets and found it funny the way she jumped for the slightest thing.

A knocking stopped her hall search. Her eyes turned forward to the single hallway window, larger than most windows in the school. Usually, it gave a view of the senior courtyard, its luscious gardens and neat branches and the large tree in the center of the yard. But, no. There was no view to see. The only thing she saw was Kenta, squatting on the sill and preparing to knock again, even if his eyes pierced her through the window. He was as tall as the window, even while squatting.

She ran over and opened the window. Surprise filled her. How long had he been there? Sazuma hadn't even turned to the window to peer outside. She was too busy with her thoughts. But all surprise faded once she remembered the reason she was in the hall in the first place.

She dragged him through the window and grabbed his collar. "You! Why are you here?" she whispered freakishly. "Why were you stalking me? It's your fault I'm in this situation." It wasn't right to blame him for *her* action, but he still had a part in this.

"Hey, calm down." Kenta choked. "If you let me go, I'll explain everything." Sazuma hesitantly let go. Her arms fell to her sides and her eyes glued on him. He now wore a short sleeved black shirt that hugged his torso; my God he had a six pack, with faded jeans and black boots. The maroon headband over his forehead remained. It didn't match his clothes. Why keep it on?

He righted his clothes while clearing his throat. Already his collar was wrinkled. Had her grip been that strong? His eyes went from his clothing to her. Sazuma froze. His eyes—not quite rubies, but close—were so striking. Sazuma could have sworn his irises swirled with something. She gulped, the lump in her throat made the action all the harder.

"Now what's bothering you?"

Coming back to focus, she turned her eyes away. The anger she once had was sliced in half. Still, she worked with what she had. "What *isn't* bothering me is the question. This morning me and my sister thought what happened yesterday was a dream, but when we tested out "abilities", it wasn't. Everything's real. I can control fire and Mary can control water. How is this possible?"

Her quick tone made Kenta grab her shoulders, hoping to calm her down. His hold was strong . . . yet so gentle. He rushed out, "You two are Element Princesses."

Her eyes touched him once more. Her anger built up, rejoining what she had left. "Okay, dude, you're gonna have to be more clear than that." Even as they spoke, their voices were low. She didn't need someone coming into the hall and finding them.

Kenta groaned. He stepped closer. Sazuma looked up at him. Dang, had he always been this tall. He must have been six-foot or six-one. He didn't tower Sazuma's five-foot-eight height, but she surely wasn't matched. Their eyes locked again. She stood in obedience. She couldn't help herself. She felt as if she was forced to stand and listen. What was wrong with her?

"You are two of the seven Element Princesses. You can control the element you are given. It is a blessing to have these powers."

Blessing? Right. Everything was considered a blessing to people. Wealth was a blessing. Love was a blessing. Friendship was a blessing. So what then? Was poverty a curse for those who deserved it? Most people in the world were in poverty and they were people who either counted their blessings, or didn't. Still, they didn't deserve it. Sazuma laughed without humor. Nothing was a blessing. This situation, in this supernatural world, wasn't any different.

Back to main matters. "So, anything fire related I can control and anything water related, Mary can control?"

"Wow you are confused. I'm making this as clear as possible." So what if Sazuma got the explanation the first time. Hearing it loud and clear satisfied her, even if the answer was already given.

"Are you stuck in fairy land or something? I do not understand any of this."

"Would you like proof that you can control fire?"

"That would be nice."

Kenta grabbed Sazuma's hand and dragged her to the now open window. They looked down. Yup, the courtyard was the same as yesterday. Flowers still bloomed in the gardens near the buildings, round iron chairs and tables sat here and there and the large willow tree in the center, surrounded by gray stones, rested in the center of it all. Its slugged leaves hung sleepily. There was no wind. Too bad. Sazuma loved when the leaves played with the breeze. It was relaxing.

"You see that tree?"

Sazuma nodded hesitantly. Where was he going with this?

"I want you to burn that tree."

Oh, that's where he was going. "You want me to kill a tree?"

"Not kill, burn. I want you to burn the tree."

"Burning is the same thing as killing."

"Can you please just listen to me so we can keep going through the lesson?"

Sazuma looked at the tree again. This might have been a lesson; however, she didn't want to burn the precious tree. Mary had once told her the tree had been there since the school's construction in 1910. The tree was symbolized as a rebirth for the town. Kayta Plains had once been nothing but land. Settlers worldwide battled for this land in the early 1900's. Then, in 1909, they came to a truce and together they built this small town. The seed of the tree was planted in the spring of 1910 and the construction of the school came soon afterward.

Sazuma didn't want to be the cause of destroying one of the many treasures this town had. Besides, she wasn't a nature devastator like most of these ungrateful people. There had to be another way to prove Sazuma could control the flame. Sadly, Kenta wouldn't allow it.

Kenta grabbed Sazuma's hand and opened it, forcing her palm to face the tree. "Now, focus on the tree. Keep it in your sights." Sazuma listened. She followed his command. "Now visualize a flame; a small flame. Turn that small flame into a ball and focus on the tree. Pour your energy into the palm of your hand." He slowed his sentence, creating a trance like state for her as she focused on her powers.

Gradually, a small fireball started to emerge from Sazuma's hand. Kenta grinned. Here was the next step. "Now, blast that energy outward to the tree." As if in a stupor, Sazuma pulled her hand back and threw the ball in the tree's direction. Her trance like state faded as soon as the sphere escaped her hand.

Sazuma's eyes widened. Her senses returned. She didn't want this, she realized. She wanted the tree to remain. She would find another way to prove Kenta's statement. There was always another way, especially in situations like this. Nevertheless, she realized this, oh, too late.

Kenta's task had been done. Sazuma had hit the tree, but it didn't end there. The fire ball flew through the tree, spreading its flames through the priceless willow and continuing on, hitting the other side of the school. An explosion caused Sazuma and Kenta to freeze.

Panic instantly hit. Sazuma's breath caught. Kenta merely stared. Screams filled the atmosphere as the other side of the campus shook from the blast. Students ran out of their classrooms, searching for the source of the screams. They rushed to the window, crowding around her as she slowly backed away in utter shock.

I did that. I did that! Tears stung her eyes but she refused to let them fall. The fire bell rang, surprising Sazuma further causing a tense ringing in her ears. Conversations flooded the halls. The fire spread even further, engulfing everything that it touched.

The willow tree, once standing and weeping in the sun, now slouched over, burning, shriveling, but still looking so elegant. Guilt chomped at her, eating away the pieces of Sazuma's soul that wasn't filled with fear, distrust and sorrow. When this was done, if she ever got over this guilt, what would be left of her? Would there be anything left?

She turned to Kenta, who had stood by her side the entire time. He turned to her as well, but he wasn't saddened by this. He wasn't even affected. He was emotionless. Sazuma couldn't read him. That bothered her. He had asked her to do this. Now that it was done, it had caused massive damage and panic. How could he be so emotionless?

"Did I do that?" she asked. Her throat dried, cracked. She swallowed air. Her lungs refused to function. Her hands shook uncontrollably. She had done as Kenta asked, but this was too hard to believe. Guilt chomped away again. Her chest ached.

"Everyone head outside," teachers rushed out as they exited the classrooms with their students.

"Kenta, did I do that?!"

Kenta didn't say a word. He closed his eyes and turned his head. Why so quiet now? Why so unresponsive now? He had encouraged that he and Mary became princesses. He had told her to test her powers by putting the willow tree on fire. Now that damage was done, he backed down. Did he always back out of danger?

"Sazuma come on." Mary grabbed her sister's arm, not noticing Kenta at all. Kenta looked at the evacuating girls, then jumped out of the window without notice. The evacuated students surrounded the front of the school and watched beyond the main building as heavy black smoke filled the air and the scent of burnt rubber mixed in the air.

"What happened? That fire was so sudden." Hiroko said as she watched what unfolded. She was just as shocked as everyone else.

"I don't know, but I hate how things like this happen when I get back to school."

"I doubt this is about you, Reiko."

"But am I wrong?" Typical Reiko, always had to have the last word. Knowing this conversation was going nowhere, Hiroko rolled her eyes. She looked around, searching for her friends from other classes. After finding a few here and there, she reassured herself.

But no matter how hard she tried, she couldn't shake the feeling of knowing she could help. She could assist in putting out the fires, but the teachers would have thought she was suicidal or trying to play the hero. Hiroko didn't want a prize or medal in her honor. She just wanted to put the flames out.

Even so, her body commanded her to run. So she had. She escaped the school and now glanced upon it. Her body, once tense, nervous, and consumed with shock, now calmed. She wondered, *Does this mean school is out?* The need to sleep washed over her that moment. Yeah, sleep sounded good.

Moans and heavy breathing snagged her attention. Hiroko followed the noises. Her gaze landed on Stella. She was clutching her shirt and rubbing her breastbone. Her eyes squeezed shut. Her face shined a hot pink. "Hey, what's wrong?" Her inner motherly side replaced the usual sensual Hiroko. She rubbed Stella's back, wanting to help, but Stella jolted. She removed her hand the next second.

"I feel hot," she answered in a grunt. "I feel hot and my chest is burning." Hiroko put the back of her hand on her friend's head. The moment she touched her, she zapped her hand back. Her skin sizzled, as if she stuck her hand in blazing hot water. "I'll go get the nurse."

"No, it's alright. This will pass, I know it." Stella panted. Yeah, right. Stella had never been so hot. Even when the summer hit temperatures over the 90s, Stella had never been so hot. She had never sweated so much, as if she had just emerged from a swimming pool.

Although she was worried, worried even more thanks to her motherly mode, she remained by her friend's side without touching her. Without calling the nurse she desperately wanted to find. Even though she couldn't help now, Hiroko knew she wasn't leaving her until Stella was truly alright.

Standing several people away was Mary. She had seen Stella's tense expression and wanted to assist her, but Hiroko had beaten her to it. She knew then that Stella would be alright. Now, she had to find Sazuma. Mary had helped her outside, but her older sister had released herself from her hold and disappeared. She scanned the area. There were so many brown-and-black-haired kids. There were some blondes here and there with a lot of redheads. There were even some pink, sky blue and light green heads. People were so weird.

There! On luck, she had found Sazuma. She had made her way to the back of the crowd, nearing the road. Too close to the road, actually. Mary rushed through, saying, "excuse me's," and, "sorry's," to people who had to be pushed out of the way, anyway.

Finally, she made it. The students around them were too focused on the burning buildings to listen in. Sazuma's back faced the school and she covered her face with her hands. Her shoulders shook, jumping every few seconds. Was she crying?

"What happened?" She hadn't seen Sazuma like this in years. Sazuma hadn't cried. At least, not in front of her. There were times after her father died that she had cried. However, that had been with a smile. "I'm free," she'd laughed while tears streamed down her face. That was years ago.

Now, this was different. As she turned around to face her sister, Mary's suspicions were correct. Her eyes were bloodshot and her face was strained. Sazuma was crying. Not from happiness. Was that guilt glistening in her eyes? Why guilt?

"I'm sorry, Mary."

On pure instinct, Mary held her sister close. One hand grasped the back of her head while the other rubbed her back. Sazuma hid her face in the crook of her neck. Her arms wound around Mary's chest. "What happened? Did you do this?"

Sazuma nodded hesitantly. Her shaking went up another notch. Her legs buckled. Sobs threatened to be released, but Sazuma held back.

"Why?" Mary asked, needing to know the answer.

"Kenta . . . I met Kenta in the hall and he told me he was going to help me learn how to control my power. He was giving me proof that I can control fire. He said this power was a blessing, but it's a curse. It's a straight up curse and I asked for this!"

Mary felt her own tears start to build up. God, Sazuma was going through so much and there was nothing to help her get over it. There was nothing she could do except hold her. Telling her "everything will be alright" was not going to help her in this case. Silence seemed to be the best way to get through this. Seeing her sister in pain caused tightness in her chest.

"I don't know what to do. I can't take it back. I know I can't, but I don't know what to do. I'm scared."

Mary nodded in understanding. Sazuma truly was scared. If she wasn't, she would have never admitted it. A slightest bit of fear would be held in and never mentioned. But this wasn't fear to her. This was terror. Horror. A true horror movie in Sazuma's eyes and she was the murderer behind the white mask.

Mary held her sister tightly. "I'm sorry," she whispered. Sazuma nuzzled closer and tried to block out the events that she caused. All conversations flew into her ears. The scent of burning rubber blocked her nose. Her eyes stung of the tears squeezing through her closed eyes and streaming down her cheeks.

"How could this have happened?" a male student asked.

"Our school! Our precious school!" a female teacher sobbed.

"Whoever did this should be ashamed." a male teacher growled.

Sazuma's heart sank. She laughed without humor. What heart? There was nothing there. Her ribcage held no heart in this body. It only held a soul that slowly deteriorated along with emotions that ravaged her chest and made their way to her mind.

More tears fell.

Sazuma was heartless. There was nothing left.

In the distance, Demonic Princesses Chikara and Emiko watched the burning building. They looked into the crowd, searched for their targets, and finally spotted them. "It looks like we found two Element Princesses," Chikara smiled. Ever since teleporting to this town, she had seen nothing but humans traveling from store to store, roaming the sidewalks, or simply standing around, leaning against buildings and watching other people live their lives.

Humans were pitiful things. They had no life. They watched others in envy or lust, never wanting anything more or less. Demons were no different, she supposed, but humans were still low on the food chain. They were worthless beings who deserved to be eaten. She had no idea why Heavenly beings would make such insolent beings.

"What's the redhead's name?" Chikara asked, getting onto the reason why they were here.

"Stella Jayberry," Emiko answered. The girl had a moderate tone, as always. Was she nervous? Sleepy? Bored? Chikara would never know. Then again, she didn't care . . . that much.

"What about the girl who's crying? Who is she?"

"Sazuma Kagami." Emiko answered again.

Chikara nodded and stood from her squatting position. They were on a business building in the distance, watching, and searching for the two targets said to attend Lane Way High School. The scent of human filled the air, excluding the two names Emiko mentioned, Stella and Sazuma. They radiated an exquisite misty aura.

It was sickening.

"Well, there are two. Sazuma is feeling guilty. She caused this whole mess to occur so I'm guessing she's the fire princess. The redhead is hurting inside, physically and mentally. Both reasons are completely different. I don't know for sure, but I think she's the earth princess."

"Which one should we bring to Derek?" Why should it matter? It was an Element Princess and Derek wanted the girl dead. Then again, he might have wanted to play with her before killing her. Bringing a princess back as a souvenir would have bumped them up on Derek's "Likeable people's" list.

"Let's get the fire girl. She's more damaged than the other child. She may be fire, but in her state, she'll be too emotionally dented." Chikara grinned ear to ear, loving what was up ahead. "And, besides, by the time I'm done with her, she would have been literally eaten alive by her remorse."

Story 3

You and *me* together

After the fire incident at school, the kids went home early. The ones who got to school by cars took their buses. The rest of the students walked home. Although parents stressed how the school wasn't safe anymore to the administrators and confusion of how the fire started was an issue, dismissal went relatively well.

In Dutchvine Middle School, in walking distance of the high school, the principal reported the students to head home due to the spreading fire from the high school. Twelve year old, Yumiko Honozoro, ran out of her middle school entrance, both concerned about her friends and excited that she got to leave early. Good thing her house was walking distance.

The young blonde stopped at the Iron Gate, now opened since the early release announcement on the intercom, and waited for her friends to come by. The twins had always walked her home after school. They passed by her middle school and her house, anyway. They were nice enough to even care if she made it home safe. They would have walked her home yesterday, but she had other things to do and didn't want to be a bother to her friends. She always found herself a bother, but her friends never thought of her that way.

She smiled. Waiting to see them was a little difficult, but she could manage. She always did. Waiting wasn't the problem. *How long* she waited was the issue. Yumiko was patient. She could wait for report cards, books being mailed, and FedEx packages. Although, if she had to wait three months for those items to arrive, that is when the edginess arrived.

For now, she could wait. She would spend the night here if she had to wait for her friends to come for her. While packing her things from her locker, Yumiko had gotten a message from Mary.

School had a fire. We will dismiss early. This should affect you too so wait for us to walk you home.

So, Yumiko had waited. This did, indeed, affect her. Dutchvine Middle was walking distance of Lane Way if you exited from the backdoors. All you had to do was travel down a circular dirt path, cross through some bushes, then you were on the other side.

The principal of the middle school had claimed the back buildings of the high school had ignited and would soon spread to the middle school if not stopped in time. So dismissal was immediate and parents were called with urgency. Fire trucks arrived on scene, in both the middle and the high school. The fire was contained but that wasn't stopping the kids from running to their parents and even crying about the day's events.

To Yumiko, this was both frightening and exciting. Frightening because your life was now in your hands and there was no one to help you but yourself. If the fire had arrived, it was every man for himself. However, it was exciting because of the sheer fact that your life was in your hands and it was every man for himself! It was a total rush, knowing you were about to die.

Sazuma must have had some kind of effect on her because this was not the usual Yumiko thinking.

Yumiko was a book fan. A book addict, actually. Well, the romance book addict. Yeah, that's better. After finishing one book, Yumiko had to have another. If she didn't, she would go nuts, wanting more books, clawing at her computer screen repeating, "I need! I need!"

At least she wasn't alone on this. Stella acted the same way. The two had formed a little book club, reading the same books and loving their manly characters. Mary had joined soon after. The book assortments had gotten better, too.

Another thing Yumiko and Stella had in common was their shyness. Approaching people was a bit of an issue and making friends wasn't as easy as breathing. Yumiko was smart, creative but mostly independent. Even though she was twelve, her ability to approach others was a bit overwhelming. People always laughed at her. People always pitied her. They always suspected she was weak, needed constant guidance and needed severe isolation.

She didn't understand people. Yumiko had done nothing wrong. Her hair might have been so blonde it almost looked white. She might have had scars on her neck and shoulders that would remain on her for the rest of her life. And she might have mistreated doctors who tried to help her with her unusual powers. But that didn't mean Yumiko was any different.

She was human. She was a girl who wanted a loving family, friends who supported her and a future she would look forward to finding. So far, she had a loving family; her older brothers Jared and Jeremy, friends who supported her; Sazuma, Mary, Stella, Hiroko, and her new friend, Reiko, whom she met at Hiroko's slumber party last weekend, but the future she looked forward to . . . would that day ever come?

"Hello, Yumiko. Anybody in there?" Yumiko blinked several times. Mary's grinning face came into view. Wow, her eyes were pretty. They might have been black but there was love in those eyes. Love and compassion, the best elements anyone could ask for in a woman.

"Yeah, good morning." Was it morning? "What's up?"

"Well you were lost in thought. We've been here a good minute."

Yumiko would have to work on that. She usually was on focus, always paying attention and stayed alert. Memories just hit her, she guessed.

Yumiko turned from Mary to Sazuma. She looked awful. Red mixed into her white eyeballs and her shoulders slumped over. She wore her black Jack Skellington jacket. Her hood covered her head, casting shadows over her face. Still, the pain in her eyes and the intensity of her frown bothered the young girl.

"Sazuma is just a bit tired," Mary said, sensing the direction of her thoughts. But, she was so sad. Had one of her other friends been injured? Had anyone in *their* group been injured?

Immediate panic struck. "Reiko! Stella! Hiroko! Were they hurt? Are they okay?"

Mary held up her hands, all innocence and truth. "No, no, they're fine. None of our friends were injured. Right now, I don't believe anyone was hurt. Just spooked."

Yumiko calmed. With the slight push from Mary, the girls started their journey home. It would be a short journey, considering Yumiko had to turn left at the intersection instead of keeping straight, but it was still a journey.

"So what's new?" Yumiko asked, trying to forget the fire incident. There was no way this was going to ruin her day.

"Uhh," Mary started, "Well nothing much. It's only Tuesday. It's not like a life changing experience happened to us yesterday afternoon after school."

Uhh, okay. That wasn't weird. "Cool," Yumiko responded in wonder. *Did* something happen after school? "What did you guys do after school?" Mary was known best for reading. Plus, she was a part of Yumiko and Stella's mini-book club, which didn't have a name yet. Yumiko would have guessed her answer was reading or studying.

"We did nothing. We were knocked out and woke up this morning in a jolt." Her response was fast, as if she was hiding what she was saying.

Sazuma, who had been inactive since the encounter, sprang to life, covering Mary's mouth with her arm snaking over her sister's shoulder. "We have to go. Call you later." With that, they were gone, disappearing down the sidewalk and making their way through the four way intersection.

Yumiko turned left, crossed the street once cleared and headed down to the one and/or two story houses past the restaurants and bakeries. Her house lied on a community known as Bakers Field. It used to be a trailer park but with economic success, the park was no longer needed. Homes were built, small but still roomy, and the income was less than $700 a month.

Her brothers were the breadwinners. Her eldest brother, Jared, was a lawyer, always on the move but handled his business on the phone rather than traveling. Jeremy was a contractor. He was also always moving except Yumiko wouldn't see him for days, sometimes weeks. He worked in local towns, cities, helping people nationwide.

Together, they could have afforded a bigger house, but they used that money for Yumiko's needs. They were even saving for her college right now. She loved her brothers. They always cared. They always presented their love to her and her friends. She couldn't have asked for a better family. A father and mother might have been missing from the picture, but Yumiko didn't mind. She didn't remember her parents, anyway.

Yumiko continued on, waving to the bakeries who were selling their fresh garlic bread. Mr. Nickels, the head of *Nickel's Bakery* even gave her a roll while she passed. She sniffed it in, not being able to wait to get home. She rushed forward, turned another left, and entered her community.

The houses were widespread with asphalt roofing. Each house was made of either red or gray bricks and had no front yards. Only a dry dirt road separated someone's property from another. Fences of iron or wood separated the remaining land.

Yumiko's house was made of red brick and square bushes rested under the front windows. She ran to her right, walked up the three stairs of her white painted porch, took out the spare house key from under the grassy *Welcome* mat and headed inside, only to be greeted by the scent of spaghetti. She was glad she was offered garlic bread.

Meanwhile, the Kagami twins rushed inside of their house. Sazuma locked the door behind them then faced Mary. She grabbed her hood and forced it down, taking strands of hair with her. "This is why you let me do the talking." Their secret had almost been compromised. Mary was never good with lying. She failed every damn time.

"You weren't speaking so it's not my fault."

Knowing she was right, Sazuma discarded the conversation and stomped up the stairs.

Mary would never understand. She might have held her back at the school. She might have offered her support by rubbing her back and being silent with her instead of saying useless things like, "everything will be alright," however; Mary would never understand Sazuma's pain.

Mary had been treated like a queen, and that wasn't only at home. Everyone at school loved Mary. She and Sazuma had the same face, but they were so different. Sazuma had had bruises on her neck from the latest beating. Mary had none.

Sazuma had worn clothes that were new but were ripped and shredded by her own father for kicks. Mary did not.

Sazuma had been isolated for weekends on end for not allowing her father's threatening and unforgiveable behavior. Mary was not.

Even now. Sazuma had used her fire ball to not only damage a tree that had no chance in defending itself but to also burn a building full of innocent students who had no idea their classroom would have exploded that today. Mary had been oblivious to it all.

It was impossible for Mary to understand the feeling of knowing you might have injured someone. It was impossible for her to understand her incident might have even killed someone. It was impossible for her to understand she had killed a weeping willow tree, whose seed was rare to have, intriguing to watch grow and was a blessing to have the time to watch that tree grow.

Sazuma had ruined it all. One mistake and it was all over.

She slammed her door, threw her bag down, plopped on her bed, and screamed into her chestnut sheeted pillow. One scream followed after another. One scream was filled with a sob. The others were filled with more and more until Sazuma screamed no more. Tears filled her pillow. Her bed shook as she sobbed. Despair hit her terribly. Guilt was no longer chomping at her but it wasn't satisfied. It continued to eat at her, slowly devouring her into nothing more than a broken shell.

To her, Sazuma was already a cracked shell. Being broken wouldn't matter.

Now exhausted from walking, Hiroko helped Stella get inside her apartment and placed her gently on the couch. Stella's apartment was all the way across town. It was a thirty minute walk to Hiroko's house from here. She ughed, already hating the thought of walking for more than five minutes.

However, it was worth it. Stella had been sweating intensely since leaving school and Hiroko's parents are working in Tokyo, which was a good two hours away, if you drove. This couldn't wait. The girls had made the walk with Reiko as one of her supports, which was rare. Reiko wasn't a fan of walking either. Because this was Stella, she made an exception.

Reiko sat beside Stella. Because Stella's head hung low, Reiko had to lean on her knees and peer at her from a lower angle. She observed her then turned to Hiroko. "Water, cold towels, and a change of clothes."

Hiroko dashed into action, getting the asked items and returning to Reiko's side, handing her the cold bottle of water first. Reiko opened the bottle. Stella gulped it and drained the contents in seconds. She panted out, not realizing how dry her throat had been. "Thanks."

"No prob," Reiko grinned. "Need anything else?"

"A shower," Stella answered. Her uniform blouse was stuck to her chest and sweat stains soaked her armpits. Her hair plastered to the sides of her face. At least she still had a floral scent. The scent always worked perfectly for her. "We'll wait out here for you." Reiko grabbed Stella's hand and brought her to her feet. Hiroko stayed behind while Reiko led her friend to the bathroom down the hall. Soon, the water was running and Reiko was closing the door. "Shout if you need anything."

"Alright," Stella answered through the door. Hiroko just hoped the girl didn't fall over from exhaustion. That was probably Reiko's worry, as well.

With a sigh, the icy blue-streak-haired girl walked into the living room.

Her hands came to her hips and her eyes wheeled around. "Nice place."

That's right. She was in Stella's apartment. Hiroko had come here once before to pick up Stella for one of her slumber parties. The experience had been startling though.

She had arrived at the apartment door, knocked, and immediately froze. A woman had shouted through the door. She was pissed, as if the knock had awoken her from a nap or bothered her headache.

"Be nice Ayano," Stella said while opening her room door with her bags in hand. She was looking over her shoulder with a smile. Hiroko was still shocked through. She knew Stella was living with a caretaker, but she had no idea the woman hated sound. "I'll text you as soon as I get there."

"No wandering off after dark." The woman's voice changed drastically. The groggy shout was now a laid back tone.

"Yes I know." Stella faced Hiroko now, smiled and exited the room. "No prank calling people for fun."

"I know that too."

"Don't play with Ouija boards. They'll fuck you up."

"Yes, ma'am."

The door was cracked now. Stella peered through. "Bye."

"Have fun," the woman said. Stella closed the door, locked it and placed the key in her pocket. Hiroko grabbed one of her two carrier bags and walked with Stella down the teal rugged, raspberry-painted hallways.

"Sorry about that. Ayano doesn't like noise this late at night."

Now, Hiroko knew the caretaker's name was Ayano. She was vile, mean and didn't like noise after six p.m. Hiroko kept a note of that for years.

Would she arrive now? Stella said the woman worked. She probably delivered papers or worked at a pizza shop. Stella said she worked little jobs, giving just enough money to get by. Who knows, she could have been a lawyer like Yumiko's brother Jared.

Why wouldn't the middle school girl get a new house with a brother as a lawyer?!

"This might be an apartment but it's kind of roomy." Reiko said, walking around leisurely and touching every surface with the pad of her index finger. Hiroko's eyes looked up, witnessing the beauty of the diamond-ceiling pattern. Each row and column seemed to shine elegantly against the single wood bladed ceiling fan.

Her eyes came back down, noticing the entire room. Dark wood hollow cabinets surrounded the rectangular kitchen behind the entrance. A single-island rested in the middle with granite as its counter. Reiko now browsed around inside the little enclosure, separated from the rest of the room by a single step. The walls of the apartment were bronze and hardwood covered the floors, each wood resting side by side in a perfect pattern. The couches, one under the single living room window and the other right in front of that one, were a wheat color. Two folded up sleeping bags, one lavender and the other black, rested beside the couch by the window with the white pillows on top.

Hiroko would have investigated further but Stella appeared from the bathroom. She wore a short sleeved orange shirt with white writing saying, 'Sunny side up'. Blue jeans hugged her hips. A white towel slept over her shoulders with her damp hair hanging above it.

Reiko rushed over to help Stella back to the couch, but Stella raised her hand, stopping Reiko mid-step. "I'm alright. I feel better now. Honestly."

Hiroko turned to the bathroom. No steam seeped through the closed door. "Cold shower?"

Stella nodded with a grin. "And it helped a lot, too. I don't feel so hot anymore."

Her pinked features were better. Her beige skin now seeped with health. Stella made her way to the couch and plopped out in a tired exhale. She rubbed her breastbone with a grunt. Hiroko and Reiko plopped to her sides, ears open, and eyes searching for any signs of pain.

Stella chuckled, "Seriously, I'm fine."

"When is your caretaker coming?" Reiko asked. She too knew about Ayano. She never had seen her either.

"I called her during the walk here remember?" Hiroko said. That had been the shortest phone call she ever had, plus the most anxious. Hiroko didn't know this "Ayano." All she knew was that the woman took care of Stella and made her happy. Maybe she wasn't a fan of people.

Hiroko had taken Stella's phone from her pocket, scrolled her contacts and pressed Ayano's name. It was the only *A* in the contacts list anyway.

"What's up? You ok?" The question had been full of concern. Yet, so tender, soft even.

Hiroko was too afraid to speak as it was, so she kept things short and simple. "This is Stella's friend Hiroko and I'm informing you that Stella is not feeling well at this time. Please come to the apartment at once and nurse her back to full health."

Yup, short and simple. Plus, she had sounded like the woman who spoke before you left a message on someone's voicemail. Great.

"On my way," the woman's tone was hard the next instant. She hung up the second afterward.

The call was nerve wrecking, but at least the task was accomplished. Now all they needed was for the woman to arrive.

The front door swung open, causing Reiko and Hiroko to jump. Their hearts leaped to their throats then floated back down with a thud. It was a woman, Hiroko realized. How did she get here so fast? She moved swiftly from the door and kneeled in front of Stella. She grabbed her cheeks and moved her from side to side, checking for injuries.

Stella laughed as if a dog was constantly licking her face. "I'm fine Ayano. Really."

This was Ayano? Whoa . . .

"Is she alright?" Hiroko stared at the mysterious woman. Her eyes were burgundy and shined with both unease and warning. She looked as if she was in attack mode.

"Yeah, she's fine."

The woman stood tall, almost towering Hiroko. The blonde stood five-foot-seven. The woman must have been at least five-eleven. Her eyes pierced her as she stared her down. She was definitely in attack mode. "Are you going to give me more details than that?" Pins shot through Hiroko's chest. This must have been true fear. Breathing got even harder. "What happened?"

"Stella's temperature was high to the point we thought we were going to have to take her to the hospital." All attention turned to Reiko. She stood straight, her eyes keeping Ayano in her place. "Sweat drenched her straight away and she claimed to have been in pain."

"But, I'm alright now," Stella interjected.

Burgundy eyes went from Stella, to Reiko then to Hiroko. "And you are?"

Ayano's rudeness was ignored. Hiroko was still a bit anxious. She was so intimidating. "I'm Hiroko. Stella's friend."

"You're the one that called me." A statement, not a question. "And who are you?" Ayano turned from Hiroko.

"I'm Reiko Takashima. It's a pleasure to meet me, I'm sure."

Reiko was ignored. Ayano kneeled down to Stella again. "Do you need anything? I'll get you whatever you want."

"I could use a nap," Stella closed her jaw, holding back a yawn that proved what she needed.

Ayano glared at Hiroko sharply. "Leave."

"Kay, bye." Reiko responded in Hiroko's place. She grabbed her wrist and dragged Hiroko out with their bags in hand. Ayano followed them to the door and slammed it behind them, causing the walls surrounding the door to shake.

Reiko flipped her silver book bag over her shoulder. "Yup, we're never visiting this place ever again. Not happenin'."

Hiroko saw why she would say such a thing. Something radiated off of Ayano. It wasn't anger. It wasn't sadness. It was a mix in between. Maybe she was misunderstood. But for what? What was the purpose? Why would Hiroko even think of such a thing?

It couldn't have been misunderstanding. Stella must have understood her. She must have known Ayano's past and helped her cope with whatever happened to her. Maybe Ayano had a happy life . . . or a troubled one. Whatever it was, it had to be something. Ayano wasn't a normal girl. She was too beautiful, too filled with such overwhelming protection for Stella.

She couldn't explain it, but Hiroko knew she was special. Maybe Stella knew what it was. She *hoped* Stella knew what it was.

"That girl is weird," Reiko said, starting their walk to the other side of town. Thirty minute walk home they come. "Ayano, I never heard that name before. There was this one dude I knew in elementary school named Ano. But, Ayano? Just hearing it is weird. Eye-ya-no."

"Such a detective," Hiroko muttered, keeping a slow pace behind Reiko.

She heard loud and clear, though. "I'm just saying, she's weird. I can't explain it, but she's different from most people."

So she feels it too. Hiroko kept that as a mental note.

"It's not like she brightens up a room. That's far from it. She might be a foreigner. Her skin was darker than most."

"Maybe," Hiroko pondered. Ayano had skin as luscious as caramel. And her hair was as blackish gray as charcoal. Maybe she *was* a foreigner. Even so, "We can't judge where she's from based on skin color. It's best to ask in person."

Reiko shrugged, "Hey, if you want to go back and face the tall foreigner by yourself with Stella not calming her little friend down, then by all means, go ahead. Me? I'm going home."

Hiroko sighed, but continued on. No way was she facing her again. One encounter was good enough.

The sun touched the horizon by the time Hiroko made it home. It didn't surprise her when her parents hadn't welcomed her or even yelled in concern for being an hour late after curfew. They still weren't home.

Her mother and stepfather worked in the heart of Tokyo, where businesses thrived and working late was considered an honor. Hiroko's mother, Kotare, worked as a stockbroker; always on the run and making deals. After Hiroko's father died in a car accident—to Hiroko, getting T-boned and swerving off the Golden Gate Bridge was not an accident—Kotare had moved to the stock market, hoping to continue working and distract herself.

Kotare had met Hiroko's stepfather, Joseph Booming, on her first day of work. She met him two years after Hiroko's father died. Although it was difficult for her to move on so soon, Kotare decided to try again at love. She succeeded and it seemed she was happy. Joseph was a kind man. Smart, loyal, compassionate and a real jokester. He never played pranks but he was good at telling the oldest jokes in the book and actually making them funny again. Hiroko had been seven when she met the guy.

She could not get over her father. Similarities between Joseph and her father are that they both had sandy brown hair and sapphire eyes. They both might have also been charming and tender, but Hiroko didn't want those feelings to mix. Even though she gave him a rough start, Hiroko learned to open up to the guy after he moved in. He never touched her in inappropriate places. He never flirted with her and he only winked at her to wish her good luck in school. So yeah, Joseph was not all that bad.

Nevertheless, they still worked their butts off. Both Kotare and Joseph arrived home late, around one in the morning and left at five, hoping to save their spots in the market and check their stocks. "We're lucky to even come home," Hiroko's mother once said. Sure, it might have been nice for them to come home, yet it still hurt returning from school and finding the house empty.

As she stepped into the house, locked the door and slugged up the hardwood stairs, Hiroko wondered, "This feeling of loneliness will never dim, will it?"

☙

After a while of thinking, Sazuma tried to get some sleep. She should have known sleep wouldn't come to her so easily. Thoughts of today's incident replayed through her mind so many times that Sazuma lost count. To see that weeping willow slowly burn . . .

Sazuma whimpered. But why? She shouldn't have cared. It was just a tree. She could personally plant another. That wasn't the point, though. Sazuma had caused destruction to an object that had stood and grew in the same place for over a century. One incident ruined all of those years of progress. Not only that, but Sazuma's meager "incident" had caused one side of her school to shrivel to the ground.

Someone could have gotten hurt.

Someone could have died.

She buried her head inside of her pillow, if that was even possible. She'd been hiding in her room for hours. Mary hadn't entered since returning home. Good thing, too. She needed to be alone. Talking was pointless. Saying meaningless things like, "Everything will be alright," and, "Don't worry, the damage wasn't that serious," would only piss her off. It was best to leave her alone.

Plus, if she was going to talk, Kenta would be the only person she would communicate with. This was his fault. He'd cursed her with this gift of fire. He had given her this "elemental orb" and didn't warn her about its abilities. She could have made a smaller flame. She could have . . .

"Accepting this gift isn't something you can come back from. Once you're given the orb, there's no going back. The human life you knew would be a distant memory to you. You will no longer be a human. As an Element Princess, you are claiming to be a supernatural being with unique abilities."

Ayano had warned them. She was clear about receiving the orbs. She must have known this was going to happen. Sazuma and Mary had accepted these gifts, without question. Sazuma had thought about it, however, hadn't truly comprehended.

Fire, an element that causes great destruction. It would burn anything, destroy everything, and re-grow nothing. Fire was also warmth and a light, nonetheless, that was all it was good for.

Why would she be given such a dangerous element? There were others. Sazuma could have had earth. She was an earthy person. Okay, no she wasn't. She could have been wind. She was breezy, and fresh and free. Was she? Doubt filled her mind.

There were other elements, right? There was light, ice, and darkness. Yeah, she could have been darkness. She liked staying in corners and reading books. Black was her favorite color and keeping to herself was her sense of peace. Isn't that what darkness is about; isolation?

There was also water. Water was Mary. Why did Mary receive that element? Water was . . . wet . . . and liquidly. What was water about anyway? You drink it, use it to refresh your gardens, and even pee it out. What was so special about it?

Couldn't twins trade elements? A speck of hope popped up. It was the first sign of life Sazuma had felt in hours. Maybe she and Mary could trade elements. They could switch powers and this problem would be over.

No, she thought a second later. If Sazuma, a teenager with a childhood that broke her trust with others, couldn't handle with these abilities, then Mary, a teenager blessed with love and respect, would have a shattered soul if a test of her flaming powers malfunctioned. Sazuma wouldn't allow that. Mary didn't deserve it. Sazuma, on the other hand. After years of fighting, cussing, and hurting others by demanding they leave her alone, after they showed nothing but kindness, proved that she deserved this ability.

This curse.

Sazuma pulled herself into a ball, wanting nothing more than to disappear.

Consequently, what she did not know was that the demon, Chikara Yamada, was watching her the entire time. Cautious amethyst peered through her bedroom window by the desk and observed the area, checking for any movements in the room. There was nothing. Chikara's eyes returned to Sazuma. She was out. Her face hid behind her pillow. Her body was still.

Chikara made her move, slowly sliding the window up and entering the room. Her heels didn't even touch the hardwood. Her weapons jingled at her belt, but Sazuma remained unmoving. She glided through the room. Her eyes raked Sazuma's body. Long white socks covered her feet. A short skirt laid on her bottom, a long sleeve shirt covered her back-a school uniform, Chikara realized, and black braids that also hid in the chestnut colored pillow sheet.

Chikara's carnation scent wafted through the room, sending a straight path to Sazuma's direction . . . and finally hitting her nostrils. The distressed teenager jumped off the bed, locking eyes with the intruder. She propelled backward, hitting the back of her knees on Mary's bed, and plopped down. Their eyes never wavered.

Who was this chick? Didn't matter, Sazuma guessed. She was an intruder. Her purpose here wasn't good, she knew.

Sazuma stood, bent her knees and faced her palms to the intruder. She hated the thought of having to use these destructive abilities again—especially knowing they might be used to burn down her own house—but if she *was* going to use them, they could at least be used for self-defense.

But would you really burn a thief? Sazuma shoved the question to the corner of her mind.

"What are you doing here?"

"I'm here to help you." Chikara answered. Her voice was settling, but Sazuma wouldn't fall for any false kindness. She had no idea what this chick was thinking, so every move Sazuma made had to be cautious. She was like that anyway.

"Who are you?" "I'm a friend."

"That's what everyone says. Don't make me have to hurt you."

"Hurt me?" Her tone was disbelieving, as if it was impossible for Sazuma to hurt her. Maybe she was right. There was a high chance at low damage to the thief. Sazuma had to try anyway. The woman's eyebrows rose. "Princess, just because you now possess fire, that doesn't mean you can control it."

Sazuma's eyes widened. "How . . . How did you know I control fire?"

The woman shrugged, pushing the lavender hair on her head up and dropping it along with her shoulders. Her hair was interesting. The woman's hair shined lilac and hung lusciously on her head. Her eyes were a dazzling amethyst with crystalline irises that were out of this world. She wore a silk gold shirt that V-ed just below her breasts, dark brown skinny jeans and gold-heeled ankle boots. Throwing stars, daggers, and guns hung on her black heavy-duty belt.

If her plan was to rob someone, she meant business.

"How did you know I control fire?" Sazuma repeated forcefully this time.

"I know things," she stuffed her hands in her pocket. "I know what happened today at Lane Way high school. I know you started that fire."

She knew. She knew about the incident. How much did she know? How did she find out? Sazuma lowered her hands. This woman couldn't be trusted, Sazuma knew that. But how had she known?

The woman continued, "I know you're feeling depressed, guilty, and you feel cursed. You were given your power by your own free will and you can't reverse your effects. Well, I can help you with your power. Just come with me and I can help you with everything."

"Everything," Sazuma pondered. She didn't know this woman but based on her looks and choice of weaponry, she had skills. It wasn't a false face, either. Maybe she could help. Maybe she could make this curse more durable.

"All I need is your faith in me. That's all I ask."

Don't do it, her conscience said. Sazuma always held a bit of doubt. What if she was lying? What if, the moment she agreed, the woman knocked her out and robbed every valuable item in the house? What if, because of Sazuma's mistake, Mary ended up suffering the price?

"I can't give you my faith. I can't give you my trust."

"Do not hold doubts Sazuma. Doubts will get you nowhere."

Was it obvious that she had doubts? Sazuma calmed, hoping to remain emotionless. This woman didn't need an advantage to take her down. Emotions slowed you down. She *wouldn't* give this woman the upper hand.

"Look, I don't know who you are and I'm sure your need to "help me" is strong, but I need you to leave."

The woman's welcoming expression dropped. "You have two choices here, princess. You either come with me willingly or I kill you where you stand. Your choice."

Funny how telling someone to leave changes one's attitude. "Get out of my house or I'm going to—"

"You're going to do what little girl?" Her tone was lethal, stern; sharp. As sharp as the black hilted dagger hanging over her right thigh, actually. "You think you really have a chance against me? I have hundreds of years of experience. You got nothing on me."

Her hands wound around, disappearing behind her back and reappearing with two daggers in her hands. Their blades were pen straight with a newly sharpened tip. Sazuma liked weapons and knew if they were worth something. These blades were not only worth it. They could finish a job swiftly.

Awesome, she was stuck. Not only was she dealing with a woman who carried daggers. She was dealing with a gorgeous woman who, Sazuma realized, had an intention to kill her. She was a skilled thief, Sazuma knew that. She had to find a way to get rid of her.

She wouldn't get Mary get caught up in this mess.

Sadly, Sazuma's hopes wouldn't be realized.

Mary burst into the room. Her hands were empty, but determination coated her features. What the hell was she doing?

"That's far enough. Whoever you are, you better leave."

Considering she was the one who didn't hold a weapon and, yes, Sazuma was on the same boat, Mary had no right to command anyone.

The woman chuckled, as if Mary had just spurted a joke. "Or what? You'll hurt me? You're just a human." Human, she'd said. So, that meant she wasn't one.

Realization hit. Maybe she wasn't human. Her appearance should have slapped Sazuma on the dot. This girl wasn't human. Small fangs poked out, barely touching her bottom lip. Her violet eyes shined with so much anticipation, she should be overdosing.

Kenta had said they were entering a supernatural world; a world filled with more than they could imagine, probably. There was such a thing as non-humans now. This was probably one of those people. But what was she?

Mary brought up her hand, revealing a bottle of water she was clutching. Was that thing always there? Mary glared at the woman just as the woman did the same.

The woman brought her hands together and shuddered in false fear. "Oooh, you're going to hurt me with a bottle of water," she dropped her façade, "Yeah, you're bad."

Strangely, Mary smirked. Her focus remained on the intruder. How could she smirk so casually? The girl was nuts. Sure she could fight, but come on, she was no hero.

Wait a sec . . . Sazuma mentally slapped herself. She felt like a total idiot. Now, if the woman hadn't figured it out by now, then the girls had the advantage. They could use Mary's ability against her and the thief would be-literally-washed away.

Too bad the theory didn't last long.

The woman's eyes widened in understanding, her options dawning on her. The intruder gulped as she shifted her weight to her right side. "You're an Element Princess?"

She knew? Sazuma stared in shock. How had she known? Who was this chick anyway?

"Bingo," Mary tilted her head in a "You should have known this" kind of fashion.

She shook her head, her purple hair following her head motions. Her arms dropped to her side and her blades hung low. "But, how? I knew there were two but three?"

Three? There's another one? Sazuma wondered to herself.

"Leave my house, *now*."

Chikara side smirked. The stupidity in these girls was something to truly hate. After years of hearing the same thing from other enemies, Chikara had had enough. She twirled her weapons in her hands and stopped them abruptly. The tips faced the girls. "Do you think you could actually stop a Demonic Princess?"

The twins paused. They were probably thinking the same thing. "Demonic princess?" they asked aloud. She was a demon. Based on the name she had to be. Because she had daggers, she was either a thief or here to kill them. Coming to this realization caused Sazuma to stiffen. Her survival was on the line. But this was different from when an enraged father arrived home. This was an actual demon. Plus, Mary's life was on the line now. She tensed up, debating on the best options to get Mary out of here.

Sazuma was willing to sacrifice herself in this situation. She wouldn't allow Mary to die because of this woman, the woman who approached her first.

"That's right ladies," the intruder flipped her long hair over her shoulder. "My name is Chikara Yamada. I am a demon ninja."

As if this couldn't get any worse, Sazuma thought.

"Now," the ninja licked her dagger's blade, "let's end this, shall we." As Chikara charged at Mary, Sazuma grabbed her sister's collar, pushed her out of the way and kicked Chikara's stomach so she landed where she started. Mary opened the water bottle and poured the contents on the floor.

Chikara charged again. This time, Mary threw up her hands and threw the water on the demon. She then grabbed her sister's hand and they both dashed down the stairs. They made their way out of the house then spotted a black-haired, green-eyed girl standing a few inches away from the house.

The girl stood straight, but timidly, as if she was too nervous about this approach. A baggy pine green long sleeved shirt covered her upper regions while faded jeans hugged her legs. Dark brown boots covered her feet. An emerald sword sheath rested on her left side. The girl's pale hand gripped her emerald sword hilt. The sword rattled. She was shaking.

Why was she scared? She was the one with the weapon.

"Get back here!" Chikara yelled as she jumped from the second floor window right above their heads, the tips of her daggers aimed for their noggins. The twins separated and dodged the attack.

Sazuma put up her hand to try a fire attack, but Chikara slashed her upper arm, ripping her uniform shirt and tearing sensitive flesh. Blood slid down her arm. A sharp pain entered her body. She knew she couldn't give up. She had to keep fighting.

Mary looked around for any water-related source. She spotted a fire hydrant two houses down and charged at it.

"San to mai . . ." Emiko mumbled as she walked closer to Mary. Seconds later, Mary was motionless. Her entire body had frozen. Her eyes widened.

Emiko walked closer to the defenseless teenager until she stood right in front of her. "Trying to escape increases your death," she said in her moderately gentle and low voice.

Mary stared at her. She wasn't a killer. She wasn't even a fighter. Her eyes were too soft. Her expression was too supple. But, with this ability that she had, there was no need for her to fight.

She had this manipulation spell, Mary knew. Her body had frozen altogether. Her mind worked but her body didn't listen. Her nerves paid her no heed. They had a mind of their own.

The black-haired woman continued, "My spell is unbreakable to you." Mary's black eyes stared right in her enemy's. The woman might have a soft expression, but her eyes seemed to stare into your soul. It seemed like she was leaving a piece of herself in you. Not only did you feel yourself fading, but there was a sadness that engulfed her very being.

The woman slowly pulled out her sword, revealing a silver blade, newly sharpened. "Before I kill you, do you have any regrets?"

Mary didn't say a word. Instead of thinking of regrets, she was thinking of ways to escape. Her mind was coming up blank. Thanks to this girl, Mary couldn't move. Because she couldn't move, there was no way to commence the plan she was thinking of; which she still didn't have. She wouldn't accept this. There had to be something she could do to save herself.

Mary's black-haired enemy raised her sword, preparing to swing in an arc. No, Mary thought, this couldn't be it. This *wouldn't* be it. Her body might have not been able to move but she could have done something! The woman's sword was swung, aiming toward Mary's neck.

Suddenly, a black whip-like cloth surrounded the woman's wrist and locked her up tight. The woman paused. Her blade touched Mary's pulse. A trickle of blood slid down her neck. Realizing her eyes were squeezed shut, Mary opened them in surprise.

Ayano jumped down from a house and sandwiched herself between Mary and the intruder. The woman's spell lifted. The woman's eyes widened in shock. Her breath caught. She stared. Using her staff, she swerved her weapon to the side, sending the woman in the air and slamming into the concrete down the street.

"Damn you Ayano!" Chikara shouted, then focused on Sazuma. Before she knew it, Kenta was running toward them with a sword in his hands. Chikara ignored the fire princess and clashed blades with the furious spirit being.

"You damn spirit beings always have to go into other people's business." Burgundy eyes narrowed. "You demons are trying to take over the world.

This *is* my business!" Chikara was pushed back. Her boots skid on the pavement. She retaliated by charging forward, colliding with Kenta's wavy crimson blade once again.

As they fought, Sazuma got up from the ground and ran to her sister. Mary unhurriedly stood. She swayed, getting used to her body movements again. She faced Ayano, both grateful and surprised to see her. "How did you guys know we were in trouble?"

Ayano shrugged casually. "Well, all Element Princesses can sense when their comrades are in danger."

"Wait, so that means you're an Element Princess?" Mary asked. "I had no idea. You don't look like that type of person." Ayano remained quiet. Sazuma stared at her. How had Mary not known? Without a doubt, she was a little slow. "What power do you have?" Mary asked, wanting to know more about her.

"Darkness and death," she answered.

"Oh that's a shocker," Sazuma muttered. Ayano simply sighed. Sazuma might have liked this girl because of her attitude and freedom, but were sighing, shrugging, and expressions of annoyance all she did?

Ayano tilted her golden staff to the side. Her black cloth pulled the woman over. Her mouth was covered now and the cloth surrounded her arms and most of her head. "Damn this girl and her spells."

Her hearing must have been awesome. The twins hadn't heard a thing. Had she been conducting a spell? "A spell, huh?" Mary said, probably thinking the same thing Sazuma was. Both hadn't noticed the woman chanting her spell. They would have to work on that.

Ayano faced the twins. "This girl is Emiko Yamada. She controls space and time. She casts spells that affect someone's time. When she's doing so, either cover your ears or cover *her* mouth." The cloth surrounding the woman—Em-me-ko, right?—tightened.

"That would help."

"Yes it would." Ayano said to Sazuma.

The team turned their attention to Chikara as she landed hard on the ground next to the twins. The sisters watched in awe as Kenta pointed his blade to her throat. "Looks like this spirit being wins."

"Not for long," Chikara hissed, then disappeared altogether, leaving nothing of her behind. When they turned to Emiko, she did the same. Ayano's cloth flopped to the ground.

"Damn," Ayano murmured. The black whip was contracted back to the tip of Ayano's staff, where a small golden sphere, matching the rest of her staff, waited for it. She then walked to Kenta. Her hips swung side to side and her charcoal colored hair played with the breeze. "What do we do now?"

"Let's have a protection group for the time being." Kenta answered as he put his sword back in its sheath. The twins froze, watching as the crimson bladed sword turned from a wavy blade to a straight and silver blade. "I'll stay with the twins while you watch Stella."

All attention returned. "Stella?" Sazuma asked, entering the conversation. Kenta answered. "Stella is the earth Element Princess."

"Really? You mean Stella Jayberry? Our little Stella?!"

Ayano glared at her. "You girls are bad at comprehending, aren't you?"

"I'm guessing all of the princesses are like that." Kenta shrugged with a smirk.

"Well, back to what you said Kenta." Mary faced him. "You can't stay with us. Our mother will be home soon and I doubt we can easily tell her a guy is going to stay at our house."

She was right. Their mother was a kind woman who showed love to all of Sazuma and Mary's friends, which was Stella, Hiroko, Reiko, and Yumiko, but she would never allow her daughters to house a guy; a muscled man who looked out of this world in their home.

"Don't worry about her seeing me. Only supernatural beings and other princesses can see me. Humans won't even know I'm here." It must have been that Spirit Being ability.

"Well I still don't want a guy staying in our house."

"I agree," Sazuma twitched. Her wound was continuing to bleed. "It's too weird."

"Fine, then I'll stay on your roof." "Yeah, that's not creepy."

"Will you two stop complaining and just go with it?!" Ayano shouted. She stomped away, wanting to get away from the people around her. "I'm going home. Good night!"

Everyone paused and waited until Ayano was out of sight. "Is she always like that?" Sazuma asked. That didn't change the fact that Sazuma still liked her. She was tough and had no manners. She was Sazuma's hero.

"For good reason," Kenta smiled. There was so much pride in his tone, as if her behavior was something worthwhile.

He turned to Sazuma, observing her wound. His proud expression morphed into anger with bits of concern. "You're hurt."

As he reached out, Sazuma gave him her back. She lowered her head, "It's nothing. Don't worry about it."

"I'll take care of her. Just worry about yourself, alright?"

Kenta paused. He sighed, "Alright. You girls should head inside, though. It's getting dark."

Kenta turn to the Kagami house. He bent his knees and pushed up, jumping into the sky, landing on a branch hanging above the home, and then made it to the roof. He sat down with his legs crossed and held onto his sword between his legs.

Although his acrobatics were awesome, the girls were too tired to comment. The twins headed out of his view. Mary closed the house door then followed her sister upstairs.

They reached the top floor and prepared to enter their room when Sazuma spoke. "Hey Mary?"

"Yes?"

"Do you think Kenta eats?" As random as the question was, which surprised Sazuma herself, Mary only giggled and simply shrugged. How was she supposed to know? Spirit Beings were weird. They could want, or need, anything. Nevertheless, right now, Kenta was on his own. This was a long ass day.

❦

This was a shame. A damn shame. How could she retreat like that? Demons never retreated even from threats they themselves caused. Even if Kenta and Ayano had appeared to rescue their princesses, Chikara and her sister should have stayed. If they died, they would at least die of honor. Man, she hated herself.

Chikara and Emiko panted as they made their way into their room. The sisters had teleported to the long hallway leading to their room. They hadn't even made it all of the way. When they landed on the hardwood floor, Chikara knew she had to get to her room before anyone unexpected—and unwanted—company appeared in the hallway. She didn't need anyone asking questions and reporting back to Derek.

Derek probably already knows about the incident, she thought. She knew most likely that she was right. Derek knew everything. He knew information even before you knew it, which wasn't surprising because he was a Demon Lord and knowing information was critical. What surprised Chikara was that he knew you better than you knew yourself. That shouldn't have mattered, but it did.

The Yamada sisters limped their way to the wooden door at the end of the hall. With a twist, Chikara entered, her enlarged room coming into view and the scent of mint whooshed into her face. It was a cooling sensation that always relieved her as she entered.

Her lavender sheeted bed with the spiral carved bed posts chanted her name. Her body slugged as she further entered, dropping her weapons to the floor, and preparing to slip off her bloody shirt. Kenta had made a mess out of her; creating bruises, scratches, and even gashing both of her thighs.

The dude had been pissed. Chikara knew why, of course, but never had she seen a Spirit being, a "warrior," as gentle as the angels he or she obeyed, in such a tight manner. His eyes glazed with fighting instinct. He was going to kill her. That had made the fight more fun, until he cut her stomach, spilling blood, and reality had hit. Maybe retreating *was* the best idea.

Her wounds were healing, however the blood stains stuck out like a sore thumb or the leftover shine in your vision after looking at a bright object. Chikara grabbed the hem of her shirt, preparing to lift it over her head, but she paused.

She had just noticed the unwanted guest. She hid the growl boiling up her throat.

"What a night it is." Lavida, one of the Three Death Daughter's said as she popped in a couple of grapes from a small plastic white cup in her hands.

The Three Death Daughters were the daughters of Lucifer himself. He was a Demon Lord who ruled at least one-third of the underworld. Lucifer was said to welcome the newcomers of Hell and teach them the ways of the underworld; killing for pleasure. It wasn't too hard, considering Lucifer was both an ass and a hot man.

Chikara admitted it, Lavida's dad was hot. But, whatever.

Lucifer's wife, also nicknamed as the Demon Queen, was said to be a woman of class and value. Maybe that's why Lucifer married her. She had looks, poise and power. All demons loved that in a woman. Chikara had never met her, but Derek had shown her a picture of the demon queen and himself while building Derek's mansion. The woman truly was beautiful. Too bad she didn't know the woman's actual name.

The Three Death Daughters got their group name because there were three daughters who had the same power levels as Demon Lords. Made sense. The eldest was Lavida, the shape shifter. Unlike other shape shifters, Lavida could become any animal in the blink of an eye. Name any animal and Lavida could become that. She was devious but didn't have a mind of her own. She is the tattletale, nevertheless, no demon dared to rat *her* out. Chikara simply ignored her as much as possible. However, because she was here, a confrontation was imminent.

At least she was not like her two siblings.

Destiny is the middle child, the body possessor. Like her power title, she possesses people's bodies, no matter what species they were. She could even rob someone of their abilities with a single touch and she could squeeze into someone's mind and command them to kill themselves. Scary stuff. No one dared to even look in Destiny's direction, fearing she could insert a voice in their head, constantly wanting them to kill themselves and those around him. Even though she has an amazing ability, she is the laid-back sister. She always wore black and wore her silver hair freely. Like Derek, her eyes were like shimmering rubies promising death. Her skin was pale and she was always seen carrying a book or reading. The girl was strange and never spoke in front of others, as if she was mute. Nonetheless, she is still a lethal opponent, but an even lethal Demon Docks member.

Then there is Diamond, the youngest daughter, and to Chikara, the most malevolent. She is a dirty blonde-haired, light brown-eyed duchess with no hint of feelings. Chikara had seen her at least ten times in the decades she's been in the castle, and each time, meeting her had felt similar to being trapped in a blizzard over thirty thousand feet off of the ground. She radiated power, and like Destiny, she promised death if you made the wrong move or said the wrong thing.

But, it wasn't Diamond's power that caused other Demon Docks members, except Chikara, of course, to fear her, but it was because she meant so much to Derek. The man talked about her all day every day, claiming to want and need her. Chikara went with the flow. Whatever Derek wanted, he had. So Chikara left him to find his "Diamond." Demons, except Chikara, feared the youngest of the Three Death Daughters for good reason. She was said to be the most powerful, considering she had the power to explode objects with merely a thought. Till this day, Chikara didn't understand that ability, but she was told by Derek that it was a rarity to have.

Still, out of all of the daughters, Lavida was found the most annoying. Right now, Chikara believed that more than ever.

"What do you want, Lavida?" Chikara asked. Her agitation was so extreme that the response was barely a question. She was being stalled. Lavida was preventing her from entering the bed that now called to her in desperation. Whatever business this chick had, she better get to the point.

"I just wanted to see how your progress went in capturing at least one of the Element Princesses." She viewed the room entrance then pointed to her. "I see you're empty handed." Her eyes went to the ceiling as her index finger pressed into her chin in speculation. "I wonder what Derek will say about this."

At the thought of Lavida ratting her out to her leader, Chikara charged. She sped forward and grabbed Lavida's collar. The knitted long sleeve, with a gray and black zebra pattern, bunched near the collar as Chikara pulled her close, making them nose to nose. Lavida's settle expression never wavered. Chikara's growl boiled over. "Watch your mouth."

"Watch your movements," she said fairly. She glared with a devilish smirk. Damn this girl was irritating! "I may look like an everyday human to you but I could kick you out of Hell, diminish your power, and become nothing but a dead shrub. I can do anything I want, because . . . I just can."

It was true sadly. Lavida was a shape shifter but with Destiny's help, Lavida would use her shifting abilities to become a constrictor, holding Chikara in place and on the verge of death. Destiny would arrive and use her ability to take Chikara's skill in battle. That might not have been a spiritual ability, but it was an ability, nonetheless. Chikara would be defenseless, knowing nothing about the skill of battle. Derek would find her as a weakness and feed her to the Demon Docks' lower leveled demons.

Still boiling with resentment, Chikara threw Lavida out of her hands. She pushed by her, bumping her shoulder hard and plopped to her bed face-first. She grumbled, having the pain from her fight course through her. Her headache, intensifying immensely now, actually, throbbed painfully.

Flip flops clipped, signaling Lavida was heading out. The clips stopped. Chikara grinned, thinking Lavida had exited. She was wrong. "And by the way, Derek saw your failure as well as I. He's very disappointed."

Chikara's grin dropped. Her heart skipped a terrifying beat.

He knew of her failure. The upcoming days would not be pretty. The days would be filled with wonder, skepticism and realization.

Wonder, because she would wonder when Derek was going to summon her and demand to know what happened. Even if he knew what happened, he wanted to hear explanations coming from people's mouths. That would not be fun.

Skepticism, because she wouldn't believe Derek would find her. She would look over her shoulder from time to time, watching for maids around the mansion who acted as his message givers. She would believe she was off the hook, hoping Derek gave her another chance to prove herself.

Then there would be realization. Derek would find you and demand you to speak true. The interrogation would be in his throne room, sitting calmly on his golden throne and staring you down with his bright rubies.

Chikara was not looking forward to the upcoming days at all.

Lavida continued, "He's willing to give you another chance, as long as you don't blow that one either. Anyway, good night and good luck tomorrow." The flip flops came again. Lavida was gone this time.

After several minutes, Chikara turned her head to the right, trying to find any sign of Emiko. She was on her bed, sleeping soundly. She only held bruises on her arms but she was nowhere as scarred as Chikara was.

Ayano must have gone easy on her. Chikara had had encounters with Kenta and Ayano many times before. The debates had been about attacking humans for pleasure and secret blood supplies. Chikara had beaten up Ayano pretty good here and there. She might have attacked her secretly, but she had to kill the girl at any chance she got; the best way she could.

But this time, Kenta had been by her side and the two were inseparable. Kenta had always been away when Chikara hunted down the little black-haired princess but, this time, he had been there and he was ready for her; he was ready for everything.

Chikara grunted, feeling her gut injury pierce her stomach. It was a mere slice wound, but the shit still hurt. She leaned in further on her mattress, crimson blending with the blanket and sheets.

She had time to think of the past and strategize her revenge. However, right now, she answered the calling of her bed and entered the darkness of sleep.

Story 4

Green ambition

Midnight. The moon was dazzling and the streets were clear . . . well that was a first.

At the Kagami residence, Sazuma, Mary and their mother were sound asleep in their beds with Kenta watching over them on their roof. He looked refreshed and well rested even though he never slept. He was a spirit being after all. His thick black locks swayed with the early breeze, refreshing the scenery and even thanking him for his twenty-four hour service.

Across the street from the Kagami's community, in the house with maple paneling and a white painted porch, Hiroko snored the night away with her sky blue bed sheets shielding the lower half of her body. Her head rested on her right side, her sunny locks splashing all over her sky blue pillow sheet. A white tank top hugged her braless torso and followed her as her chest rose and fell. Her arms flattened above her head while her legs parted, taking up all the space of her queen sized bed. The night was good.

Reiko was sleeping with her door locked and her pale painted balcony doors open. The breeze elegantly blew her white unsullied curtains into her room. Unlike Hiroko, Reiko was relaxed. Her right cheek smashed into her white pillow, her belly flatted on the mattress and her hands anchored up under the pillow. Celeste blue sheets hugged her mattress and caressed against her silky black, spaghetti strapped night gown. Like always, her house chilled at a frosty forty-six degrees, and she slept idly.

Yumiko and her brothers were also sleeping firmly in their small, but comfortable, home. Yumiko's room was a good size with just enough room for a twin sized bed, a dresser, a single closet, and an enlarged bookshelf; all of which were made of pine wood. The young girl rested in her violet sheeted bed while having a soundtrack on her iPod on repeat. It was a score for *Iron Man*, a soundtrack she could strangely sleep to. She wore a smile as she slept; having a dream she most likely wouldn't remember.

But, at Ayano's apartment, while the owner of the apartment room slept, Stella was wide awake. She had woken up fifteen minutes ago and found herself staring at the ceiling.

Her chest wasn't pained and throbbing anymore, and her heat flashes had faded, but she felt different. She felt as if she could run through a whole forest, run through the night and wouldn't be tired hours later. Energy sparked through her. She'd never felt this way before. The only time she'd held such energy was when her family was still alive. Ever since they'd passed, that energy had diminished.

Where was this coming from? Why so suddenly?

Stella looked over, doing her daily wake up and look around check-up, and saw Ayano knocked out on the couch under the window. The back of her left hand rested on her forehead and her left knee propped up on the armrest while the other leg was straight. Her right hand hung off the couch, hanging vividly. Maybe even swinging a little. She still wore her gray T-shirt and short black shorts. At least her thigh high boots were off, exposing her pretty black painted toenails.

The day must have been rough, Stella figured. She would know too. She'd been in pain all day with no mercy. She understood incredibly.

Stella slowly and silently slipped out of her sleeping bag, watching Ayano as she rose, and headed to the kitchen. The hardwood was chilly below her feet but she was used to this chilliness. No matter that season it was, the floor was always cold.

She got a glass from the cabinet and closed the door while watching Ayano still. She didn't want to wake her. She would feel guilty afterward for waking her friend after such a tiring day.

Just as silent as she was being, she turned on her faucet and collected half a glass of water. She pressed her lips against the rim, preparing to sip the cool liquid, but she stopped, stared. Her attention turned to her plant cup on the counter by the sink. She put a sunflower seed in a plastic cup over a month ago and watered it when the soil got dry. It now had a small little root poking out of the soil. She knew it took a while for plants to grow, but her cup in general just wouldn't appreciate the kindness and patience of its planter.

With a sigh, Stella picked up the cup and observed it. The soil was moist, probably still soaking up the feeding from three days ago, and placed it close to her mouth. "I wish you would grow," she whispered. She knew speaking to plants would help intensity their growth—something about carbon monoxide being absorbed by the plant and stuff—so she hoped this small talk session, which happened frequently, would help the plant thrive.

She placed it back on the counter. She gulped down her water, placed it in the sink then traveled back to her sleeping bag. Ayano hadn't moved a bit.

Stella grinned as she placed her head back on her pillow, wiggled herself into comfort, closed her eye, preparing to head into another slumber.

"Are you good now?" Stella grinned. She should have known Ayano was awake. She was such a light sleeper and noticed every little thing. Stella hadn't made any noise. Not even the floor creaked. But, she still shouldn't have been so naïve.

"Yes, thank you," she answered with her eyes still closed. Ayano said nothing else, allowing Stella to enter her slumber. Several minutes later, she did.

༄

"Stella!" Said girl jumped up. Dizziness welcomed her as she tried to zoom in to wherever her name echoed from. "Stella, come here!"

Stella rushed up headed to the kitchen, not without tripping over her two feet several times. Ayano hurried to her and grabbed her forearm, acting as Stella's support. The tired teen smiled nervously. Maybe she took this situation a little too seriously.

"Come see this," Ayano walked her to the kitchen, right by the sink. Stella's smile widened. Right on the counter, in her plant cup, was a large, fully grown sunflower. Rich chocolate-brown colored the center and lively and perky pedals surrounded it, brightening up the room and even lightening Stella's day.

She clapped with joy, not knowing what else to do. She didn't want to overreact by grabbing the flower and swinging it around. That would only kill it. Keeping her modest smile was enough. "I did it! I made the sunflower grow!"

Stella turned to her. Ayano was smiling, but also false. Ayano wasn't a big fan of plants like she was, but a little bit of excitement would have been nice. "I talked to the plant last night and now it's fully grown. I can't believe it." she beamed.

Ayano's false smile dimed. She didn't even grin now. She was saddened, Stella realized. Ayano watched her through dull eyes, as if this event was a bad thing. Usually, Stella would grow a flower or two and once fully grown, she and Ayano would plant them in Lune Park about a mile out of town. The whole event wasn't too bad and Ayano had even loved coming along.

What made this so different?

Now, Ayano grinned back. She rubbed Stella's already messy hair and motioned to the flower with a tilt of her chin. "That's good. I'm happy you got what you wanted."

No, she wasn't. For once in her life, or for as long as she knew Ayano, the woman she had known for so long had not been happy for her. Her smile had been false; her expression had showed sadness not excitement. Stella shouldn't have been as upset as she was, but she was. Ayano had always appreciated Stella's ideas and supported her desires. Why was she saddened now?

Asking what was wrong would have to wait. Stella had a long day ahead of her. She had to go to school . . . wait, because of the fire, did that mean no school for Stella? There were no school phone calls stating as much. Still, she knew going would answer her question.

Now able to make it around on her own, Stella slipped out Ayano's decent hold and headed to the spare room for her uniform. Her mind wandered as she placed her clothes down and headed to the bathroom. Her friend's sudden change was interesting but it didn't ruin her promising day.

"Nice hair," Mary complimented.

Sazuma turned to her and rubbed her thick violet bangs. "Thanks," she murmured, a pinkish blush dabbed on her cheeks.

Mary had heard noises from the bathroom around three last night. With a metal baseball bat in hand; one she hid under her bed—she slowly headed to the bathroom, ready for anything. Maybe that lavender-haired chick had returned—Chikara was her name, right? Maybe it was the black-haired woman—Emiko was her name, Mary knew that.

But when she peered around the bathroom entrance, Mary only found Sazuma with a bottle of hair dye in one hand and the other was clutching the side of the sink. Mary lowered her bat and entered, standing at her sister's side, peering into the mirror. Sazuma had dyed her bangs purple. The rest of her hair remained black and braided, falling just over her shoulders.

Last night, the dye had looked so dark, Mary could barely see where she changed her hair. Now, as the light of their bedroom shined down, giving Sazuma a friendly spotlight, her new hairstyle showed clearly. It actually looked cool, Mary had to admit. She would never dye her own hair, but it looked good on her sister.

The twins grabbed their bags from beside their bed—Sazuma carried a plain black book bag while Mary had a black carrier bag with white stars and hearts ironed into the material—and made their way down the stairs.

There was no need to say goodbye to their mother. She left early this morning. It was something the twins got used to nowadays. Mary was glad her mother was working and living life how she wanted to. Before, she had never been so free. She didn't understand why her mother was a stay at home mom until her father died. Mary's eyes opened from that day forward.

Mary had no idea of the unforgivable things her father had done to her mother, especially her sister. Mary found out the actual events happening in her home hid from her shaded eyes. She realized that screams were toned out by music in her ears. She realized what happened behind closed doors and she recently found out the scars hidden under her sister's clothing. Yes, her eyes opened. She vowed they would *never* close again.

The twins headed out, locking the door behind them. Sazuma placed the spare key under a small frog statue beside the front door. As they stepped into the street to begin their walk, Kenta had landed in front of them. He'd jumped off of the roof, Mary realized after calming from her mini heart attack.

Kenta stood tall and proud with a welcoming grin. Mary gulped. He was so handsome. She never met a guy so tall and well-built. His name might have been Japanese but he looked nothing like her native people. He looked like a foreigner with full burgundy eyes, perfectly sloped nose and inviting lips. His black T-shirt hugged his torso and his faded, ripped jeans and black boots made him look even more bad than usual. His weapon rested on his left side. He looked kind of intimidating.

Mary didn't mind at all, but carrying around a sword might raise suspicion. "Good morning." Kenta said, stepping to the side to join the girls in their walk.

Mary grinned, unable to help herself. "Good morning. Are you hungry?" Last time Mary checked, he hadn't eaten all night.

"No, but thanks." Kenta put up his hand freely, stating he wasn't and still wasn't hungry.

"Let's get going. I want to get to school before we walk so slow we miss the bell." Sazuma yawned. Dying her hair must have tired her out.

"Nice hair," Kenta complimented. "It fits you."

Sazuma rubbed her bangs between her fingers with a blush. She lowered her head. "Thanks," she murmured. She wasn't good with compliments, obviously. Mary giggled. Sazuma walked in front while Kenta and Mary walked slowly behind.

What adventure would this day bring? Mary sighed. She was surprised she hadn't gotten a phone call from the school stating it would be cancelled. The fire had happened only yesterday. Sazuma had started it and Mary knew she would suffer from it. She already did and the event yesterday hadn't helped her case. Even so, Sazuma needed help with this situation. There wasn't anything Mary could do, but maybe Kenta...

Kenta. He was the driving force behind Sazuma's actions. She had told Mary about the whole incident before heading to bed. Sazuma told her how Kenta was going to assist her with her powers by shooting the willow tree in the senior courtyard. When the event went completely wrong, he had said nothing, and soon disappeared, then reappearing when Chikara and Emiko attacked.

He was responsible for Sazuma's pain and inner turmoil. With every fiber of her being, she should have hated him. She should have despised the fact he could remain here, walking by her side without any bit of apology. Why didn't she hate him? She found the situation troubling but she didn't detest him one bit. Why?

"I want to confess something," Kenta spoke. Mary turned to him. She continued her walk. Before she could respond, he continued, "No apologies will make Sazuma's pain subside, but I still feel as if I should apologize."

"I'm not the person you should be apologizing to."

"You're wrong. I said my apologies to Sazuma last night before she dyed her hair. She said she can't forgive me right away. Her inner pain had been too strong for her to simply forgive. I told her I understood and the conversation ended there. But, now," He faced her, "I'm apologizing to you. I've affected you as well."

The fire might have surprised her but he hadn't physically done anything wrong. He might have affected the lives of hundreds of teens, with Sazuma's help, of course, but he'd done nothing wrong to Mary. "It's alright," she answered, anyway. "But I too can't forgive you so easily. Anyone who hurts Sazuma hurts me."

Kenta nodded, "That's why I'm apologizing."

What was that emotion in his eyes? It wasn't guilt. It was more of understanding. But was that it? Mary probably would never know. At least he cared enough to apologize at all. Maybe she could forgive him—just this once.

That aside, she changed subject. "By the way, can you really help us with our powers?" Sazuma might have had enough with her fire abilities, but Mary hadn't had any real experience. She might have seen the fire hydrant before Emiko froze her body; however, she hadn't messed with it in the slightest. She wanted to do the real thing. She wanted to use her water for defense. She wanted to be the true water princess.

Strange, knowing you now held an orb that allowed you to use one of the earth's elements. Being an Element Princess might really have been considered a blessing depending on the extent of the element.

Kenta nodded, grinned even, "Of course. Why do you ask?"

She shrugged, "Well, I was thinking last night and I realized that Sazuma and I can't handle ourselves in a good fight, especially if it's against a demon ninja and a time possessor." Mary hated feeling defenseless. That would change. "Sazuma can barely cause any fire to arrive so she's defenseless," she completely took the school's incident out of her thoughts. That was practice gone bad, not skill, "and the only thing I can do with water is make people wet." Water was more than that, Mary knew.

Kenta chuckled as they turned a corner and headed further down the sidewalk. The trees acted as a shield against the rising sun. The wind blew gently, sending a floral scent through the air. Kenta's black locks played along with the wind, just as Mary's did. His sun kissed complexion mixed with the morning scenery beautifully.

Mary continued, as if she didn't just stare at him, "I want to learn how to defeat my enemies. If you and Ayano can help us, then I would appreciate it."

"Well, I can't do anything until we find the others. As soon as we do, then I will train all of you and help you control your powers."

All for one and one for all, huh? Understandable, she guessed. "Alright, but I have another question. Is it true that Stella is the earth princess?"

Kenta turned from her, his grin slowly fading. Was it bad for her to know? "That's true."

"Why didn't you tell me?"

"Ayano and I found out about this yesterday. We are planning on telling her about her powers tonight."

"I want to be a part of that. When you tell Stella about her powers, I want to be there with you."

Kenta nodded. What else was he going to do? Turn her down? He had no right even if he was going to do so. After everything he put Sazuma through, they didn't deserve anymore deception.

"I will let Ayano know, then we can all tell her together."

Mary nodded. Could Stella take the news though? "Hey so guess what, you're something called an Element Princess and you control earth. By the way, you're going to have to fight demons in order to survive." The poor fifteen year old would have a heart attack.

Stella had been through a lot as a child. She lost her parents and remained homeless for some time, but Ayano had taken care of her. That was probably what saved the girl from this cruel world.

She had been through too much already in her too short life. She didn't need more stress and surprises on her. It was too late, though. There was no going back for her. At least she wasn't alone in this.

⁂

"Oh yes, that's very nice." Derek exhaled with lust. He held one of his maid's in his hands and sucked on her gaping neck. He had bitten the long black-haired maid. Obviously, that hadn't been enough. His thirst was too strong. He had slipped one of his daggers out from the holder connected to his weaved dark brown belt and stabbed the woman's neck, slicing through muscle and veins. She died instantly. After he was finished with her, his minions could have her flesh. Derek wasn't interested in the meat aspect of a meal.

Diamond watched as her master continued to hold the maid. She crossed her thin, yet occupied, legs and watched the scene in front of her. She was a woman of no emotion. She always was. She wasn't even jealous of the fact he was mixing the blood of a random woman with his. She could have at least pouted. But, no. Those lush lips stayed in a mulish line. Such an impassive woman.

Derek smiled as he watched Diamond staring at him. He slipped his fangs out of the maid's neck and licked his lips. She tasted of grapes and smelled like watermelon. It was a pleasurable taste but nothing compared to Diamond's sweet cherry blood. Just looking at her made him want to feed on her again.

"What's with that look Diamond? Would you like to join me?"

With a roll of her eyes, Diamond stood form the window platform she rested on and made her way up Derek's stoned throne stairs.

He licked his lips. He had a clear view of her straight and attractive frame. Today she had on sky blue short shorts with a tight red shirt, exposing her belly button and was shoeless. Her dirty blonde hair hung high in a ponytail that matched the swinging motion of her hips. He threw the maid to the side—her skull the first to meet Derek's floor—then slid his hands around Diamond's body. She was true beauty. Derek's mouth watered, yearning to once again taste his sweet Diamond. He smirked when she begun to unbuttoned his white long sleeved shirt, revealing his peach colored skin.

Diamond lowered her head, hovering her lips above his pulsing artery. His hands shook uncontrollably. Tasting her would have been better but to have the pleasure of being tasted? Now that was a blessing all its own.

He grabbed Diamond's hips, his nails digging deep. She straddled his waist so fittingly it should have been a crime to fit him so well. Without warning, she bit down, taking him in. He moaned on impact. To have the feeling of daggers for teeth piercing you was beyond intoxicating. Although, to have the woman he cared for more than anything, mixing her blood with his, was just downright addicting.

Damn this was good! His blood rushed upward, from his chest, to his shoulders, through his neck and finally entering Diamond's awaiting mouth, leaving him deliciously hollowed. He leaned his head back, allowing her more access. She accepted without hesitation.

This was always the highlight of his day. His woman would drink from him, loving his blood and wanting more while hugging his body in want. Maybe even need. Besides, he could deny her nothing. Diamond was precious, lovely and worth any sacrifice. Her name was perfect for her.

As the owner of something so precious, Derek would allow no other man to behold her. She was his and his alone. Derek didn't share. Anyone who thought he did deserved to die. Plain and simple.

After mere seconds of increasing ecstasy, the couple was interrupted. Derek growled as he heard his throne room doors casually sliding open, revealing Lavida dressed in a plain tan long sleeve, black jeans and white flip flips.

She noticed the scenery immediately and stiffened.

Oh yeah, Lavida did have a thing for him, didn't she? She confessed to him several times. He turned down her love but not her body. It must have been hard to see her own sister in the arms of the man she dearly adored . . .

Derek grinded against Diamond, urging further contact. "Do you want something?" he asked through an exhausted breath. Diamond ejected her fangs and pushed up, preparing to leave, but Derek would not allow that.

He pushed Diamond back down, slamming her body into his. The sensation caused him to groan. A growl boiled in his throat.

She grumbled. Diamond? Grumbling? Why? Shouldn't she like being held by her lord? Shouldn't she want to be closer to him? She had taken his blood, leaving him closer to emptiness that usual. Now that he thought about it, she had sucked more blood than usual. Derek's hands even numbed. His suspicions rose. Something was wrong with his girl.

"Lord Derek, I came here to inform you that Chikara has left her room without Emiko by her side."

Attention back to the jealous visitor, who now sounded betrayed, by the way, kept her focus on him and Diamond, refusing to look away. She was here on a mission, he figured. He was going to hear her message.

Derek worked his fingers through Diamond's thick hair and ground against her again. She growled in warning. He ignored her. Something was definitely wrong with her. "She might have gone to try and get an Element Princess," he said to Lavida, "That's alright as long as she doesn't get herself killed." He liked Chikara and he intended to keep her.

"Would you like me to assist her?"

"No," Derek grinded once more, testing his theory about the woman in his arms. The moment his lower body touched hers, she smashed her fangs into his shoulder blade and used her knives for nails to stick into his chest.

The action should have pleasured him. It didn't.

That shit hurt!

Most definitely something was wrong with this girl and he would find out. But he needed a clear room.

He focused on Lavida again, ending the conversation. "Watch her and keep me posted. I don't want her doing anything stupid. We don't need the entire supernatural world knowing the Demon Docks are back. Stay cool and stay sharp in case any other species decides to mess things up."

Lavida nodded. She brought her hands up, clutching them and pressed them against her chest. She lowered her head and gulped hard. Betrayal was a wicked scent and the girl was covered in it. What was up with *her*?

"Is that all you need, my lord?"

Duh. What else would he want from her? Money? Blood? Sex? Been there, done that. The sex wasn't that good anyway. She always did what he told her to do. A little feistiness would have been nice.

Diamond gave him feistiness, determination, and sugar coated rebellion. Too bad she never took that to the bedroom. She always pushed him back or threatened him whenever he tried to get too close. The threats wouldn't have bothered him if she didn't have the ability to blow something up with only thought. She could have exploded his vital organs without even touching him. She was that dangerous.

Even if she was deadly to have around, he wanted to know why she acted like this. She should have been kissing his ass-literally-for allowing her to be in his arms all day, every day. She should have been grateful to be named Diamond Southbound, the woman of the Demon Docks leader. Any woman wanted such a title. Why she didn't, Derek would soon find out.

Lavida exited the room, leaving the room doors open and her head inclined downward depressingly.

Derek grabbed a handful of Diamond's hair and pulled her up from his shoulder. She didn't protest. She didn't squeal in shock or pain. She merely glared at him through light brown eyes, holding no fear.

"What the hell is wrong with you? You will show me nothing but pleasure, understand?" He hadn't been this forceful in years. There were times when Diamond lost her cool for unexplained reasons—reasons that were now coming to mind.

Derek's eyes narrowed. "You spoke with Kouta again, didn't you?"

Diamond glared this time. "Don't bring him into this."

That was a yes. Kouta is another Demon Lord who controls another percentage of the underworld. He is the ruler of the Vampire Demons, vicious beings who need termination. Diamond had known him in the past; however, Derek severed that relationship.

Or, at least he thought he did. Every time Diamond acted up, Kouta was nearby or communicated with her. All demons held a telepathic ability. Maybe that's how they spoke. The idea made Derek's blood boil. The bastard needed to die.

"If you spoke with him . . ." he threatened. He didn't know what he would do to her, but without a doubt he knew he was getting rid of Kouta.

"I didn't speak with him. I didn't speak with anyone outside of this castle. I never do." There was a hint of truth in her tone. Nevertheless, she couldn't be believed. Demons always lied. Even though Diamond was important to him—a precious puzzle piece to complete the puzzle he'd been working on for thousands of years—he still couldn't trust her enough to know she was telling the truth.

Punishment would be given. Today. Here. Now.

Without further warning, Derek's four inch fangs spiked out venomously and sunk into Diamond's neck before she could protest, or at least he thought they did. One instant, Diamond was on his lap. In the next, she was gone, disappearing out of sight.

Teleportation . . . smart girl. But, this was Derek's castle. No one could hide in this place. Derek stood and stretched, preparing for a day of cat and mouse. Too bad little mousy didn't know, the cat always wins.

✦

The walk to school had been casual for the most part. Mary and Kenta had a little talkie-talkie session about god knows what. Sazuma didn't care. Her sister was happy, that's what mattered. Although she was happy with the same man who caused her pain and suffering . . . well, that couldn't matter now. She had realization to face. Woo.

How was she going to survive this? Sazuma had to face the destruction she caused up close and personal. She and Mary were the only people who knew she caused the fire. That was good, Sazuma guessed. She wouldn't have to deal with other's hatred towards her for ruining the school. She would only have to face herself. That was the worse pain to face, in Sazuma's opinion.

As they approached the school, Kenta said his goodbye and disappeared; here one moment, gone the next, leaving Mary bewildered. Chikara had done the same thing when she made her retreat. Maybe it was some kind of supernatural skill the girls knew they would never possess.

It must have been cool to disappear when people needed you most. Kenta must have been a pro in that department. Sazuma stopped herself. *Flashback*, she thought. Moments of the past always affected her present, making her personality change completely based on the situation. She would have to work on that.

The twins were welcomed into the classroom with silence. Yes, this was weird. Usually, Reiko, Hiroko, or Stella would be commenting on their dreams, books or complaining about the school uniform. This morning, there was nothing. Stella focused on her reading, Reiko was bobbing her head to music-hip hop, most likely, and Hiroko slouched in her chair, staring directly at the gray paneled ceiling.

Mary entered and conducted conversation with Stella. Sazuma made her way to Hiroko. There was no point trying to get Reiko's attention. Music was her life, other than fashion. It was alright though, teenagers could relate.

Sazuma knocked on her friend's desk, grabbing her attention. Hiroko blinked out of her trance and grinned. "Hey," she said groggily. Sazuma took her seat behind Hiroko. The seemingly tired blonde readjusted to face her.

Hiroko looked different. Her long hair, which usually hung in a neat ponytail, was now hanging loosely over her shoulders and piled on Sazuma's desk. In the sunlight, her hair beamed the richest gold with highlights of sunshine yellow. Her usual blue eyes now shined a rugged turquoise. She still emanated beauty.

"What's up? You look . . ." She had to approach this smartly. If she messed up Hiroko's mood, she was in for a world of silent treatments and death glares. Plus, saying she looked horrible was a lie, because right now, Hiroko looked more beautiful than anyone she'd ever met. She approached wisely, "You look tired." Yeah, that's good.

Hiroko slid her fingers through her thick mass of hair, catching her split end with a sigh. "I had a strange dream last night." She answered in a low tone, as if it was unusual to have bizarre dreams.

"Was there an unknown creature flying in the sky with you? Maybe a dragon or a two headed beast?"

"Sazuma, I'm serious." Hiroko blinked. In that split second, her eyes watered. Sazuma's joking demeanor slipped away. Hiroko wasn't usually serious. The fact that she was caused Sazuma to worry. Was her dream that bad? "I . . ." she lowered her head, her bangs casting shadows over her eyes. "I dreamed of my father's accident."

Sazuma's heart sank. The world zeroed in on them. They were the only people in this world. The water in Hiroko's eyes piled up, forcing their way to escape. A lump formed in Sazuma's throat. There was nothing she could say. There was nothing she could do to make her friend feel better. What could you say to something like that? Nothing, that's what.

Hiroko had told Sazuma and the others about this. Hiroko's father was a businessman who made deals overseas. He was gone for long periods. On the other hand, when he returned for several months, he gave his family love and tenderness; much more than any family could ask for.

On one of her father's travels, he traveled to California to confirm a future business transaction. On the way to the airport, there had been an earthquake, which caused a massive traffic jam on the Golden Gate Bridge. Struck with fear, citizens exited their vehicles and hoped to make their escape on foot.

Others decided to push their way past the cars by using their own. So many panicked citizens had pushed vehicles. In the end, those trapped inside of their cars and ran on foot lost their lives to the careless drivers behind the wheel.

Sadly, Hiroko's father had been one of those trapped in his car and pushed off of the bridge. He happened to be hit on his left side and pushed off without a care by the pusher. The man had drowned, not even having a chance at survival. She mentioned that police on scene found her father's body on the edges of the San Francisco peninsula, not in the water. He didn't even carry a wrinkle on him. It was as if he washed ashore, the water not taking his body as its own.

The only time Hiroko brought up her father was his birthday and the day he died. Sazuma and her group, including little Yumiko, had accompanied Hiroko to her father's grave on those days. They had watched as her tears sprang free without protest and listened as her sobs and cries echoed through the cemetery.

The fact that she had dreamed about him raised a red flag of suspicion. Why dream of him now? "I'll listen to your dream if you will let me."

Hiroko nodded and wiped her damp eyes. No tears fell but her long black eyelashes were moist. Hiroko knew if she cried, then other kids would ask questions and wonder what was wrong. It was none of their business but kids were nosy. Hiroko didn't want unneeded attention so she hid back her tears.

Sazuma knew, if these two were alone, then Hiroko's tears would slip from her eyes and create a river of sadness. The fact that she hadn't shed a tear caused Sazuma's heart to swell. Hiroko was so much stronger than Sazuma would ever be.

"It was as if I was in my father's place. I was in his car, watching as the earthquake shook the bridge. I heard the screams of the people around me and watched as they dashed out of their cars with their families, leaving their car doors open." She sobbed, not even holding back anymore. "I was stuck. My father was stuck. There was no way to get out. Cars and car doors blocked all exits. There were so many screams."

Hiroko's shoulders shook uncontrollably. Her face slammed into her awaiting hands. Sazuma grabbed her shoulders. "You don't have to go on if it's too painful. Hiroko, it's okay."

But she continued, "People pushed past, not caring if they ran people over or crushed people between the vehicles. They didn't care! My father's car spun, pushing other cars and one finally hit his left side. The car pushed and pushed, even honked at him, until he . . . until he . . ."

"Hiroko," Stella and Mary flanked Hiroko's sides. Between the two, Sazuma didn't know who said her name. It didn't matter. Reiko bent down, blocking the students now watching the scene. Sazuma's focus remained on Hiroko.

"I saw black," Hiroko sucked in a breath. "I saw black, and for sure I was going to wake up or something, but no. I was still dreaming. My eyes opened, and I was looking at the bottom of the bridge. I lay out on land. The earthquake had ended. But . . . I couldn't think. I tried to move, but I couldn't. I tried to speak, but I couldn't. I tried to breathe but I just couldn't! But . . ." as she exhaled an exhausted breath, she raised her head, locking eyes with Sazuma. "There was a man. He was on his knees, looking down with saddened eyes. There was a woman right beside him, watching him as well. They had so much concern, it was a blessing. He told me, *"Everything's going to be alright. I'll take care of your loved ones. Rest now. I'll guide you to heaven."* My father's eyes closed and then I woke up."

She smiled in shock. Her hands fisted. "An angel saved my father." Her smile faded. "It all happened so fast."

Sazuma was speechless. Silence filled the room. The girls were too amazed, not knowing the right words to say; probably unable to find words to say at all. If anyone was going to understand Hiroko's situation, it was going to be Stella. However, even she was astounded. Sazuma never realized how much her friends had been through. Compared to her, their situations were far more painful.

"This isn't drama class girls. If you have business to take care of then take it outside." The group's attention turned to Mrs. Salter. Her fists were glued to her hips and her glare was raked at them. The class, which was now full, zeroed in on them, watching their every gesture. The girls glared at Mrs. Salter in pure hate.

It figured she would think this was some sort of drama. Teachers never understood. They didn't care either. Some teachers might have at least asked if Hiroko was alright, considering the group resided around her, but it was those teachers Sazuma never met. She was stuck with this woman, this black-haired, brown-eyed woman with so many freckles that connecting the dots would be impossible and a white coat that made her look like a doctor.

Without another word, Hiroko threw her bag over her shoulder, grabbed her black leather jacket and headed toward the door. Reiko dashed to her desk and packed as well. Hiroko didn't stop her. Neither did Mrs. Salter. The two headed out, probably just heading home.

Mrs. Salter turned from them, to the remaining members. "Do you care to leave, too?"

"Don't tempt me," Sazuma said. She slouched in her chair and crossed her arms. Stella and Mary merely took their seats. Mrs. Salter nodded and turned to the board, continuing the day.

Sazuma made a mental note to check on Hiroko later. She knew Reiko was with her, acting as her shoulder to cry on, and an ear for listening. Sazuma still wanted to know if she was alright. First though, she would need time to heal. Right now, Sazuma's mind wandered, hoping time would pass without any attitude from her troublesome teacher.

Close to noon, the students were sent home early again. Because half of the school burnt down that meant half of the day would be taken away for students who still had their classrooms. The students who had their classes burned did not come to school at all. Lucky bastards. Why the school just couldn't tell the kids not to come until reconstruction finished, Sazuma would never know.

Stella led the way to her apartment, urging the twins to see the sunflower she held so much pride in. "It was small one moment and grew awesomely. You'll love the sight of it." To Sazuma, Stella's smile was all she needed. The innocence of her smile was utterly brilliant. Nothing compared.

On the way there, the girls were surprised to find Hiroko and Reiko sitting on the bench of a bread store. They were chewing down on spaghetti with right-out-of-the-oven garlic bread. Both teens grinned as the rest of their friends approached.

"What's up peeps," Reiko waved as they came near.

"You guys have been here the whole time?" The girls nodded to Stella's question.

"Tommy's grandfather owns this shop. He said we can stay as long as we buy some lunch. So that's what we did," Hiroko said, then popped a piece of bread into her mouth. She moaned in goodness. Tommy is one of the silent students who blocked himself from the world around him. It was funny how Hiroko had the most complex friends. Being one of the said friends Hiroko had, she had every right to talk.

"So . . . care to join us to Stella's place?" Sazuma asked. She was about to ask if she was doing better, but she rethought the idea. Maybe it was too soon.

"Bring it on," Hiroko and Reiko answered in union. After taking down the rest of their meal, they threw their trash away, thanked the store owner—"Come back anytime," the male Italian elder smiled—and headed off to the apartment. To Sazuma's surprise, Reiko didn't complain. It was a thirty-minute walk from the school to Stella's apartment and it took ten minutes just to reach the bread store. Still, the rich teen didn't complain. She walked to Sazuma's right side while the others continued on in front of them. "You probably want to know what happened, huh?"

Sazuma turned to her friend. The teen stood at five-foot-ten, and that was without heels. Her black hair with icy blue highlights swung gently with the breeze, tickling Sazuma's arms. "What happened after you guys left?"

Reiko stuffed her hands in her skirt pockets. "We left the school then and there. No one stopped us, because of my wealth status of course." She patted her chest and smiled with awesomeness. After realizing this conversation was in the direction of "Talking about Reiko", she cleared her throat. "We headed to the bread shop while Hiroko calmed down. But on the walk there, she gave me the man's appearance."

Sazuma's eyebrows lifted. Back at the school, she hadn't described the angel who sent her father's soul to heaven. But . . . "What about the woman?" Reiko shook her head. "She said the image was too blurry to see. She did see locks of black hair from her." Sazuma nodded. Reiko continued, "The angel on the other hand," she sighed in longing, "He sounds so dreamy. He had silver hair, hazel eyes and dressed in nothing but white. His skin was peach-tinted and he was muscled. Oh, I wish I could have seen him myself."

Seeing him would mean she wished to be in Hiroko's father's situation. Then again, the girl might have been able to see the angel herself. In this world, now supernatural filled, anything could happen. By the way, she, Stella, Hiroko and Yumiko didn't know about Kenta and Ayano and this Element Princess stuff. They would have to explain once in a while, just not now.

"So is Ayano at home?" Hiroko asked to Stella, who walked to her left side and Mary on her right.

"She shouldn't be. She should be at work."

Work—right. Stella surely didn't know about Ayano's *"work"*. Her eyes searched the area, looking for any sign of the stalking couple. They had stayed on a business building rooftop the entire time she'd been in school. They were the king and queen of stalkers . . . and they were spotted on an apartment building a block away.

Too bad they stuck out like a sore thumb though. Ayano was at least squatting while Kenta stood tall with crossed arms over his black shirt. Their hair played with the wind, creating a mystic aura around them.

They looked awesome, Sazuma grinned. They always did. Something told her they always would.

Mary must have spotted them too. She had turned her attention upward for a couple of seconds then lowered her head with a grin. And a blush even. Was that a blush? Indeed, it was. Her cheeks had heated a light shade of pink.

For Kenta? Most likely.

After a few minutes—twenty minutes to be exact—the girls arrived at Stella's apartment building. It was more like a hotel, in Sazuma's opinion. There was a main lobby filled with antique furniture, rugs with cheetah patterns placed at every entryway on the hardwood floor and paintings of modern marvels stationed in threes all around the teal painted walls.

There was a dark brown-haired woman at the front desk, dressed in a fluffy white shirt with her hair kept in a tight bun. She stopped her typing to watch the arriving guests. Once her hazel eyes reached Stella, the woman nodded and allowed them to continue without a word.

Down the hall from the front desk were three platinum door elevators only on the right side. They took the middle elevator up to the second floor. There was no music to accompany them; thank God. If Sazuma heard another upbeat song that involved singers who you *knew* were totally smiling while recording the song, then Sazuma was going to go nuts. It's as simple as that.

The doors opened, revealing more teal painted walls and maroon carpets with a gold diamond design. They walked to their right, heading to Stella's room. The hallway was narrow for the most part with a dark brown ceiling.

"The designer must have been a total ass wipe when it came to styling the place." Reiko would be the one to comment. But the designer didn't have to be an ass wipe. They could have just had bad taste. The place did leave you feeling like you were in the middle of a horror movie and you strangely see a shadow figure making its way to you.

Apartments weren't Sazuma's favorite places to live; she lived in a house all her life, so she wouldn't know about living in an apartment anyway, but this place just gave her the creeps. She didn't know how Stella could live here without fearing who would be outside her doorway at night.

Finally, the group made it to Stella's place. The tired teen unlocked her door and allowed everyone inside. They entered with an exhausted exhale. The walk had clearly killed them, except for Mary. The girl wasn't winded or anything. She hadn't even broken a sweat. It was summer man! She could have at least been panting.

Reiko plopped on one of Stella's beige couches, the one resting under the single window. One leg laid on the arm rest while the other draped over the couch. Mary and Hiroko took their places on the other couch in front of Reiko. Sazuma leaned against the wall while Stella ran around the corner, probably going to put away her things.

The girls placed their belongings on the floor and took a breath themselves. "So what's going on? Where's the plant?" Hiroko asked, a bit curious to see it.

Brief moments passed. There was no response.

"Stella," Mary called. Nothing. Maybe the girl was hard of hearing.

Stella's blood rushing scream proved Sazuma's suggestion was false.

In one swift motion, the teens raced to the back room, preparing to assist anyway they can. The journey from the living room to the guest room in the back was short; however, it felt like slow motion had taken time's place. Sazuma couldn't explain it.

There was more to this than just Stella's scream. Plus, this wasn't a normal scream. This was spine tingling, stomach churning, blood rushing. It was a scream of true fear. And it had come from Stella, one of the most innocent people in the clique.

The group came to a halting stop. Sazuma pushed past, trying to view who resided inside of the room. Sazuma glared at the sight. Lavender hair flowed as she turned to face the newcomers of the room. Weapons rattled as she readjusted the unconscious Stella under her arm. The dark brown body suit she wore hugged her body swimmingly. Amethyst eyes watched the teens as lush lips peeled back, revealing straight pearly whites.

"Chikara!" Sazuma snarled. How could she not have known? She should have expected something like this. She was involved in the supernatural world; she was a being said to fight demons. How could she not have expected a sneak attack by a woman she was supposed to take out?

Chikara blew a kiss to the teens then disappeared all together, leaving Hiroko and Reiko dumbfounded.

Hiroko inhaled and exhaled rapidly, trying to contemplate what just happened.

"Stella? Hey, what's going on?!" Reiko freaked. Her attention went to the twins, who were rooted to the floor. What were they supposed to say? How could they explain this without sounding utterly insane? There was no way to explain without sounding insane, was there? "Well?!" Reiko shouted in rising anger. Panic was taking over.

The girls jolted when a bang sounded. Footsteps pounded in the living room and increased as they approached ever so closer. Ayano and Kenta quickly entered the room, observing the area and checking the girls.

Reiko and Hiroko stared in shock. "Ayano?" they asked together. They didn't even focus on Kenta.

His attention was squarely on the twins.

Ayano spoke, "Sazuma, Mary, come with us."

"What? Why only them?" Hiroko asked.

"It's not your concern." Ayano said.

"Hey!" Reiko shouted. All awareness moved to her, "Stella is our friend. She just disappeared in front of us and now you're telling Sazuma and Mary to leave. Whatever the hell is going on, I want to know what it is right now!"

Reiko had every right to be pissed, but she didn't understand this new world. She didn't understand that there were forces at stake. She didn't understand that . . .

Ayano sighed. "Stella was kidnapped by one of the Demonic Princesses."

"Demonic Princesses? What are those?"

"Explain later," Kenta told Ayano. "We need to leave before we lose them." Why didn't he say anything to the girls though? They were standing right in front of him.

"Listen," Mary started, stepping up to the still stunned teens, "I know this is strange right now, but Sazuma and I are needed. We promise to explain everything when we get back."

"There will be no explaining when you get back. You explain this shit now!"

Sazuma had never seen the rich girl so infuriated. She always had nothing to be upset about so it would make sense to always see her happy or mellow. This was another side of Reiko, a side Sazuma never wanted to see again.

"Go," Hiroko said. Her bottom lip quivered. She trembled in worry. Bravely, she stood strong. "I don't know what the hell is going on, but I know my friend was kidnapped by someone—something. And if you guys are the only ones to get her back then go. We'll wait here for your return. And you better come back with Stella safe and sound."

Pride and self-assurance swelled the twins as they nodded. "We will." Mary reassured.

"Let's go." Ayano said. Mary and Sazuma wasted no time following Ayano and Kenta out of the apartment and down the empty street. *We'll get her back,* Sazuma thought. *I promise.*

Story 5

Talent comes in many *sizes*

Chikara darted from rooftop to rooftop with a grin on her face and anticipation in her eyes. She turned around every now and again to make sure no one followed her. When the coast was clear, she continued on. Stella was still unconscious under her arm. As the wind blasted onto her, causing her wardrobe to swing left and right, she grew overwhelmed with righteousness. Her anticipation grew stronger.

"I did it," she beamed. The success was too much for her, "I finally did it. Now Derek has to appreciate me. I can take this girl back and get the respect I deserve."

Derek would have loved her, she thought, then and there. He would love her forever for this. Not only did she bring back an Element Princess, but also Chikara had the opportunity of personally slaughtering her in front of her Demon Lord and her comrades, proclaiming she was the strongest of the Demonic Princesses and be worth the name Chikara Southbound, woman of Derek Southbound.

Even though there were rumors going around that another Demonic Princess, Diamond, had that title already, Chikara couldn't-wouldn't-let that stop her. She was going to get Derek's respect. More importantly, she was going to get his last name.

Hair was flying. Clothes were ruffling. Breath was getting hard to catch. Adrenaline rushed through veins. This was how it was to travel with mystical beings.

Sazuma and Mary were piggy back riding on Kenta and Ayano's backs. This was the fastest way to catch up to the ninja. Running on the ground would have just slowed everyone down. Then again, the girls didn't have a choice in the matter. They were pulled onto their backs and entered the air, landing on the apartments and one story houses on the way.

Their speed was faster than regular human speed. You might as well have called them 'the Supernatural Cheetahs'. Kenta and Ayano's speeds matched and their thoughts seemed to be the same. They were in sync, matching each other perfectly, stepping together as they dashed through the air.

Mary couldn't help but notice them and even want that power just as much. Ayano was an Element Princess, so this speed could be achieved. It probably just took practice. Lots and lots of practice.

Mary looked to her right and left. Ayano and Sazuma kept their pace to her right. Mixes of colors zipped past her vision. The environment was so blurry now. The wind was too much for Mary's eyes, causing them to water from dryness. Still, it was a rush to dash through the world, in a life where there weren't just humans, animals, and normalcy.

What was not cool was that Stella was in danger. *Not for long though*, she promised herself.

"You guys alright?"

"Yes," Mary answered in Kenta's ear. Her legs wrapped around him fittingly and her arms held on for dear life, but left enough room for him to breathe. His arms, which were wrapped under her legs, pushed her up just as he jumped onto another building. She huffed, not expecting the sudden movement, but calmed when his grip on her tightened.

"I'm good," Sazuma answered. Her twin braids flopped up and down as the wind ravished her. Her kung fu grip didn't seem to bother Ayano though. She didn't answer Kenta's question, either. Her focus remained straight, as if ignoring all those around her.

"I'm sorry Ayano." Kenta said in a low tone. "I got Stella involved in all of this and now she's in danger."

"Don't remind me," she buzzed. Her anger was full force. Her expression remained focused. "But, its fine. Now that I know she has this power, I can feel safer with her. She can learn and grow and soon she'll be able to protect herself. Until that time, I'm going to protect her with my life."

"Such devotion that I never expected from Ayano." Sazuma teased in her ear.

"If you don't shut up, I'm going to drop and leave you."

"If you leave me, then I'm going to burn you."

"You can form the fire but you can't throw it. Prime example, Lane Way High."

Now, that was just cold.

Still, Sazuma liked this girl. She seemed to have a fire in herself. She hoped they could be better friends.

"Hey that's enough you too. We're getting close." Kenta sped his stepping pace as well as Ayano. They continued on and entered the outskirts of town; a place no townspeople dared to travel to.

With most of the humans out of range, Chikara would have a better shot at escaping this place. She didn't need witnesses for what she was planning to do. Torture was her idea. The kid was going to die by her hands anyway, but what was the point if there was no fun in the kill, huh? Confidence, Deception, and then Death. That's what the kid was going to go through, Chikara promised. Chikara continued her run on foot, where she entered an area filled with thick canopies, tall trees and rich soil. She traveled down a dirt road, leading further in, passing a wooden sign with large white letters saying, "Welcome to Valla Park."

If humans were currently in this *"park"*, then Chikara would end them. She didn't want witnesses. Men, women, children, it didn't matter. They would die. End of story.

On the other hand, there were no humans in this Valla Park. Chikara faced a large mystic-like area. The park was no children's park with a playground and other things human children used as pastime, Chikara realized. The park was scenery. A large pond-half the size of a football field—rested in the center of this vast tree-filled place. A stoned mini waterfall poured past three stoned layers and entered the lily pad covered pond. The scent of upcoming rain filled the area. The shining sunshine could barely peer through the thick ceiling of the canopies.

She threw Stella to the moist dirt, not even caring about her wellbeing. Her dark brown boots squished on the dirt as she approached the pond. Several frogs, once unseen, plopped into the muggy water, disappearing; probably fearing Chikara's presence.

She bent down, picked up a hand full of water and splashed some on her victim. Stella didn't stir. "Maybe I punched her a little too hard." It was the girl's fault anyway.

She had entered the room, all cheery and shit, but stood frozen when she spotted her. Chikara didn't even have to ask if this was Stella Jayberry. Power shined from her. It was as if a green aura surrounded her. It wasn't shining bright like the twins did—Sazuma held a dark crimson aura while Mary carried a calming blue—but it was enough to say she was no longer a human.

Before Chikara had even said a word, the girl had screamed. It was high pitched and filled with innocence and fear. This girl had probably never been in this situation so, of course, she was scared. It wasn't every day that someone was kidnapped by a demon anyway.

Another pick up and splash of water. Stella finally woke up. She didn't jump up, however. She remained still on the ground. She lifted her head and looked around. Her right cheek was smudged with dirt. Her hands acted as her support as she made her way to her knees. "Valla Park? What am I doing here?"

She really asked such a stupid question, huh? Realization must have hit. Her eyes widened in shock and her attention finally came to Chikara, who stood at her quarter profile. The teen's clothes were wrinkled and now carried smears of the moist earth. Amethyst locked with frightened chocolate browns.

Chikara could say this much, she was brave enough to remain where she was. Usually, humans would have ran by now, which called for a chase, which always ended too quickly. Too bad she didn't end her life in a hurry. Now that she stayed, she ensured her guaranteed torture.

"Hello Stella," Chikara grinned.

The girl didn't respond. She merely observed her area, probably looking for the best exit points. She wasn't escaping though. The little redhead should have known that much. "Don't be frightened."

"I'm not afraid of you."

Chikara's eyebrow cocked up. "Oh, really."

"Yeah," she answered with attitude. "I might be afraid of the Boogeyman, but not you."

This girl was an idiot. Chikara *was* the Boogeyman. No, she was better than that, asshole. There was a Demon Docks member who was actually nicknamed as the Boogeyman. He hid under the bed and in closets of the humans and scared them late at night. He was so lame he wasn't even considered a foot soldier. The wuss.

"I know you're trying to be smart and all, but don't be an idiot. It's alright to wonder who I am, what I want with you and what I am going to do with you."

"So you're a pervert."

Now she was asking for it. Chikara's eyes narrowed. This kid, no, this child, was looking at her through the most relaxed eyes she'd ever seen. The frightened look she had before was completely gone. It must have been masked by that smarty face. It better have been.

Chikara approached her while slipping out a dagger from her front holder. Stella's fear returned. There it is. "Say another word and you're dead, understand?" Stella nodded without hesitation. She dragged herself on the dirt, creating stains in her navy blue skirt.

Chikara stepped closer. "I don't expect much from you, princess. All I need is a favor."

"I don't care what you want. Leave me alone." Bold, but not fierce. She would have died by now if she had been taken by anyone else. What was Chikara waiting for?

Slow death, she reminded herself. Oh yeah. If so, then she had to make this quick. She could sense Kenta and Ayano coming fast.

As quick as lightning, Chikara rushed forward, using her speed to move faster than any human, any animal, grabbed Stella's bronze stitched, auburn shirt and threw her over her head. Stella landed on her back with a thud. Chikara's heels touched the top of her head.

The smirking ninja twisted her body and bent down just as Stella tried to squirm away. "Oh no, no, princess. That was just a warm up." Stella grunted and tried to scream. Chikara threw her once more, this time, skidding on the ground and almost falling into the pond.

Just as quick as her first attack, Chikara slipped out one of her throwing stars, aimed and fired. The weapon hit Stella's thigh. The shocked teen screamed in pain. No one could hear her though. But, then again, she knew Kenta and Ayano would hear and come rushing by. *Make it quick and pleasurable.*

Another star shot out of Chikara's hand with a mere twist of her wrist, aiming for Stella's neck, but she had dodged it, placing her head to the ground. She yanked the throwing star from her thigh and threw it to Chikara. The demon had caught it and again threw the star; aiming in the same spot she had been struck. That earned Chikara another spine-tickling scream.

Messing with this girl was wondrous. She was innocent, never experienced pain and this was truly killing her. These were the best victims to have. Those who already felt pain would always hold their grunts and cries in. But this girl was a releaser. Chikara loved every minute of it.

Company coming our way.

Right. Back to business. Chikara sped to Stella, and gripped the dagger she never released from her hand. She brought her hand back, preparing to stab anywhere—it would be much more fun if she missed her vital point—and lowered her arm. Before she could hit her, Stella punched Chikara's throat, causing her to stop for brief moments.

Stella stood, making her run for it, but Chikara caught up to her, oh too soon, and stabbed her right shoulder. There was another scream just as Stella fell to her knees. Actually, those were two screams in Chikara's ears. One was Stella's and the other . . .

Ayano dashed from the forest in a war cry. She jumped on Chikara, punched, kicked and threw her into the pond with everything she had. Chikara rose. She couldn't even make another move. Ayano's black whip wrapped around her neck like a desperate boa constrictor and dragged her from the cold water, only to be skid on the ground and thrown into the air.

Chikara finally made her move. Dizzily, she cut Ayano's black cloth-like whip and severed all contact with the thing. She landed on the ground, only to have Ayano rushing back at her. As they came together, the women threw fists, catching contact here and there.

Ayano's lip, Chikara's throat–in the same spot Stella had gotten, Oww!—Ayano's stomach, Chikara's temples. Finally, Chikara caught her opening. She dropped down and kicked Ayano's stomach, causing her to bolt into the air and skid on the dirt on her back.

Amethyst eyes searched the area. The other members of the club were gone. Oh no, they weren't leaving so easily. Before Ayano could stand to retaliate, Chikara sniffed the air and followed Stella's bloody trail.

*

"Hold on, Stella. Don't give up on us, okay."

Stella was shaking violently. Paleness bleached her skin. Her blood coated Kenta's black shirt. Her breathing was rushed and she sunk lower and lower into Kenta's hold, ensuring surrender.

Mary was scared. No, she was terrified. She and the others had arrived just as Chikara reached Stella. How she managed to make it from the pond and over to Stella in less than a second, Mary didn't know. Then, Chikara had stabbed her. Stabbed her! A defenseless and petrified Stella!

Ayano had dropped Sazuma then and there and lashed out with a growl. Mary had caught Stella in her arms and removed the blade. Kenta had collected her in his arms and entered the forest once more.

It had taken longer to get here. It was such a large woodland area. But that was no excuse. They should have reached Stella before this happened. They should have been well prepared for anything and moved quicker. Valla Park was at least an hour or two from town. Nothing resided out here. There were no police stations, no clinics, no food shops or resting places. There was nothing!

Stella needed help, and she needed it now.

"Get out of here."

Kenta turned to Mary without stopping his run. "No."

"Stella needs help and keeping a human's pace won't help her. You need to get to town now."

"I'm not leaving you girls without protection."

"We can protect ourselves." Sazuma said. Good, she and her sister were on the same boat.

"There's gotta be something we can do. We have to at least stop her wound."

"You're a spirit being right. You're all supernatural and shit. Can't you heal her?"

Sazuma didn't have to be so rude about it.

"I cannot. I don't have that ability."

"Well we have to do . . . ," a gasp, "Mary!" Sazuma pushed her sister out of the way, just as a two throwing stars came into view. Mary hit her back on a tree trunk. Sazuma was hit on her left side. She didn't scream. She didn't grunt. She flinched and sucked in small amounts of breath.

Kenta turned and pulled out his sword. The silver blade morphed the moment it reached the atmosphere, turning from a straight blade to a wavy shape. The silver turned to ink, sliding down, entering the blade's hilt, leaving behind nothing but red.

His blade collided with Chikara's the moment he turned. "I want my pet back." She glared.

"She's no pet," Kenta pushed back, jumped and slammed his heel in Chikara's face. She tripped over her own feet and fell to the ground, only to stand back up and dash again. Kenta placed Stella against a tree and went to Chikara once more.

Cautious of her surroundings and the battle taking place just inches away from her, Mary crawled to her sister, scraping and cutting her exposed knees on the way to her. This was nothing. This pain, these wounds were nothing compared to Sazuma and Stella's. She would live from this. But would *they*?

"Sa . . . Sa . . . ," She couldn't even say her sister's name. Her hand trembled. Sazuma's left eye stared up at her. The onyxes of her eyes were polished. Tears threatened to fall. The cries were well hidden. The pain must have been unbearable. Mary swallowed a single drop of spit down her suddenly dry throat. "Hang on, okay. I'll help you."

Instead of removing the stars, Mary pulled at Sazuma's shirt and dragged her to Stella.

"Let me go," Sazuma exhaled. Mary released her but stared in shock as Sazuma brought herself to her knees and yanked the throwing stars from her side.

"What the hell are you doing?" Cussing wasn't a big thing of Mary's. The word came freely as she watched her wounded sister.

"It's not like I can't walk. I'm fine. Now let's go."

Let's go? Let's go?! Sazuma must have been hit in the head somewhere. She couldn't move in her condition. And, if she could, she wouldn't get far. Even now, the reluctant girl's left side was coated crimson, even extending to her thigh. Paleness advanced forward.

Also reluctant, Mary turned to Stella, bent down and picked her up. She was cold, Mary realized. She was breathing, but her temperature was dropping.

The girls moved forward, heading back to the town. The road there was clear, but in Mary's vision, there was nothing but trees. The clashing of blades echoed, letting Mary know Kenta still had Chikara occupied. Terrifyingly, at this rate, Sazuma and Stella weren't going to make it. Sazuma was already slowing down and even tripped over her own two feet. Finally, after several more times, Sazuma dropped, landing on her stomach with a grunt.

Worry drastically hit. Mary turned to her preparing to drag Stella and her sister back into town. Sazuma shook her head in protest as she brought herself to her knees. "Go on without me. I'm slowing you down."

Mary had left Sazuma behind many times during their childhood. She always traveled places with her mother while Sazuma was stuck at home with their father. Pained expression coated Sazuma's face every single time Mary returned home from a day full of fun.

No, Mary wasn't leaving her again. Not mentally or physically.

She grabbed Sazuma's arm more forcefully than expected and dragged her to her feet. Sazuma followed suit, pushing herself from the ground and hurrying forward. "I said leave me."

"Correction, you said go on without me and you're slowing me down. Both of which are immaterial."

Mary's load had doubled, but she didn't care. She continued on in her rushing pace, determined to make it back to town, where someone, anyone, could help them.

To her misfortune, the moment she realized the colliding of blades no longer echoed was when assurance came crashing down. Were they out of range to hear the battle? Or was someone defeated?

Mary continued on nonetheless. She hoped, she prayed, her friends were alright. Kenta and Ayano were strong. They were courageous, willing and daring. They survived these supernatural worlds' years before Mary even knew them, she bet. So they would be alright . . . she extremely hoped.

Suddenly, the scent of carnations hit Mary's nose. A shadow hit a beam of light shining through the trees. The twins looked up, eyes widened. Chikara appeared through the canopies with her blade in a swinging position. Acting on intuition, Mary handed Stella to Sazuma and pushed the two to the nearest tree. She was wide open now, prepared for anything Chikara gave her.

"Mary!" Sazuma's scream of horror echoed through the forest.

There was no water to use. There was nothing to shield her. Chikara was too fast. She was too ready while Mary was trapped in her state of shock. Oh well, she figured. This was alright. If she was struck, and if she died, then it would be alright. Sazuma had been through worse pain. It was time Mary felt some pain in her life was well.

Chikara pulled her arm back further and swung, aiming for Mary's middle.

A flash blinded Mary's vision as the sunlight came overhead. When the blindness faded, Mary froze. Her breath caught in her lungs. Time slowed.

Someone was standing in front of her. But who?

A tall, silver-haired man stood in front of her now, wearing what seemed to be a dusty gray one piece. A matching clayish blade with no hilt resided in his hand. There was only a blade that seemed to come out of his left palm.

Chikara was frozen in air; blade touching the newcomer's and shock straining from her features.

The man made a husky chuckle. "You got a lot of nerve attacking a defenseless teenager."

Chikara's eyes narrowed. "You have no right scolding me."

Another husky chuckle, "You're right, except I have every right to kill you." The last part was sultry, as if so much pleasure would be given to him while he took her down.

In one measly push, Chikara was thrown back, pushing past branches, leaves and even flying through an entire tree trunk. The tall tree slowly fell to its right side, missing Mary and the others.

Mary's fright morphed into surprise as the man peered over his shoulder. Her heart sank into a pool of . . . something. Those had to be the most beautiful eyes she'd ever seen. They were a shimmering hazel and welcomed any woman into his arms. His skin was a healthy peach color. His nose sloped handsomely and his lips were delectable.

He was gorgeous. Out of this world, even.

"You alright, Mary."

Her shock bolted out of her, as if hiding and beaming in a corner of her mind for the sheer fact that he spoke to her. "Yes, I'm . . ." Wait. How did he know her name?

Without even letting her finish, the man turned to Sazuma. She was limping over with Stella in hand. The man stepped forward, arms outstretched, hands free of a blade. Where did it go?

"Hand her to me," he said without much patience.

Sazuma held the injured teen closer. "No. For all I know, you could be another demon."

"Or, I could be someone who could save your friend. She might have a shoulder and thigh wound but she could die from blood loss. A matter of fact, so can you."

Mary did notice Sazuma's legs were buckling and she was far more pale then just a few minutes ago. It was good to suspect this unknown savior would be another demon, but Mary felt no evil from him. She didn't even feel the evil, if there was any, when he pushed her back. Where had she gone anyway? Another surprise attack?

"Chikara teleported out of here right after breaking the tree," the man answered, as if reading Mary's mind. He was bent down on one knee and holding Stella protectively. His right hand placed right over Stella's shoulder wound. After seconds of impact, his hand shined a dazzling gold.

Coolness filled the air. There wasn't a breeze. It was coming from the man's hand. It wasn't even a minute after he touched her that Stella's skin plumped back to health and the blood that stained her shirt was disappearing.

Stella took a deep breath as she opened her eyes in realization. She was healthy, whole again.

Sazuma and Mary smiled, relieved and overwhelmed with gratefulness.

The man helped Stella to her feet. She only reached the man's chest bone while Mary and Sazuma reached his shoulders.

The man gave her a brief grin then turned to Sazuma. "You're next." He motioned her to come closer with the crook of his finger. She hesitated, but she approached. His glowing gold hand reached her wounded side and kept there. The bloodstains were disappearing. The blood that had created a river down her leg was sliding back up, leaving no hint that it was ever there.

Like Stella, Sazuma took a deep breath as the stains dissolved away and the man pulled back his hand. He placed his hand to the side. The glow dissipated. Sazuma turned to him and he too gave her a brief grin.

"Thanks. Who are you?"

She could have given him more of thanks than that. He deserved a better gratitude.

The man shrugged. "As long as you girls are alright, then I don't see why you have to know my name."

"Not meaning to flirt or anything, but you are kind of like a knight in shining armor."

The man turned to Stella and winked with a smirk. "Thank you."

Leave it to Stella to think of those kinds of things. She was right though. The grayish material he wore shined like armor but there were no armor-like plates. The material looked like clay a bit, with designs that looked similar to symbols Mary had never seen. Where his blade went though, she still wondered.

"Mary," a familiar voice said. Kenta approached her. She jumped. Why was everyone appearing out of nowhere?

His arms wound around her; embracing her tighter than any hug she'd ever been given. His hand rested on her lower back as his other hand held her protectively. It was . . . nice. His hugs were nice.

Her face heated as she brought her arms around him, returning the hug. It was nowhere near as passionate as his, but it was something. She couldn't find anything to say. His warmth had shut her up completely.

He pulled back too quickly, taking his warmth with him. She mourned of the loss. She came back strong. *I can take the cold.*

Mary searched him. His shirt ripped and his jeans were even worse. The rips on his thigh and calves were not a part of his ripped-jeaned fashion. There was no blood, though, so he must have been fine. His hair plastered to his temples and his headband kept intact. His sword, straight blade now, rested in its sheath.

"Stella," Ayano breathed in relief. The tall caramel skinned woman grabbed her friend lovingly and waved her from side to side. Stella took everything in longing. "I'm sorry. I'm so sorry. I should have protected you better. I should have known this was going to happen."

"It's ok." Stella's words muffled in Ayano's shoulder, "You came for me. That's all that matters."

Sazuma joined in on the reunion, hugging Mary and then hugging Stella once Ayano backed away, which she did halfheartedly.

Mary turned to Kenta. He faced the unknown savior. Kenta glared. The man glared with a smirk. Kenta was at least an inch shorter than the man was. Funny, though. That didn't stop the hated stares. Why stares of hate though? He probably thought the unknown man was a demon. Made sense.

"Leave Damon," Kenta growled.

"It's nice to see you too short-stuff."

Short-stuff? Kenta wasn't all that short. The man's husky voice remained, but it was filled with playfulness; so much playfulness he didn't seem like the same person.

"You could at least thank me for healing them," the man sighed as his shoulders slouched. "It's a shame really. How could you possibly protect these girls if you can't even heal them?"

Kenta's hand moved to his sword hilt. The man's blade appeared once more, slipping out of the palm of his hand. The man-Damon, was it?-gripped the blade, its tip aiming for Kenta's forehead.

"Hey, knock it off." Ayano stepped in the middle, palms facing both of the threatening men.

Damon looked her up and down, ignoring Kenta completely, "Since when did you hit puberty? You look hot."

Ayano turned to him. She bowed her head to him and brought it back up, "Damon, good to see you. You're voice is still a little pitchy, I see."

"Ho ho ho, you're so cute," he glared with a smirk. Damon lowered his hand, his blade disappearing in his gray coated material once more. "Well, I took care of business. I'm out of here."

Kenta's hold on his blade finally soothed, relieving Mary, strangely.

Damon peered over his shoulder. "Don't worry kiddies. I'll be in town if you need anything else. Dr. Damon will always be there to help." With that, he disappeared. That must have been some kind of awesome supernatural thing.

Kenta dug his fingers into his scalp. "I had no idea that idiot was in town. I should have sensed him."

Did he hate Damon or something?

Ayano turned to him. "I don't see why you still hate him."

Mary noted, case proven. "Did something happen?"

"His birth happened," Kenta murmured with increasing hatred. He wasn't answering Mary. The answer was more for him.

For the first time in Mary's presence, Ayano chuckled. It was soothing and brought such a shine to her that she was a completely different person. "Come on now. Damon's a nice guy."

"I don't see how you could like him." He faced her now, ignoring the other girls completely.

"He was nice to me. You only hate him because of something that happened over twenty years ago."

"You act like that's a long time."

"For a human, it *is*."

Mary had never seen Kenta so worked up before. It worried her. He should have been less stressed. This whole event must have taken a toll on him. Gently, Mary placed her hand on Kenta's firm shoulder. She shivered. Her warmth returned. "Kenta?"

His tense shoulders dropped just as his hands did. He faced her, stress completely terminated, leaving no evidence it was ever there. His burgundy eyes stared her down, staying there, freezing time, leaving only them. She gulped. Her cheeks heated again. *Again*, she found no words.

"I'm sorry," he lowered his head and put his forehead on hers. His eyes closed. His warm spearmint breath fanned her face. "Are you alright?"

He investigated her before, she knew, yet he cared to ask her anyway. "Uh huh," she answered, no other words forming. With a grin, Kenta wrapped his arm around her waist and pulled her in for another embrace.

"I'm glad," he whispered in her ear. All self-awareness was cut off. She surrendered into his embrace. Her nose rubbed against his muscled chest. He smelled like coconuts. How he did it after not even entering the house and showering up, she didn't know. Didn't care at the moment.

Sazuma cleared her throat and shouted for attention. "So yeah, I want to go home."

With that attitude, Mary knew she was fully healed.

Mary pulled back but kept her hands on Kenta. He hadn't released her either.

"Sure thing," Ayano said. She handed Stella her gold staff and wrapped her arms around the grinning red head and Sazuma. "Because you've never teleported before, I'm going to give you some instructions."

Mary grinned ear to ear and wrapped her arms around Kenta once more, knowing he too was going to teleport. Her eyes closed anyway as she relaxed against him and welcomed whatever teleporting had to offer. He tightened his embrace once more and brought his head down to Mary's ear. He said nothing.

Ayano continued in a higher toned and cheerful voice, "Please keep your hands and feet in my personal bubble at all times. Do not attempt to leave or even understand what's going on at this time. If you have any questions, please ask me later when I'm not tired and in the mood to kill something."

The wind picked up in a split second. Mary launched off her toes. Kenta's firm hold never wavered. She puffed in some air in shock and clutched Kenta's shirt. Seconds later, she was standing on a hard surface again. The surrounding was utterly chilly and the scent of cooked noodles filled the air.

"You guys," Hiroko and Reiko's voices got Mary's attention. She opened her eyes, realizing she was in Ayano's apartment. She smiled, even as Kenta released her. The two relieved teens rushed over and came together in a group hug.

❧

Chikara appeared back in Derek's home. Blood, scrapes, future scars, and wood splints coated her from head to toe. A splitting headache pounded in her skull and breath barely filled her lungs.

Her luck seemed to not have changed. It had only gotten worse. Ayano had attacked head on and would have cracked her neck if Chikara hadn't been more skilled in this kind of combat. Once taking her out, or at least pushing her back, she had gone after her prey. Then Kenta came into the picture and ruined everything.

It had taken longer to push him far enough for her to teleport to the girl's location. But once she found her opening, Chikara had punched and kicked her space open and moved on, finally reaching the girls and even about to take out the water girl.

Devastatingly, Damon had stepped into the spotlight after over a hundred years; since the Kyushu island invasion. He had been one of the spirit beings to come into the battle of Kyushu Island and assist humans, although it was stupid of him to try. The battle had lasted over two hours. The Heavenly Beings had retreated and the island belonged to the Demon Docks.

Now, he seemed to have changed. His hair was cut short—which looked pretty good actually—and he wore a dusty gray material she had never seen before. Whatever. He was going down anyway. He not only was bothersome in the past, but now he was a pest. He had pushed her back, causing most of her injuries. Chikara had teleported once a stick embedded itself in her right thigh.

Awesomely, her fucked up day didn't end there. Just as she teleported home, echoes of sheer laughter entered her ears. She looked up wondering who had invaded her room; however, she quickly realized she was in the middle of Derek's throne room. She recognized these beige walls. She recognized these gold framed paintings of her fellow Demonic Princesses and even some of the Demonic Princes. There were numerous paintings of Derek and Diamond, either heavily clothed or somewhat naked, barely covered with blankets.

The gang was all here. There was Lord Derek and his wife Diamond, the mischievous Lavida, the quiet Destiny with a dark green book in hand, Emiko-silent as ever, and the Demonic Princes, the Nakamura brothers.

Lavida was sitting on Derek's throne armrest and laughing at Chikara.

Emiko, who was sitting on the ledge under the large window, remained silent. She hadn't noticed her sister's appearance. Once she spotted her, Emiko darted up and ran to assist her sister.

Chikara pushed her away and righted her ripped up and slanted clothing.

"That's one impressive sight," the cat demon Riku Nakamura said as he looked at his comrade. The demon had snow white hair that reached the back of his shoulders. The sides and front of his hair were short, reaching his ears. He had emeralds for eyes with silver cat ears and a matching tail. He was a skinny kid with more bark than his bite. He was attitude incarnate. "I never would have thought to see you like that. You surely are hopeless."

"Shut up," she muttered. She bent down and pulled out the stick in her thigh. She stood straight with a sigh. Her thigh still throbbed. She expected that pain for the next hour or two.

Diamond walked down Derek's throne stairs and stepped to the side while Derek followed and faced the exhausted and injured ninja. Whatever he had to say, she could take it, she reassured herself. Derek had scolded her before. She handled it then and she could handle it now.

"My dear girl, what happened to you? What silliness have they done to you?"

No disappointment filled his tone. Good. "Nothing, they just gave me an unexpected move and it happened like this. I assure you it won't happen again."

"I know it won't." Derek stroked Chikara's hair. "That's why I'm suggesting you stay here for a while. You need to increase your strength and you have to be reminded of who you really are. You let yourself be defeated." The more he spoke, the lower and more menacing his tone became. "Girls like that with weak powers should have not taken you out so easily."

Chikara gulped. Derek's aura thickened. "I apologize."

He grinned, the thick aura slowly, but surely seeping away. "It's quite alright, my dear. Now go." Chikara bowed then limped out of the room. She closed the door on her way out. She couldn't help the weep escape her as she rushed to her own room. It was bad enough to miss her destination and landed in Derek's throne room. Now, she and her other *"comrades"* had witnessed Derek's darkened aura. He was pissed, she knew. But there was nothing she could do now but rest. So rest, and forget the world—she would.

In the throne room, Derek's gentle and reassuring face directly changed to annoyed and sinister. He glared at the door. "What a useless girl."

"I say we send her back to Hell," Riku said.

Derek sighed, greatly considering the idea. "No, she's still needed around here. We just need someone who can take care of business in a more organized and professional manner." Derek thought Chikara had that quality. It seemed like she was only good at taking out angels. But Kenta was a spirit being. How come she couldn't handle him? Derek sighed again. "We are demons after all. We need to have style and class with the things we do."

"She might be the last demonic ninja ever. Nevertheless, that doesn't mean she's special," Lavida said. She sat on Derek's throne arm rest. Her short caramel dress with crystals woven at the hems rose up as she sat. She crossed one black ankle high booted leg over the other. "All she has is sex appeal."

To Derek's surprise, Emiko remained quiet. Her head was lowered. She hadn't spoken a word since her sister pushed her away. "Let's have little Emiko step up to the plate. The midget hasn't had her debut yet." Lavida's voice sizzled with anticipation.

"That's true." Derek grinned, liking the idea. Derek called the black-haired girl's name. Her head rose. Her green eyes stared him down, even watering. "How would you like to go into town and try to take an Element Princess?" Key word, *try*.

"I would be honored." She choked back some tears.

Fine answer. "Good, now listen carefully. Don't be like your sister and be reckless." There was disgust in his voice. He hoped Emiko understood his message. "Try to find the other Element Princesses and find one that you can bring back here."

Emiko nodded and wiped her face. She inhaled deeply, lowered her head again, then teleported away.

"Man, that girl is so weird," Riku exhaled. He stroked his fingers through his hair.

He turned to his brother, Nao. His daring green eyes were turned to the window, viewing the shore. He was completely out of the conversation.

The young Nao Nakamura was the cast out but he was still a Demonic Prince. Derek didn't know anyone who actually thought of him as one, but in Derek's mind, he was one.

Riku rolled his eyes and focused in as Lavida spoke. "From what I remember, the Yamada clan was filled with strong ninjas who didn't dare follow orders. How you got your hands on two of them Derek, I will never know."

Technically, Emiko's not even considered a ninja, Derek thought.

Riku spoke once again. "Well, same goes for you, Destiny and Diamond. You three are the daughters of Lucifer. You can do anything, go anywhere, become anything, and, yet, you stay here with Derek."

"As a Demonic Princess to a Demon Lord, and a handsome man," she winked at Derek, "it is an honor to stay here."

"Either that or your lonely," Riku murmured.

"That's enough," the two demons silenced themselves and turned to their leader.

Derek stuffed his hands in his black jeaned pockets. "Kenta now has four princesses on their side. We have to find the other three before he does. One of my girls couldn't do it. I now sent Emiko, so she might succeed this. Lavida, I want you to use your animal skills and track down Emiko's progress. I also want you to find either Kenta or Ayano and spy on them. We need all information possible. I refuse to let them gain another princess."

The demons, now including Nao, rose up, bowed in respect and exited the room.

As they exited, Diamond went to join them. Derek stopped her mid step. "Where do you think you're going?"

Her shoulder hunched up, hiding her irritation, he knew. "Going to my room." She was being infuriatingly rude. She knew to face him when she spoke. The least she could have done was look over her shoulder.

"You're not going anywhere. We have progress to check on in the underworld and you're coming with me to the update center." The update center was a room stationed with computers all over its walls. At least ten foot soldiers were placed in the room and monitored the section of the underworld

Derek controlled; the human region, where damned humans were sent to and morphed into the hideous creatures all beings of the world saw.

"It sounds like an easy job. You don't need me."

She still didn't face him. Derek's fury rose. He was on the verge of spinning her around and slapping her. Derek knew better, though. She would explode his organs if he did something like that. She had done so many times before, anyway. If so, then why was she holding back? She could have killed him a long time ago. What was with the hold up?

"Diamond Southbound, you are my wife and I command you to do as I say. Come with me to the update center."

With a sigh, she finally faced him. Her light brown eyes stared him down, hating him with every fiber of her being. Slowly, his fury drained until . . .

Diamond stood tall and proud and introduced Derek to her middle finger. She teleported after mere seconds.

Derek's fury rose once more, boiling over and threatening to burst.

❦

"Are you sure you're going to be alright being home by yourself? I hate leaving you here at such late hours."

Yumiko grinned, "I'll be fine. You go to work, get lots of money and remember, smile when hanging up the phone."

"If it's a good deal then sure thing," Jared smiled as he slipped on his classy black work shoes. His company *"Yamamoto Lawyers"* had called him on short notice. They were short on staff and needed assistance. Being as humble as he was, Jared decided to go and assist.

Jeremy had called before dinner—fried chicken with mashed potatoes and peas, all of which were so American, by the way—and said he would be home late. He had a job in Tokyo and that was a good distance away. Kayta Plains was so isolated from everything. Yumiko thought it wasn't even on a map.

Overwhelmed with worry, Jared had dressed in a buttoned up white shirt with dark brown dress pants and a suit jacket while asking Yumiko countless questions. "Are you sure you want me to leave? Do you want to order a movie? Do you want to know the safe password so you can reach my gun?" He was the safety prone.

Yumiko giggled and answered with yes and no. She said yes to the idea of ordering pizza late at night and ordering some movies, though. Jared even approved for her to have a friend over. Maybe she could invite her friend, Kimi, from math class; Tokuya, from Language Arts; or Abby, from the tennis team.

She shook her head. Her high school friends were so much cooler.

Jared pressed his lips to Yumiko's forehead and ruffled her hair. "You call me if anything is wrong. And I mean *anything*. Call even if you think you see a shadow in the corner or a figure in the window."

"Okay, Jared, okay." She waved as he exited, closing the door behind him.

Her eyes remained on the door.

Three ... two ... one ... "Are you sure you're good."

"My gosh, Jared, bye!" Yumiko waved her arms hysterically. His head peeped through the door. He smiled wide and laughed full heartedly. She was lucky to have such a caring brother. Brothers, she corrected.

Jared waved goodbye and closed the door. Yumiko ran to the window and watched as Jared entered his silver convertible. He backed up, placed on his black sunglasses—he always felt cool while wearing them—honked the car horn to signal his goodbye and headed off. Yumiko waved. Her smile faded.

Silence greeted her.

He said it was fine to call even if she saw a shadow, right?

Yumiko shook her head. She was crazy to even consider the idea of calling him. He just left mere seconds ago. Yumiko closed the white window shades, blocking the afternoon sun from the inside of her living room and exhaled as she turned.

Yumiko's living room was a bit on the narrow side, with yellow walls and a plush white carpet. A single white couch sat in the center of the room, a few inches away from the thirty-two inch flat screen. Beyond this living room were the kitchen and the backyard door. White carpeted stairs were in the kitchen and led to the second floor of the house.

She looked around. She had all this space to herself. The sun was setting and her stomach was full from just eating dinner. She nodded. *Yeah ... I like this.* she thought ... and thought ... and thought some more.

Hiroko and Reiko were at her house ten minutes later. "I couldn't do it," Yumiko said as she opened the door.

Reiko nodded in understanding as Hiroko laughed. "And, that's why we're here, my love."

The lively girls entered and ordered pizza, on Reiko's debit card of course. Yes, the girl had a debit account filled with her monthly allowance. Instead of her parents personally giving it to her, they enclosed it into her account. Reiko's parents found it crazy to personally give their teenage daughter one million dollars in cash. Silly, right?

Anyway. Yumiko listened in as her friends described their day. There was Hiroko's dream, which brought Yumiko to tears. The whole ordeal was shocking and caused all girls to eat ice cream afterward—chocolate ice cream for Yumiko, Cookies and cream for Hiroko and Reiko. And yes, they brought their own ice cream.

That conversation led to traveling to Stella's house to see the sunflower she was going crazy about. Then, Reiko explained how some lavender—haired woman stole her and Sazuma, Mary and Stella's caretaker Ayano had went to save her. Then after an hour or two they returned, appearing in the living room out of nowhere. Everything turned out fine though.

Except, Hiroko thought Mary was going a little crazy. She was hugging and talking to the space beside her, as if she was conducting conversation with a ghost. Yumiko hoped not. She had paranormal experiences in her previous house. Those were scary times.

Reiko had finished the day's fun times by saying, "We were on our way home when we both got your text message"—Yumiko had sent them both the same message "Jared just left. Come over, please and thank you."—"So you know we had to grab our stuff and come see you. It was a necessity."

Yumiko nodded with a grin. She was grateful. She could sleep with some well-being. She wasn't good with darkness. She feared the dark for multiple reasons. She had seen horror films, she had encountered ghosts and she had witnessed a robber enter her house through her very own bedroom window. She had every reason to fear the dark.

She was highly grateful to have Reiko and Hiroko; one could sneak out of the house without her parents calling 911, and one could simply leave if she promised to return home safe and sound. She couldn't ask for better friends.

The chat session and ice cream chewing had lasted until ten at night. The girls had eaten two cartons of ice cream—Oops (Wink, Wink).

Jeremy had returned home around an hour afterward, surprised that Jared was gone and replaced with two teenage girls. He allowed them to stay, however. The nineteen year old liked Yumiko's friends; liked them in an, "I'm glad my sister has such caring friends," sort of way.

As he retreated upstairs, the girls got ready for bed—well, Yumiko was actually the one to enter her sleeping bag. They were going to nap together in the living room, like a real slumber party. Yumiko entered her violet bag and observed as Hiroko and Reiko engaged in a fantasy video game. Hiroko was the player, Reiko was the supporter, claiming to having finished the game so many times-, and Yumiko was the watcher who slept while the people played.

It didn't take long for the young girl to enter her slumber. She placed her head on her pillow and drifted off.

In her mind, she saw her school, a red bricked building with too many windows to count, her town; a decent and American early 1900's feel, her brothers; a blonde-haired and brown-eyed Jared and a shaggy light brown-haired and brown-eyed Jeremy; she saw the things that made her happy.

All of her restful images swirled together, mixing as one and slowly faded into the darkness of her mind. Yumiko focused in on where her images had disappeared to. A small white dot blinked, on and off. On and off.

As quick and random as it appeared, the light shot forward, blinding Yumiko even further. She shut her eyes to block its intensity. From a bright light to the complete black, Yumiko opened her eyes to see where the light had gone.

Standing in front of her was a woman. No, not a woman, but a girl. Her outline was shining an eerie green, but Yumiko saw her perfectly. Long black hair swayed behind her shoulders in a wind Yumiko did not feel. Eyes of jade glared at her. Yumiko's school uniform, a long sleeved button up shirt with a tan skirt that reached her knees and black or white sneakers, was this girl's wardrobe. She must have been a student, she figured. But, why was she dreaming about this random girl?

Appearing in the girls hand from thin air was a sword. Yumiko's panic mode kicked into high gear. She tried to move but she froze in place. She was rooted into the darkness of her mind with no hope in escaping.

"There you are." The girl's voice echoed through her head. It was a gentle tone laced with lethal intent.

Move Yumiko, a voice told her. It wasn't her conscience. It was a male voice she never heard before. She tried to follow the command, but it was futile. *Move Yumiko. Come on darling, move.* Still nothing.

The girl brought her sword up in an arc, prepared to strike.

Wake up Yumiko! The male voice shouted. *Wake up!*

The girl swung.

Just as the black-haired girl brought up her sword and was about to swing, Yumiko had woken up. She shot up, seeing nothing but darkness. She moved her head left and right, her room slowly coming into view. The TV was turned off and her friends rested on her left and right sides. They hadn't woken up at the slightest.

Yumiko didn't even want to see what time it was. She figured it was late and she needed more sleep. She wiped her damp forehead with the back of her hand and cuddled back down, placing her head on the pillow, taking a deep breath, closing her eyes and entering sleep once again.

Story 6

I'm simply *brightening* your night

Instead of returning home like she thought they would, Mary and her sister remained with Stella, informing her of the world she was hidden from; the world she was forced to enter. After Hiroko and Reiko left for the night, Ayano figured this was the perfect time to confess everything, and she meant everything.

Stella was informed of the supernatural world and given details about the Demon Docks; the group Sazuma and Mary had to defeat. Overall, Mary was proud of her friend. She handled everything in stride and didn't panic in the slightest. Kenta had even told her who started the school fire. Sazuma's head lowered in shame. Stella held no grudge.

"Your pain from Sazuma burning down the tree was proof that you were in fact an Element Princess; the princess of earth." Kenta said. The group resided in the living room and focused on Stella, who sat on the couch under the living room window. Ayano sat beside her. Sazuma, Mary and Kenta took the other couch in front of them.

"And you're sure about this?" Stella asked, trying to confirm Kenta's thought. Mary thought Stella wanted to get involved. Kenta told her about the upcoming war, the training, the lies she would have to tell her friends—she didn't have parents so that worry was out of the way. But Ayano would worry for her. She was the closest role model Stella ever had, Mary knew.

Kenta nodded. "The Mother Angel, Saki, had given me a list of names and descriptions of the women I was needed to search for. There was Sazuma; black hair, black eyes, and a heart of warning. There was Mary; black hair, black eyes and a heart of love." Mary's cheeks heated as she heard her description. *A heart of love, huh?* Kenta went on, "There was Ayano; black hair, blue eyes and a heart of poison."

The girls' heads tilted to the side in confusion. Black hair, yes. Blue eyes, no way. All eyes turned to Ayano. Most definitely her eyes were burgundy; not as dark as maroon, but not crimson either. They were a shimmering beauty.

"Long story short, it's a perk from my element orb," Ayano said, answering anyone's question, most likely everyone had the same question though. If her eye color was a perk, then was her hair the same. It was a charcoal black, otherworldly for sure. In addition, it matched her caramel skin perfectly.

"What was my description?" Stella asked after observing her friend, probably trying to imagine her with blue eyes.

Kenta grinned lovingly, answering, "Red hair, brown eyes and a heart of therapy."

"Therapy? As in healing?"

Kenta nodded to Sazuma's question. His eyes never left Stella. "It makes sense. You healed Ayano even when I couldn't. You allowed her to truly smile and love someone dearly. You're a healer, for sure."

"You brought smiles and love to my life as well." Ayano said to Kenta. The words rushed out, as if urging him to believe her.

"I know I have. I witness it every day since day one, but Stella is your true healer. You can let me go in battle and don't have to watch over me. Can you do that for her?"

Ayano turned her head, knowing she couldn't. Stella was too important, Mary knew.

Kenta nodded, knowing he was right. He leaned on his knees, interlocking his fingers and hung them between his legs. "Stella, I can't tell you enough about the dangers of entering a world like this. Because you can see me, it proves you have entered this world, but," he pressed his lips together. He sighed roughly and shook his head, "We're not one hundred percent sure you're the girl on the list. There are other Stella Jayberry's in the world that could hold the same features you do. We don't know if . . ."

"It's alright," Stella said. She grinned and pointed at herself with her confident thumb. "I'm your girl. I want to enter this fight. I know there will be training and I will have to deal with the thought of killing another living creature, but it's not a kill in vein. It's not a pointless kill. I can be able to say I helped someone. Plus, to be with Ayano, I'll do anything. I don't want her fighting this alone." She turned to Ayano, who stared at Stella with thankful eyes. "I'll never let her fight again." The conversation finisher had been meant for Kenta but the words were meant to touch Ayano's heart the most. And it had.

She turned her head away, eyes closed, lips pressed tightly together, turning them pale. "I can't . . . I just can't."

"Can't what?" Stella asked. She reached out to touch Ayano's shoulder, but on the moment of contact, Ayano jumped to her feet and began to pace the room. Her voice got louder, "You have no idea, no *idea*, what we have been through, how many teens we had to kill."

"Kill?" Stella stood.

"We?" The twins turned to Kenta, who now stood as well.

"Ayano . . ." he said, with regret slowly eating at him.

Kill? They'd killed before. Mary didn't know what to think of it. She had no idea what to say. Her throat dried and her breathing quickened. Sazuma stared in shock.

Ayano whipped her body around to face Kenta. "What if we're wrong again? What if she's not our girl? What if she changes her mind when the going gets rough? We'd have to kill her and I can't stand to kill anyone else!" Her lip quivered and her eyes turned glassy.

Stella was the same. Her legs shook, her lower lip vibrated. She huffed, suddenly struggling to breathe. "This has happened before?" she huffed again. "You've killed those who resisted leaving?"

Ayano turned her head away. She covered her mouth and faced her back to the group. Kenta walked to her. He reached out to her and grabbed her forearm. She pushed him away, getting out of his hold. He kept on, grabbing her again and pulling her into his hold. She didn't resist this time. She allowed Kenta's arm to wrap around her, both hands caressing her back. He leaned his head on hers. His eyes focused on Stella. He answered, "We had no choice."

One step, then another. Stella backed away. Her eyes shined with tears that threatened to fall. Mary stood just as Sazuma did. Sazuma was closest to Kenta and Ayano. She glared at them with rising hatred and confusion.

The room seemed to increase in temperature. The moderately cool temperature had turned into temperatures in the eighties. It didn't take long to reach the nineties. The increased heat had come from Sazuma. Her hands fisted at her sides. Flames crackled around her knuckles. Her lips pulled back, releasing a growl of pearly whites. "You better tell us what the hell happened in the past. And you better tell us right now."

Ayano pulled out of Kenta's hold. She wiped her face but refused to face the group. Kenta turned to his saddened friend. "They deserve to know."

"Damn right we do," Sazuma answered for her. The temperature was rising. Beads of sweat slid down Mary's cheek. The same was happening to Stella. She was rooted to the floor, staring at Ayano, waiting for answers. Mary faced them as well.

Ayano faced the group again. She wrapped her arms around her middle.

Kenta put out his hand and presented the couch. "You might want to sit down."

"We prefer to stand." Mary said. Her need for answers was rising. What *had* happened in the past?

"This happened before," Ayano began. "This happened so many times before." Ayano lowered her head and choked on a puff of air.

Kenta rubbed her back and continued, "After finding Ayano, we traveled together around the nation in search for the Element Princesses. We read from the list the Mother Angel had given me and in Tokyo, we thought we finally found our girls. The descriptions matched and their eyes shined with willingness." Kenta swallowed. Gulped, was more like it. "But once we gave the orbs to the girls, they had changed their minds completely."

Silence filled the air. Ayano continued this time. She inhaled deeply, "After realizing they could see demons and control the elements they were given, they wanted to give the orbs back. One by one, the girls had come to us and demanded we take out the orbs we stuffed into their chests. The orbs hadn't gone willingly, which surprised us at first. But now we see where we went wrong."

Mary understood. The fire and water orbs had gone to her and Sazuma willingly, pretty much jumping to their breastbones and merging themselves with their owners. If the orbs were shoved, then that means those were the wrong girls. Kenta and Ayano hadn't known that. How could they? They were never told so knowing was impossible. So how did they get the orbs back?

Kenta went on, "Ayano and I wanted to give the girls their lives back, and sadly there was no way to remove the orbs without damaging their souls. If their souls were damaged, then it would have been the same as dying. I asked the Mother Angel what I should do, how should I proceed with this. She told me the only way to retrieve the orb was to annihilate the host."

"They had to die in order for you to get the orb back." Sazuma's crackling fingers stopped. The crackle was no longer there. Her temperature dropped, but it was still hot. Mary thought her sister had calmed down . . . but she was wrong. Sazuma returned back with a vengeance. The temperature rose once more, now reaching over a hundred degrees. Her fists were consumed by a red-orange flame. "You killed them anyway!" she screamed. "You could have left the orbs and made some more."

"It wasn't that easy," Kenta stepped closer, facing off with Sazuma. Sweat beaded his forehead. Ayano lay against the wall and stared, not knowing what else to do. Kenta shook his head, "The Mother Angel could barely create these orbs as it was. They were power she only achieved on luck. She created orbs to create a team that protected the world when she could not. Angelic Warriors and Spirit Beings weren't enough to protect the humans. You girls act as the human's defense."

"I didn't tell you to give me a story of the creation of these damned things in our bodies. You didn't have to kill those teens."

"Their sacrifice led us to find you, the real princesses."

"And, what if I asked you to take this thing out of me? Would you kill me?"

Kenta merely stared. He had to think about the answer? He really had to *think* about it? He should have said no. He should have said something. Mary blinked repeatedly, fighting back the tears, the sadness, and the heartache. She understood why those girls had to die, but they didn't have to.

"Would you kill me?" Sazuma repeated. She wasn't about to last, Mary knew.

"Yes, we would," Ayano answered.

Stella turned to her, full on shock consuming her. She swallowed hard. She was still rooted. "How many?" Ayano's eyes turned to her. Her head remained low. More forcefully, she repeated, "How many?"

"How many what?" As if Ayano had to ask.

"How many people did you kill?" Stella's tears locked tight in her eye sockets. Her shoulders shook. Her legs buckled.

Ayano lowered her head further. Her hair acted as a curtain to her feelings.

"Ayano Matsumoto, you look at me when I'm talking to you." So much authority came from this fifteen year old. Ayano followed suit. She truly followed suit. Her head raised and she stood straight. Her eyes glued onto Stella. "Now, how many people did you kill?"

She inhaled roughly. "Are you asking how many *I* killed or are you asking how many *Kenta* killed?"

Mary's heart sunk. She knew Kenta had taken out the girls from his past. Hearing it from Ayano, who spoke vividly and true, was the most painful thing Mary had ever endured. To hear that Kenta, a man she trusted even though they had met mere days ago, had killed them. Mary shook her head. She couldn't speak. She didn't want to think anymore. She didn't know what she wanted to do.

"How many were killed all together?" She found herself asking. She hadn't even known the question had formed in her mind. Her reddened and glassy eyes stared at Kenta as his pained burgundies stared at her.

"Over a hundred," he answered.

Stella was straining. Her knees bent, threatening to fall, but she rose up and wrapped her arms around her chest. She sobbed once but held the others back. Mary's heavy breathing heaved.

"Give an exact number," Sazuma demanded.

"One hundred and fifty teenagers," Ayano answered.

Stella dropped to her knees. Her cries released. Her shock boiled over.

Sazuma's flames dropped. Her fire disappeared in a snap and her heated aura dissolved as she too dropped to her knees. Mary was the only one standing—barely though.

This was too much. This was far too much to take in. So many innocent teens were exposed into this supernatural world and killed because of the wrong choices he and Ayano had made. In the beginning, Mary would have never thought these two had killed the humans she found redeemable. She had no idea the two people who seemed otherworldly and rare would be murderers of her fellow humans.

Were they murderers? It seemed too strong of a word. Still, a life was a life, and Kenta and Ayano had killed one hundred and fifty innocents. What about the families of the teens who died? Who told them what happened to their daughters? Who told them a Spirit Being and an Element Princess had killed their child? To them, the deaths of their daughters were random and the culprits would never be captured.

Because the culprits were standing right here.

"You bastards," Sazuma mumbled. Her anger was still there, but through the dryness of her throat, it was hard to get out a growl. "You damned bastards. You deserve to die by the demons you hunt."

"Sazuma . . ." Mary said lowly.

"You deserve to burn in the flames of Hell that you yourselves despise."

"Sazuma," Mary said louder.

"You should be killed by the very princesses you've been out to search for!"

"Sazuma, stop!" Sazuma's head whipped around. Mary's tears escaped, sliding down her cheeks and mixing with the sweat she held. "Just please, stop."

She couldn't handle this. She couldn't handle all of these facts given to her. Too many details lingered through the air. Mary should have agreed with her sister and hate the man and woman standing in front of her, but she didn't. She should have wanted them to burn in Hell, but she didn't. She should have possessed the need to kill them herself, but she didn't. She should have demanded to give the orbs back even at the risk of her life, but she didn't.

She should have not held the understanding and nobility for their decision, but she did.

Mary stepped forward. Her sneakered feet skidded on the hardwood. She turned to Stella, who remained on her knees. Her head hung low, her forehead touching her knees. Carrot orange hair concealed her face. Her body was still. She was still processing everything. Mary hoped she was listening, because these next few words would affect them all.

"You deserve punishment, that much is true," Mary sniffed. She took several more steps. "Justice will be brought to you, that much is certain." She took her steps to Kenta. He hadn't moved an inch. "You have committed the worst of the worst and left hundreds of people with bottomless ominous holes of perplexity and sorrow in their chest." She reached him now, staring up at him. Her tears continued to fall, freely allowing him to see her grief. Kenta brought his hands up and grabbed Mary's cheeks. His warmth returned to her, shivering her body. She brought her hands up, resting them on top of Kenta's. He stared down at her painfully, regretting the deaths he caused. She huffed, "I can't bring myself to hate you."

"Please don't hate me." Kenta's pain released through his voice. Mary knew he truly hated himself. He despised himself. He hated the idea that he had killed those girls—with every right—but Mary didn't want that. He and Ayano had probably carried more guilt than anyone Mary had ever met. They didn't enjoy their kill. They had lived with the names and faces of the young girls who died. She didn't know how many years had passed since their killing spree—saying the word felt so wrong—but she knew their previous kill would indeed be their last.

"You told me I had a heart of love, right?"

Kenta hung his head low. He gripped Mary's cheeks tighter. She welcomed the pressure. He nodded his head to answer her question.

She nodded, "Then, let me love you."

"I don't deserve it."

Angels in Heaven knew he didn't deserve it. Mary didn't care. To her, he and Ayano needed it gravely. "Maybe," she answered anyway, "but that won't stop me from loving you." He faced her once more, shocked as can be. She grinned, "You're already a part of me."

And he was. Not only was he a part of her, but so were the girls from the past. Mary now connected to every single teenager who possessed the water element; just as Sazuma was connected to all of the fire possessors.

"Let me love you," she repeated to Kenta. She brushed her knuckles through his thick black hair and slid them down his dampened cheek. Sazuma's temperature blast had affected everyone. "It's alright Kenta. You don't have to hold . . ."

Mary's words were soaked up as Kenta moved in and pressed his lips onto hers. She froze, not knowing what just happened. The feel of his soft lips caused lightning to flow through Mary's veins. He was so warm. Had she always been this cold?

As quick as he kissed her, he pulled away and embraced her tenderly, holding her the same way he held her in the forest; one hand behind her head while the other went to her lower back. He hadn't done this for Ayano to calm her down. Maybe she *was* special.

"How could you just forgive him?" Sazuma's angered voice clouded the room. It wasn't that she didn't understand why she did it. She was just upset with the fact that she could forgive so easily. Mary was always the kind one who forgave people as long as their reason was valid. With Sazuma, there was always hate and misunderstanding. Forgiveness never came easy for her. Once you broke her trust, you were forever untied from her life.

"He had a valid reason." All eyes turned to Stella. Her head was brought up again. Her tears dried over her cheeks. Her glassy eyes lingered. She rose from the ground, standing on wobbly legs. As her knees bent, ready to fall, Ayano rushed over and caught her before she hit the floor. Stella's arms quickly wrapped around Ayano's neck and pulled her into a tight embrace. "I'm sorry. I'm sorry I never noticed your pain. Please forgive me."

Ayano chuckled without humor. She squeezed Stella's body and hid her face in the crook of her neck. "There's nothing to forgive," she sobbed.

The tense aura in the room died down immensely. Mary turned to Sazuma but remained in Kenta's arms. The harsh glare she held before died down to a moderately confused expression.

She still didn't understand, did she? Or if she did, she simply did not want to forgive.

"I'm sorry," Kenta said. Mary looked up. He had faced Sazuma, as well. Their eyes met. "I cannot undo the past, I know that well. Now, I know for a fact that you are the right girls. You are the girls we've been looking for. We have others to find. At the very least, understand what I did. You can hate me all you want, but don't let your hatred stop our cause."

Sazuma turned her head, unable to face him. She shook her head. Mary prayed. Just this once, could she give them a second chance?

"Sazuma, please," Stella said. Now that she was in on the plan, she had every right to ask her friend to reconsider leaving.

Sazuma sighed, "I never said I was leaving." She responded as if she read their thoughts. "It was just difficult for me to come to terms with their actions. I understand you wanted the orbs back, but you hurt so many others for your mistakes. I know you know that too." She turned back to Kenta. "I'm still in."

Mary smiled. Kenta sighed, releasing a breath he probably didn't know he held. Ayano and Stella did the same.

"However," Sazuma continued, harshly this time, "If *you* decide to change your mind and want to take these orbs back, I will not hesitate to kill you with the powers you gave me."

Kenta rubbed Mary's back up and down. He nuzzled into her hair as he answered, "Of course."

Just as the final bit of harshness dissipated and forgiveness filled the room, everyone but Stella jolted. It was as if they were struck by lightning. Intense urgency swam through Mary's bloodstream and the need to run consumed her. Ayano stood to her feet, the need hopefully filling her too.

"The girls," she said, grabbed her staff and returned back to Stella.

Kenta nodded, understanding Ayano's thought process. "You ladies stay here."

Sazuma glared, "Why? What's going on? What's this electric feeling I'm getting?"

So, she felt it too.

"Element Princesses get signals of when their fellow princesses are in danger. Someone is in danger."

"I'm getting something," Ayano said. "Head to Yumiko's house."

"Yumiko?" Mary asked in surprised. How was little Yumiko involved in this? Was she . . . ?

"Yumiko is on the Mother Angel's list isn't she?"

Sazuma asked. "Yes," Kenta answered.

"Okay, what other shit have you not told us about."

"You can be pissed at us later. Right now, we have to go." Ayano dashed out of the room, Kenta on her heels.

Sazuma grabbed her book bag. She grabbed Mary's and threw it at her. "You know we're following, right?"

"Heck yeah," Stella said. She put on white nurse-like sneakers, a highlighter green hoodie, and moved out first. The twins followed close behind.

Mary figured this would happen the second Kenta and Ayano exited. They might have been pissed to follow them in the first place, but her friends were right. They would always follow the supernatural beings. They were a part of this fight now, too.

Bang! Bang!

The girls zapped up to a sitting position. Their eyes zoomed in on the dark room, looking for the cause of the banging. It had come from upstairs. That wasn't enough to calm these instantly frightened teenagers and the single twelve year old.

Bang! Bang!

Not upstairs, Yumiko realized, but the roof. It was coming from the roof. Okay, explanations.

It might have been acorns. Acorns didn't fall that loud. Explanation one, failed.

It could have been little rodents playing on the roof. With the intensity of the bangs, there was no way the creatures would have been small even if they were rodents. Explanation two, failed.

Maybe it was fireworks gone wrong. Okay, that's just stupid.

Bang! Bang!

"Jeremy?" Yumiko called. Her brothers always responded with haste when she called them. At this moment, there was nothing. He couldn't have been sleep. The noises were too loud, echoed too vividly for anyone to sleep to. "Jeremy!"

"Oh, my gosh, this is like a movie I saw." Even though this was a scary situation, Yumiko listened to Reiko anyway. "There were these kids in this cabin and they were isolated from the world and then one night, the last night of their week long expedition, they realize the area has been rare for Sasquatch sightings. So, the group is attacked and their cabin went bang, bang. And they were all eaten one by one."

Hiroko nodded confidently. "I think I saw that movie. Wasn't it on Sci Fi?" Yumiko stared at them. They had completely forgotten the reason they had woken up in the first place. But Yumiko did once hear that there was a large eight foot tall creature in Japan. Could this have been an attack?

Bang! Bang!

"Yumiko..." the calling had come from a feminine whisper. Not a whisper. A chant. The chant echoed from the walls, surrounding the group no matter where they turned. "Yumiko..."

"*What* did you *do*?!" Hiroko shouted and pointed in a tone of "I don't know what you did but I know you did it."

Yumiko's palms faced them in innocence. "I didn't do anything." She was nice to people. She waved with a smile when people waved to her. She had a kind soul. Was that a crime?

Yumiko's name chanted again, still puzzling her. She slipped out of her sleeping bag. "Jeremy," she called again. Once she heard nothing, she made her way to the kitchen. It was a good size with white cabinets on the far wall with a dishwasher under the metal sink. A marble counter separated the sink from the gas stove. Sandstone acted as Yumiko's flooring.

Her feet patted as she moved to the stairway leading upstairs. Darkness greeted her as she looked up the white carpeted stairs. The stairs led to Jared and Jeremy's separate bedrooms; one bedroom was on the left and another was on the right. Yumiko's bedroom was beside Jeremy's down the hall.

Oh, how she loathed darkness. You never knew what resided in that said darkness. Anyone could have been hiding behind you. Anyone could have been sneaking behind you and prepared to strike. Anything could have been happening around you. Sound would assist you, but to Yumiko, sight was power. Darkness declined your chances of winning many times over. She felt powerless, even now.

"Je... Je..." She never thought her throat would constrict so dangerously. Her warmth was disappearing, leaving nothing but a hollowed girl stuck in a terrifying yet familiar place.

The night the robber had entered her room had truly destroyed any remaining sense that Yumiko had. She was once a child, so she didn't have much to begin with. Just looking back on it made her want to drop to her knees and cry out for her brothers, just like she did all those years ago.

"Jeremy," Hiroko called. Yumiko turned to her right. Hiroko stood there, her hands gently resting on Yumiko's shoulders. She was looking up the stairs, just as Yumiko had been. When Reiko, too, called his name, Yumiko turned to her. When had they followed her? How long had they been standing there?

There was no response to Hiroko and Reiko's call, which worried Yumiko gravely.

"I'll go up and check on him," Reiko took two steps up the stairs. "Maybe he's got headphones in his ears or . . ." She froze. She stared up at the top of the stairs. Yumiko and Hiroko froze along with her.

An ominous figure stood at the top of the stairs. Eyes of Jade stared down at them. The eyes were big and round, staring and staring and staring. They were buckeyes, watching your every move. It only appeared the minute Reiko touched the steps. Yumiko's eyes watered. Fear swallowed her up.

"Jeremy," she called fiercely, her voice cracking. Appearing inches down from the eyes was a pearly white grin reaching from ear to ear. A sword appeared out of nowhere, its silver blade beaming in light Yumiko never realized was there. "Jeremy!"

The dark figure rushed forward, sword held up high in an arc. Reiko jumped down the two steps and followed her friends out of the kitchen. She screamed at the top of her lungs, not knowing what else to do but run and scream. Grunts were heard as the sword in the woman's hand was waved and made contact with everything else but her targets; the frightened girls.

They dashed outside, not even thinking about turning around. Their bare feet pounded on the dirt as they rushed out of Yumiko's property and made their way to the community's exit. It was right in front, so close yet so far away. They could make it. They could make it!

The shadow figure misted a few inches away, standing in the middle of the exit.

They skidded to a stop, their heels digging into the dry dirt.

"Turning... and we're turning around," Reiko said as she started running in the other direction.

She didn't know what possessed her, but Yumiko turned around. The shadow figure was no more. It was a girl. The same girl she had seen in her dream. Her long black hair shimmered in the moonlight overhead. Her eyes filled with determination. Instead of wearing Yumiko's school uniform, like she was in her dream, the girl wore a long sleeved black shirt with a turtleneck and navy blue jeans. Black flats covered her feet.

She brought her arm back with her sword in hand. She was going to throw it, Yumiko panicked. On instinct, she pushed Hiroko, causing her to land in a neighbor's bloomed garden. Next was Reiko. Yumiko grabbed her friend's arm, twirled around and threw her to another neighbor's yard. Before she could move out of the way herself, the sword was thrown, aiming at her chest.

Time slowed. All she saw was the girl's sword coming nearer. Soon now, it would pierce her. The impact would be a pain all its own. The blood loss would most likely kill her if her heart attack didn't. The sword came closer, closer still. Her heart stopped. She was rooted to the ground.

"Yumiko!" Hiroko screamed. Her hand pushed up, reaching out to her. Just like that, Yumiko pushed back. She felt as if her body had been punched. Her back touched the dirt. The sword flew past her and pierced itself in the ground. What was that? A blast of wind had come at her, pretty much saving her life. Where had it come from? Wherever it came from, Yumiko was grateful. She froze like a deer in headlights. She would have died without the help, no doubt.

Yumiko brought her head up. The girl was running at her. She shot up in a panic, but she wasn't quick enough. The woman pounced in the air, planning to slam her foot into Yumiko's head. Before she even fell back to the ground, a black whip-like cloth wrapped around her neck. She was pulled back and slammed into the ground.

Reiko made her way to Yumiko and helped her to her feet. Hiroko joined them, inspecting Yumiko's body for injuries. Finding none on both her and Reiko, Hiroko calmed and turned to the scene in front of them.

The woman slept solidly. She wasn't exactly sleeping. It sure seemed like it. The black cloth still surrounded her neck. A tall caramel skinned woman stood behind her, keeping her eyes on the unconscious body. She had thick long blackish-gray hair and eyes of shimmering burgundy. She was beautiful. She was *striking*.

The black-haired beauty looked up from the attacker to the group of startled girls. "You guys alright?"

They slowly nodded, uncertain if that was the right answer.

The woman turned to her right and paused. She nodded her head after several seconds. "Getting rid of her shouldn't be a problem. I'll take care of this."

What was she going to do with the girl? Yumiko knew the girl had scared and tried attacking her and her friends, but it wasn't right to just throw her away somewhere.

"Thank goodness you were here, Ayano," Reiko said. She was grinning, "We would have been so screwed. But in all seriousness, where did you get that cool staff? It's so awesome."

Ayano? That was the name of Stella's caretaker, right?

Ayano picked up Yumiko's attacker and threw her over her shoulder. She completely ignored Reiko's question. "You guys get some sleep. This girl here casted a spell, ensuring that everyone in this community entered a deep sleep." That explained why no light came on during the screaming. "Forget what happened here and you should be fine."

"Easier said than done, don't you think?" Hiroko said. A calm breeze swished by, blowing Hiroko's straight blonde hair on Yumiko's arm. Her bubblegum pink silk nightgown blew lovingly, making Hiroko look like royalty. Reiko's nightgown was strapless and reached her ankles, unlike Hiroko's, which reached to her knees. Reiko's nightgown was sky blue. Her black hair danced with the wind. She looked like a million bucks. Ironic, because she was worth more than that.

"I'll say." A man's voice came from behind them. Yumiko stiffed as she swished around with Hiroko and Reiko. Indeed, there was a man standing behind them. He was tall. Taller than Reiko even, who stood five-ten. His skin was peach colored. The moonlight shined on him beautifully. A short sleeved indigo shirt hugged his torso and black jeans covered his legs. Black boots covered his feet. The breeze played with his silver locks. His eyes closed, hiding his eyes. She wished he would open them.

"Popping up out of nowhere, huh, Damon."

The man opened his eyes with a grin. Hazel eyes peered past the girls and focused on Ayano. "Now that you're back in town, I have the right to, do I not?"

"Yeah, yeah. But since you're here, take this junk back home. I don't have time to do it personally."

He tilted his head to the side, "Where do I take it?"

"I don't know. Throw it out or something. You're creative. Surprise me."

They were treating this girl as a piece of trash. It's like they forgot she was a person. She was somebody's baby . . . once. She might have attacked her, but saying how she was nothing was just wrong.

"Excuse me," Yumiko spoke up. She didn't know what possessed her to do so. She continued anyway, "I cannot let you just throw her anywhere."

"Yes you can," Reiko said while nodding. "He can take her to a faraway land where she will never return. Send her to the States."

"I like your friend," Damon smiled.

"No, no, no," Yumiko protested. "Her family might miss her. They could be out looking for her right now."

"I'm guaranteeing you right now; her family doesn't miss her at all." Ayano approached the group. The girls turned to their sides, making conversation between the two much easier.

"You don't know that."

"She knows full well, kid." All eyes turned to Damon. "Chikara most likely knows she's out here doing Derek's work, but doesn't care to give her back up. Little Emiko is screwed."

Chikara? Emiko?

"Chikara," Hiroko pondered, "Isn't that the same name Sazuma and Mary said when Stella got kidnapped?"

"Yeah." Reiko answered, the memory of earlier today popping into her mind. "And this dude," she pointed to Damon with her thumb, "said the black-haired girl had family. So . . ."

"They're sisters." Hiroko answered for her.

"Nice work Detectives Blondie and Black. What other mysteries are you going to solve?"

Hiroko glared. She was never good with people, other than her friends, giving insults. "Why don't you go back to wherever it is you came from, okay?"

Damon licked his lips. His eyes raked Hiroko up and down, lingering in certain places. "I like you. So feisty." The echo of a slap entered the scene.

Yumiko pressed her lips together. She was speechless. The dude did ask for that one. Hiroko hated perverts and this dude was indeed a pervert.

"Alright, let's end this now. Here," Ayano handed Damon the black-haired attacker. He whisked her over his shoulder. The attacker's sword was also given. Damon took it with a grin. "Anything else, 'Person who always appreciates my visits?'"

There was a pause. Ayano turned to her right again, focusing and listening . . . as if someone was standing right beside her. Yeah, Yumiko was missing something here.

Damon snickered, "I know you secretly love me Kenta. Don't show me so much hatred. I know you want me." He lifted his eyebrows twice in a playful motion. He disappeared seconds later, leaving no evidence he was ever there.

"I like him," Reiko grinned, pointing to the spot Damon once stood.

"I know him," Hiroko muttered. Yumiko was the only one who heard. No one else seemed to acknowledge her.

"Don't mind him. He's a friend of mine. If he arrives again, just know you can trust him." Ayano turned to her right again and grinned. "You just hate him, that's all."

She was talking to someone now? Ghost, maybe?

"Ayano!" Sazuma, Mary and Stella arrived, entering the community.

Ayano narrowed her eyes. "You were told to stay at the apartment."

"We had every right to follow," Sazuma said, coming to a stop when she reached the group. She turned to her friends. "You guys alright? We got a signal. Were you guys in trouble?"

"Not really. We were just chased by a shadow woman with a sword. Normal night, really." Yumiko and Hiroko left the sarcastic tone to Reiko.

Mary sighed, "People just keep coming." Her tone was concerned. This had happened before?

"I've had a pretty messed up day so anyone want to tell us what's going on? Obviously, this whole ordeal isn't normal."

Stella shook her head. "They deserve to know."

"I don't want them to get involved." Mary rubbed her arms. She was still wearing her school uniform. It was smudged with dirt and even ripped here and there. Sazuma and Stella's uniforms were the same.

"A demon attacked them. They're already involved,"

Ayano sighed. "Demon?" All three attack victims' outburst. Yumiko did not see that coming.

"It's a conversation that's going to have to wait," Sazuma said. A light flickered on the house to the Yumiko's left. People were waking up. Sooner or later, if this continued, people might have asked questions; questions they didn't need.

"How do you possibly expect us to continue the night like nothing happened?" Reiko asked.

"Continue the day you mean," Hiroko faced the horizon. Bits of blue shined through the darkness. The moon was setting.

"This is going to be a tiresome day," Sazuma said.

"We continue this tomorrow. Try to get some sleep." Ayano turned around. She wrapped her arm around Stella's shoulders.

With a wave, the twins made their way out of the community. As they turned left and headed out, a car pulled up and into Yumiko's driveway; which she realized the moment it came up the driveway.

Jared emerged from the car, utterly stunned with squinted eyes. "Yumiko?" She ran to her brother, thinking of the best way to explain this situation to him. *Well, we were possibly attacked by a demon and ended up almost stabbed. It's not that bad, though.* There was no way Yumiko could tell him that. What was she supposed to do? Lie?

"Hey bro," Yumiko smiled, as if it wasn't bad to be outside early in the morning.

Jared panicked instantly, "What are you doing out here? Do you know what time it is? What business do you have being out here?"

"Hey, what's up Jared," Reiko grinned ear to ear.

His eyes narrowed on her. "You brought her out here? Why?"

"No, no. Jared you have it wrong." Yumiko said. It wasn't right to let her friends have the blame for this. It was the attacker's fault, not theirs. Plus, if she told Jared about the attacker, his freaking out levels would skyrocket. He would ask more questions. One of those questions would be, "Where was Jeremy when this was happening?" and that would lead to an all-out argument. This whole situation was just not good.

She grabbed her brother's hand. He always responded best to contact. "We needed some fresh air and decided to go for a quick walk." She despised lying, but it was needed.

"And you decided to take a walk with bare feet and lingerie?"

Yumiko wouldn't have called their clothes "lingerie". Besides, Yumiko was wearing baggy pants and one of Jared's shirts, which bagged on her too. "We're sorry about leaving. Let's put this behind us. Please." Yumiko smiled brightly, hoping this would reassure him.

Luckily, it did. He sighed, knowing he couldn't resist his sister. "Just, get back inside. You have a few hours before school starts. You should try sleeping."

Based on how awake she was, there was no way she was sleeping again.

*

"You Yamada's are a damn shame."

Lavida had been giving crap to Emiko for the longest time. Ever since she returned to the mansion, actually. She had teleported in her room with mere bruises. Outside, she had bruises but inside, she had ruptured her lungs and broke a few ribs. She received massive injuries and teleported away. She was a damn shame.

The Yamada clan was a clan of demonic ninjas that were ruthless, chivalrous, and downright awesome. Some clan members, such as Emiko, had strange abilities like mind reading, shape shifting and time possessing. Lavida had even had a few friends in that clan, but they soon drifted, claiming they had better things to do then hang around a daughter of Lucifer. Now, the clan is on the endangered species list. Thanks to a mass murder, only Chikara and Emiko are the only remaining members of the clan and are the only ninjas left in the supernatural world.

If they kept getting their asses kicked like this, the Yamada clan would be finished for good.

"Just leave her alone." Chikara said. Lavida had been in the Yamada's large bedroom, hanging over Emiko's sleeping body and ranting how messed up her fight was. Now, it was Chikara's turn to be messed with.

Leisurely, Lavida swayed playfully as she made her way to Chikara's bed. The girl was still recovering from her fight in the forest. She should have healed by now. It was only a few wounds here and there. Then again, the girl was stabbed by sticks. The Yamada's *were* pitiful.

"You Yamada's are pitiful. You can't even defend yourself against some measly humans who were given boosts of power."

Amethyst eyes glared up at light browns. "You don't know what we've been through."

"I actually do. Kenta entered the scene, saved the day and you couldn't even handle him. He's a Spirit Being for crying out loud, and you can't even defeat him."

"Kenta's not the one who fucked me up."

Lavida pivoted a laugh. "Come on now. Ayano's one tough bitch, but she couldn't have done this to . . ."

Lavida stopped. Chikara's constant stare was enough to say who had done this to her. It wasn't one of the princesses or their Spirit Being for a pet. It was someone else. "Who?" she asked. It could have been anyone. Lavida hadn't used her manipulation ability and followed them with one of her chosen animals. She hadn't seen a thing. She should have done her orders by Derek. She hadn't. She'd been too lazy; too caught up flirting with foot soldiers working out and keeping tabs on Derek—who happened to be with Diamond at the moment. Who could have ruined these Yamada's so easily?

"It was Damon."

All hint of playfulness died immensely. Their injuries began to make sense. Kenta was a good fighter from what Chikara had seen from other foot soldiers, but Damon had over thousands of years of training and fighting on the front lines. No wonder the sisters had been beaten so easily. "What happened to Emiko?"

"She told me she woke up to find Damon over her body. He had thrown her around, smeared her face in dirt, and kicked her more times to count. He didn't touch her sexually, and that is something I'm grateful for."

That was the first time Lavida had ever heard Chikara give a damn about her sister.

Lavida paced against the room. She sighed and scrubbed a hand down her face. "What do we do? We have to stop him. What *do* we *do?*"

Chikara shrugged. "Tell Derek."

Story 7

Found *Elements*

To be a Demonic prince, one must have the usual elements: adversity, authority and, the most important, affection. Adversity was needed to understand the reason and purpose for fighting on the side of the Demon Docks. Authority was needed to get their enemies in line; terror was always needed in this case. Affection was needed to trick females into the prince's dirty work; affection was also used to trick these said females, Element Princesses, no doubt.

But if you asked Demonic Prince, Nao Nakamura how it was to be one of the elite of the Demon Docks, he would probably give you a definitive answer; it sucked.

There were better places to be and this place was not it. There were nations to journey to. There were other countries calling his name. There were people who were dying to meet him. No, he thought next. There was no one who wanted to meet him, see him, or even want to deal with him. He was a demon; nothing more, nothing less. People would want him dead.

That didn't matter to him at the moment. He wanted up out of here. He'd been in this castle for years, only leaving the mansion to lose himself on the shoreline. The seawater breeze would fill his nose. The plush white sand would squish under his feet. He would smile, truly smile, at the thought of not being a demon, not being a member of the Demon Docks, not being a Demonic Prince. If only that worked every day, but it didn't. There was always someone who interrupted; someone who had to ruin Nao's mood. A.K.A, everyone, except Derek.

Derek was actually kind enough to give the demon his private time. Derek only called Nao for small jobs: clean this, help this person, train this person, or, to put it simply, leave. Yes, Nao usually got requests, even from Derek that told him to leave. They weren't questions, they were commands. "Leave the room, could you please? But, don't leave the mansion." Yes, those were words said by the lord of the Demon Docks himself.

Not even Derek appreciated him, but he didn't care. Nao had food, a roof over his head and the opportunity to meet new people. Unfortunately, it failed every time. Everyone here is ruthless and only craves blood. Meeting new people was a waste of time, but at least he still had victuals and shelter.

Being a prince wasn't always fun to begin with. You always had the Demonic Princesses to deal with, and for Nao, having to live with them every day was torture.

Chikara is the "No mercy ninja". She would boil you in a cauldron if she wanted to. Emiko is the silent type, but she would have been the stir girl who added the vegetables in the pot Chikara threw you in. Lavida would be one of the girls who ate you today, ate you tomorrow and continued to eat at you until there wasn't a drop of you left. Destiny is the silent one in the corner who stared you down with her ruby eyes and forced you not to run away while you slowly boiled to death.

Diamond... well she was another story. Diamond would eat you, and enjoy you for sure, but she would have given you a small silent funeral afterward. That's *if* you were lucky, though. Nao might have been one of the lucky ones. He always stayed out of her way when she walked by in the hallway and acknowledged her as Diamond, not Mrs. Southbound, like the other demons around here did. Nao knew well that she hated the name and wanted to be the one person who respected her enough to at least address her by the name she was given at birth.

Nao wasn't weak. He was just kind.

It obviously was a problem for his brother. Riku, his older twin, despised the fact that his brother had a kind heart. "Toughen up, idiot," he had once said, emphasis on *idiot*. So many years had passed and Riku held the same hate for Nao as he did back then. Nothing had changed in Nao's opinion. Then again, his opinion was never favored.

"Hey demon, get over here and help me out." A blonde-haired, blue—eyed foot soldier commanded of him. Nao was in one of Derek's many exercise rooms. Foot soldiers, demons such as him, who possessed advanced abilities in combat and looked similar to humans, filled the room. They worked on their biceps, forearms, abs, legs, everything. Nao was the "Special Helper" today. Once again, Derek had asked him to assist the foot soldiers who needed assistance. He waited near the double doors that entered this place; barely missing the smacks of the door as more muscled soldiers slammed their way inside.

"Hey demon! I know you heard me." This foot soldier in particular had blonde hair and blue eyes, of course, but he was as pale as a bed sheet and no taller than five-eight. Nao was five-eleven, so he could have taken him out.

That would mean a fight though. Nao didn't want that right now. Plus, the act would disrespect Derek, and you never wanted that on your conscience.

Nao made his way over to the soldier. He and his group were on the far wall, watching as he took his sweet time walking to them. The blonde soldier hung with four others; one was a dark haired male, two were fire red-haired women and the last was also blonde. All had pale skin.

They're total vampires, he thought.

"What is it?" Nao asked, crossing his arms over his chest.

"Don't get snippy," one of the redheads said. The one speaking to him had emeralds for eyes, like he did. The other had chestnut browns. "We need you to move this weightlifter and put it over there." She pointed to the other side of the room.

"And, why do you want it moved?"

All soldiers shrugged. "Just because," the dark-haired said.

For one, this was a large room. The room was cloud white with a domed ceiling. Equipment and comrades—assholes in Nao's eyes—consumed the room so moving it would A. be a waste of time. And B. cause much more effort that Nao wanted to give. And what do you know; there was a similar machine that matched this one on the other side of the room.

Why was he here again? Derek, he reminded himself. Right.

"Just use the one over there," Nao sighed. He was tired of these guys. Couldn't they mess with someone else?

"We want this," the red-haired, brown-eyed female pointed, "Over there," she pointed to the room's other side.

"And this," Nao pointed to the machine, "is staying here," he placed his palm to the Oakwood floor.

The blonde soldier who summoned him punched his cheek, swinging Nao's head to the side. He rolled his eyes. Yeah, that shit hurt, but this means conflict. One punch would lead to another and soon everyone would be fighting each other for the sheer pleasure of possibly cracking someone's skull. Demons were so irritating.

"Don't get so cocky," the blonde said.

Of course, he would think Nao was being cocky. All demons thought that way. Jeez.

Nao's head came back around, only to be punched once again; same cheek, same force.

His black locks casted shadows over his face. His tongue rolled on his left cheek and pressed against it. Yup, there would be a bruise. He brought his head back up, waiting for something, anything, but there was nothing. The soldier stood straight, an expression frenzied with horror. Why? He was the one who made the first move and Nao wasn't all that scary.

All expressions were pale. Nao listened in. All minor conversations had ended. No one spoke. He looked around. Every person stood straight with astounded and terrified expressions. They all faced in Nao's direction, but their eyes weren't focused on him.

Apprehensive, he peered around his shoulder then turned to his side.

Diamond stood a few feet behind him. Her hands were on her hips. Her shoulders were lazed, as if she hadn't a care in the world. Her dirty blonde hair hung over her slender shoulders, covering most of her V-necked long sleeved black shirt. Her long legs were covered by ripped black skinny jeans and matching heeled boots reached just below her knee. Her light browns glared at him devilishly. No, she wasn't looking at him, but beyond him; to the group.

"Get out of my way."

Nao swiftly moved to the side. There was no need to act stupid on purpose. You know when Diamond was speaking to you. Act like a fool and she might blow you up without even blinking. Her powers were extraordinary. That was exactly why Nao didn't act dense around her.

One step of Diamond's booted heels caused every single person to jump. Even Nao had moved. The walk had been unexpected. There had been moments of silence once Diamond had been seen. That fact that she was here caused the soldiers' hearts to kick into overdrive.

She took another step, then another, and reached Nao's puncher in the next second. Nao had blinked and missed the intense walk to him. Alarm didn't course through Nao's veins, it was pleasure. Smiling was getting harder and harder not to do.

Diamond grabbed the blonde's white shirted collar. The "soldier" yelped as she pulled him in, making them nose to nose. "You have a lot of nerve punching my friend."

"Friend?" he asked in absolute shock. Nao was just as shocked as he was. "I d-didn't know he was your fr-friend."

"He is and you punched him."

"No I didn't." Bad move, Nao thought next. It only took two seconds for Diamond to rip off the soldier's head and throw it into the petrified crowd. They rushed back, eyes wide. Nao couldn't stop his grin.

As the corpse fell to the ground with a thud, blood rushing out into the floor, approaching her feet, her attention turned to the others. Their grinning faces were there no more. "You touch him or attack him behind my back, facing Derek will be the least of your worries."

They bobbed their heads, their chins probably bruising their bodies.

She turned completely, her lovely hair flying. Her hands fell to her side. As she passed Nao, she crooked her finger without anyone noticing. He followed close behind, leaving the demons to exit their shock and stare at the corpse continuing to bleed.

Diamond led the way through the dark brown hallway, passing by enlarged windows, shining slices of the rainbow in the corners of the mirrors. Their footsteps on the white flat carpeted floor echoed as they made their way down another hall then making a sharp left. Diamond opened a sliding glass door. The salty scent of the sea brushed into his nose.

They descended down three stoned stairs then stepped onto the white sands. On pure instinct, Nao slipped off his black and red sneakers and his white socks. He moaned in ecstasy as the warm sand caressed his feet. He picked up his belongings and caught up with Diamond, who had continued onto the beach. She stopped a foot away from the shoreline and stared out.

Nao joined beside her, looking out, knowing there was another—a better—world out there. Humans might have inhabited that land, but those were free people. They had government, had to follow rules and even pay a thing called taxes-Eww. But those were people with choices and options. Would such a life ever be given to Nao? He hoped and even prayed to the Heavens for it . . . it was something Riku despised. Still, he wanted out. He wanted help. One step at a time, he supposed.

"You alright, kid?"

Nao was brought back. He focused in. Diamond hadn't faced him. He pushed his blowing hair behind his ear. "Yes, I'm alright. Thank you." He couldn't forget to be formal. Being rude got you killed.

"That dude has always been messing with you, hasn't he?"

Nao looked back. Yeah, he had. Nao never knew his name though, and he didn't care. The dude always pushed him around, commanded things that were just plain stupid and threw a punch here and there. Derek had done nothing to stop the abuse. "It's demon playfulness," he'd merely said. "Yes, he has. Thank you for getting rid of my problem."

She rolled her eyes. "He wasn't your problem. He was *a* problem."

He nodded. "Thank you for helping me."

"Yeah, whatever."

That had to be the kindest thing anyone's ever said to him. A smile broke out. "If there's anything I can do for you, please let me know." Saying he would do anything was risky for species like him. When someone said *anything*, it could be *anything*.

"I don't need anything." She pushed her hair behind her back, revealing her diamond studded earrings. He just noticed she had on a red shade of lipstick. She was gorgeous. "But . . ." her head lowered a notch; not as confident as she once looked.

Nao stood motionless. She could ask for blood. She could ask for his skin, to nibble on of course. She could ask for his organs. They would grow back and some foot soldiers liked organs from other living beings. Why did he say he would do *anything*?

"I-I," she paused again. She brought her hands together, locking them just above her belly button. She turned away nervously. And, what the hell? Was that a blush? Her cheeks highlighted pink. Whoa, this was a rarity. "Never mind, just leave."

A smart demon would have left. A genius demon would have scurried. But Nao, he remained. "Whatever it is, I will do it." She would have killed him if he didn't anyway. *Would she kill you?* Nao thought. He shouldn't have placed the question in his mind. It was there now.

Diamond faced him. Yes, she was blushing. Barely, but Nao knew a blush when he saw one—sort of. He wasn't good with women, but he knew when one was nervous, scared or happy. He knew the basics. "I need a comrade and you're going to be him, okay. Bye." She walked off. She had said it so fast. Did Nao even hear that right?

He turned to her. He was greeted with her back. "Hey."

She turned back to him. He froze. He had shouted at her. He was dead. So dead. He should have dug his grave in advance, but no. He was stuck. Goodbye cruel world, and damn it you knew you were cruel! Nao waited, watching as Diamond kept her attention on him.

He didn't blow up. His organs weren't everywhere. He didn't feel inner pain from an organ blow up. He was saved!

"What?" Diamond asked.

Never mind, he was still screwed. Wait, maybe not. She had responded kindly; shocking Nao completely. She hadn't shouted the "What" to him. She had merely asked him without a thread of threat. He grinned.

"I'll be your comrade." Wait, he thought a second later, turning his grin into a smile, "I'll be more than that. I'll be your friend." A comrade was someone you knew and worked with. A friend stuck with you through thick and thin. If he needed to, if he was allowed to, Nao would do that for her. He knew Diamond needed more than a comrade.

She looked around, surveying the area. When she looked back to him, her frown turned upside down. She swung on her heel, made her way to the door and waved over her soldier, yelling, "Yeah, whatever."

<hr>

"Good, we're all here." Kenta placed himself on Ayano's floor and observed. As he said, the gang was all here. Mary, Sazuma, Hiroko, Reiko, Yumiko, Stella, and Ayano sat in the circle with Kenta to Ayano's right. They were in perfect alignment and placed exactly as they'd been named.

A whole day had passed after Yumiko's attack. After a day of rest, and forgetting about the new changes of their lives, the gang had decided to meet, to understand the situation once and for all. All girls were involved in the supernatural world now but more girls were informed more than others. The time to explain was now. Ayano thought it was best to get it over with. Kenta had agreed and asked Mary to assemble the group. She had followed the request. Now, they were all here.

"I've had a whole day of being human. I'm so bored," Reiko said, leaning on her knees. Her legs were crossed, making leaning down a little easier.

"I hope you enjoyed your human life, because you are never going to get it back," Ayano sighed. She was uneasy. She had every right to be. They had news to give the girls. Kenta only hoped they didn't take it the bad way.

"We need explanations Ayano." Hiroko said. She was anxious, probably still worked up over the attack. He didn't expect the girls to heal after one day anyway. Hiroko's left over panic didn't surprise him.

"First off, who's the guy?" Reiko pointed to Kenta. The fact that she saw him proved that she was now into the supernatural realm. Her human life would be no more.

"My name is Kenta. I'm a Spirit Being."

Reiko wagged her eyebrows. "Hello Kenta," she leaned closer with the biggest smile he'd ever seen. He knew that was a flirtatious gesture. He grinned. It was cute. The gesture didn't tempt him at all.

"What are Spirit Beings? Like angels?" Yumiko asked, ignoring Reiko.

Kenta turned to the curious middle school scholar, "Not exactly. Spirit Beings are Heavenly Beings that act as doers for the higher ups. We're warriors who carry out assignments on Earth. Angels assist humans, give humans ideas to help others and watch over them in secret."

"So you are an angel. You're our angel." Kenta turned to Mary. Her grin alone brightened up the room. She was sitting beside him, listening in on the explanation. Her scent filled his nose. It was a scent of light jasmine with a hint of the healthiest moon flower. Her shower soap had to come from Heaven. Her scent was so addicting. Kenta sniffed again then turned away, stopping himself; and hoped he didn't look like a weirdo.

He must have because Sazuma was staring him down. Through the blackness of her eyes laid nothing but hardcore protectiveness.

"I wouldn't say I'm your angel," he said to Mary's comment, "I'm a Spirit Being carrying out a mission."

"Mission for what?"

He turned to Stella, "To find the seven Element Princesses."

The brightest smile spread on Stella's face. She pointed in understanding, "The seven Element Princesses of Heaven. You mean that story is true?"

She knew what he was talking about?

"It's true," Mary smiled. "I was surprised about it too, but it's all factual."

"I'm going to need a story. Please and thank you." Reiko leaned on her knees again.

"Long story short," Ayano started, "There's seven princesses who bring down a group called the Demon Docks. We take them down, save the world, and you guys get back to whatever human life you have left."

Kenta pressed his lips together. She didn't have to make it sound so bad. But with a situation this drastic, it's no wonder she made the explanation as blunt as possible.

Hiroko turned to her left, looking at the twins. "Are you guys these *'princesses'* he's talking about?" Without his permission, Sazuma, Mary and Stella had appeared at Yumiko's house, wanting to help their friend. Kenta had scolded them, or tried to. Mary's smile had blocked him from giving a lot of damage, and they were forgiven. Kenta wondered why the blonde hadn't turned to Stella.

The twins nodded.

"Well good luck with that, you guys." Reiko smiled wide. "Make sure to send me a postcard from wherever you're going and get back safe."

Kenta and Ayano turned to each other. They both grinned. This was a good time to announce the news Kenta had realized yesterday. And, when did Ayano start grinning in front of people other than him? He liked this new change.

He turned back to the group. "On contraire princess, your name is on my list as well." The twins and Stella stared in surprise.

The other three held confusion. "What list?" Hiroko asked.

Ayano explained, "Before searching for the princesses, the Mother Angel had given Kenta a list of names of the princesses he was said to find. He found the twins, we even found Stella, just as he found me."

All heads went to Stella. She shrugged nervously, not expecting all of the attention.

"You're a princess, too?" Yumiko asked.

"She isn't," Ayano answered for her. She was far calmer about this than before. Kenta was grateful. "She hasn't received the earth element orb, so no; she's not officially a princess."

"You act like I know what the flip you're talking about." Reiko waved her arms in the air. Kenta leaned back. He'd never seen a girl act with so much energy. It was as if she had sugar every single day. If she did, that would have made so much sense.

"These girls had to get their powers from somewhere," Ayano leaned on her knees as well. "The orbs that Kenta holds freely enter the princess's body and allow her to use the gifts of their element. The orbs were made by the Mother Angel to give to the chosen kids. A Spirit Being is assigned to assist the girls on their journey. Kenta isn't only our caller. He's also our teacher."

Yumiko shook her head, misunderstanding. "You keep saying *'our'*. We're not in this fight. We only know that not only humans and animals exist on this earth. Why do you keep saying *'our'*?"

"I mean *'our'* as in all of us." Ayano moved her head clockwise, peering at every girl. "Every single one of us."

"Hold on now," Reiko sat up straight. "We're not in this fight. We were attacked, that's it."

Kenta spoke this time, "Your names are on the Mother Angel's list. I have no doubt you three are my remaining princesses."

"So you want us to join a fight with demons, as in demons of the underworld?" Hiroko said, more a statement then a question.

After brief and anxious silence, Reiko laughed loud without humor. "You're nuts."

"But I speak true," Kenta was unfazed. He was getting his point in. He needed these girls to at least listen to him; hear him out. "This is your decision a hundred percent. But I truly have faith that you are the princesses we've been searching for."

"How long have you been searching?" Yumiko asked.

"Ten years," Ayano answered. "I was found first and assisted him at an early age."

"You got her involved at age nine?" Sazuma was the one to freak out this time. They hadn't discussed ages before, have they? "That's crazy."

"Well I'm twelve and I'm involved in this fight." Kenta's head jerked back. Yumiko just said she was involved. Did that mean she would become a princess? He only hoped the orb would react to her with as much intensity as it had for the twins.

"We're not involved in this fight. We're not doing anything you guys want us to. This is too much and seeking a favorable answer right now is impossible." Reiko shook her head. She was on overload, Kenta knew. He didn't want a single one of them to surplus on information, but they deserved to have the whole story; nothing more, nothing less.

"This is my decision," Yumiko went on. She faced Kenta. "I'll do it. I'll fight with you."

Instead of smiling, or even grinning, Kenta's eyes narrowed. "There is no going back once you become a princess. You could . . ."

"Sazuma told me the whole story on the way here. Hiroko, Reiko and I know the girls you killed in order to retain the orbs. We know we'll die if we decide to give them back. But trust me, I won't give it back." She lowered her head and gripped her ironed uniform skirt. "I understand what I'm asking for. I understand that the world might, no, will depend on my shoulders. I've experienced darkness and inner turmoil once before. I don't want anyone to ever feel that way." She raised her head again, "If I can prevent that turmoil, then I will stop it."

Determination swirled in those coffee browns. She wanted this. She truly wanted this. Looking at her now, Kenta knew this was the light princess. She might have been twelve but she was becoming a fine teenager. *"Yumiko Honozoro; Platinum blonde hair, Brown eyes, a heart of growth.* That is the light princess saying. You are this princess," he prayed.

She grinned. "Yes, I am."

He grinned as well. Her confidence brightened his.

"You can just agree? Just like that?"

Yumiko turned to Reiko. "I feel as if I should join. There's never been a calling like this. Opportunities like this only come once in a lifetime."

"Yeah, because the moment you want to give that "opportunity" back, they end up killing you. Some lifetime!"

"I'm in, too." All eyes turned to Hiroko. She faced Kenta as well. She, too, clutched her school uniform and inhaled deeply. "My dreams mean something. I've always wanted to fly. Because I dreamed of it, nonstop for months actually, I believe this is my calling as well." Her grip loosened. "Is my name on the list?"

Kenta nodded. *"Hiroko Kotani; Blonde hair, Blue eyes, a heart of clarity.* You are the wind."

Hiroko exhaled. She too grinned. She clutched her shirt, rubbing her auburn neck ribbon between her fingers. "I've never felt so needed before; so wanted."

"We'll always need you," Mary said. "Element Princess or not."

Hiroko smiled.

All eyes turned to Reiko. She was pawing the floor, scraping her nails against the hardwood over and over. Her bangs acted as a shield for her eyes. Was that a nervous gesture?

"Reiko you don't have to join us," Stella said. Concern swam through her voice, hopefully entering the nervous teen's ears.

"There are demons out there, coming here to kill us and you're telling me you want to join the supernatural police squad."

That was a little harsh. Princesses were no police squad. That was definitely an insult to the Mother Angel. "As Stella said, you don't have to join. It's up to you."

"Quit telling me that!" She shouted at him. She rushed to her feet and begun to pace the room. She dragged her fingers through her thick black hair, the icy blue streaks shined as she stepped into the window, catching the left over sunlight of the day.

Out of all of the girls, he expected at least Hiroko or Reiko to freak out. Thankfully, Reiko hadn't freaked as much as Sazuma and Stella did. She was lost, confused. Maybe skeptical, even. Maybe she just needed some self-assurance. She needed absolute resolution. Could Kenta give that to her?

"*Reiko Takashima; Black hair, Hazel eyes, a heart of intensity,*" Ayano spoke with subtlety. Her words were a caress. "You are the ice." Reiko's tense shoulders sagged a bit. She wrapped her arms around her middle, seeking comfort, Kenta knew.

"If I join," the slightest bit of hope dripped in her voice, "What is needed of me? Will my family be implicated?"

"If you want them involved, then they are welcomed to know, but they cannot join this fight. Each of you girls has that choice." Kenta hid his grin as he spoke. He didn't want to push Reiko's resolve. "Family is welcomed to know but your human friends must *never* know about you being princesses. In this world, you can trust no one. Anyone could be a demon. They'll attack at your most vulnerable and spring into action if they get the chance. Know that well."

"We'll assist you if you have doubts about certain people," Ayano added. "You are allowed to have friends, we just want you to stay cautious and never let down your guard. The supernatural world is deceiving. It's a cruel world, just as the human world is."

"Why us?" Hiroko asked. The best question of the day. It was the question Kenta didn't have an answer to.

"Not even I have an answer for that," he said anyway. "I was only given the list and the box the orbs reside in. I was told to summon the team, and I have."

"Then what?" Reiko turned away from the window to face Kenta. "You summoned the team, now what? You're going to leave? You're going to continue through life and complete other missions?"

"You think low of me." He was kind of ashamed by that. She thought so lowly of him. That hurt. "I will never leave you girls. I have spent years finding you. There is no way I'm letting you go now. I've come to want to know every single one of you."

"Some more than others," Sazuma muttered.

Kenta ignored her. However, he couldn't hide his grin. "I will never betray you. I swear this."

She raised her head. Disbelieving? Contemplating? He wasn't good with reading girls. She could have made her expression a little more emotional, though.

After brief silence—silence that almost made Kenta so nervous, he broke out in a sweat—Reiko nodded. She rejoined the group, this time sitting on her knees. "I'm in."

Kenta released a breath he didn't even know he was holding. His shoulders relaxed. When had he been so stiff?

"You're with us too, right kiddo?"

Stella grinned and nodded to Ayano's question. "Most definitely."

Kenta turned to the twins. Sazuma shrugged. Mary winked. Yeah, this was the right team. His team. Always.

Kenta reached into his faded jeans pocket. The red and gold orb containment box slipped out. He placed the box in his left palm. The smooth material box fit Kenta's palm perfectly; big enough to hold the orbs, but small enough to easily hide.

All girls stared in wonder and absolute curiosity. Their eyes looked just like puppy dogs now, waiting for a new chew toy or a recently bought bone. Slowly, Kenta opened the box, revealing the emerald, silver, crystalline, and golden orbs. The liquid contents inside the orbs swirled, moving in a circular motion and shimmered of its own radiance.

The orbs rattled, bounced even. They were anxious. Waiting was no longer an option. With a few more rattles and even some rolls, the orbs shot out, swerving in a cross motion, searching for their princesses. They reached them and shot at their breastbones. They reacted the same way as the twins did. Their bodies shook. Bewilderment plastered to their faces. Power radiated from them as their orbs pushed their way into their bodies and soon disappeared altogether.

The girls dropped to their backs, thudding the hardwood, automatically unconscious.

Kenta couldn't explain how relieved he was. The orbs had desired them; every single one of them. They dashed out to them and entered their bodies without the slightest bit of protest. These were his girls now; all seven of them. Finding the princesses was a lengthy and difficult chapter of his life.

He sighed. Too bad that was only chapter one.

✺

Derek had every right to be pissed. It wasn't like anything was wrong. His allies followed and respected him, as they should. His Demonic Princesses and Princes were by his side, as they should. On the other hand, his woman wasn't acting like his woman, like she should have been.

A little birdie, a foot soldier who decided to inform him about the incident this morning, has decided to inform Derek of Diamond's actions.

Nao Nakamura, a prince also nicknamed, "The Powerless Demon," because the young man had no powers once so ever, had been summoned to assist whoever needed assistance. Derek's informant had said Nao refused to move a weightlifter and was punched because of it. Diamond had rescued him and killed the blonde soldier who had punched him. They were seen leaving the room together. That bothered Derek greatly.

No one was allowed to touch Derek's woman. She is Diamond Southbound, Queen of the Demon Docks and the wife of the Demon Docks leader. She is his property. He owns her. She belongs to him. Nao knew full well who Diamond belonged to. He knew better then to talk or even look at her. But the fact that he was seen leaving with her pissed him off greatly.

Derek thought long and hard contemplating how to approach this situation. He didn't want to overreact to a situation that might not have even been happening. It wasn't like Nao and Diamond were in a romantic relationship. They barely talked or encountered one another anyway . . . at least, that's what Derek thought.

What if they met up secretly? What if she traveled to his room and they spent the day together, wrapped in each other's arms, kissing fervently, caressing each other, bodies mixed between the sheets?

Oh hell no. *Oh hell no!* Derek rushed down the hallway. He was heading to his room to relax, but at the thought of Nao and Diamond's passions, he pivoted and to Nao's room he went. They couldn't escape him. They couldn't hide their passions from Derek. He is the owner of this house. He is the Demon Docks leader! Nothing would be hidden from him. Nothing!

Shades of orange, yellow, and red brightened the dark hallway through the glass ceiling. Every few steps rested large wooden doors with golden crystal knobs. Down Derek went, continuing on, locking on Nao's pine scent and tracking him down. The bastard didn't even try to hide from him. Maybe Nao planned to face him head on. Foolish of him. He should have known he was no match for Derek. No one was a match to Derek, except Diamond. That's why he married her. She was his equal. His eternal partner. His everything.

Why did she despise him?

Nao's scent grew stronger. He was closing in. Closer now, closer still. Derek stopped in front of the last wooden door in the hall. He inhaled. Yes, Nao was inside. He didn't smell Diamond. She wasn't here yet. She would come. He knew it.

Derek grabbed the glass pentagon shaped doorknob. Its sharp spikes jabbed his hand, causing them to bleed. He turned and entered, uncaring of what was happening inside.

Nao was spotted. He was sleeping soundly, uncaring of the rest of the world. The walls were painted lime with no windows. His ceiling was made of glass. It was the only room in this hallway with a glass ceiling. He had a modest queen sized bed, lime green sheets with a dark wood head post and legs. Matching dark wood nightstands rested on both sides of the bed and a furry white carpet lain on the left side of the bed on the, of course, dark hardwood floor. The bathroom, located to Derek's left, had a closed wooden door. That, too, had a crystal knob.

Nice room, but Derek's was better.

Nao hadn't moved since Derek entered. The demon should have been smart enough to lock his door if he was sleeping. Anyone would have entered and murdered him on the spot. Many demons here wanted him dead anyway. That didn't include Derek. Whatever the little demon had coming for him, it was his fault.

And, if he was having relations with Diamond, Derek wouldn't stop his minions from slaughtering then eating him.

Derek entered. His boots clicked on the floor. Nao was motionless. How asleep was this guy? He approached the left side of the bed, looking down at Nao. The shades of the setting sun shined on him, giving him more radiance than he deserved. This demon deserved nothing but darkness. If he had that, he might just understand to lock his door, even if he wasn't sleeping.

Nao's chest rose and fell as he inhaled and exhaled. One hand slept over his head on the edge of his fluff white pillow while the other rested on his stomach. He wore a dull gray short sleeve with black jeans that hung low on his waist. His feet were shoe and sockless. He was relaxation incarnate.

That would have to end. Right now.

"Awaken Nao." Nothing. He didn't even shift. A muscle ticked in his jaw. He should have jumped up and stared in shock. Then he should have bowed his head in apology and respect. What was wrong with this demon? He needed to be taught the basics of this castle.

Lesson one, always respect Derek.

Lesson two, always follow Derek's orders. No matter what they are.

Lesson three, no touching Derek's woman. Ever.

"Nao?" He said, heightening his voice this time. Still nothing. Not even a fucking twitch came from him. No one could be that good a sleeper.

"Nao Nakamura!"

Finally, the reaction he'd been waiting for . . . well sort of. Nao shot up, scooted to the other end of the bed, slipped a hand under his pillow and pulled out a .45. He aimed to Derek's forehead. He was prepared to fire.

Derek stared. He just stared. Self-restraint held him back. Nao had better pray to Lucifer for not ripping him to shreds.

Realization hit. Nao lowered his gun as his shoulders dropped and his exhalation was released. "My lord," he swallowed hard and made his way off of the bed. "My apologies. What are you doing here?"

He didn't even ask if Derek was alright. Nao was so rude. Pitifully rude, actually. All that aside, he got straight to business. "What happened when you and Diamond exited the gym?"

Nao shrugged and scratched the back of his head. Any wise demon would have answered on the spot, even if it was a lie, but demons that lied always got their punishments. "I thanked her for getting me out of that situation. She told me 'whatever' and went on with her day." He hadn't even questioned how Derek knew about the incident. He knew he could hide nothing from Derek. Maybe Nao was smart after all.

That still didn't save him. He knew more happened then that. If she had the audacity to save him then there must have been a . . . Derek paused. Derek's attention zeroed in on Nao's shoulder. He turned on his heel, took several steps and reached Nao, who had been staring him down the entire time. His hand came out and gripped the speck of hair on his shoulder. He hadn't noticed it before.

The color looked familiar. This was Diamond's hair. He knew dirty blonde when he saw it.

He gripped Nao's collar and pulled him in, making them nose to nose. Nao didn't panic in the slightest, which caused Derek's blood to boil. He should have been squealing. He should have at least been writhing. "Did you touch my woman?" Possessiveness was taking over.

"I never touched her."

Truth or lie? Derek didn't have the ability to detect such things. "Diamond's hair is on your shoulder and you're telling me that you two did not touch?" Derek was so calm he was scaring himself.

"I tell you the truth, my lord. I did not touch Mrs. Southbound."

Derek couldn't help it. He grinned. He loved when his minions called his woman by her new and eternal name. His boiling blood came to a simmer. He still didn't like that her hair ended up on his shoulder. At least Nao got Derek's message loud and clear.

He backed away and brushed off Nao's shoulder. "Sorry about that, good man. As her husband, I have every right to suspect her of trickery."

Nao tilted his head, utterly puzzled, "How could you say such a thing? As her husband, shouldn't you have faith in her and expect nothing but trust and promise?"

What kind of fairytale world was this boy living in? He chuckled, "Dear prince, relationships like that only end in betrayal and suffering. Diamond and I possess a relationship made for royals."

"Uselessness?"

This kid was asking for a beat down. Derek cleared his throat. "No. Diamond and I possess a relationship of interest and restlessness. It's the most important traits in any relationship."

Nao merely nodded.

Derek was starting to think why he was even here. He made his point, so there was nothing else to discuss. He stuffed his hands in his pocket. "Continue on with your day, Nao. Tomorrow you will continue your job in the gym and assist those who—"

A heavy cool sensation swept over Derek. Nao must have felt it too because he rooted in place, eyes widened, breath caught in his lungs. The creatures outside the room walls roared in protest and aggravation. Derek was about to join them. Redness blinded his vision. His once simmering blood over boiled in a matter of seconds. His teeth elongated, poking out and sticking his lower lip. "Lord Derek! Lord Derek!" Lavida rushed into the room. Her body was tense. The chilling sensation caused goose bumps to dot her lovely tinted skin. "The princesses my lord. They have awoken."

Kenta had found them all. All of the seven princesses had been reunited; ready to attack and ready to defend. Heaven had gained major points for collecting all of the chosen females. But no longer would they be allowed to make a move. Derek would make sure of that. No more chances. No more mercy—if he was giving any.

It was time for Derek to make his move. All drama would have to wait.

Derek turned to Lavida. His brown hair swung as his head came around. Redness still tinted his vision. "I want a princess." His voice was a deep grovel. Lavida's knees buckled the moment he spoke to her. "I want a princess in my presence. Think of a plan. Think of anything! I want a princess and I will have her!"

Lavida rushed out with heavy whimpers, probably already thinking of a plan.

All anger with Nao was gone. All hatred he had for Diamond betraying him had faded. Right now, he needed them now more than ever. All insecurities would be postponed.

Story 8

Darkness always has a past

Reprieve; that's the only word that described the feeling in Ayano's heart. She'd never been so grateful in her life to be able to say, "I can give these girls a chance." Now that she found her remaining comrades, she didn't have to worry about killing them. She didn't have to worry about ending their lives early and retreating out of the city, leaving behind another family who questioned how their daughter had died to unexplained reasons.

That burden no longer rested on her shoulders. She prayed and thanked the Gods and Goddesses of Heaven. Maybe now, she could think of starting a real, a true friendship.

Baby steps though, she reminded herself. Her kinder nature might have frightened the others. They had to wake up first, however.

After dropping the hard sleepers at home, Sazuma and Mary decided that Stella could stay at their house. They had been at the apartment too many times and the Kagami house was feeling a little empty. Sazuma didn't care. She just wanted to sleep.

Ayano couldn't blame her. A nap did sound nice right now. Strangely, Ayano was too tired to sleep. Sounded weird, but her mind was so worked up that her body just continued to work, processing the memories of the past and replacing them with the memories of the new. This never happened before. It explained why sleeping wasn't much of an option for her.

Sazuma led the way to the Kagami house. The lampposts flickered on as they continued down the empty sidewalk and made the right hand turn, entering Sazuma's community.

Stella walked on Ayano's left side while Kenta and Mary were taking their sweet time behind them. Ayano didn't have to ask what was up with him. He was going through Puppy Love. This happened at least twice since the ten years they had known each other. Kenta wasn't a "Search for a girlfriend" type of guy. Nevertheless, when the two girls before Mary caught his eye, the Puppy Love had begun.

The first was Haley, a tourist from Britain. She was a friend of one of the chosen princesses; the earth princess, Ayano thought. Haley was in her early twenties with lovely brown hair and hazel eyes. Haley was also a medium, so she could see and speak to the dead. She noticed Kenta right away and claimed he was an angel. She was half-right. Kenta didn't care. His interest in her was automatic.

Together, the two had met in the woods, ensuring their private time together. They talked, played tag, and even kissed here and there. Yes, Ayano knew and saw it all. As a child, all she knew was to follow Kenta, no matter where he went or whom he was with.

Anyway, the moment Haley's friend wanted to return the earth orb, that's when everything changed. Haley was enraged and feared the demons that now attacked her. Her older brother had been attacked and ended up in a coma. Her parents were in the hospital for stab wounds. She wanted to give the orb back dearly. She even offered her life, trying to end this constant chase.

Kenta personally gave that to her. His hand misted through Stella's chest and pulled out the orb. It sucked away Stella's very life force, draining her energy and strength. She dropped to the wooden land that he and Haley once played on. Stella dropped to her back. Her arms and legs separated and her shoulder length red hair splashing around her head, her lips shaded blue and her green eyes closed forever.

Haley witnessed it all. She watched as her friend plunged, motionless and unbelievably pale. She cursed at him, punched him, threw rocks, and even a boulder, at him. Kenta took it all. He took it all so much that he refused to move once the police echoed around the area. He hadn't even noticed that Haley had called the police.

Using all of her strength, Ayano pulled Kenta along and teleported out of the town. Haley's cries and curses echoed with them as they left.

Was it a doomed romance? Ayano would guess so but stating that to Kenta was too much for him. Right now, they had no idea where Haley was or what she was going. There were times during the year when Kenta would disappear for at least a day or two. He would be visiting the graves of the girls he killed. Ayano would ask him to send her condolences. It was too painful to return to the towns from which they came. Plus, she couldn't hide herself from the human eye like Kenta could. She had to take care of Stella anyway. That was only an excuse.

"They make a nice little twosome, huh?"

Ayano peered in the corner of her eye to see Kenta's smile and Mary's grin as they continued their muttered conversation. "I guess," she said to Stella.

"Kenta's a Spirit Being right? He must have lived for a long time. He must have had a lot of girlfriends."

"Not really," she responded with a shrug. One crush loathed him and the other one-his first girlfriend in his entire life, both as a human and a Spirit Being—passed away. "Relationships romantically aren't his focus."

"He at least had a girlfriend right?"

He had a girlfriend all right, and he vowed never to love another like he loved her.

Her name was Hiroko. She was the wind princess of, course, but she was nothing like the Hiroko Ayano knew now. This Hiroko was the silent type. Her shyness was unbelievable. One grin from Kenta and her face was as red as a tomato. She agreed to aid their cause, feeling she could save the world in a way.

Once she received the orb, her and her friends dashed into actions. When demons attacked their home, they fought back. Their family members remained safe and out of harm's way. Hiroko and her group were incredibly strong, in both the mind and body. No Demonic Princesses or Princes had attacked them, but they kept on anyway, learning to control their elements and even balance out their social lives.

Ayano liked this group. Kenta *loved* this group. They lived on Kyushu Island, near the Nagoya prefecture. There was no other fighting force like them. After ten failures from the others in the past, this group seemed to be worthy of keeping the elements. Hiroko acted as their leader, guiding them from attack after swift attack.

Kenta was by her side all the way, just as Ayano was by his.

The two had fought together. Interestingly, Ayano never thought they had a romantic relationship. One night, while traveling around Hiroko's house, which was ironically as tall as the current Hiroko's house was, Ayano had found the couple in the girl's bedroom, making out with roaming hands and moans echoing throughout the room. She had merely peeked through the door and seen it all.

It was far more than Ayano needed to see. She was clear on their relationship from that day forward.

They had spent four months with Hiroko and her team. Kenta and Ayano believed the group was strong enough to face the Demon Docks foot soldiers. They were stronger, better and faster than what the girls were used to. They said they could handle it. They said they would fight them with everything they had.

But that wasn't enough.

To everyone's revelation, Derek's foot soldiers invaded the Nagoya City, murdering over hundreds of people. The princesses were among those killed.

The group had separated at the time, trying to protect as many people as they could. Ayano had teamed up with Hiroko, watching her back and keeping her safe not only to protect her friend, but to protect the one person who meant the most to Kenta; his girlfriend.

As the numbers were counting down, Ayano truly believed they had won the battle. She was wrong. The soldiers were merely hiding in the shadows, waiting for the girls to let their guard down. And they had let it down alright. The moment she turned her back to the patch of shadows behind her, Hiroko had been stabbed in the chest and the stomach; two blades had struck her by the same foolish soldier. Ayano had retaliated. She whipped the soldier's heads off by the dozens, piercing them with her staff and releasing her inner fury; fury a teenager shouldn't have ever had.

Ayano watched as Hiroko bled out. There was nothing she could do. She wasn't a healer and everyone in the area had been annihilated. She was too shaky to teleport anywhere, much less to touch her friend. Her body had shaken terribly, to the point where she could scream.

Kenta had arrived after Gods knows how long. He was just as shaken as Ayano was. None of the others was with him. There was no trace of them. Without a word to Ayano, he made his way beside Hiroko and placed her into his arms. He placed her head in the crook of his neck and squeezed his eyes shut. "I'm sorry," he repeated over and over. As he did so, he placed his palm to her breastbone. Tears streamed down his eyes as his hand misted through her chest and received the silver element orb. Whatever remained of her life force diminished as the orb exited her. She lolled her head to the side, forever still; forever in peace. She died with a peaceful expression.

Ayano knew Kenta never got over that. Out of all of the graves he visited, Kenta always traveled back to Nagoya to visit Hiroko's grave. It was difficult to return there, but she and the other princesses who died in battle deserved a little companionship, even after death.

Every year, Kenta cried. He would drop to his knees, the pain returning to him, and he would release his tears freely, giving no care in the world. Ayano would stand behind him and shed several tears of her own. She missed Hiroko dearly. She missed Sazuma and the others too. This was the only team who fought bravely and strived for excellence. Somehow, Ayano hoped they stayed together in the afterlife, staying as the team they were obviously born to be.

"Earth to Darkness. Come in, Darkness."

"I don't think anyone's home," Sazuma's voice was heard.

Ayano blinked. She was standing in front of the Kagami house. When had they reached this place?

"I've never seen you look so dazed," Stella said, a bit concerned.

"Everything alright?"

She peered over her shoulder. "Yeah, I'm good," she said to Kenta. When memories returned to her, her body was on autopilot. Sometimes, most of the time actually, that wasn't a good thing.

"I've never seen you spaced out to the point where you're not even responding. Are you sure you're okay? What's on your mind?" Stella was too troubled about this. It was just a blank out.

"I'm fine." Ayano ruffled Stella's hair. "I'll be on the roof." It seemed too inviting up there. She couldn't resist the urge to head up there and blank out without a bother.

"You don't like my house?" Sazuma asked. She didn't look it but she was offended. Sazuma had a nice house—the fact that she had a house was good all in itself—but the roof . . . it was just calling her name.

"I like it, I do, but I rather go up there. I can protect you better that way."

She shrugged and headed into her house. She walked past the garden to her left and reached the side ladder. It was wood and white and reached up to her new favorite relaxation spot. She climbed up anxiously and quickly reached her destination.

The white tiled roofing was cool the moment her hand touched it. She sighed of longing. It had been years since she lain back on a roof and watched the sky above her. The moon was a crescent tonight. Beautiful. She placed her staff on her right side, placed her back to the chilling roofing and exhaled. One by one, stars twinkled in the distance as the sun finally set, welcoming the darkness of the evening.

The fresh breeze, the chilling tiles and the stars popping here and there; everything was just so relaxing.

Ayano couldn't stand it.

The feeling was gone. Being on the roof was boring.

Damn that was fast. What changed the mood?

"Hey," Kenta's voice was heard. Ayano rolled her head in his direction. He climbed up the wide stepladder and joined her, placing both hands behind his head, his elbows facing the sky.

Yeah, she found out what ruined it; the approaching of the uninvited. She loved Kenta dearly, but come on. This was her idea first!

"Hey," she responded. She could have kicked him out. That wouldn't be right, though. She could do that to the others, but not to Kenta.

There was silence for a while. The two friends stared to the sky. More stars appeared. It was times like this when Ayano wished she had a microscope. Darkness always surprised her. Or, at least the darkness of the sky did. She wondered how something as beautiful as stars could survive inside of the abyss of the universe and shine down on earth. This planet didn't deserve such beauty.

"Are you going to tell me what's really on your mind?"

Ayano should have known he was going to ask that. She would have thought of a vivid answer if she put two and two together. Still, nothing false came to mind. How could she bring up the past girls without bothering him? That's the problem, she couldn't.

"No," she said, hoping to stick with her answer.

"Are the things traveling through your mind that terrible?"

He had no idea.

"I won't bug you about it. Whatever it is, I'm bound to find out sooner or later."

That was the other problem. No matter what it was, Kenta always found out about it. Whether it was suspecting someone of being a demon in human form, the amount of training you needed or even not liking a certain TV show on at the time. Kenta always found out what was wrong with you. This was no different. Somehow, someway, he would realize she was thinking of the past, how she was noticing his crush on Mary and who knows what else.

"So, what's really bothering you?"

And, he said he wouldn't bug her about it. Well, this wasn't bugging. Kenta could bug if he wanted to. Thank the gods he decided not to, knowing it was annoying to be the buggy and being the bugger. "Flashes of the past."

"Ah," he grinned. "Remembering how far we've come and how many years it took to get here."

"How many mistakes we'd made," she added dryly.

His grin gradually vanished. "I was trying to avoid that conversational path. Guess there's no avoiding it."

Maybe she shouldn't have gone down that path either. Too late though. Might as well go all truth. "It's been ten years." Saying it caused realization to arrive. Had it only been that long? She didn't know if she should be surprised or shocked. All she knew was that that amount of time had passed; and those years had been spent with Kenta.

"I can't believe it either. But this is it. The next chapter in our lives has arrived. Let's just hope this book ends in a neutral note."

Why neutral? He should have been saying, "Let's hope for the best," and, "We can certainly defeat the Demon Docks." He was usually so positive. This time, they had every right to shout positive comments. Why be unbiased? "Less enthusiastic, are we?"

He shrugged, "I don't want to get my hopes up." Guilt and pain came through this time. The past was haunting him. So many tragedies and they would forever be locked within his mind. Ayano was on the same boat as he was.

"I have high hopes for these girls. If I believe in them, then you should support them more than I."

Kenta shrugged again. That was his answer.

Silence took over them again. She guessed this conversation was over. Her focus went to the sky again. It didn't last there long.

"You've noticed Mary and I, haven't you?"

No hiding it now. "Yeah."

He nodded. His hands came down from his head and intertwined just over his belly button. "While walking here, I tried to stop myself from smiling. I tried to hold back my awareness of her. You know I failed, right?"

Based on how much he was smiling, he failed immensely. "I've noticed," she hid her grin. "I don't mind if you date Mary. She's a pretty—"

"No," Kenta rushed out. Ayano turned to him. "I won't date her. I can't."

If she died the same way Hiroko did, Kenta's pain would grow. Ayano knew that. That didn't stop her from wanting Kenta's happiness. He deserved solitude, a resolution. A *favorable* resolution.

Ayano leaned to her side, propping her elbow up to support her head. This was actually a comfortable pose. "Don't let the past affect your future."

He turned his head to her. "You don't understand the pain of losing a loved one."

True. She never had a lover like he did. She had one person she cared for, an old woman who cared for her at a young age, but that was it. Ayano hadn't loved her as much as she should have and as much as Kenta loved Hiroko. At the thought of Kenta dying in battle, her heart ached. "Maybe not, but love never dies. It only lives on in another woman."

He grinned, but it was not reassuring. "Lives on, huh? Where'd you hear that from?"

"Princess Intuition." That was good enough for Ayano. When Kenta nodded, she knew it was good enough for him, too. She grinned as well. Now it was time to tease him. "But she's a pretty one, huh?"

This grin was lively, as if thinking of her as he spoke. "Utterly beautiful. I've never met anyone like her. Mary's of the past don't even come close to this one."

Yeah, he was thinking about her. His cheeks were even shaded a light pink. Now the teasing could really begin. "Her hair is so long. Her eyes shine so lovingly. When she smiles at you, it's like ruling the world, because you know you caused that smile."

"Damn it, Ayano." He was smiling wide now. His pink cheeks reddened now. He hadn't blushed this hard before. At least, not in front of her. "Now you're just being mean."

She chuckled, "It's not my fault your body reacts well to details." A question jumped into her mind. "Why Mary though? Why not Sazuma?"

Kenta licked his lips, thinking of a definitive answer. "Well . . . I . . ."

"You just don't like her."

"Not that way." His shoulders sagged as he chuckled himself. He knew his mind was blank. Ayano asked this question once before, after she found him and Hiroko in her bedroom. She asked why he didn't like Yumiko, who was a nineteen year old instead of the twelve year old they had now. The girls had looked the same in the facial expressions and their hair was surprisingly the same, reaching their waists with strands of white. He answered the same way, not knowing the answer but liking Hiroko all the same.

"I think Mary's cute for you. She's smart, willing, easy to talk to . . . And beautiful," Kenta exhaled dreamily. He was definitely thinking about her.

"Why, thank you." The friends jumped to a sitting position and turned to their left. Mary watched them from the side ladder. Her forearms were placed flat on the arched roof. Her chin placed on top of her hand and her black eyes mirrored curious puppy eyes.

How long had she been there?

"How long have you been there?" Kenta parroted his mental question.

Mary's head lifted as she shrugged. There was a lot of shrugging going on lately. "I wanted to check on you guys, to see if you were hungry or anything, of course."

"Of course," Kenta smirked. His eyes were fixated on her. There was the Puppy crush again.

She made her way up and placed herself on Kenta's other side. She wrapped her arms around her legs and sighed with a smile. She slightly rocked back and forth. "I'm allowed to stay right? This is my roof after all."

"By all means," Kenta propped up one knee and wrapped his arms around it. Ayano sat up and kept her hands by her sides.

"We're not hungry or anything, but thanks anyway," Ayano said. If Mary was up here for that reason, she had her answer.

She nodded. "Alright." She thumbed to the side ladder. "Sazuma and Stella are knocked out."—what time was it? Eight, maybe nine?—"I thought I could join you with star seeing."

"You're more than welcome."

Of course she was. Kenta obviously forgot his secret vow to not dating her.

"Did I interrupt something?"

How doubtful could this girl get?

"No, no," Kenta waved his hand innocently. "You're fine. We were just discussing some things. Like how long it's been since we've known each other." He knew Ayano would ask what they were talking about. Answering her future question was a smart move. *How long have you two known each other?*

"Oh," she grinned, "That's nice." Her attention went to the sky.

What? No pester? Was this girl not a bugger either? Well that's one thing she and Kenta had in common. Well, there was that and the fact they were involved in the supernatural world. Two things right there. Element Princess Couple here they come!

Another breeze kicked in, blowing Ayano's hair onto Kenta's arm. His black tresses played gracefully over his headband. Mary's hair whipped around her and tapped her shoulders several times. They each inhaled and exhaled together, unplanned and unexpected.

Mary broke the sudden silence, "You know, I remember coming up here with Sazuma and just watching the sky like this. Every time we couldn't sleep or we just didn't want to, we came up here. I miss my childhood sometimes."

Missing a childhood. Ayano couldn't relate. She was glad her childhood was gone. Thank goodness.

Mary turned to them. "What about you guys? How were your childhoods?"

Ayano should have known she was going down this road. She was not a good road predictor, was she? Maybe not now, but she was a pro before.

Kenta shrugged. "I don't remember much. Spirit Beings sometimes lose their memories when they die. I don't have much to say."

All attention went to Ayano. "And you?" Mary asked.

Those puppy dog eyes must have worked wonders for her because Ayano couldn't help but want to confess her inner secrets. She wanted to tell it all, share it all and expect nothing in return. She had hidden her childhood from the others. They hadn't known long enough to gain her trust in order for her to tell them of her past. Ayano hadn't even told Hiroko, whom she trusted dearly. Would sharing this with Mary be worth it?

Kenta nodded, allowing her to continue. He now had trust in this new group. Sharing secrets wouldn't be difficult anymore. She could do this. She *would* do this.

Ayano brought up her legs and wrapped her arms around them. She did this when feeling uncomfortable. This confession would be a struggle. There were memories she didn't want to reopen, wounds she didn't want to cut again and wait to replenish.

Mary slouched down nervously, "You don't have to share."

Ayano continued before she could stop herself. "I'll tell you what happened. This conversation stays with us. If I want to repeat it to the others, then I will."

Ayano's point of view

When I was younger, I was always running. Running from people, places, past memories. It didn't matter what it was, I was just running.

My parents abandoned me. I don't remember much about them, but that's better for me, I believe. It makes space to put something else there in my memory. Sooner or later, I did find that replacing memory.

I met this woman who took care of me. She was on the older side with wrinkles here and there. Her skin was peach tinted. And her smiles would warm your heart. She seemed as lonely as I was, but then again, I didn't know what loneliness was. I felt so many emotions and had no idea what I was feeling. What swirled inside of me, I didn't know. What would soon become a part of me, I had no idea.

The woman took me into her home on the outskirts of Itoshima. She provided food, water, and a roof over my head; the basics. She never forced the needed items onto me. I took them without a care, not wondering if the food was poisoned or touched by others before me. It never was. The food was always fresh, the water was always bottled with a tight cap—a cap so tight that I asked the woman to open it every time I received a new bottle—and the bed provided for me ensured I had a good night's rest.

I stayed with her for a month when she decided to name me.

"You can't go through the world without being named," she said. Her voice was raspy with a hint of exhaustion. Her smile stretched the slight wrinkles around her mouth. "I shall call you ... Ayano. That's my grandmother's middle name. And to be honest, I think it suits you."

"What does it mean?" I asked, suddenly curious. I had short hair that reached my ears back then and more split ends than I could count.

"It means 'My color.'" That made no sense to me, but she elaborated. "Right now, you're so ominous. You're lost in a world where no one is kind, gentle and just." She giggled wholeheartedly. "I believe you will fill in the blanks of this gray world. You will bring color to this world once more." I believed her. I believed I could somehow *"Save the world"*.

So, I spent my days as Ayano, the girl with no last name. I lived with this fire red-haired, brown—eyed woman that always had a smile on her face. I was happy, for the first time in my life. The funny part was that I didn't even know her name. It didn't bother me either. Every time I needed something, I would tug on her pants or skirt leg. All attention would turn to me. Back then, I couldn't help but smile at her.

After a year of living there—I was probably six or seven years old now—there were men she allowed into the house. I might have been very young, but sadly, I remember it like it was yesterday.

"Ayano, these men don't have a place to stay. They'll be here for a week for two." One man had short brown hair and a full out gray beard that echoed loudly when he scratched it. The other man was completely bald and had a uni-brow. Both wore trashed and dirty clothes. Nothing but filthy vibes came from them.

I had no idea they were registered sex offenders who broke out of jail just weeks ago until I left that town. Why she took them in, I guessed she was at gunpoint.

I nodded to the woman's announcement and stayed in my room with the door closed. Not even thirty minutes later, outside of the door, I heard livid and ravenous men. I heard those voices for more than a solid week. They stayed at the house for a month, then a few months. Those months turned to a year and a year turned to two.

The woman who kept me never turned me away. She never told me to run. There were times when money was short. She would repeatedly tell the men that they needed to pay for their stay here but she would only end up getting slapped and thrown around. She was a woman who didn't deserve to be abused, but what could I do? What should I have done? I was a kid, fearful of my own shadow. How could I help her when I couldn't even help myself?

During those times of poverty and insecurity, she kept my room door closed, leaving me in the universe wallpapered room with several lamps on. There was a chest full of toys ranging from Barbie dolls and cars to large plush dinosaurs I loved to hold. I even thought that would protect me from those insidious men. Child imagination, I guess.

She never told the men that I lived in the house. The day she introduced me to them, she told them that I was simply visiting. They didn't know I was living there full time. If they did know, I guarantee I would be more traumatized than I already am.

She called my room the storage room so no one went inside. She would sneak food into my room and give me fresh clothes and things to wash myself with when the men weren't around or weren't looking. Every time she visited me, she always had a smile on her face.

Why she was smiling, I always wondered. With men like that and how bruised her cheeks were, to me, there was absolutely nothing to smile about. No matter what, she smiled at me and that was enough for me to remain in the house. I didn't feel like a burden or someone's extra package. I felt like a person. I felt wanted.

One day, one bone chilling day, I heard her screaming behind the door. I put down the Barbie dolls and grabbed the plush pine green T-Rex, seeking comfort and protection. I didn't want to approach, fearing someone would barge inside. I traveled forward anyway.

The shouts of protest echoed into my ear the moment it was pressed against the wood. "I told you I'm not doing this anymore! I won't let you control me and I won't let you use me!" The woman screamed some more. One of the men, the bald one, I think, was cursing at her, acting incredibly rude and vile. The entire night, I heard loud and muffled screams. I stood at the door and listen to what they were doing to her. I didn't know what it was, but I knew she was suffering.

I was lost. How could I stop them? How could I save her? Was there a way? There was always a way, but me, being a child always on the offensive, should have known better than to interrupt something I was not involved in.

Afterwards, it might have been six in the morning, the woman limped into my room. She braced herself against the door as she opened it. I stared up at her. My eyes must have been saucers because I could see every single inch of my caretaker's features and found more bruises, scratches, puncture wounds, and hand imprints that I could count, and back then, counting from one to ten was difficult enough.

She headed to me. I dropped by T-Rex and ran to her, somewhat catching her as she slopped to her knees, unable to hold her own weight. She pushed the door, leaving it cracked. She stiffened the moment I touched her shoulders. Her long sleeved violet shirt hid her injuries. They must have hurt, I figured. I couldn't see her face clearly, the dull room acting as a hiding place for her facial injuries, and I knew there were some.

"You look tired Ayano," she said scruffily. "We must have kept you up. I'm sorry. But please, get some sleep alright." I nodded. I didn't know what else to do. She kissed my forehead, tried to stand but fell back to her knees. My hands faced her, attempting to push her up. I didn't touch her. She delicately pushed my hands away anyway and eventually stood with a grunt. She ruffled my already messy hair before turning around to leave.

"Hey woman! Where are you?" A man asked. The door opened an instant later. It was the bald man with the uni-brow. He hadn't changed a bit. He looked in and smiled as he saw us. His smile was wicked and left a pit in my stomach. "Oh, I thought this little shrimp left already. Oh well, there's another girl we can play with."

"You leave her alone. She had nothing to do with—"

"Shut up," the man charged and slapped the brave woman. Her remaining energy drained and she fell back to her knees. The man took one step and reached me in no time. I was rooted to the floor, left to defend for myself, with nothing in hand.

The woman grabbed the man's leg and bit him with all she had, which wasn't much but enough for the man to holler and take a few steps back. My senses returned. My focus reappeared. I was no longer rooted. The woman jumped to her feet, grabbed my wrist and dragged me to the single sliding window. She slid it open, picked me up and pushed me out. I landed on the dead grass after my two foot fall.

"Run Ayano! You have to live! You must live!" I couldn't believe what she was saying. She wanted me to leave her with those men. "Get out of here!" Her voice croaked at me. There were even drips of blood dotted beside her mouth. The moment I heard the men's voices approaching, I looked at the woman one last time and ran down the street.

Without even knowing it, tears strained from my eyes and slid down my cheek. My instincts told me to run, but I shouldn't have. I should have stayed and protected her to repay my debt to her. In this act of escaping, I could at least do this much. I could do what she commanded of me and run like she said. So I did.

I turned back around as I made my way into the town we resided in. What possessed me to turn around, I don't know. The men from the house were following me. There seemed to be more men behind them, though. What started as two men ended up being three and soon became eight. All eight men were coming after me. Their legs were longer. Their strength was stronger. How long could I keep this up?

They wanted their way with me, I realized. They wanted to claim me as their own or merely use me and throw me somewhere where no one could find me. I had heard cases like these, where men prayed on helpless children and "played" with them until they were no longer wanted.

I wouldn't surrender myself to them. I was a child who wanted to live. My legs kept me going. My lungs heaved and my mind screamed at me to run. My heart fueled more energy, allowing me to travel faster. There was no hesitation in my steps. The thunder roared as the black clouds lifted above my head. The heavy, thick rain poured down, causing my clothes to instantly soak and slow me down. My eyes were blinded from the sliding raindrops, but I continued on.

I ran through two-way alleys, bumped into people and got lost in crowds. Somehow I lost them. I didn't know where to go from there. I couldn't go back to the woman's house, so I was on my own. This realization terrified me. I had been on my own before, but I had no idea my life would change drastically in one measly night.

For the next several weeks, I stayed in boxes, hid in empty garbage cans; which was rare, and I even stayed underneath house decks. I lived this way until nine. It was a tough couple of years and, although dodging cops because they wanted to take me to a foster home, and freaks of the night because they were just as their name said, was interesting; the thrill of it opened another side of me I never realized I had; bareness.

I was bare, empty; lost, as my caretaker would say. Homelessness helped me believe I truly was lost inside of a world that ruined you for sure. I was the lowest of the low now; with no hope of getting to the top. I had no education and I didn't know much about everyday life. How I survived this long, I had no one to thank but the woman.

At some point, the need to return to the woman came at me. I was a good mile out, taking refuge under a foreclosure house's deck. It was spacious, too, with moist dirt that acted as a chilling mattress. I had no idea why I wanted to return after so long, but I did, and I did so without regret.

I returned to the woman's house, staying in the shadows. I never knew who I would find, so I remained low. Good thing, too. While hiding on the sides of a building in front of the woman's red-bricked, sunshine yellowed doored house, I overheard the bald man who stayed at the house talking to his friends. It had been years and he had remained. He was still bald and his allies looked as raggedy as ever. The woman who took care of me was nowhere to be found. If they had harmed her . . .

I listened in as the men continued to chat. The bald one told his allies to be on the lookout for me. He wanted to sell me to one of his other *friends*. After hearing that, I quickly and quietly dashed off into hiding again. I did whatever I could to hide from the men that chased me, only because "they wanted something to play with."

Unfortunately, one of the men had spotted me. He called out, calling me his "Little Baby." I only took off faster than I ever thought. I didn't look back this time, fearing to see how close they were. My lack of healthy food caused my energy to become lower than usual. Still, I couldn't let that stop me.

I knew I was far away from the woman's house, nevertheless, I knew they were still following me. They were men. They wouldn't have ever given up on a pretty little kid so easily.

Just like the night I ran away, torrential rain hammered down, blinding me once again and even causing me to trip, allowing the men to gain up on me. As more rain fell, I turned around to see if anyone was chasing me. I was in another unknown area, yet I still wanted to see if anyone was behind me. As soon as I saw the coast was clear, I turned around but I ended up bumping into someone. I fell to the ground on impact, looked up and saw a tall lightly toned man with black hair.

It ended up being Kenta. He had on a closed up black jacket that reached his ankles with matching boots. He was wearing his headband on his forehead and his usually spiky tipped hair was drenched down. I couldn't believe my eyes. He was so stunning. I wasn't scared in the slightest.

"Hey, why are you running in the rain? You're going to get hurt."

His voice was too soothing for words. I closed my eyes in longing, wanting to hear him again. His words were warm, worth listening to over and over again.

Men's voices were heard. The bone chilling sensation I had once before returned. I had to run. I just had to! I jumped up and tried to dash off, but Kenta grabbed my arm. "Do you want my help?" I looked at him desperately. I didn't answer him. "I can help you."

Could he? Was he another freak just like the others I had been running away from? With all of my hopes and prayers, I nodded. Whatever happened to me next was my own fault, good or bad. He pulled me to the left side of an alley. The men ran past us without even noticing us hiding from them. They continued to run and soon they were out of sight. I had never been so relieved.

I looked at Kenta again and thanked him. I should have been smarter and headed out without another word. But being the kid who was thankful every time something good happened to me, I stayed. He bent down and asked what my name was. "Do you have a last name?" he asked. I shook my head.

"Well Ayano, I'm sorry to ask you this, but are you alright?"

I nodded.

Kenta smiled, revealing the pearliest whites I had ever seen. Just his smile made me want to burst into tears of gratefulness. The tears stayed locked away. There would be no tears. All of my overwhelming emotions of loneliness and despair overflowed the moment Kenta wrapped me in his arms in a reassuring embrace. Comfort, the one thing that I have wanted ever since I left the house, was right in his arms. I was so gullible back then.

"I'm scared," I told him. "I don't know what to do and I don't know where to go. I don't want men chasing me anymore and I don't want to hide. I don't know what to do." Kenta patted my head. Why I pretty much summed up my life story in a little sentence, I didn't know. The words slurred out before I could even function myself forming them.

"I can take you away from here." I pulled away and looked at him. Was he serious? Was he another freak with a welcoming demeanor? "I can take you away from here. I could give you a new life and everything. But it comes with a price."

So he *was* a freak, I pretty much thought. "A price?" Kenta nodded and placed me on my feet. I was as tall as his chest, barely reaching his chin. I stared up at him through slit eyes. The rain was still strong, too much for me to handle.

He unzipped his rain coat and took out a red and gold box. "There are orbs in here that give you the power to do anything." I had no doubt this guy was a freak. Still, I couldn't help but listen to him. His voice was too warm to turn away.

"Anything?"

Kenta nodded. He was so sure. He was adequate. I truly believed him. "There are seven orbs in here and there's one calling your name."

"Mine?"

"Yes Ayano." Kenta grinned. "If you take the orb that's calling your name, then you have to help me find the others who have orbs calling their names. If you do this, you can also have a better life. You can change your name if you want to. You can wear different clothes, eat where ever, and do whatever. So, what do you say, will you help me?"

To travel where my heart desired, to be wherever I wanted to be, and even have comrades along the way. Without hesitation, I nodded. I had no idea what I was signing up for but I took the job, wanting to be anywhere but here . . . as long as I had this man.

Kenta opened the box and a midnight colored orb zoomed out of the box and hit me. I fell out instantly, but I didn't feel afraid. As the orb merged with me, combining us together, I allowed the darkness of my mind to grip me, suck me in and trap me within its hold.

When I woke up the next morning, Kenta was by my side. He stroked my forehead with his knuckles as I woke up. I was on the ground, which I wasn't surprised about. He helped me to my feet and pushed my hair behind my ears. He was so warm. So deliciously warm.

He told me I was an Element Princess. I had the powers of Death and Darkness. That meant I couldn't kill people with it, but I had the ability to sense spirits, suck the souls out of people's bodies, and even blend with the shadows more than any demon ever could. I was scared that I had those abilities. Then again, it didn't matter to me as long as I could control it. Besides, how bad could this ability be?

"So where would you like to go?" Kenta asked me. He asked so curiously, as if he really wanted to know.

"I want to visit somewhere before I leave permanently."

Without another word, Kenta put me on his back, carrying me piggy back style and I told him where to go. Since I was lost, I had no idea where we were going. Once I remembered, we followed a winding damp road then made it to my old house; the same house where the woman took care of those men and me.

The ride there was incredibly fun. I had never felt such a rush. The wind blew my hair and even dried my clothes. The colors around me were smudges as Kenta and I continued together in the direction of my destination.

Anyway, we finally made it. The house was the same. Nothing had changed. The men were even gone this time, leaving the house in its original glory. We approached the front door and knocked. Why we knocked, I have no idea. I didn't seem to care who or what answered at the time. When no one answered, I grabbed the round silver knob and opened the door. The old hinges didn't even squeak. Maybe the house wasn't so old, after all.

There was dust and cobwebs everywhere. Once entering the house, there was the living room in center view. The white carpet I remembered was a dirty light brown, filled with dirt, dust and some shoeprints. The yellow walls were faded and the chandelier on the sun kissed ceiling had broken bulbs. Two beige recliners were all that remained in the room along with a coffee table with a glass center. There were newspapers scattered along it with some cards.

Kenta searched the house, wondering if anyone was inside. I didn't have the strength to look around the house. Just knowing my caretaker wasn't there anymore broke my heart. Had the men dragged her away? Had they hurt her? Had she finally run from them? Where had they gone?

After rolling my head left to right, remembering the good times in this place without those men, I decided to go through the scattered newspapers and cards. I found a piece of paper that shocked me to my core.

It was a funeral information sheet for a woman named Tammy Matsumoto. The picture in the front of it was the picture of the woman who cared for me.

My heart dropped. My lungs stopped. I choked on a piece of air lodged in my throat. I read the paper and found out that she was murdered and found dead outside of her house. A single gunshot to her head had ended her long sixty-three years of life. She was drained of blood. She was a single, unmarried woman who always wanted to raise a child.

Tears rained down then and there. My lungs and heart functioned again. My inner pain grew at rapid speeds. Her funeral had been two days ago. I didn't even attend her funeral, which ripped at me, tearing me to shreds.

"What did you find?" Kenta asked me. He had returned to the living room. His thumbs hid inside of his jacket pockets. His eyes were so sympathetic. They weren't filled with pity and I was glad for that. I did not seek pity. Could I be read so well?

I told him everything I found. After wiping my tears and breathing started to even out, I placed the paper back on the table.

"We can go now." I told him. "And, I already know the first thing I want to do for changing my life."

"What is that?" He asked with a grin. He could obviously read me.

I looked up at him with confidence. "I'm changing my name. My name from this day forward is Ayano Matsumoto." It was only right to continue a name I could always remember. She had taken me in, fed me, provided for me and gave me more love then I could ever ask of a motherly figure. If she didn't have children, then I would be her unexpected child.

Maybe that's why she always smiled at me, I grasped.

Kenta grinned. "That's a beautiful name."

Mary wiped away a tear that lingered down her face. It was the only tear she allowed to fall. Her eyes were utterly glassy, revealing a pool of tears wanting to fall. Ayano grinned. If Mary cried, then she would have let her. "I had no idea your life was like that." Her voice was groggy. She wanted to cry, alright.

"I know you didn't. That's why I told you." Ayano leaned back again, focusing on the stars. "Now you know why I'm always grumpy or whatever."

"Well she smiled now." Kenta turned to Mary. He delicately wiped away her tear with his thumb.

"And this fool never changes!" Ayano busted out, almost seeming to laugh. "In all the ten years we've been together, his face has not aged a day."

"That's because Spirit Beings don't age. I'm guessing you forgot I told you that too, huh."

Ayano rolled her eyes again.

Mary giggled then wiped her face. "Well I am both appreciative and honored that I got to hear about your life story."

All attention went to her. "You're sleepy now huh?"

"Yes," she answered Kenta.

"I knew it." Ayano sighed. She brought one leg up and threw the other one over it.

"Don't be mad just because she's sleepy after listening to *your* life story." Kenta said then helped Mary down the ladder. Ayano knew she was supposed to take offense of that. Both she and Kenta knew she didn't.

Mary reached the ladder and prepared to climb down. She paused. "Good night," she smiled up at him. Their eyes locked.

"Night," he said to her as sweet as could be; as lovely as could be. Puppy love could do that to you. He watched as she went in the house. With a sharp click, the window was closed shut, leaving her and Mr. Puppy Love outside for the rest of the night.

"And you're telling me there's nothing happening between you two."

"That's exactly what I'm telling you," Kenta smiled. He rejoined her on the sightseeing. The moon had finally caught up with the stars and joined them in the night part of their own. Their hands locked behind their heads and they both exhaled in relaxation.

This night continued on in silence. Soon, Ayano's eyelids got heavier and heavier. She yawned several times, but refused to drift. "I'll watch the girls. You rest now."

Ayano grinned. Spirit Beings didn't sleep so he meant his word when he said he would watch them. However, there was a difference between watching them in protection and watching them like a pervert. Kenta was such a tease.

With another sigh, she allowed him to take charge for the night. Her eyes closed. Sleep arrived.

Story 9

The *Chilling* training

If you asked, or if you cared to even wonder, how it would be like to have the abilities to possess the bodies of anyone of your choosing, you would either respond favorably or deniably.

Destiny had a favorable answer.

Her powers are unique and valued by many others of the Demon Docks. Foot soldiers would approach her asking questions and wanting to know the feeling of being possessed physically and mentally. They were foolish to want to know the feeling. It was strange how they had the audacity to approach her in the first place.

Destiny's powers worked wonders. They not only control the victim's body. It controls their body, their willpower and their very soul. Everything belonged to Destiny. Everything would always belong to Destiny. The soldiers soon realized that. The moment she exited the body of the chosen victim, he had ended up in a coma for half a year. Even afterward, his brain functions were lacking. He was slower than he usually was and his attack patterns were swerved. Deeming him unworthy, the soldiers killed their friend and ended up eating him for their next meal.

Destiny held no sympathy. He had volunteered. She hadn't warned him what would happen to him. Besides, the results always varied.

That's probably why Lavida had summoned her; for her abilities.

The distressed blonde had entered Destiny's room without so much as a knock, closed the door and started off their conversation with, "We need a plan."

Correction, *she* needed a plan. Destiny was minding her own business in this spacious room of hers. It looks like a green house. The entire room is made of glass that revealed everything outside but blocked those outside from observing the inside. Dark hardwood covered the floors and the glass stretched high, coming together and creating a point, acting as her ceiling.

Two long chained swings with a wooden seat hung over her bed, over ten stories in the air. Her queen sized bed with silver sheets and a midnight blanket hung below one of the swings and the bathroom rested to her right. The door was closed at the moment. A black painted, metal rocking chair with horizontal prongs as the arm rests was placed a few inches from the bed. That was where Lavida currently resided.

Destiny swung on her swing, the one farthest away from the bed and gave a perfect view of Lavida and her pitiful form. She wore a long magenta dress that reached to her ankles and was made of wool. She had a turtleneck as an added bonus. It wasn't even that cold outside. Destiny would know. Her room's temperature was the weather outside. Summers were a nightmare.

Lavida rocked back and forth with her hands intertwined around her chin. She stared off, contemplating ideas.

Destiny stood on her swing while rocking along with Lavida's speed. Ruby eyes stared down at her sister's desperation. She couldn't focus much though. Lavida's outfit was just not doing it for her. When Lavida dressed like this, she was in real disrepair. Derek must have really gotten to her.

A few hours ago, an extremely cold sensation breezed into Destiny's room. She knew the princesses had been brought together. All seven had been found and the entire Demon Docks army knew about it. She had heard Derek's fury cries so she knew some demons would be messed up from witnessing their master's rage.

Lavida had been one of those victims. She hadn't shed a tear since being here, and that had been hours ago. It was the break of dawn now. Nothing came to her mind. Destiny wasn't even going to help her. Lavida was more than welcomed to visit her and even shuffle through her mind here.

Key word, visit.

No rush though. The sooner she thought of a way to kill the princesses, the better. Derek's fury was feared by all, even by Destiny. She wasn't a wimp, but when your leader was pissed as hell, you wanted to scurry to the nearest corner you could get to. That's why Destiny had stayed in her room when Derek shouted his anger. The farther away you were from a raging bull, the better.

"We could kidnap . . . no never mind."

That had been the eighth time she said that. It seemed like that was all her mind could think up. Destiny had already thought of ideas and they could have worked. She wasn't going to share them though. She figured Lavida would figure it out. Out of the Three Death Daughters, Lavida always was the dumbest.

The girl was loyal to ones with the power. She followed father like an excited prisoner. She followed Derek as if he was her lover. Every single person in this place knew Diamond was married to him. Destiny's precious little sister always got the perks and Lavida hated every minute of it. Lavida had claimed to love Derek once. They even shared a bed and their bodies together. He chose Diamond; her own sister.

Their father had laughed. Lavida had cried. Destiny didn't care.

"We have to get rid of them. We just have to."

"Think of an idea, and it might happen," Destiny said. Her voice was emotionless. She didn't sound bored or boring. She always had a voice meant to chant someone's name or be a silent, secret thought. She always talked like this. She liked it. It explained her personality greatly.

After hours of sitting,-from the late evening to now—Lavida stood and begun to pace. Her legs weren't even affected by the constant sitting session. She locked her hands behind her back and peered to the floor. Her white flip flops flopped. "If we kidnap one of the princesses, the others would come and rescue her. We can capture them and Derek would be pleased." She sounded insane, deserving to be a part of a mental facility.

"Maybe, but what if none of them come and that princess's hero is Damon?"

Lavida froze.

Everyone heard the news. The Spirit Being Damon Sasaki was back in town, big and bad, now based on Lavida's report. She informed Derek about him, and, of course, he was pissed. Damon was a big and bad Spirit Being who kicked ass better than any Spirit Being she had ever seen. He could take out hundreds of demons with his eyes closed. Rumor has it that, when he was away, he gained a newfound power. Why he disappeared in the first place, Destiny didn't know. Didn't care.

"Damon would murder us all. I know it."

The fact that she was doubtful proved just how messed up her head was. Derek must have truly been pissed. Destiny had never seen her sister so jumpy and cynical. "There are different ways to capture them. We could just send a horde and kill them all. We've done so with others from the past." Kenta and Ayano had tried recruiting other princesses but none of them ever let off a cooling sensation like this team did. This was a real deal. They had to move fast or the Docks were done for good.

That's what everyone believed. Destiny just played along.

With a sigh, Destiny jumped off of her swing. Her small angelic wings popped out fluttered as she made her way elegantly to the ground. Lavida turned to her, hoping she had an idea. She did. "I'll go."

Lavida tilted her head. "Go where?"

She rolled her eyes. *Put two and two together, idiot.* "I will go and kidnap a princess for you." Honestly, she was tired of Derek's fury and the demon's fears. They were demons! Fear shouldn't have even been in their vocabulary.

Lavida smiled ear to ear. She brought her arms out wide, preparing to hug her sister.

Destiny raised her hand, stopping her. "No touching."

Demons never hugged. Ever. *What the heck is wrong with this girl?*

Lavida cleared her throat and dropped her arms. "Of course. Be on your way then."

How was she going to tell Destiny to leave when Destiny was the one who decided to leave? This girl is indeed the dumbest of the sisters. Destiny might have been shortest but she was smartest.

Lavida was forced to leave. Destiny refused to leave this wondrous and tranquil room to her unbalanced sister. Once she was gone, Destiny locked her enlarged wooden door and teleported to the princess's location; the town known as Kayta Plains.

"Man I feel so awkward!" Reiko over-exaggerated as she chatted on the phone with Mary.

The laid back water princess grinned and even popped a chuckle. "I know. When you wake up, you could swear yesterday's events were a dream, but they weren't. You really do possess an element."

"This is awesome! I feel even better than I did yesterday. I feel stronger somehow. Oh! I forgot to tell you. This morning, I woke up and guess what I did in my sleep." Reiko's attitude traveled faster than most people could catch. Mary caught up easily.

"What did you do?"

"I froze my bed! Can you believe that? When I woke up, my entire bed was ice. I slipped out of the bed and fell on my ass. Best/Worst feeling ever." The teens laughed.

"That's interesting because this morning my mattress was soaking wet."

"Bed wetter . . ."

"Uh no, the liquid was clear. You know what, never mind. Anyway, is that the only reason you called me?"

Mary had woken up to a phone call. It was Reiko, of course, and her voice had been so high pitched, as if she drunk over three cups of coffee with extra caffeine. She had done that before, actually. That had to be the funniest school day ever.

"Yeah pretty much," Reiko said, still as happy as could be. "Wait, did I tell you that school was cancelled today?"

"Yeah, this is the fifth time you've told me . . . on the same phone call."

"Oh, well I'm gonna tell you again. School was cancelled for the next two weeks thanks to the fire at school. They found out that they have to rebuild and the fumes might affect the kids. The middle school students down the street are out, too."

Man this girl is hopeless. Mary thought. "Oh, and another thing!"

"Yes Reiko?" What else could she possibly have to say?

"I called Kenta to tell him I slipped out of the bed and I told him about school. He told me to call everyone and meet in Lune Park at noon."

"Oh, the open area on the outskirts of town." The place held for annual carnivals and fairs but once the events were over, people moved out and there was nothing left but a large football field wide area surrounded by the thick, lush forest.

"Yeah. It's eleven, so I'll see you in an hour."

"Alright, see you later." The girls hung up.

Mary looked over at Sazuma. She was sound asleep. Her snoring proved that she didn't know what was going on around her. Ayano had taken Stella back home early this morning. "We don't want to overstay our welcome. Thanks again." How were they over staying? Mary wondered. They had left around six in the morning. There was no overstaying.

Back to the present, Sazuma was too comfortable for her own good. Mary picked up her pillow and threw it at her sister. "Hey! Kenta wants us to meet at the park at noon."

Her snoring ceased. She gave a tired hiccup. "What time is it?" Sazuma mumbled.

"It's eleven O' one."

Sazuma nodded, rolled to her side and cuddled to her pillow with a yawn. Mary sighed. *Three . . . two . . . one . . .*

Sazuma shot up. "Eleven O' one? What's today?!"

"Saturday."

"We're missing school!"

She obviously was still asleep. Kayta Plains didn't have school on Saturdays. Mary rolled her eyes and went along with her game. "School was cancelled today. I told you that already but you pushed me away and went back to sleep. Now come on, we need to eat breakfast, fix ourselves up and meet Kenta and the others at the park."

She pouted. Mary was stunned. Sazuma was no pouter. "Why?"

"I don't know, just come on." Mary got up and headed to the bathroom. Sazuma sighed, slugged out of bed, and followed.

Element Princess

❦

"Good morning!" Mary waved at her comrades as her and her sister arrived at the park. Ayano's head rose from the ground. Her arms crossed over her chest. "You're thirty minutes late." Ayano said. She might have given an authority image, but Mary wasn't falling for it.

"I'm sorry. Sazuma wouldn't move quickly. A Linkin Park music video played on the TV and she wouldn't move until it was over."

"Linkin Park?" Yumiko asked happily. "Was the song *"New Divide"*?"

"Heck, yeah," Sazuma grinned. She loves music. It's one of the things she loves to research. Music is her life . . . or a small part of it. The conversation continued on with no end in sight.

"Girls," Kenta began. Mary guessed there *was* an end. The girls gathered in the middle of the empty park. "To your left, right, front and back, there are trees. The town is a few miles away so when we do this, we won't affect anyone."

"What's going on?" Hiroko asked. Her cotton hoodie covered her upper body along with her head. The chilling winds touched the navy blue material but had no affect with affecting the cooled blonde.

"We start training today." Ayano answered. "Something tells me this is going to hurt."

Sazuma muttered. "It is."

Mary knew this was going to, too. Mary was the fighter, not Sazuma. "Don't say false things Ayano," Reiko said. She clapped her hands together. She wore no jacket. Reiko merely wore a short sleeved white shirt with glittered words saying "*Ice Princess.*" Faded blue jeans covered her legs and the edges of the material hid under high-heeled black boots that reached below her knees. "So how do we start this training of yours? It sounds interesting."

"Well we're going to start with volunteers and see what happens," Kenta answered.

"I'll go." Reiko stepped forward. "I am ice, after all. What's the worst that could happen?"

She could have said better words than that. Mary thought.

"Alright," Kenta continued, "Before we work with our elemental powers, Ayano will help you learn physical combat."

"Cool, I learned a lot of Kung Fuji on TV."

"It's pronounced Kung Fu," Ayano said plainly. She picked up her staff and got into a fighting stance. "I bet I can beat you by the time my staff comes back to the ground."

"I doubt it," Reiko smiled. "I have skills."

The skills of failure. The thought had formed in Mary's mind before she could comprehend it. That was a little mean to say.

"Fine then. Come at me."

Reiko paused, took a deep breath then recklessly ran to Ayano. She threw up her staff then jumped. Her body turned clockwise. Her booted heel poked out and landed smack dab on Reiko's cheek. The impact threw her back on the ground. Ayano landed back on the ground then grabbed her staff as it gravitated back down.

Sazuma and Yumiko had their mouths opened wide. Ayano looked over at the rest of the girls. "Who's next?"

Hiroko pushed Sazuma out of the crowd. She panicked at first and glared. Hiroko glared back. She was far more intense though. Hiroko could be scary sometimes. With a shrug, shaking off the panic, Sazuma stepped up. The group stepped back a couple of steps. Mary was quick to join them. No way was she going in there.

Sazuma dashed to Ayano, less recklessly than Reiko. Whatever was going on in that mind of hers, Mary just hoped Sazuma had a good hit. Ayano threw up her staff. Sazuma lowered herself to block the kick attack that Reiko received. Just as she did so, Ayano lifted her knee and it made contact with Sazuma's jaw.

"Oooooooo . . ." the girls stiffened and Yumiko covered her face, somehow feeling the pain of her friend. Sazuma hit the ground while Ayano caught her staff. "I'm not going out there! I'm not going out there! I am *not* going out there!" Yumiko freaked and tried to run. Mary grabbed her back collar, keeping her in place.

"This is just day one of training. We'll be fine."

"You haven't gone out there so you don't know!"

Very true and she still wasn't. "That's not true Yumiko. Everything will be fine. Right Stella?"

Stella shook her head in rapid speeds.

"Alright here's what I'm going to do." Ayano took a step closer. The girls quickly took a step back. Instinct kicked in. Ayano is a killer. She is going to murder them. Mary was sure of it. Running sounded like a good idea right now. "I won't ask you all to come and approach me. Instead, I am going to warm your bodies up. We will be doing exercises and warm ups. Then we will work with combat. And at the end of training, we will work on our elemental abilities."

She wanted to think of this idea after bruising two of her friends? Very dark-like.

"That sounds fair," Hiroko sighed in relief.

"In exchange, you all have to stay in my apartment on the weekends." "Darkness and Death chick, say what?" Reiko said trying to stand from the ground. She tried to lift herself but she was still dizzy from the kick. There was a circular red mark on her cheek. How was she going to explain *that* to her parents? "If I give you this format of training, you have to stay at my house Friday and Saturday nights for the next few months." "Months?" Reiko asked, shocked.

"Is there a problem?"

"Nope, not at all." Stella answered for her. She was just as scared to training as everyone else was. Sazuma was still on the ground by the way.

Ayano turned around. Mary's eyes followed her until they spotted Kenta. The guy had been sitting on the ground with his legs crossed. What surprised Mary was his posture. His eyes were closed and he was motionless, as if focusing in on something—or someone. In this world, anything was possible.

Mary refocused on training as Stella and Hiroko helped Sazuma to her feet. There was no bruise. Mary knew there would be later on. Sazuma's only current side effect might have been an extreme headache.

Ayano faced the group once more, legs apart and hands behind her back; full force authority. "Alright, let's start the real training shall we. Everyone get on the ground and give me twenty pushups."

"Push ups? I can't do those things," Hiroko said in a crying manner. "Trust me, I've tried and failed miserably."

"You know," Ayano stepped closer. The girls stepped back again, "every minute counts as more pushups that you have to do. Right now, you have to do twenty-two instead of twenty."

"That's bogus," Reiko said.

Ayano's eyes narrowed, the burgundy piercing deep. "Twenty five."

"How did you get from twenty-two to twenty-five pushups? It hasn't even been three minutes yet."

"Your mouth causes more pushups. You have to do twenty-eight now."

"But Ayano!" Stella cried.

"Thirty one!"

The girls dropped to the ground then started doing their best pushups. Hiroko struggled her way up. Her arms wobbled as she completed one push up then dropped to her stomach, already out of breath.

Stella did a few, then quickly started to get tired.

Yumiko started feeling the same way.

Sazuma and Reiko were having hissy fits.

Mary simply kept going. She went up and down as she did her pushups without any effort. She was stronger than most, hiding her minor muscles under her clothes.

"What the..."

"Yeah, she can do that." Sazuma panted to Reiko's comment.

"Come on girls," Ayano said as she walked around observing. "You each have thirty-one pushups to do. None of you leave until you do your thirty one."

"I can't do this!" Yumiko panted and complained.

"Girls your age can do many things," Ayano said. "Now come on. One, two, one, two..."

"I'm gonna die," Reiko exclaimed.

Up and down Mary went until she completed her number. She pushed to her knees and inhaled a deep breath. Ayano allowed her to rest, knowing she completed her task.

Her attention whipped to Kenta. He was looking at the girls now, watching them as they trained. He looked so amused. Ayano wasn't breathing down his neck so of course he would be amused. His eyes went from Sazuma to Mary's left and then reached her.

Mary froze. He was looking at her. His gaze screamed fascination. At her? Why? Mary wasn't all that interesting. She looked just like Sazuma except their personalities were very different.

As his eyes turned away, now focusing on Stella to Mary's right, her heart kicked back in gear. When had it stopped? What was wrong with her? Guys looked at her before and she never nearly acted as surprised as she was. Kenta was just a guy. He was a guy who now assisted them with defeating the enemy.

You know that's a lie, she told herself. She was right. Kenta was no ordinary guy. For one, he carried around a black sheathed sword that curved when released from its hold; a sword which rested to his right, by the way.

He is tall with copper skin. Mary had never seen anyone with such beauty. But that was only his skin. He was muscled from his broad shoulders, to his long arms, to his tight torso, to his buff thighs and long legs. His hair was a curtain of shining black that hung just below his ears. His mahogany headband pulled back most of those masses of hair but allowed just enough to hang over his forehead. His eyes were like shimmering rubies that froze Mary's heart wonderfully as he looked at her... like he was doing now.

She turned her head away. How long had she been looking at him? Had she been raking his body while she explained to herself why he was different from other guys? Her eyes went back to him. He was still looking at her. He was smirking this time. She had been raking him, hadn't she?

Kenta placed his elbow on his knee and crooked his finger. Mary had never seen a more lustful of an act. He was still looking at her, so he was talking to her, right?

"Come here Mary." He crooked his finger again.

Mary jumped to her feet. She jumped up so fast she surprised herself. *Why are you so desperate?* she asked herself. She didn't know. Her feet guided her as she filled the distance between her and Kenta. She dropped to her knees in front of him. *Hide the grin. Hide the grin!*

Kenta snickered. He leaned down, getting closer to her. "Why are you staring at me?" He was definitely amused.

Hide the blush. Hide the blush! Heat rushed to her cheeks anyway. He was so close. Not close enough for a kiss but . . . his lips were so inviting; lush, vibrant, and warm.

"Do you want to kiss me?"

God yes! "No, I'm sorry. I can't help but stare." What was up with her? Her mind wanted to be all over Kenta. Hug him, kiss him, and roam her hands around him. She was most definitely going crazy. Why the sudden urge? More importantly, would it ever go away?

A gust of wind rushed by, causing Mary to shiver. Her hair whisked over her shoulder and tickled Kenta's face. Curse her long hair!

Kenta snickered again. It was a lovely sound, filled with amusement and love. He was lovely. That's all Mary could think about him. She didn't know much about him and she knew he had killed the princesses in the past. She still could not hate him for that. She never could, she knew.

He pushed the strands out of his face and even pushed the hairs behind her ears. Warmth slurred through her as his fingers stroked her skin. "You don't stare at guys all of the time do you?"

"Nope, just you." She mentally slapped herself. Did she have to be so honest?

He grinned, "I guess I'm a lucky man."

Mary melted. Kenta was too sweet for his own good. He looked like a warrior, fought like one too. She had seen his battles with Chikara when she attacked her and Sazuma at the house and when trying to retrieve Stella. He was fast, strong, brave, and everything in between. Mary was the lucky woman. To be able to meet Kenta was a blessing all its own.

"You're staring at me again."

She immediately turned away. Her eyes pointed down. She grabbed the hem of her long gray shirt and rubbed the material together; a nervous gesture of hers.

"You're a strange one, aren't you?" Mary looked back up again. He was still grinning. His eyes shined as they zoomed down at her. Their eyes locked as he brought his chin down to his awaiting hand. His index knuckle placed itself on the curve of his bottom lip. "I like it."

Heat returned to Mary's cheeks. This guy was too much for her. He was too handsome, too lovely, too much of a teaser. He teased her without even noticing it. Mary inhaled. His mint scent locked in her nostrils. She didn't mean for that to happen, but it couldn't be helped now. "You are quite a tease."

"Says the girl staring at me as if she was stripping me with her eyes."

Was her stare that bad?

There was nothing to say. Nothing came to mind. She would allow Kenta to win this conversation. She couldn't win even if she tried.

Kenta opened his mouth to speak. Nothing came out. His expression changed then and there. From fascinated to alert. He turned his head, looking behind his shoulder and focusing there. Mary looked over as well. She saw nothing but trees.

Kenta turned back around and rose to his feet. He grabbed Mary's hand and dragged her up as well. He picked up his weapon. "Stay close to me." Mary received Kenta's back as he faced the area in warning. "Ayano."

The alert princess was at his side a second later; her staff in hand. "What do we have?"

"Demonic Princess."

"Which one?"

"Not sure, but she's close."

Mary's comrades flanked her sides. They were confused, just as she was.

No one spoke, fearing they would throw off Kenta and Ayano's concentration.

Stay calm. I have to stay calm. Mary inhaled, exhaled, and repeated the process. She didn't know what was going to happen next. The anticipation was killing her. Was someone out there? Was there some*thing* out there? It could have been anything. It could have been everything.

A sharp squawk echoed. A shadow flashed by, blocking the group's sunlight for a brief moment. All eyes went to the skies. Creatures with wings circled around the park. No, those weren't creatures, they were humans. Humans with wings.

"Bat demons," Ayano growled. She swung her staff, releasing her black whip-like cloth. Another swing and the cloth became longer. Her ravenous eyes held so much hatred. Mary knew she was readying for battle.

Kenta pulled out his sword. Once again, the silver of the blade inked into the hilt, crimson red replacing it. The blade maneuvered in a slithering shape with a razor sharp tip. "You girls listen to me." His focus never left the wall of woods. "When I say run, you run damn it. No "If's", "Ands" or—"

Reiko screamed. A bat demon was soaring down right behind them, nowhere close to its friend above their heads. Ayano swung her whip around. Her cloth wrapped around the demon's neck. With one meager tug, the creature's neck snapped. It shattered into dust as it made impact with the ground. More swooped in, aiming for the group now centered on each other.

Snarls entered Mary's ears. Busting out the forests were more humans.

They ranged in height and complexions. They were still taller and stronger than Mary's group.

"Shit," Ayano hissed between her teeth, just now taking out another bat demon.

"Burn them, Sazuma," Kenta commanded.

"How?" She panicked. Using her powers might have endangered them. Mary understood her sister's fear but she needed to do something.

"Release your flame," Mary commanded, as well. The men approached, dashing forward in speeds Mary didn't even understand. "Sazuma, now!"

Sazuma threw out her arms with closed eyes. A wave of fire released, hitting the soldiers in reaching distance. They shouted and withed as they burned to the ground. Their bodies turned into dust. The other soldiers continued on, reached out and even grabbed Stella.

Ayano's rage ignited. She raced forward, flipped her staff in her hand, and stabbed Stella's grabber in the forehead. She pulled out. Black blood stained her staff. The attacker turned to dust instantly. That's how demons died, huh? Everyone was consumed by shock. The man had been killed so violently, so viciously. "Hiroko, use your wind to give us some extra room."

Following the command, Hiroko stepped up, inhaled deeply through her mouth and blew out. The mass of soldiers were picked up and thrown back into the forest.

"Good, now Stella, use your earth to create a rock wall."

The terrified redhead was shaking. She still freaked about the way her attacker died. He had grabbed her neck, attempting to end her life immediately. Then Ayano had arrived and stabbed the man's forehead right in front of her eyes; she had heard the cracks of a skull, the gushes of a pierced brain. It was a surprise that she was standing on her own.

"Stella, come on." Mary shook her friend's shoulders. She had to be strong. They both did. Mary was scared too. She was now surrounded by demons determined to end her and her friend's lives. Kenta and Ayano had warned them that this would be their new life if they agreed to obtain the orbs. She might have been terrified however, she regretted nothing.

"Stella please," Hiroko rushed to her, grabbing her hand and shaking her. Stella's eyes were wide. She couldn't hear them, Mary knew. "You have to work with us. We need to survive. Stella, please!"

Flickers of heat rushed by Mary. Sazuma had thrown out another wave of fire, one after another. They had reached a group of soldiers coming at them, causing them to burn and wither away.

One by one, Kenta sliced and arched his blade, slicing through throats, piercing torsos and even decapitating heads. Ayano was pulling down bat demons and slamming them into the ground, causing them to die on colossal impact.

"Stella!" Hiroko shouted. She slapped Stella's cheek. A red handprint formed with no waiting period. Stella was refocused though, stunned that she had been slapped in the first place. Before she could protest, Hiroko shouted, "Make a rock wall. Now! Do it now!"

"I don't know how."

"Move your hands and make some kind of motions. Say some magic words. Do something!" Hiroko's panic mode had been activated. Her hood now hung on her shoulders and her hair was fuzzy, as if she had currently had a session with a balloon.

More men rushed out. More bat demons soared down.

Stella raised her hand. A block of dirt rose up eight feet in the air. Several men busted by it. Wide eyed, Stella tried again, forming more walls in separate locations. All walls were busted through.

"Make the wall stronger."

"I'm trying," she rushed out to Reiko. "I'm barely forming the wall to begin with."

"Reiko, freeze the men." Yumiko shook her friend's T-shirt violently.

"Yeah, that requires close range," she pointed to the approaching soldiers.

She faced Yumiko, "I am not going anywhere near those demons," she shouted forcefully.

Yumiko was unaffected by her shouts. "Can't you make ice crystals or something?"

"Does it look like I know how to control this element?"

"You haven't even tried!" Yumiko threw her arms in the air.

One of Stella's walls shot up, stopping the soldier aiming for Reiko and Yumiko. This wall stayed up, nice and sturdy.

"That was a good one," Hiroko said, but she didn't calm. "Keep at it."

Stella's arms rose and fell, rose and fell. Walls popped up here and there and they remained sturdy. The soldiers went around them. Stella blocked their path. The demons who got by were handled by Kenta's blade, Ayano's whip and Sazuma's flames.

Hiroko threw her hands in the air, sending the bat creatures further away. They remained in the air, afraid to get too close and end up having their necks snapped by Ayano.

Soon, the group was surrounded by sturdy dirt walls. The protests of the men outside of those walls were heard, but ignored. There was no way those guys were getting through. The build of the wall was firm and tall. Mary was proud of her little friend.

Stella dropped to her knees. She panted. Her hands were flat on the ground, holding her up as her shoulders shook.

Ayano bent down beside her, grabbed her shoulders and pulled her into her embrace. "Nice work, kiddo." She pushed her hair out of her face and praised her some more.

"Nice work to all of you," Kenta said. His sword returned to a straight silver blade and slid it back in its sheath. He reached out. Mary's hand joined with his. His warmth cascaded through her, making her legs weak. He reached out to Sazuma and took her hand as well. "Let's get out of here."

The remaining girls touched Ayano's shoulder as she commanded them to. One second passed, then another. Nothing happened.

"Damn it," he cursed.

"Something's blocking us from teleporting," Ayano answered. She was looking around, observing the walls. The men outside stayed out there and the bat demons remained in the skies. Could demons block the ability to teleport?

Suddenly, a black shadow slithered on the far wall. Kenta must have seen it too, because he tensed. Ayano's eyes looked to the side, watching her own back, probably sensing the shadow as well. Everyone noticed once the shadow encircled them, moving around and around, waiting for the opportune moment to strike.

"Destiny," Ayano muttered, but everyone heard loud and clear.

Kenta released Sazuma's hand and pulled out his sword once again, the blade returning to its crimson glory. He released Mary's hand, as well. He wrapped his arm around her waist protectively. "Stay close," he whispered to her as his eyes followed the shadow.

She wasn't planning on leaving, anyway.

"Do I throw fire at it?" Sazuma asked, her eyes too following the shadow. Her tone wasn't filled with fear. She liked this position she was in. She was even grinning.

"Don't do anything until I say so," Kenta said. No one moved.

The shadow's quick moments slowed, slowed, became slower still, like a slowing spinner, until it stopped completely, directly behind Reiko. Her eyes wandered. She knew the shadow was behind her. The group contemplated how to move.

A seemingly devious chuckle swerved through the group's ears. "So you are the current princesses. You're no different than the ones Kenta chose in the past. With the right amount of fright, you will be running to Kenta in desperation, just as the others did."

The voice was feminine and emotionless. Mary never knew someone could hold such plainness.

"What do you want, Destiny?"

"It's nice to see you too, Ayano." Destiny slithered. The shadow behind Reiko remained. She hadn't moved an inch. The shadow had even morphed into a figure. An outline of a woman standing at tall was Yumiko. Based on what she could tell, Mary figured she had long hair. The shadow had strands flowing, as if swaying breeze could touch it. "I don't want much. I only want a princess; a heart of intensity."

Intensity. Mary had a heart of love, so she wasn't it. Who was ...? Before Mary could complete her thoughts, Ayano reached up to grab Reiko's hand. She was too late. The shadow came up an upward position. Appearing out of the dirt wall was the upper section of a woman. She had silver hair, eyes of rubies and pale skin. Her black-gloved hands reached out to grab the startled teen. Reiko whipped around and threw out her hands in protect. Ice shards shot out. The woman slipped back into the rock. A shard had hit her shoulder.

The moment she left, crumbling shook the ground. Stella's walls were falling. She had regained her strength, now standing on her own, except the wall's sturdiness could only last so long. The crumbling continued, causing urgency in Mary to grow. They had to get out of here. They just had to.

"On the first opening, you run."

Everyone nodded to Kenta's command.

His attention went to Hiroko. "You blow us an opening." He turned to Sazuma. "You give us a barrier." He turned to Mary. His determined expression was one only a strategist would have. "You and Yumiko watch Reiko's back. You summon your power however way you can. I'm sure you guys will be fine."

Another wall collapsed. The roars of the demons escalated.

"What can light do?" Yumiko asked, not having a clue what special abilities her orb had. She probably thought all she could do was blind people. Mary hoped she was wrong.

"Make them blind," Ayano answered for her. "It will give us time and distance to separate ourselves."

Yumiko's shoulders sagged.

"What about water? There isn't a source around here."

Kenta turned to Mary again. "The past Mary's have learned to take moisture out of the air."

Ayano looked at them. "It took them weeks to master that move anyway. If they made it that long."

She had to go there, didn't she.

Mary dismissed Ayano, focusing on Kenta as his eyes looked at her with ... something. "I'll be defense. Nothing to worry about."

Kenta's strategized demeanor faded as he nodded. That glassy look of his eyes vanished as sounds increased. He focused up ahead again, ready to dash out.

As another wall dropped, this one far closer than the others, Hiroko stood in front of the group, feet apart and ready to inhale.

A loud gulp was heard and even seemed to echo. Reiko spoke, "Ten . . . nine . . . eight . . . seven," Mary knew she was terrified. The girl never counted down for anything. "Six . . . five . . ." Anticipation rose. Beads of sweat formed and slid down Mary's cheek. Kenta's sword was in the ready. Everyone surrounded Reiko, watching for more shadows and listening to the increasing devilish snarls. "Four . . . three . . . two . . ."

The wall in front of Hiroko crumbled, revealing a six-foot tall beast on four legs, brown fur and a saber tooth face. It roared, giving a wave of foul breath to the group. Clumps of saliva spat out and hit Hiroko's face. Ignoring the breath, she inhaled and exhaled her whirlwind of air, sending the creature and several others like him into the forest.

The entrance to the park, which was nothing but a rectangular space, was a good foot away. They could make it. They could . . . a soldier popped into the opened area, reaching out for Hiroko. She threw her hands, sending another wind of air, blowing the soldier and his comrades back.

They took this chance to dash out. Sazuma exited behind Hiroko. A barrier of flames shot a straight path to the exit on both sides of them. No demon dared to move through the fire—at least they didn't at first. Weapons shot at them: swords, throwing stars, even bullets.

The group charged, hoping to make it to the exit. Soldiers stepped in front of the path. Hiroko sent them away. Sazuma's flames danced. They soon began to spread, enclosing the group in this narrow space. The path seemed farther now then it was before.

A curse sounded. It was Ayano. Mary wanted to turn. She focused on the task at hand. Reiko was in her sights and so far, so good. More weapons zoomed through the fire. The team dodged and ducked. Another curse from Ayano sounded. Then Kenta released a curse. Mary didn't turn. She refused to turn. She had to focus. She had to go on. They were almost there. So close yet . . .

A sharp pain exploded through Mary's body. She tripped on her own feet and fell to the ground. She cried out, not knowing what just happened. The pain came from her left side. Every muscle, every vein, every single nerve, focused on that spot, which increased her agony tenfold.

"Mary," Kenta hovered over her. His eyes scanned her body. "Oh Saki," he exhaled a harsh breath. Before she knew it, she was picked up and carried down the path. Her vision blurred, her lungs were slowing down. She reached out, not knowing what else to do. "Ken . . . Kenta."

"I'm here sweetheart, just hang on."

A scream sounded. It was Hiroko. A holler sounded, this one coming from Reiko. There was just one scream after another. Through her vision, she saw Destiny grabbing Reiko then teleporting away. Hiroko was on the ground. Yumiko pulled Stella before she fell in Sazuma's flames.

She had to do something. She had to move. The moment she did, her pain intensified, surging through her veins and consuming her entire body. One side injury could affect her so dearly. She heaved in breaths, finding difficulty in something that should have been second nature to her.

"Reiko," her voice gurgled. A tangy taste flooded her mouth. She coughed up, spitting something out. Blood, she realized. It was her blood.

The heat of Sazuma's flames cooled, until Mary felt nothing. That didn't make sense though. The flames still danced around her. There should have been heat caressing her skin. Not even Kenta's warmth got to her. There was nothing. Blurriness strengthened.

"Mary, my God, sweetheart. Please hang on."

She tried, she truly did, but she failed. Mary's eyes closed. She entered darkness.

"Very nice, Destiny. I like this one."

Derek liked any girl with large breasts. Diamond rolled her eyes.

Destiny had teleported into Derek's throne room and summoned Derek and his loyal soldiers here to witness her capture. Diamond had arrived first, taking her spot on the ledge of the large window overlooking the shore. Derek arrived through the entrance moments later with Lavida, Riku, and Nao. Chikara and Emiko were still damaged from their encounter with Damon so they remained in their rooms.

Diamond knew Damon. Not personally, but she knew him well enough to not get in his way. On an enemy basis, they had no past fights. The others though were placed high on his Kill List.

Derek circled the girl. After everyone had reclined in one of the sitting area in the room, Destiny had slipped herself into the protesting teenager's body. Her stiff and rebellious body slowed, calmed. Her hazel eyes were replaced by apple red irises. Destiny had complete control. Derek smiled at that.

He was a real Sicko sometimes.

That Sicko is your husband. She mentally gagged. The thought of Derek and the word husband in the same sentence was just damn wrong; a disgrace really. Derek brought his hand up and locked a piece of princess's icy streaked black hair between his fingers. He looked her up and down, lingering in places he should have been forbidden to see. "Very nice," his voice slurred, holding back saliva.

"She's pretty hot," Riku said. He was sitting on Derek's stoned throne stairs, watching her just as bad as Derek was.

"What is she called?" The Demon Docks leader continued his stroll around her.

"Reiko Takashima," the teen said, a mix between Destiny's voice and, Diamond guessed, the girl's natural voice. She must have been a preppy girl, based on how high toned her voice was. She looked like a rich girl. She was tall with flawless black hair. The highlights were too straight to be said she did those by herself. Her nails were squared and painted dark purple. Her wardrobe was nice; white shirt, jeans and boots, and she was tall and cute enough to be a model. An icy aura surrounded her, chilling the room the moment Diamond had entered here. There was no doubt she is the princess of ice.

Derek's smile turned into a grin as he made another trip around her. "Reiko, huh? She doesn't look very Japanese."

And she didn't. Her eyes were too full, too luminous.

"I still like her," Derek smiled again. His fingers slid around her shoulders as he moved. He finally reached her front, gliding his hand down her slender shoulder and lingered at her breasts before bringing his hand to his side.

"Send her to my room, my lord." Riku stood and put his weight to his right side. His hands fisted in his jeaned pockets. "I'll take *real* good care of her."

"Too much care and you might end up killing her."

Riku shrugged his shoulders in innocence. There was nothing innocent about this white-haired Demonic Prince. He is selfish, takes what he desires and dispatches it afterward. Most likely, in his care, Riku would take the girl when she was down, taking what he wanted whether she wanted it or not. In the end, she would be thrown back to Derek and probably used again.

She was going to have one hell of a time here.

"Alright, as long as you don't damage her, then you are allowed to keep her." He turned to Destiny again. "You know what to do."

The teen's head nodded and was teleported out of the room. Riku's hands exited his pockets. He rubbed them together. "I'm going to love this."

He's a Sicko in training.

As Riku exited by foot, his brother remained on the throne stairs. He hadn't moved or said a word since the meeting. Derek made his way to the door. His hand was outstretched, urging Lavida to join him. She had placed herself against a wall. The wall was forgotten the moment Derek summoned her.

Nao stood and headed to Diamond. She hadn't moved. He placed himself on the other side of the window platform, facing her direction. He stared at her. Her left leg arched up. Her hand hung over her knee while the other leg touched the ground. Her right hand slept on her thigh.

Nao sat as polite and retarded as a demon could get. Both feet touched the ground firmly and his hands sat on his knees. His head lowered. His eyes stared at the golden platform cushion. "I hope I'm not overstepping any lines between us, Ms. Diamond."

"You're really going to use such politeness with me?" she asked in a friendly fashion, something she never thought she would be able to do, other than him of course. Nao was the only demon who treated her with the kindness and respect she thought—she believed—she deserved. At least in this place, that is.

Plus he didn't call her "Mrs. Southbound". That earned him extra appreciation points.

"You're still a higher being than me. You still deserve respect."

"Friends don't respect each other." Did they...? Diamond had friends, but they hadn't been seen in so long. A hundred years, to be exact.

Nao finally faced her, his emerald eyes watching her; making sure this was the right action to take. Smart dude. Usually, Diamond would have blown up someone by now, just because they were in close proximity. Nao knew better than to cross a line he knew he shouldn't cross, especially a line he'd never come close to.

Maybe making him her ally wasn't so bad.

Diamond had doubts at first. On the other hand, right now, this moment, she knew she made the right choice. He would stay by her side, not betray her and be a small buddy around this enormous mansion.

She knew she needed someone to keep her sanity in check. She was lucky Nao was in trouble back in the gym. It was the perfect time to approach him and ask to be her friend. It sounded more pitiful than it was. She needed this. She had noticed Nao for a while and treated him with respect just as he did for her. Sure they hadn't spoken. She still liked the little guy. He was too cute to be a demon.

Even now, while watching as his nervousness was increasing with the silence and his cheeks heated to a gentle pink, he was illuminating cuteness. That had to stop.

"What do you think of Derek's plans? Has he told you anything?"

Diamond viewed the room. She sniffed the air. Derek's scent was far gone along with the others. No one was seen or smelled in the area. Knowing it was safe to speak, she shrugged, "Whatever Derek has planned, that's his handlings. I'm only the wife, remember."

"You are not Derek's wife," he rushed out louder than intended. Realizing his outburst, he lowered his head again. "At least not in my eyes."

Diamond liked this guy even more. "Thanks for that," *Really, thank you,* "but I honestly don't know much. All I know is that he wanted to end the human race and bring his demons to earth, fucking up everyone and everything. Any of this ringing a bell?"

"The end of the world," Nao nodded.

"For humans, yeah," Diamond nodded. Demons weren't affected in the last. Humans were the ones to fall. And, so were the Heavenly Beings. Other than that, they were good.

"What will you do if Derek's plan succeeds and everything is destroyed? Where will you go?"

Diamond leaned her head against the wall behind her and sighed. It was a good question. Would there be anywhere to go? Derek would control a majority of the ravished earth so there would be nowhere to hide; nowhere to call home. She was tired of calling Derek's arms her home and calling Derek's bedroom hers. She might have been given his last name but that was all they shared.

Diamond didn't know what she would do. Somehow, she knew she would soon find the answer.

She answered Nao's question, saying, "Anywhere but here."

Story 10

Such a *windy* situation

Kenta thanked the gods. He thanked Daisuke, the angel of healing, the angels in general and most definitely the Mother Angel. His girls were alright. They were shocked and Reiko was now in the hands of the enemy, but by Saki, Mary was all right.

A bullet had entered her side while she was trying to catch up with Hiroko and Sazuma. Terror and rage coursed through Kenta the moment the bullet lodged itself into Mary's left side. He had caught her and hoped the bullet hadn't hit any major organs. It had barely missed her intestines. She wouldn't know that though. All she knew was pain. Kenta cursed. He would never wish such a thing for her.

Mary's injury wasn't the worst of it. Ayano had been shot as well. Hiroko had been stabbed in the leg with a single throwing star. Stella dodged a bullet but almost fell in Sazuma's fire blockade. If it wasn't for Yumiko, the young redhead would have burned. Only Sazuma and Yumiko were uninjured, although their worry for Reiko's safety grew with every passing second.

They would get her back, he vowed, but Ayano had protested to the group going after her. "We need backup," she'd said. Kenta knew exactly who she was suggesting.

"We need to heal the girls before we make any moves." Kenta had teleported the girls to Ayano's apartment, thinking that was the safest way to go.

His teacher mode activated as he instructed Yumiko how to summon her healing abilities. As the light princess, she had the ability to heal injuries without suffering the injury of those she healed. As he suspected, Yumiko was shocked she even possessed such an ability. Her hands shined a dazzling auburn as she hovered her hands over Hiroko's thigh wound. It slowly healed, surprising both girls.

While they healed, he traveled with Ayano around the corner to discuss private business; business he already knew he would hate.

"These girls aren't ready to face the Demon Docks," she said. Kenta knew that. "They can barely handle an attack," Kenta knew that, too. "Much less go to the headquarters of the demons they're supposed to destroy." He knew that very well.

"That doesn't mean I want *his* help." He wasn't stooping as low as to ask that revolting Spirit Being for backup.

Her arms crossed over her chest. "You can't hate Damon forever."

Yes, he could.

"The least you could do is give him a chance. He's a healer. He's an excellent tracker. He's far more skilled than you are."

He glared at her.

She ignored it. "Reiko is out there. We know where she is and we can get her back but we cannot do this without him. Please get over the insecurity that you rarely have and open your eyes. We need him."

She was right, but saying, "We want him," made him feel a little better. With reluctance, Kenta agreed. As soon as the girls were healed, and Kenta knew a hundred percent that they could continue, they headed out in the Saturday afternoon, following Ayano as she led the way to Damon's location.

Ayano was a tracker herself, able to sense people through the air instead of sensing spirit trails like other Heavenly Beings could. She's like the princess with heightened hearing, smell and reflexes. She is a vital ally to have.

The group headed down several sidewalks, passing the array of shops and the mall in the center of town. They headed further out of town, heading to an area he'd seen before. The lush forest was, oh, too similar and a floral scent breezed in the air, filling the area with peace.

A dirt path led them down further into the abandoned area. When Kenta found broken tree branches, splintered trunks and blood stains, he knew exactly where they were going. The wooden sign with large white letters confirmed his suspicions. They were headed to Valla Park.

It was once a battlefield with Chikara Yamada on one side and Kenta and the princesses on the other. He remembered the battle well. He had almost lost his friends, just as he did today. He lowered his head. Maybe they weren't ready for this world.

"So who is this *"he"* Kenta keeps moping about?" Sazuma asked. She walked in the center of the group; Kenta again acting as the caboose. Mary was by his side. She hadn't said a word since being healed and taking this two hour journey.

"We're visiting Damon," Ayano answered.

"That silver-haired guy at Yumiko's house?" Stella asked. Ayano nodded.

"So why the mopes?" Sazuma asked, glaring at him over her shoulder. Why so curious?

"Kenta doesn't like Damon very much. Something happened in Heaven. I don't know what, but it seemed to affect Mr. Grouchy Pants in the back." Ayano thumbed at him. And, when had she used such a charming word as "Grouchy Pants"?

"Jealous?" Yumiko wondered.

"Never," Kenta grouched. Mary cracked up a giggle. All grouchiness was abandoned. He didn't turn to her though. He strangely didn't have the courage to.

Because you allowed her to be shot. His mind raged at him. He was right. If he hated anyone, it was himself. He watched as the bullet hit Mary's side. He should have been in that spot, taking the bullet instead of her. He should have known better. Obviously, he didn't.

"You must not like Damon a lot. You're moping immensely." Hiroko had said that to him. She too peered over her shoulder. All attention except Ayano's went to him. Even Mary was looking at him, which made his heart race dangerously. Just her eyes on him caused his blood to rush through his veins and his eyes to wander anywhere else except for where she was. Was it so hard to act casual around her? Yes, it was.

"It's just been a tiring day," he lied.

"The day didn't even start yet," Ayano said, enlightenment in her tone.

She might have been right. Unfortunately, this morning's attack snatched whatever energy Kenta had. He'd been ready to step into the training when Ayano was finished with them, but no. The whole afternoon had been screwed up. Demons always had to ruin everything.

"You guys go ahead. I have to talk to Kenta for a moment." All eyes turned to Mary. Kenta's heart skipped a beat, and not in a good way. He was going to be alone with her. Everyone would be out of hearing distance, leaving him to defend for himself.

And what was the problem with that? He would be alone with the girl he'd come to like. She was beautiful, fearless, and strong. Kenta had seen the way she completed her pushups back in Lune Park. The girl must have had muscles hidden behind her clothing. Being with someone so beautiful should have been an honor. And it was, but . . .

The problem was, Kenta almost lost this precious girl. No, young woman. Mary was no mere girl. The fact that she was an Element Princess made her special. Compared to the others though, she had to be the strongest princess he'd ever met; excluding Ayano of course. Hiroko had been similar to how Mary was now. However, Mary held so much vibrancy, veracity and love.

How could you allow someone so special to suffer a critical injury?

He couldn't be alone with her. It would do him more harm than good.

"We can chat later. We have to meet Damon." Kenta continued forward. He stopped the moment Mary latched her hand on his bicep and glared up at him.

"Stay." So dynamic. So demanding. Why did he find that sexy?

Kenta stayed put, staring down at her in surprise. He knew Mary was tough, but he didn't know she could be forceful. He should have known. What was wrong with him? His ability to sense people's emotions and inner doings was dissipating.

Knowing her sister better than anyone, Sazuma pushed everyone forward, rushing them further into the forest and head to their destination. If Mary was getting demanding, that must have meant she was getting serious. Did Sazuma have to rush them away with urgency, though? He wouldn't have minded if they stayed a bit longer.

Mary faced him, looking up and peering into his eyes. Her onyx eyes swirled from demand to concern. Her hold on his bicep remained. Her grip loosened. "Now tell me what's wrong."

His eyes turned from hers. "Nothing." What was there to say? *I'm sorry would be nice,* his mind mentally slapped him; a slap he deserved, both mentally and physically.

"I hate liars, Mr. Shiroyama." Her hands turned into fists and they hooked to her hips.

Personally, he liked his new nickname. "Mr. Shiroyama" might have been the polite way to say his name, but when Mary said it, it was considered an endearment. "I'm not lying, Ms. Kagami. I'm saying it's nothing for you to worry about."

"Whatever is going on through your head most likely will affect us later. We don't need any distractions."

She was right. If he let his fears of being unable to protect his team get in the way during battle, the number of injuries would increase because of the sheer fact he wanted to prevent those injuries. Life always happened that way.

Might as well confess, "The demons injured you and it bothers me that I couldn't prevent your damage."

Mary nodded, "I figured as much." She figured? Was it that obvious? She released his arm and grinned at him. "One injury won't take us down. Trust me, the wounds hurt but they're nothing compared to the pain you've been through."

Kenta had been injured plenty of times. They hadn't been severe. His wounds were nothing, she and Kenta knew that . . . so . . .

"I might have endured many weapon wounds. I'd rather suffer your pain than my own."

She shook her head. "I don't mean your physical pain," she placed her palm to his chest, right above his heart, "I mean your emotional pain."

The killings of the past, Kenta realized. His heart swelled. She still believed he held the pain and harsh thoughts of the princesses of the past. She believed he suffered every day for the pain and confusion he caused so many families.

Mary was right, yet again.

Kenta did blame himself. He was the murderer; the last thing those girls saw before their orbs were sucked out of their bodies along with their life force—their very souls. Ayano had only to hold the girls down while Kenta slipped his hand into their bodies and watch them slowly pale and eventually cease moving. She hadn't once shed blood but she was just as responsible as he was. Scarred for eternity, they were. Kenta held the most damage. He made sure of that.

It was damage he hoped he would never again endure.

He gently placed his hand on Mary's, pulled it up, and gracefully pressed his lips on her wrist, right where her veins pulsed. "I'm alright. There's no need to worry."

Her cheeks flushed bubblegum pink as she exhaled a wobbly breath. Her eyes went from Kenta's lips, to his eyes. "For how long?" she asked, reveling in him, ensuring what he said was true.

He pushed a lock of black hair behind her ear and kept his palm in her heated cheek. She leaned into him, wanting more. He couldn't turn her away. He answered her, saying, "As long as I'm with you."

Her cheeks heated further as she closed her eyes and absorbed his words. It took a minute for him to realize what he'd said. He had said something so promising, telling her he would forever be fine as long as she was well. He had meant it. There was no point in holding anything back. He knew that now.

Before he continued this moment further, allowing himself to stare at her, picture every pore movement, and blush on her face, Kenta pulled away completely, keeping his hands to his side.

Mary moaned, which surprised him. It was a moan of longing, wanting more, but could not receive. Oh, how he would give her anything right now. He silently sighed. If he did, he wouldn't be able to stop. He didn't want to take things too far, and this most definitely would take their relationship to the next level.

It was too soon. Far too soon.

Right now, they had to focus on getting Reiko back. Kenta nodded, keeping that as his main focus. With a gentle push, he moved Mary forward. She grinned over her shoulder then faced the front, heading down the dirt path the others had disappeared on.

It didn't take long for their déjà vu to arrive as the center of the park's scenery came into place. There was the large pond consumed with lily pads along with the stoned waterfall. The water bypassed three rock layers and emptied into the pond. Several frogs lazed upon the pads, rotating around and around at their own pace.

Kenta approached the area. His friends had waited before entering entirely.

"About time," Sazuma said. Her hands were stuffed in her gray sweatshirt pockets. Her eyes narrowed on Mary, checking for something.

"We didn't want to proceed without you," Yumiko admitted. Kenta was grateful. At least someone cared. Knowing Ayano, she would have handled the business without him.

Then again, in situations like this, Kenta might have preferred Ayano handled this business alone. That's probably why she waited, Kenta thought next. Made sense. She was such a conundrum.

Kenta made his way past the group. Ayano hit his left side while Mary hit his right. The remaining princesses followed inside, entering the enlarged moist landed area. Standing at the ledges of the pond was indeed Damon. His silver jacketed back faced the group. His weight swung to his right side. A woman stood at his left side, standing to his shoulder and wearing nothing but a black bodysuit with pink ruffles around the waist.

Without a word, Damon turned to them, giving the group his shoulder. The woman did the same. Their eyes—one pair of lightning hazels and the other pair dazzling violet—were unreadable. One thing was for sure, Kenta was not going to like this conversation.

Out of nowhere, the woman gasped. Her fierce expression changed drastically as she pointed her finger in Hiroko's direction.

"That's her! That's the girl from your picture Damon." Her voice was high pitched, child-like. Her long navy blue hair swung as she turned from Damon to Hiroko and repeated several times. "I know that's her." She kept her stare at Damon this time. "You know I'm right."

He passively waved his hand, silencing her. He turned to the group fully with a playful grin. "I honestly didn't think you'd come, Shiroyama."

All wonder of the woman's actions faded. "We have a friend to save. I'll take whatever drastic measures it takes to get her back."

He nodded, "Now you're getting the purpose of being a Heavenly Being. Tell me, how's being a Spirit Being doing for you? Getting your share of women?"

Kenta gritted his teeth. He *would* bring women into a conversation like this. Damon is lecherous, vile and not even worth Kenta's time. But Damon was needed. He would have to deal with it. "There's no time for stupid questions. You know why we're here."

Damon glided his hands through his thick mass of hair. He looked off into the distance, "Yeah. I sensed Destiny somewhere in town with her minions. Your ice girl is gone, right?"

Ayano's eyes narrowed, "You knew we were in danger and you did nothing to assist us?"

"I figured you could handle it. I only sensed them in town. I didn't know how many there were until they left."

"You still could have investigated." If Ayano was angry with him, then her trust in Damon was fading. Was this a good or bad thing?

"Damon," Hiroko pushed past the group, standing between Mary and Kenta now. Her arms crossed over her middle. Her eyes focused on him. Her shoulders shook a bit. There wasn't a breeze. It was fairly warm. How could she have been cold? "Your name is Damon, right?"

"That I am," all sense of playfulness vanished. He zeroed in on her as well. It was a change Kenta did not see coming.

"That *is* her," the woman gasped again. "Wow, she really aged."

Hiroko turned to the woman, "Why am I so special? How do you know me?"

"Ignore her. Focus on me." Still so serious. "I know my name wasn't all that you wanted to ask me."

"I wasn't going to ask you a question. We need your help and you're going to give it to us." Bold, Hiroko was.

Damon grinned. His playfulness was still absent. "Am I now?"

"Yeah, you are." She was still shivering. Her tone was bold and her chin arched confidently. She meant business.

"Help us get Reiko back. We know you know how. You've been in our enemy's headquarters many times before, am I right?" There were times in the past, back in Heaven, where Saki sent Damon into enemy territory to observe the demons way of life. Damon had been one of those to enter the enemy lines and make it out alive.

"I've been inside. What makes you think I'll help you?"

"Damon," the navy blue-haired woman scolded.

He continued, ignoring the woman, "One of you hates me, the others know me but don't have faith in me and one of you actually demanded that I help." "What are you? A sissy?" Hiroko unwrapped her arms and brought her hands to her hips. "You're supposed to be some amazing Spirit Being. Your abilities should be more advanced than Kenta's will ever be . . ." That hurt . . . "so how come you're whining about your lack of authority?"

Damon disappeared a second later. He was in Hiroko's face the next second, grabbing her shoulders and putting them chest to chest, nose to nose. Her shivering shoulders ceased as her eyes locked with Damon's.

Sazuma rushed forward. Damon stopped her, seeing Sazuma through his peripherals.

"Damon," Kenta warned. If he did anything to her . . .

"Shut up," he snarled, and it was a deadly sound. "You have a lot of nerve, you know that." All attention went to the woman in his face.

She was determined, fearless, willing even. It was as if a living breathing, thousand-year-old Spirit Being had not frightened her. "Someone has to stand up to you. Otherwise, we'd be your little peons and I'm not having it."

Seconds passed in silence. Kenta and the princesses watched cautiously, incase Damon decided to make any further movements; movements that would be fatal to Hiroko. She just healed from her thigh injury. She, and Kenta, didn't need any more physical blows.

Damon waved his fingers on Hiroko's shoulders. His grin returned as he released and backed away from her. His hands moved to his ripped navy blue jeaned pockets. His hazel eyes lingered from Hiroko to the group. "I like this one."

"We like her, too, so don't touch her." Sazuma glared. She was obviously the protector of the group. Nevertheless, wasn't that Kenta's job?

You're just the teacher. He reminded himself. Yeah, just the teacher.

The hazel-eyed Spirit Being shrugged, all innocence, "I like her, that doesn't mean I want her." Hiroko glared at that. He went on, "You want my help, you got it."

All it took was a mental teaser and being in close proximity of a beautiful young woman. Kenta rolled his eyes. Would Damon ever change for the better? Probably not, he thought a second later.

"So what's your plan of action?" he asked. When no one answered, turning to one another, Damon sighed, "Right, you came to me to be the rescue man."

"You're our tracker. Nothing more," Kenta said.

"You could respect Damon a little better," the woman grouched. She approached Damon and wrapped her arm around his, pressing her small breasts into his bicep.

"Okay, who are you?" Ayano asked, her patience wearing thin.

Damon pointed to the woman with a tilt of his head. "This is Aurora; a Spirit Being. She's a partner of mine. Don't mind her though. Your focus is with me."

"Aurora, the goddess of the dawn?" Mary's expression brightened with curiosity. Aurora looked at her in question. "I read about the goddess of the dawn, the one who rides across the sky announcing the sun's arrival. Your siblings are Sol and Luna, right?"

"She's not that special," Damon said, as if she really wasn't special at all. "That's just her name. Aurora."

"I'm glad we're making new friends and all but seriously, we need to get down to business and get Reiko back," Sazuma stepped up, approaching Damon full force. His eyes watched her approach. As she did, he fanned himself and blew out a breath.

"You're on fire, princess. Might want to turn the heat down before you really burn something."

"Your face looks like a good volunteer to be burned," she growled. The tension was immense. She was right, however. It seemed like everyone was right, or Kenta was always wrong.

"We need the location to the Demon Dock's headquarters," Ayano said, stepping up to Damon was well. Soon, the entire group surrounded him, only allowing his back to breathe.

The hazel-eyed Spirit Being rose one of his black eyebrows. "If I'm not mistaken, shouldn't you princesses be able to sense each other no matter the distance?"

"Yes, except range and longitude count in these cases," Ayano answered, "Plus, we never been to the headquarters so we can't teleport there." Spirit Beings and the Darkness Element Princess have the ability to teleport from one location to the other with a single thought. The problem is, they cannot teleport to places they'd never been before. They had to do this the hard way.

"How long have the princesses gained their powers?"

"It depends which princess you're talking about," Kenta said. He remembered each princess's orb giving's vividly. Damon was going to have to be specific.

"You mean these girls don't have a single clue on what they're doing? Do they even know how to defend themselves without a weapon?" Aurora had stared at the princesses with pity, as if they were a waste of time and space.

She didn't look at Ayano that way though. She had been glaring at her for a while now, watching her every move.

Damon slid a hand down his suddenly irritated face. "You all are hopeless." "That's why we came to you, Mr. Damon." Stella said. He turned to her with a grin. He bent his knees and elegantly bowed down to her. Hiroko's eyes narrowed on him. Kenta did the same. He had better not have been getting any ideas. Damon's mind was a constant creation bomb. Anything could, and would, explode, leaving Kenta and his team bewildered.

"You're earth right, redhead?" Stella nodded. "I like your politeness. If I'm not wrong, you have a heart of therapy." She nodded again.

"What does this have to do with anything?" Sazuma asked, her patience too wearing thin.

Damon turned to her, "Your orb descriptions help me determine which one of you I take with me to the headquarters."

Kenta's protective mode activated. "No way are my girls going in there. I will go and get Reiko."

Damon's eyebrow cocked up, "You can barely prevent one of your girls from getting kidnapped."

"That's exactly why I'll be the one to save her."

"I was supposed to be her guard. I'll go with you." The moment he heard Mary's voice, Kenta turned to her. Her eyes were on Damon, filled with willpower and courage.

"I will too," Yumiko jumped in, speaking for the first time since arriving here.

Damon's head went from Mary to Yumiko, back and forth. He pointed to Mary, "a heart of love," he pointed to Yumiko, "and a heart of growth." He went back to Mary again. "You're coming with me." He turned to Yumiko, "You stay here."

"I can go," she protested.

"You're twelve," he said dryly.

"Your point?"

"You're too young to even be involved in this mess." He turned to Kenta, "You let a child get involved with this?"

"Fate is fate," Ayano said, hurrying this conversation. "I'm going with you."

"Of course," Damon nodded.

"And what are we supposed to do?" Hiroko asked. "Wait for you?" Her tone was disbelieving, as if saying "How dare you make me wait for you?"

"You girls could spend your time training," Damon said, pulling out his hands from his pocket and cracking his fingers. "No one said you had to wait. Aurora can assist you."

Aurora said nothing. She merely nodded. Her expression screamed she was shy to help them. It surprised Kenta. He believed the girl didn't want to help them, period. Maybe there was more to Aurora than possessiveness for Damon.

"I'm not putting my sister in the front lines."

"I won't be," Mary reassured Sazuma. "I guarantee you. Damon wouldn't allow me to even encounter a demon."

"I wouldn't allow it either," Kenta said, and he meant his word. If any demons harmed Mary, or even had the nerve to face her direction, those demons would be annihilated by his hand, and his hand alone.

Damon smiled, "So you're coming too, kiddy Kenta?"

Kiddy Kenta? Oh hell no. He is not keeping that name.

"Of course, he's coming." Mary rubbed his arm. They faced each other again, her eyes glowed with reassurance. "I wouldn't be able to function without him."

Just hearing that brightened Kenta's day, his evening, his week, maybe. It is one thing to say he is needed. It is another thing when someone cannot function without you. Maybe that's how he felt about his girls. They were separating, causing his ability to recognize their emotions and thought process to lack. That made more sense than anything right now.

"Alright fine, come along. But don't get in my way. I won't be coming after you."

"Likewise," Kenta's eyes narrowed, promising Damon's claim.

"None of you are going anywhere." A feminine voice coursed through the atmosphere, surprising everyone but Damon. The decadent scent of holly berry swirled through just as a breeze entered the scene. Kenta's hair played with the wind. His senses were sharp, alert.

Damon merely grinned, which pissed Kenta off greatly. Was this a trap? Was there an ally of his whom just now decided to make its appearance and attack them? He knew Damon couldn't be trusted. If he called in someone to get rid of them, Damon would forever be the lowest of the low.

The scent blew in stronger, stronger still. The breeze kicked into a vast wind, swishing everyone's clothing and hair. All heads turned left and right. All noses stuffed in air, trying to find its origin. There was nothing. Damon's eyes touched the moist dirt and remained there for several moments.

As suddenly as it came, the wind came to an abrupt stop. The scent remained.

Aurora jumped a bit, puffing up a gasp.

"Hello there, Kenta."

Kenta threw his focus behind him. He stepped back with alarm, pulling Mary with him. He blinked, making sure he was really seeing this. A woman floated right where his head had been. Her arms stretched out wide. One leg was partially bent while her other leg held her leg up so high, her calf touching her butt. She wore a cloud white Komon Tsumugi; a type of kimono worn for casual wear. One side was long while the other cut off at her thigh, revealing black heeled boots that buttoned on the sides and black leggings reaching her thigh.

Her skin was pale white, with the slightest bit of freckles on her nose and cheeks. Her hair was long, reaching below her butt even when her white hair hung high in a blue bowed ponytail. Her eyes shined silver; swirling with liveliness.

He had seen this woman before.

His eyes squinted. It couldn't be. "Jezebel?"

She slowly smiled, revealing whites of the shiniest pearls. Her radiance caused Kenta to even go blind for mere seconds. "I'm surprised you remembered me."

"I'm surprised I can even see you," he joked, all form of startle and cautiousness left.

Just seeing her again made Kenta smile. He and Jezebel had communicated in the past. She had been the female friend Kenta always craved. Before Ayano, Kenta was alone. He could confide in no one. Sure, the angels of Heaven were kind, welcoming, and loving. To Kenta, Jezebel was different. She took risks, she took chances, and she hadn't cared what her fellow angels thought. She had a free spirit and Kenta loved that about her.

He had told her about Saki wanting him to travel to Earth to search for the princesses. He expected Jezebel to cling to him and beg for him not to leave. She had done the exact opposite. She had patted his shoulder and blessed him with a hearty farewell. They hugged, kissed each other's cheeks, then Kenta was off, never to see her again . . . until now.

She hadn't aged a day. She was still full of life, still bright with action and still looking at him with companionship. She always looked at him this way. The feeling would never abscond. And Kenta was glad for that.

Jezebel floated down with a squeal and landed in Kenta's arms, wrapping her legs around his waist and her arms around his neck. The scent of holly berries had come from her, for they inked themselves into his nose, insuring that every time he smelled the fragrance, he would be reminded of her.

He hugged her back with a smile. He had his friend back. It had been too long. Like usual, her hug was strong, taking the breath out of your lungs. Her beauty already took your breath away, but when she hugged you, whatever breath you had left, she took. Jezebel was too amazing.

"Hey you two. Let's not get frisky." Damon approached them.

Jezebel slipped out of Kenta's grip with a giggle. "Sorry about that." She wrapped her arm around his waist, "You know I couldn't continue this conversation until I hugged my friend. He's my favorite Spirit Being."

Damon patted his chest, just above his heart. He pouted, "I'm so hurt. How could you pick him over me?"

She grinned, "Because he's not a woman-crazed, single-minded pervert like you. You might have lived longer, but it's the committed and respectable guys that the ladies love."

Damon shrugged, his pout gone in an instant.

Jezebel turned to Kenta and clutched his cheeks. She was least two inches taller than him. Back then they were the same height. He hoped *she* had gotten taller. He couldn't deal with the fact that *he* was shrinking. "Look at you," she smiled like a proud mother, "You've really grown. It's been, what, ten years?" Her hands slid down his broad shoulders, to his wrists. "You're so buff."

Ten years of searching for teenage girls could do that to you. He praised himself. Buff was nice. "Thanks," he smiled.

She brought her hands to her side and looked to each and every member in the area. "Hiya," she smiled with a bounce.

"Whoa," Stella said. She was hiding behind Ayano, peeking from her right side. Yumiko was the same way, except she peeked on Ayano's left side. They were probably getting over the fact that an unknown woman appeared out of nowhere.

"You're Jezebel?" Mary asked, disbelieving.

Jezebel turned to her. Her hand came to her hips confidently and she pushed to her toes and came back down. "Yup, that's me."

Mary's stunned expression went to straight excited. "Wow, you're really Jezebel. I read about you. You were once a princess. You were the daughter of the Hebrew king Ethbaal, right?"

Although shocked by the sudden informational question, Jezebel continued to grin. "I don't know about that. I *have* been around the world, speaking different languages and even encountering several physics and mediums. That was fun."

Even when faced in a weird situation, Jezebel was unaffected. It always seemed like nothing surprised this girl. She had lived for years, based on what she'd told him. Probably nothing *did* surprise her.

"Welcome to Earth, Jezebel," Aurora greeted.

The angel gave a thumbs up. "Thank you, thank you."

"Let's get down to business shall we," Damon said. "First off, you guys need to stop gaping."

Kenta now noticed Sazuma, Mary, Hiroko and even Ayano were gaping at the gorgeous angel. He knew they had never seen anyone so stunning and vivacious. Stella and Yumiko still hid behind Ayano. Stella and Yumiko continued to gape behind Ayano. The nineteen-year-old princess didn't even seem to mind two girls hiding at the back of her.

These girls had better prepare themselves. Heaven had many surprises in store for them, both power and people wise.

The girls' focus returned after Damon's comment. Yumiko took several steps outward, appearing more into view. Half of her body hid behind Ayano, still. Getting used to Jezebel would take a little time.

"So what's this business about us not going anywhere?" Kenta asked. He remembered Jezebel's entrance statement. She must have forgotten, as well, because she snapped her fingers in remembrance.

"That's right." Her tone lowered. It was still lively, "You guys aren't going anywhere. The less people going to the castle, the better."

"But we're going to need backup," Mary said. Her focus on Jezebel was no longer based on her past, but for the upcoming demonic conflict.

"No," Jezebel corrected, "*They're* going to need backup. That's why Damon summoned me."

Kenta peered over his shoulder. "You knew we would come to you?"

He shrugged, "You're too predictable."

That bugged Kenta a bit. To be predictable was to be vulnerable. Vulnerability was to be averted. He didn't need that on his already overflowing plate. Dealing with Damon already took up most of his plate.

"I have no problem with assisting you all. Besides, I can be very helpful."

"Yes I know." Whenever he needed assistance, Jezebel was always there to answer the call. Kenta might have needed help from the simplest things like watching humans intently, to learning how to flash from one place to another. Jezebel had been his teacher, his friend. She was powerful too. He had never seen or heard of Jezebel's "special abilities," as she liked to call them. But he knew she held power. It radiated from her, probably mixing with her already beautiful face.

She is the Element Angel of the Wind, after all.

"How long will you be gone when you leave?" Mary's voice held concern. Kenta was grateful. It was an honor to have her concerned about him. Just moments ago, she had eased his worries about protecting them. She was such a loving girl. She deserved to have the title as the Water Princess.

"That depends on how fast we find Reiko and how smooth we are at leaving the place," Damon answered. "The Docks mansion is vast. There are thousands of rooms and Reiko could be in any one of those rooms."

"I'll track her down," Jezebel volunteered, a hand raised in the air in a swinging motion.

Damon nodded, "Yeah I know." As the angel of the wind, Jezebel could track people based on their voice vibrations, tone and breathing patterns. Kenta was beginning to see why Damon summoned her. "Knowing Derek—his cocky ass, he'll probably want Reiko by his side or in the hands of someone he trusts."

"She'll probably be with one of the Demonic Princesses or Princes." Kenta finished for him. His strategizing side released. "Derek might know we're planning a rescue, so sticking her in his room might not be a good idea." He had to think like a Demon Lord. If he were a Demon Lord with his enemy right in his grasp, what would he do with her? Not anything sexual, that's for sure.

"Let's split up," Damon suggested. "I'll go after the princesses while you handle the princes."

"Going for the women again, huh?" Kenta wasn't surprised in the least.

"I'm not going to stoop so low as to date a demon."

"But you would bed one, right?" Jezebel's eyebrow rose along with her grin.

Damon rolled his eyes but, he too, grinned.

All jokes aside . . . "We have a plan. We have a mission. Let's do this."

Damon and Jezebel nodded in union, their expression glowing of anticipation.

"But Damon," Aurora pouted. She was so concerned for him it was actually touching.

He patted her head and ruffled her navy blue hair. "Watch these princesses. Don't wait up for me."

"I can't sleep anyway," she stuck her tongue out at him. He knew Spirit Beings never slept. Why that was so, Kenta didn't know.

Kenta faced Ayano. Both Yumiko and Stella had come out of their hiding places. The princesses came together, huddling around Kenta, leaving his back exposed. Damon, Jezebel, and Aurora moved out of the circle. Kenta heard little murmurs of conversation about Damon's new hairstyle and the woman now traveling along with him.

"You better make it back with Reiko," Sazuma said. If that was supposed to wish him good luck, it strangely did.

Kenta took it with a nod, "I will."

"Happy travels." Stella.

"Kick butt like a ninja." Yumiko.

"Don't let Damon affect you," Hiroko said. She had no idea how much Kenta would keep that in mind.

"I won't, trust me."

"I'll keep an eye on these guys. I'll train them until I see the slightest bit of muscle on their wimpy bodies." All eyes went to Ayano.

"You're going to kill us, aren't you?" Sazuma asked in knowing.

"It's only right that I do," Ayano winked.

Kenta nodded with a grin. He knew these ladies would be fine. They were different from the princesses of the past. They were stronger, wiser, and diverse. The fact that they hadn't ran to him, asking to take back the orbs, showed that these were the princesses he'd been looking for. He was missing one member and he intended to get her back. This wasn't his entire team. He was positive he would make it whole again.

"Good luck warrior," Mary grinned. She punched his shoulder playfully.

His expression softened. He pushed a strand of hair behind her ear. His hand came down slowly, caressing her cheek. She even leaned into the touch. Her eyes closed for brief moments and opened the moment contact severed. "Thank you, Mary."

"Kenta has a girlfriend? What!" Jezebel's cheery voice hyped up a notch. Mary turned her head away.

"Let's get going," he said, just as he saluted to his girls. And yes, they were his girls.

"You didn't deny it!" Jezebel pointed and jumped up and down.

He hadn't denied it, had he? Oh well. He wasn't going to.

Kenta, Damon and Jezebel took several steps away from the group of girls near the entrance of the park. They watched as the descendants came together, preparing to head to their destination. Because Damon had been to the Docks headquarters before, he was able to teleport there. Contact would have to be made in order for him to teleport with him, which he did not look forward to.

Stella yelled, "Don't talk to any demon you don't know."

So, don't talk to anyone. No problem.

"Please stay safe," Yumiko yelled.

Come on. It wasn't like this was a forever goodbye.

If Kenta wasn't careful, this might have actually been a forever farewell.

Damon wrapped his arm around Jezebel's waist. She wrapped her arm around his neck and gripped his shirt, ensuring her personal teleporting safety. Nothing could go wrong with teleporting, right? Wrong. You didn't know where you were being teleported to and you didn't know how many people, in this case, demons, you would encounter once you arrived.

Teleporting was an issue at times. It is an amazing gift to have though. Ayano had once said those words. How would the other girls feel about having such an amazing ability? Damn it, he missed his girls already.

Mary, his favorite girl, watched idly. Her arms wrapped around her middle, her head slightly tilted to the side and her lips spread into a sad smile. Her long black hair swayed to the side amorously. Her black eyes watched his every move, she hadn't turned away one bit.

Kenta winked at her, promising his and his comrade's return.

She smiled, brightening the scenery. She was as beautiful as Jezebel; probably even lovelier than his angelic friend.

"Let's do this," Damon said, unable to hold his need for action much longer.

Kenta grabbed his arm, not wanting Damon's arm around his waist. That wasn't happening, at all. In one moment, he was witnessing his girls, watching as Stella and Yumiko waved, Sazuma watched, Hiroko grinned, Ayano rubbing Stella's head and Mary smiling. Aurora had even said her goodbyes.

Now, Kenta saw darkness. Or, at least, darkness mostly surrounded him. They were in a narrow hallway, barely able to hold two people in a single hall. Metal torches with fire sparked, acting as their only light. The torches were carried on the walls, a copper holder acting as their support. They continued down both sides of the hall, entering other areas and other halls. Dirt walls flanked them left, right and below. The ceiling held solid stone.

An exhale from Damon calmed Kenta down only a little bit. The scent of holly berries whiffed the air, proving Jezebel was here as well. They had made it, but where in the mansion were they located?

"Welcome to the Demon Docks mansion," Damon muttered.

Miles away in the mountains near Kayta Plains, millions of trees rooted to the expansive land. The environment chirped with birds, branches cracked from surrounding wildlife, and pitter patters of footsteps tapped as insects grabbed their food and retreated home.

None of these animals bothered the strongest animal in this desolate place.

There was a creature who ruled these mountains...well, she self-proclaimed these mountains. But there was no doubt; she was stronger than all of these animals combined. Everything ran away from her. No, not ran, scattered, as if in one false move, then they were dead for sure.

These animals were smart, because they were right.

Akira would have murdered them. She had to eat, after all.

All thoughts about survival and environmental fear vanished.

The Wolf Demon, Akira Suzuki, noticed the sudden wind change.

Power...liveliness...and holly berry. There was an angel in the area.

Another whiff of air grasped her nostrils. Man...power...determination. There was a Spirit Being as well; two of them, she realized.

That wasn't it. There was something else. Femininity...bravery...and...

"Ayano," Akira grinned. Ayano was in town, in this town. The Spirit Being must have been Kenta. One did not travel without the other.

Right then and there, a visit was in order. Akira had only arrived here at the beginning of the week. She had resided in the trees, pouncing and devouring her prey when necessary. If she had known her old friend resided here, as well, she would have made her appearance days ago.

How come she just sniffed her out now? Had she just arrived?

Questions would be asked later. Right now, visit time. Akira leaped off of the branch she rested on, flying past more branches and leaves. She landed on the ground with a stomp, her brown steel-toed boots indenting the ground.

Her orchid-haired, single-braided ponytail flew side to side as she stood straight to her full six-foot-five height.

In a mad dash, she zoomed off, following Ayano's addictive raspberry scent. She zapped past thick oak trees and became nothing but a dark shadow making its way through the mountain and into Kayta Plains.

Her mind flew as fast as her dash. Only one thought dwelled in her mind, "What adventure lies before me now?"

Soon, she would find out.

Story 11

The *howls* of friendship

She was a pretty one, this Ice Princess, Reiko Takashima.
Her glare was icy all itself. She hadn't moved since being brought to Riku's room. Destiny had chained her to Riku's bed. She hadn't even protested as she was dropped onto the bed and connected to the dark wood headboard. Even when Destiny left, leaving her and Riku alone, Reiko had not moved. She only stared, her hazel eyes showing no mercy.
Appearance wise, he liked her since he noticed her in Derek's throne room. She hadn't moved then, either. Destiny had been in control of her, so it made sense. Even now, she wasn't doing anything but blinking and breathing. Riku wished she did more though. This was the first time he'd seen a girl like this. One so pretty, it actually hurt to look at her.
Riku moved from his dark wood dresser on one side of his tan-painted room to the bed in the center of the room. His gray sweatpants scuffed into each other as his thighs rubbed together. He placed himself near the foot of the bed, Reiko on the other side. Her arms were on her sides, silver handcuffs acting as her holders. Her legs were brought to her body. She sat on Riku's beige pillowcases. His beige sheeted and tan blanketed bed worked wonders. She looked good on his bed. Her black, icy blue streaked hair splashed over her shoulders. Her bangs acted as curtains over her eyes. Her eyes peered through, watching Riku's every move.
He pulled down his long black long-sleeved shirt. The temperature had plummeted the moment she entered the room. Riku even swore he saw his own breath when he exhaled.
He grinned, unaffected by her. Or, at least, he tried acting like it. "You're mine, girl. You got that?"
No reaction. Just a stare. Fine, she wanted this the hard way. He never offered her the easy way, but this would make things more fun.
He pushed himself up, bringing himself a little closer to her. Still, no reaction. "Derek gave you to me. I can do whatever I want to you." His eyes

raked her up and down. He should have looked at her as if she was nothing but a delicious lollipop ready to be sucked on. He didn't see her that way. Why the hell not? "You're so damn fine."

He brought himself closer, crawling to her this time. Still nothing! What did it take for her to respond to him? He guessed physical touching would cause her to speak, or at least flinch.

"I like you princess. You're real nice."

Nothing! Okay, this was frustrating. How was he going to take her if he couldn't get a reaction out of her?

He approached her fully. They were nose to nose. She smelled of frosted mandarins and vanilla, mixing together in a combination he had never smelled before. It was a scent he hadn't expected. He added this to a list of things that surprised him about her. His list was growing.

Up close, her eyes were dazzling. Her skin was pale, but pinched with pink, as if flushed. She wasn't peach colored, she had a skin color all her own.

"Can't you say something? Anything?"

Obviously not. She just stared.

"Damn you're annoying."

Reiko inhaled one moment and spit something out of her mouth in the next. He shouted. Sizzling pain shot through Riku's cheek. He pushed himself off of the bed, hand going to his cheek and rubbing on a slick, chilling surface. He grabbed the unknown object, pulling his fingers away several times—it was so cold—then finally grabbed just enough to pull it out and place it on his palm.

It was a crystal, he realized. It was a small diamond shaped crystal with grooves on every side of it. The ends were razor sharp. One side was clear while the other was covered in his blood.

Ever so slowly, Riku faced her.

She was grinning ear to ear.

That was her plan, huh? Smart, he had to admit. He didn't see that coming. She proved how smart he had to be next time he approached her. She could do more than spit out ice crystals, he knew.

At least she had reacted to him. Maybe he had a chance to do . . . what? He didn't know. All he'd wanted was for her to react to him. Now that he had that, he had to think of a next goal.

"Very cute," his teeth rubbed together.

She blew her bangs up, pushing them out of her face. She still grinned. She was lovely, even if her grin was devious.

He shook his head. She was not lovely! She was a damn prize. That's all she was.

"You have a lot of nerve attacking me like that." That was nothing compared to what she could do, Riku knew, "If I were you, I would listen to my master."

"That's why you're Derek's bitch." She spat with disgust.

Finally, she talked! She even spat at him. This was a miracle. It had to be.

But, her voice. It was high pitched, as if she was a person who would shout to the world that she broke her nail. She was a screamer. A downright, break your eardrum screamer and Riku was looking forward to . . . wait. Did she just call him Derek's bitch?

He stalked to her. She didn't move again. She stared with a grin. He got in her face, making them nose to nose . . . again. "I am no one's bitch."

"And yet you're doing everything he says. You don't have any freedom do you? You never have, have you?"

What did that have to do with anything? He pulled back, giving them more distance but was still close enough to smell her fragrance; Riku's new favorite scent. "Every one of us has to start somewhere. We follow those who will lead us to higher places and power. When the earth turns to rubble, you humans will grovel at my feet. Of course," he slid his finger down her jaw. She was freezing, "you'll be my most important slave." He was keeping a special place for her. Where though, he was still figuring out.

She rolled her eyes, annoying Riku further. "So, because I'm a prisoner, that means I get my one phone call, right?"

This wasn't a human prison. "No phone calls." One call to her friends and they would be screwed. Then again, those Spirit Beings and princesses were up against a household of Foot Soldiers. They would lose for sure. They might even end up on tonight's dinner table.

Reiko sighed. It was a long sigh of annoyance. "Well, if I can't have anything then leave me alone. I don't want you staring at me."

Is that what annoyed her? Him staring?

Riku placed himself on the bed, his knees touching her feet. She pulled back as far as she could go. She sat on the beige pillows. Her back touched the headboard. Riku stared. This was her punishment for shooting the crystal into his cheek. It was a smart move; one that he didn't see coming. She would pay dearly, later. Right now, this was a good way to extract his revenge. This had to be the lamest revenge strategy he ever had. He was just glad this worked on her. Her grin morphed into a frown, filling Riku with pride.

The two stared . . . and stared . . . and stared. Did she even blink? She didn't, he noticed. This was a staring contest. Who would win? It would be Riku. He always won, end of story.

He blinked two seconds later.

Reiko grinned again. "Loser."

Okay, he was pissed, again. He didn't respond. He blinked, allowing moisture into his eyeballs.

Before he could retaliate—demand another blinking contest—a knock was heard from the door. He moved off of the bed with a bounce, landing on his feet and dragging his feet to the door. Whoever thought to interrupt him would pay.

He grabbed his hexagon shaped crystal doorknob, turned and swung it open. His shoulders dropped. His heart stopped. His lungs ceased functioning. He stood frozen.

A woman stood at his entrance; a woman he'd heard descriptions and warnings of but never thought too much about them. He'd seen pictures of her and told never to cross her path. Riku had listened but never paid attention to them for the sheer fact that he would never cross her path . . . until now.

She was exactly as she was in the pictures and descriptions. She was tall, standing six-foot-three with tanned skin. Her dirty blonde hair was longer than from the images. Before it had reached her slender shoulders, but now, her hair hung freely over those said shoulders, reaching just below her breasts. A short sleeved olive green shirt hugged her torso perfectly. The shoulders were a diamond shaped design, exposing her shoulders. White skinny jeans glued to her legs. Olive four inch heels stuck to her feet.

Her narrow light brown eyes gawped down, and gawped down hard. "Hello, little demon." Unlike Reiko, this woman's voice was on the deeper side, yet, still held femininity.

He gulped, the lump in his throat making it hard to do. At least his heart was pumping again. His lungs were gradually coming back to life. "Good . . . ," What time was it? Morning? Noon? Night? "Day. Good day, Lady Mayu."

She smiled, revealing her straight white teeth and canines that only a vampire should have. "I would like to come in, if you don't mind."

As if he released from a thousand years of standing in the same place, Riku scurried to the side and opened the door as wide as it could go. With the click of her heels, Mayu entered the room, making her way to the bed. To the princess.

Reiko was struggling. She pulled at the headboard and pushed her body away from Mayu, desperately trying to get free before she reached her. One step, two, Mayu took her time getting to the bed. The distance wasn't long. It was torturous watching as she continued to step forward. Even Riku felt tortured. Just watching Reiko struggle so much, waiting for her to approach. It was too much. Riku was rooted to the floor once again.

Why was Lady Mayu here? If she had business, she would have visited Derek or someone else. She was here for Reiko, Riku knew that much, however, it was still a shock that the Demon Queen was here in the first place. It was an honor, no, a blessing, to be in her presence alone. If she so much as said a word to you, you should have killed yourself, then and there, for being so lucky.

How long had she been here? How long was she going to say? Chaos followed wherever she traveled. In no time at all, something was going to happen to this mansion. Maybe something was going to happen to him, because she had visited him. Whatever it was, Riku was ready . . . maybe.

Mayu sat at the edge of the bed, giving Reiko enough room to squirm. And, she was squirming alright. She was still tugging and pulling on the handcuffs. Her eyes even watered. Mayu watched her. The edges of her lips quirked up. "Don't be afraid, princess. I won't hurt you." Mayu reached out. Reiko yelled. She wasn't quite screaming but she shouted with alarm.

"Go away! Get away from me."

Mayu leaned closer, pushing onto the bed and continued to reach out. The moment Mayu's violet-painted nail grasped her jaw, Reiko screamed.

Riku was right. She was a screamer. She shouted long and loud. Still struggling, still squirming. She writhed as tears slid down her cheeks. She was smart for having so much fear. She wasn't alone on that boat either. If you didn't fear Mayu, you were a damned fool.

Mayu bent her index finger, her claws for nails slicing Reiko's flesh and drawing blood. She pressed her finger pad against the wound, coating it with as much blood as possible. She pulled back, bringing the blood to her mouth. Her black tongue slipped between her red-lipstick lips and took all the blood she captured. Her finger was clear with a single lick.

She moaned, "I prefer warm flood, but you're an exception."

Was she going to . . . ? "Lady Mayu?"

She crawled onto the bed. Her legs trapped Reiko in a death grip. She straddled her waist and grabbed her head with one hand. She tilted it to the side—the side Riku could see her entire face—and pushed back her black strands with the other. She turned to Riku, her canines coming into view. "What is it, boy?" It was a slurred response, one on the climax of pleasure.

"What are you going to do?" He already knew the answer. Shock coursed through him. He didn't know how to respond to this. *Make her stop*, he thought. But, why?

Mayu turned her attention back to the terrified princess. "You know what I'm going to do. I'm tasting the enemy." With that, Mayu's fangs elongated further and sunk into Reiko's petite neck.

Riku thought she screamed before. He was wrong. Now, Reiko truly screamed. Her tears became a river of fear and pain, coming down her cheeks. They kept coming, never stopping. There was no sign they would stop, either. Those screams became loud whimpers. Her eyes squeezed tight. She tried to pull away. Every movement cause Mayu to sink further and further into her.

Her eyes opened, revealing the hazel eyes he terribly hated. Why was there a sharp pain in his chest? Why did his hands fist to his sides? Why was he able to move again, the roots to the ground severing the moment Mayu straddled her waist?

Stop her! Stop her right now! Riku didn't understand. Reiko had attacked him. *She spit a piece of crystal at you. That's nothing!* His mind was siding with the enemy. How much of an idiot could Riku be? He debated to stop the demon queen, a woman who could plug out his heart before he even realized she moved, and help Reiko—a girl who was his enemy yet had grabbed his attention like no other.

"What a disgrace my mother is."

Riku jumped. Diamond stood at his left side, watching the scene in front of her with her arms crossed under her chest. Her gaze shouted disgust. She shook her head, not wanting to see anymore, but she didn't turn away.

How long had she been there? When had she arrived? Her actions and appearances were random. There was no doubt her authority was absolute, though.

Like mother, like daughter, Riku supposed.

Mayu's head flung back, her hair tickling her back. She faced the door, mouth covered in crimson. She licked her lips, taking anything she could touch. She wiped her teeth, revealing her whites again. A crimson sheet covered Reiko's right side. Riku hadn't even noticed she stopped screaming and yelling. She was unconscious and so much paler than how she was before.

"Diamond," Mayu said, still licking her lips. She slid off the bed and sped to her daughter with open arms.

Diamond's eyes squinted. Instantaneously, Mayu doubled over in agony. She released several yells herself while wrapping her arms over her middle. The hollers of pain were stomach churning. The sound of her pain made him cringe, as if he felt her pain inside of him. "Revolting," Diamond spat. She threw a wad of spit in Mayu's glorious hair then teleported away.

"Damn her," Mayu grounded out. "She ruptured my stomach."

Riku's eyes widened. She'd done it. She truly did it. Diamond actually used her power of explosion to blow up her mother's stomach. Never in his long life had Riku seen such a spectacle.

She deserves it.

"Do you need assistance?" Riku asked, without a rush.

Mayu rose, standing as straight as she could. Her back hunched. "I'm fine . . . just need . . ." She teleported, leaving Riku alone with the princess. He slammed and locked his door. He was at Reiko's side the next second, observing her. His hands hovered over her, not knowing what to do. Why did he care how she felt? He shouldn't have. Sadly, he did and the feeling couldn't be stopped.

His hand came over her wound. Two puncture wounds gave their welcome to him. Her blood surrounded those areas. Her frozen mandarin and vanilla scent was replaced by a metallic tang. He could have taken this time to suck her blood. As a Cat Demon, he didn't need blood to survive like other species, but it was a nice little treat here and there.

Having Reiko's blood, having her coursed through his veins, caused him to shiver. Maybe it was the temperature. No, it was him. Her chilled demeanor was gone, leaving warm luscious skin. Her powers must shut off when she sleeps . . . or in this case, knocked out.

He wanted to touch her. He wanted to push her now damp hair out of her face. He did nothing. He did nothing to *her* at least.

Riku needed . . . something. He had to get out of this room. Obviously, she was affecting him in ways he did not like. If she had reached him mentally, then he was forever screwed.

He pushed from the bed and headed toward the door. He would go to the underground facilities. There were rooms where women would reside and give all of the pleasure anyone could ask for. There were men's rooms too, where the females would travel if they were in situations Riku was in.

Yeah, he'd travel there.

He opened his door. He paused. He couldn't leave her. What if someone came after her? What if she was kidnapped by anyone? Demons never liked to keep their noses to themselves and possessing other people's properties was a necessity.

He peered over his shoulder. She was still motionless. Her hair still splashed over her tight face. *She'll be fine*, he thought, then closed the door. He headed down the hall, hoping he was right.

❦

Ayano might have lost a friend today, and so have the other girls, but training had to continue. Waiting for Kenta, Damon, and Jezebel to return was a waste of time. While they got their business done, hopefully returning home safely, she and the princesses had business to take care of themselves; their powers.

Not wanting to go far in case the departed team arrived back here, the group stayed in Valla Park. She looked around the place once the three savior's teleported away. That was a good place to train. They were in an open space with enough room to expand and they could use their powers without affecting the lives of everyday humans. They would stay, she decided. So, stay they did.

Ayano observed as the others focused on combat. They chose partners, fighting one on one, and giving and taking kill shots. No fist or finger hit the other. Right before contact, they stopped and pulled back, just as Ayano had instructed. Some girls fell, some girls tripped the other, and one girl actually got hit. Sazuma took it like a pro and kept up the combat with her sister.

While they practiced, her mind wandered. They needed to defeat the Demon Docks, that was a given. They had to save the people, also a given. They needed to save the world, of course. Training the princesses, sure thing. Now that Jezebel was here, it could surely be done. Random attacks, they could manage. All out war, no way. Hell no. Not happening.

These girls could barely handle a horde of demons. Lune Park had proved that these girls were different from the princesses of the past although it also proved they were nowhere near as strong as they needed to be. That was a given of course, considering they received their powers some days ago. Was there a way for their orbs to kick into overdrive?

For Ayano, she had ten years to grow, learn and explore. Kenta had strengthened her body physically. Along with his guidance, he assisted her mentally, teaching her to remain calm, assertive and cautious of everything. Encounters with some of Kenta's heavenly friends had assisted her, as well.

Ayano hadn't met that many of Kenta's allies, but she was grateful to meet who she did.

Two years after becoming a princess, they had run into Tamaki, one of the Mother Angel's archangels. She and Kenta had been passing by a small village on Kyushu Island, before the Docks had taken over. They had just taken back orbs from another group of failed princesses. It was the third killing that month. Honestly, Tamaki appeared at the best time.

He had appeared out of nowhere, claiming he was watching over the Nagasaki Prefecture for at least a year. Pollution had gone out of control. An oil refinery had had an accident, affecting the water in the area. He'd said he was sent to secretly and leisurely purify the water. At the time, Ayano was too upset to care about anything. It never got easier, hoping to make friends and defeat the enemy you were destined to destroy.

Feeling sympathetic—he must have known she hated pity—Tamaki had taken them to amusements parks at night, when every human returned to their homes. Tamaki smiled. Kenta fought his grins. Ayano hadn't cracked once. How was she supposed to find fun when her hands were coated with invisible blood?

They left the park at dawn and traveled to the outskirts of town, approaching a small murky lake. It was late—early actually—and Ayano didn't want to have "fun" anymore. To Ayano's surprise, no fun would take place at this time, in this night.

They had approached the lake, stopping right on its edge. When he pointed his hand straight ahead, Ayano had looked. She froze. There was a cemetery. It reached at least two football fields with gray marble headstones engraved with names, dates and messages from loved ones. There were even dead and fresh flowers placed below the stones, touching the stone platforms where the coffins rested.

"Welcome to the Nagasaki Peace Park."

Ayano's heart plummeted. Her eyes stung and watered. Her throat dried. Her fingers shook. She might have been young but she heard of the 1945 Nagasaki bombing, ending the lives of innocents; just like she had been doing. There were so many headstones, so many people. There were probably many loved ones who missed their deceased members greatly.

"You're not the only ones mourning," Tamaki had said. The wind kicked up, blowing a harsh, chilling wind, causing Ayano to shiver furthermore. Her tears fell. "Even now, people mourn for the loss of the family member they always loved, never met, expected to see but never saw, met one time and that ended up being the last time, and who knows what else."

Tamaki's angelic gray hair blew lovingly to the side. His apple red eyes looked ahead, watching the land whispering silent prayers. The breezed kissed his tanned skin. No goose bumps came over him.

"I never thought about life this way," Kenta said, fighting his own tears. Ayano knew what he meant. He never thought about waking up and not seeing your death arrive in the same day. He never thought about how precious life was and that all you had was this one life. Even if you had another chance in the supernatural world, you would never be a human again. That life was over.

In the end, Tamaki had taught them that they weren't alone. However they were feeling, someone else, someone around this world, was feeling the exact same way. The prospect of life was introduced and Ayano's eyes cracked open. It was a shame those eyes had opened far too late.

But the second person Ayano had met was the Wolf Demon, Akira Suzuki. Akira was a bit of a shocker for Ayano. She had never seen a Wolf Demon before and, at the time, the demon had towered over her fifteen-year old body. Kenta and Ayano had taken a break from searching and decided to take a mini vacation to the island of Shikoku. They headed to Hiroshima, where their vacation would be in a place called Itsukushima Shrine.

Ayano hated the long name. Not the place.

It was beautiful. The shrine was literally built on water and said to blend well with the sea and the pine green mountains behind it. It stood in perfect harmony with its surroundings, which brightened Ayano's spirits even more. Kenta really knew where to travel.

He was a Spirit Being for crying out loud. What part of the world hadn't he seen?

Tall copper red entrance gates were built in the water along with the shrine. A main shrine was centered in the sea, with white walls and copper red wood holding up the structure. Other small rooms surrounded the main shrine with brown hardwood floors and black paneled ceilings.

Commoners were welcomed, except the sick, and pregnant women approaching labor could not enter. Good thing Ayano was neither one of those. And thanks to Kenta's connections with the people, they had an all access pass with a private tour and a personal room. She shouted her love to Kenta that day; her love that he knew people, of course.

Kenta had once appeared here and prevented a terrorist attack on the mainland, before they could step into the shrine's pure land and demolish the hard work hundreds of people put into building the structure. The shrine's keeper, an elderly woman nearing death, had welcomed Kenta into the shrine along with Ayano. She claimed to be a psychic and sensed he was a Spirit Being; a being of wisdom and purity. She hesitated when it came to Ayano, suspecting she held darkness inside of her, but she allowed her inside for the sheer fact she knew Kenta.

The woman was right on, too. Ayano did hold darkness inside of her, literally.

They were tourists anyway, so it all worked out in the end.

Inside of the shrine, the frail gray haired woman with squinted eyes, wearing a pink kimono with yellow sunflowers on it led them to their room in one of the quarters near the main shrine. She slid the white door open, revealing a woman already inside, dusting off the paper walls. That woman had been Akira.

Her business in the shrine; watch the old woman until she passed.

Akira had told Ayano the woman had saved her life. A bear trap had caught Akira's foot, causing her to be immobile. Villagers had run up to her with knives in hand. They believed strongly in villainous demons and wanted to butcher her. The woman had stepped into the scene in her day's quick movement and forced them to stop, saying the girl had belonged to her. The villagers exited the scene with hesitation, but left all the same.

Since that day, Akira had spent several years at the shrine with the woman, waiting for her to pass so she could wrap her in a white cloth, cremate her then place her into the sea, rejoining the rest of her family. It was the woman's dying wish, after all. Akira intended to make it happen.

The vacation was not the vacation Ayano expected. There was moping, dusting, polishing, hanging laundry, patting out sheets, washing dishes, and cooking for the tourists, which were over three hundred people. On the plus side, she fed Koi fish reaching a few feet in length; star gazed with Kenta and Akira and even swam with the fish she fed.

When the kind old woman had gracefully passed in her sleep, Kenta believed it was time to go. As promised, Akira placed her corpse inside a long white bed sheet and slowly wrapped her up, giving her the respect Ayano knew she deserved. She cremated the woman's body with the help of several cremation experts, placing the sheet inside of an oven and watching her burn through a rectangular window. A black stoned cylinder case with a diamond shaped top held the ashes. One of the shrine's keepers, who happened to be a specialized diver, took the case to the sea, placing it under the construction poles of the shrine and put her in one of the many stone chambers where the keeper's family resided.

Now held with relief because she had fulfilled her promise, Akira too decided to move on. "Let's meet again," she said, hugging both Kenta and Ayano at the same time.

"Of course," Kenta said.

Akira ruffled Ayano's short black hair. "Grow up so we can one day battle together one on one in real life." The girls had played video games and professed to have awesome fighting skill on and off the gaming world. Ayano nodded, wanting to keep her promise.

The two headed their separate ways. Akira had been Ayano's first female friend. She had also been her first demon friend. The princesses of the past weren't considered her friends back then. She hadn't met the twentieth choice of princess's which happened to be Hiroko, Kenta's girlfriend, and her team.

Ayano would have called but Akira didn't have a phone. It had been four years since meeting Akira. She sort of missed the orchid-haired, blue—eyed demon.

A shout echoed. Ayano's focus returned to the present. Stella was flat on her butt. Dirt pounced onto her dark blue jeans. Hiroko, her opponent in this case, reached out a hand. Stella took it with a giggle and was brought to her feet. Both girls got into their fighting stance—fists up, legs apart, eyes locked on the other—and went for each other again.

Stella ducked and aimed for Hiroko's stomach. Hiroko blocked with her elbow and kneed Stella's stomach. She had made contact. Stella hunched over, loss for breath. She dropped to her knees and heaved.

Ayano didn't stand. In cases like this, actual contact was encouraged, even if it was accidental. If you didn't know how it felt to be punched, kicked, kneed and slapped, then you needed to learn how it felt to be punched, kicked, kneed and slapped. Ayano would do it personally if she wanted to. These girls looked like they were good, anyway.

"I'm so sorry," Hiroko said. Her hands hovered over Stella, not knowing what to do.

"Don't apologize," Ayano said, grabbing Hiroko's attention. "You wouldn't apologize to the enemy, would you?" God, Ayano hoped she wouldn't. Knowing Hiroko, she just might. "Don't hold back. Let loose. This is training. Act like this is a real . . ."

A ledge of dirt shot out right under Hiroko's feet. The startled blonde flew back, landing hard on her back, getting dirt all over her hoodie. Stella stood to shaky legs. She got into her fighting stance once again. This time, with a grin.

"How was that?" she asked Ayano boldly.

She couldn't help but grin herself. She'd grown so much stronger from years ago. She used to be timid, afraid of her own shadow. Currently, she was bright, expectant and simply vibrant. Who knew a week in the supernatural world could do that to you? "It was good." She couldn't praise her too much. "You've got more skill than you realize. Show it to me."

And she did. Stella brought her fist up, mimicking an uppercut. Another ledge popped out just as Hiroko stood straight. She was flipped this time, still landing on her back. Another fist up, another ledge. The air punches continued until Hiroko barely fell into the pond.

Just as Stella brought her arm back, preparing for another punch, Hiroko threw out her hand, creating a blast of air, hitting Stella's chest. She was pushed back, her feet coming off of the ground. Both arms came up, creating an even taller ledge. Hiroko shot up and landed straight into the pond just as Stella landed on her back.

Everyone's attention went to them.

Hiroko brought her head up. A lily pad acted as her hat. On that lily pad was a small lime green frog with shining black eyes. "Ribbit," it croaked. Knowing exactly what was on her head, Hiroko freaked. She launched herself out of the pond and threw the pad off of head. The frog was long gone.

She threw her hoodie off and checked herself. Her sky blue, sparkle studded skirt stuck to her chest. Her ripped faded jeans hung low on her waist. Her white nurses like sneakers were soaked. Her hair, which she had in a ponytail before practice, now hung freely, the edges reaching below her waist.

She grunted, "Great."

"Look on the bright side. You can dry yourself off." Sazuma said, watching the whole scene.

Mary helped Stella to her feet. "You guys were pretty serious."

"Training is serious," Ayano said. She pushed herself off of the tree she leaned on and approached the group. "You have to give everything you've got. You'll be giving and taking blows. It's best to know what those blows feel like." She stopped, reaching the group now centered on her. "You'll be taking out living, breathing demons whose mission is to murder and even eat you. Training is an extended version of battle. Don't hold back, but don't kill each other, either."

No fear. No hesitation. The girls nodded; even Aurora, who acted as Yumiko's opponent. Their eyes, ranging in colors gazed at her as if she was their teacher, their protector, their friend. No other group had held such looks. Ayano's heart swelled.

Maybe she truly had found her friends.

Hiroko turned to Stella. "Let's go again."

Stella shrugged, "Okay." She brought her fist up, creating another ledge. Hiroko shot up again. This time she landed on her feet. The ledge had also hit Yumiko. She landed on the ground, but rose up.

"Wait, wait," Aurora said. All eyes went to her. She was smiling bright. Her eyes gleamed with an idea. Kenta had the same eyes whenever something popped into his mind. "Why don't you guys have an element circle or something. Stand in a circular formation and randomly throw your powers at the person you choose."

That had to be the smartest idea Ayano ever heard. She didn't even think about that, and she was the teacher in this case.

"You don't have any powers," Sazuma said to her frankly. It was true though, she couldn't participate and based on her skinny figure, she needed training more than any of them.

Aurora shrugged, "I'm good watching, trust me. Yumiko tired me out." See, she did need training.

Ayano stepped up anyway as the circle formed. Mary stood closest to the water. With one blow, she might have landed in the pond like her blonde-haired friend. All princesses, except for Reiko—sadly, *We're going to get her back. Don't be such a downer.*—turned to one another, watching to see who made the first move.

Anticipation rose. This was the first time Ayano had felt such anticipation that didn't involve demon attack. Her senses heightened. Her fingers wiggled, unable to wait. Her eyes went from Mary on one side of the circle, to Sazuma on the other side. Yumiko and Stella stood in front of Ayano and Hiroko flanked her left side.

All girls bent their knees, ready for anything.

The anticipation was killing her. Who was going to make . . .

Sazuma shot first, aiming a fireball to Yumiko. The twelve-year-old ducked and pointed her finger to Hiroko, shooting a beam of sunshine yellow light. Hiroko bent her body to the right, missing the attack. She threw out her hand, sending a blast of wind Mary's way. She was blown to her right, skidding in the dirt. As soon as she caught her feet, she brought her hand back.

A string of water zapped out of the pond as she brought her hand forward, aiming for Ayano. She blocked the attack with her forearm. The water scattered, landing near her feet and soaking her arm. With her staff, she swirled it around. Her black whip released and aimed for Yumiko. She dodged as one whip missed her neck and another whip missed her ankles. She brought her cloth back just as Yumiko shot out another beam, aiming it to Sazuma.

The playoffs kept coming, going to one person and then another. Hiroko had even attempted to blow Ayano away. She even released a whirlwind, causing her to lift from the ground. The attack was strong but she got her revenge by using her whip to latch around her ankle and lift her in the air. Everyone had gotten their air dosage, except Sazuma, who burned the cloth, ensuring her safety on the ground. Stella had ledged Hiroko into the pond so many times that it kept getting funnier. Ayano had even started laughing.

That grabbed everyone's attention. They stared at her in disbelief, as if hearing her laugh was such a rarity. It *was* a rarity, even to Ayano. She chuckled here and there, but she never released a hearty laugh, one that was deep yet feminine. Sure, her voice was lower than a usual girl's was. To her, she was still womanly.

After the little shocker, the girls continued. Aurora even shouted the name of the person she thought had the most skill. She picked Stella. Stella threw her fists to her chosen target, the earth acting as her fists. She was focused, determined, a little shaky but willing all the same.

Ayano agreed with Aurora. Stella was strong.

An echoing howl stole the group's attention. Their eyes turned to their surroundings. They couldn't pin an exact location. As soon as the howling stopped, it echoed yet again. The howl was firm; steady and filled with an emotion Ayano couldn't decipher . . . it was a howl she'd heard before.

The howl was from a wolf, she knew. Was this *her* wolf? The howl came again. This time Ayano turned around, knowing it came from her direction. The princesses flanked her sides, looking into the thick forest. There was nothing but black and pine green.

Could it be? Ayano howled this time. She sounded like an idiot. The girls looked at her questioningly. Their opinion of her was most likely to change, thanks to today.

This time, the howling stopped. Heavy footsteps replaced the howling, coming fast. The girls took their stance, preparing for a full on attack. That wasn't what they got though.

It was what Ayano got.

A woman jumped out of the forest. Time slowed. The orchid hair, the navy blue eyes and the smile Ayano couldn't resist to save her own life. The brown furred ears on her head, the cream colored skin and the apple blossom scent that stuck to Ayano's nostrils for four years. Ayano's arms reached out, prepared for the pounce of her life.

Normal time returned.

Akira pounced, locking her arms around Ayano's neck and her legs around her waist. They both fell back. Ayano took most of the fall, not surprising her at all. She didn't mind. This didn't bother her one bit.

Stella squeaked, shocked about the entire situation.

Sazuma stared in attack mode, igniting her flame in her hands and preparing to fire. Noticing Akira's affections, she lowered her hands, her heated temperature faded.

Akira nuzzled into Ayano's cheek. "We meet again, little Yano."

And there was the nickname. "Nice to see you too, Kira."

Akira's chest pressed into Ayano's as she deeply inhaled and fell as she exhaled. "You still smell like raspberries."

"Really?" that had surprised her. Back at the shrine, Ayano had used raspberry shampoo and body wash. Since leaving, she hadn't used any soap with that scent. There was no way it could still linger after four years.

Her friend finally pulled herself back and got into a sitting position. She still sat on her legs, making Ayano immobile. She smiled, "Yup, you're still my caramel raspberry."

Raspberry, because of her scent, and caramel, because of her skin. Because Akira had been her first female friend, she and Ayano created so many nicknames it was crazy how much they could actually use. Some they both hated. Others, they both loved. With her here, she was sure those nicknames, good and bad, would resurface.

"It's official, this is the weirdest day of my life," Hiroko said, staring down at the women, talking to no one in particular.

Akira rose to her feet, taking Ayano with her. "Whoa," Akira gaped, staring at Ayano. She patted her head, "You're not so little anymore." Akira was still taller, at least six-inches taller than she was. To Ayano, those inches mattered. She wasn't as short as she was when she was fifteen. She still couldn't beat Akira's height. Damn.

"You're . . . a demon," Mary said in recognition. She must have noticed the brown outside furred ears on top of her head. The fur inside was tan, and matched Akira's creamy skin perfectly. She was flawless.

The Wolf Demon turned to her, navy eyes shining bright with wonder. "Yeah." She sniffed in Mary's personal space, inhaling deep. Her eyes raked her up and down until they landed on her face. "You're the Water Princess." She sniffed again, little puffs this time. "Have you and Kenta been in close contact?"

Mary's cheeks heated, answering Akira's question.

"I thought so," the wolf grinned. Her ears flopped as she searched the group, eyeing every girl who crossed her eye. She stopped when she reached Stella, who was at the edge of the group, standing to Akira's right.

She just stared, unmoving, not even breathing. Stella gave her the same look, but her look was concerning. She rubbed her hand on her face, checking to see if anything was on her. She looked down her body, checking for stains of anything. There were smudges on her jeans. Other than that she was fairly tidy.

Ayano was starting to wonder why she was staring, as well.

After brief moments, Akira sniffed. "You're earth right?"

Stella nodded, not knowing what else to do.

She nodded, then turned back to Ayano, "Where's Ken-Ken?"

And there was Kenta's nickname. "He went to the Demon Docks mansion to rescue Reiko, one of the princesses."

"You're missing one?" Akira counted the group, including Ayano. Her mouth opened in understanding. "Okay, what happened to her?"

"Kidnapped by Destiny."

"And you're honestly telling me you allowed one of the Demon Docks members to kidnap one of your girls?"

Akira had known about the Demon Docks and their intentions to dominate the world. Kenta and Ayano didn't have to inform her about that. She was well aware.

Ayano rolled her burgundies, "We were ambushed."

Akira crossed her arms, "Yeah, that's an excuse."

Ayano had forgotten her little demon friend was a determination freak and a strategist. That is one of the things she and Kenta had in common. Those two combined could infiltrate an enemy territory and end up returning home scot-free. It didn't surprise her that Akira would make a fuss about Reiko's kidnapping. There was no excuse, was there?

"Kenta, Damon and Jezebel went after her. While they're gone, we're working on our skills."

"Damon's here?" Akira freaked. A smile popped full bloom, revealing her canines. Had her teeth always been that sharp? And how did she know Damon? Did everyone know him?

"How do you know Damon?" Aurora asked, transforming into her possessive mode.

"How do *you* know Damon?" Akira asked, leaning down to the five-foot-eight lady.

"Damon is my savior and the savior of us all," she answered. She threw out her arm, as if it made her point.

Akira smirked, "You're his fan girl, aren't you?"

"He had those?" Hiroko asked, anger rising. Why was she angry? Ayano wondered.

Akira nodded as she crossed her arms. "Heck, yeah. Last time I saw him, he said he had several ladies waiting for him back in his apartment. I paid no mind, considering I wasn't one of those girls."

"I knew he was a player," Sazuma shook her head. How would she know? She barely knew the guy.

Hiroko's eyes were distant. She frowned and her eyebrows arched. She was mad about Damon? Did she like him and found this news troubling? She hoped that wasn't the case. Damon's handsome, smart and powerful, Ayano would give him that, but he doesn't seem like the long term relationship type of guy. Ayano had no room to judge. She thought Kenta would be forever single, but look what happened—two girlfriends in under ten years.

"I am no fan girl," Aurora raised her chin stubbornly. "I am a Spirit Being he's been with for over ten years. He means more to me than life. If you know anything about him, I demand to know at once."

This was the first time Ayano had been told the connections between Damon and Aurora. They had met years ago. Damon had lived for thousands of years, alone most likely, except for his fan girls. Why carry on the responsibility of another person after so long?

Akira poked Aurora's forehead and kept it there. Her long clear nail dug into her skin, leaving redness around the spot. She grinned, "Calm down kiddo. You're a little too possessive. Damon doesn't like possessive," she turned to Ayano, "At least he didn't when I met him."

"When was this?" Yumiko asked, entering the conversation. She must not have been a conversation type of girl because this was the second conversation where she appeared out of nowhere.

Akira dapped her chin with her free hand. "About two years ago. Long story short, we had a fun night, then he left."

All eyes widened. Aurora was gaping. Hiroko was glaring. What did she *do*? Noticing the glares, Akira threw up her hands, all innocence. "We didn't have sex. We snuck into malls, stole some movies, sat on a skyscraper and star-gazed while chatting. Nothing sexual. Damon's not my type, anyway."

Everyone calmed. Hiroko closed her eyes. She sighed tiredly. "Enough about Damon. What is your business here?"

Akira shrugged, "I smelled Ayano's scent and I had to say hello. Now that I did, I took care of business."

"Don't go," Stella rushed out, hurrying forward, clutching Akira's forearm. They stared at one another once again, but it wasn't as long as last time.

Akira gave a sweet grin. She rubbed Stella's head, ruffling her hair ever so softly. When had she been so gentle? Ayano must have missed Akira's transformation during those four years. "Don't worry princess, I won't leave. I'll stay, if you'll have me."

Stella smiled. Her head swung to Ayano. Her brown eyes went big and the puppy dogface formed. "Can we keep her?"

Akira was no dog . . . she was a *wolf*. There was no way Ayano was keeping a *wolf*. It was hard feeding Stella. She didn't need another mouth to feed. Plus, with Kenta popping in here and there and snatching some ramen without her knowledge, food was hard to come by.

Alas, how could she resist that face? Stella knew the puppy dogface would work. It always did because she rarely used it. The first time she used it was when she wanted a poster of some boy band from the nineties. That one mall shopping trip had turned Stella into an observer and a consumer. Although she wanted everything, this poster she truly wanted. She'd given Ayano the puppy face, the cutest thing she had ever seen. She bought the poster, costing fifteen bucks, and that was all they bought because that's all they could afford.

Now, not only was Stella doing the face, but Akira turned to her, stuck out her bottom lip and gave her own version of the puppy face. Because she had wolf blood, the face worked to her extreme advantage. Her navy blue eyes widened and watered, creating the need to take care of her; the *want* to take care of her. She whimpered, her doggie sound mixing with her own human whimper.

They were players. Every single one of them.

With a roll of her eyes, she sighed, "Fine."

With a smile, Stella hugged her new best friend. Akira picked her up, surprising Stella completely, and squeezed her tight. The excited redhead laughed. This friendship started fast; a little too fast. Maybe, because Akira was a Wolf Demon, a protector of the Earth. Stella is the Earth Princess so it makes sense. Did she really have to be the family pet, though?

"This whole situation has me tired," Yumiko scratched her head.

"No kidding," Sazuma yawned. She was always tired. She had no right to talk.

"We can't just leave," Mary said. "What if the gang returns?"

"What makes you think they're going to return here, to this very spot?" Sazuma asked, pointing to the dirt she stood on.

"I don't know," Mary said sadly. She made her way to the pond, sat down and crossed her legs. "But, I'm staying here."

"Okay, bye. I'll let Mom know you were attacked by a demon if you don't come home." Sazuma left, entering the pathway leading to and out of the park. Hiroko followed after, not believing Sazuma left her sister—her younger sister—to defend for herself. Aurora followed, not knowing what else to do. Mary didn't move.

"My brothers will be wondering where I am," Yumiko said, playing with her fingers. "They wanted me home at least an hour ago."

What time was it anyway?

Ayano turned to Akira. "Could you take Yumiko and Stella home? I'm going to stay with Mary." The Wolf Demon nodded. She placed Stella on her feet and grabbed her hand. She walked to Yumiko. "I run fast, so hold on tight, kiddo." Akira wrapped both arms around the girls. She peered over her shoulder. "Call if you need anything. You know I'll hear you."

She nodded. Akira dashed off, taking the girls with her. The sound of Yumiko's shriek and Stella's "Yippee" was the only evidence they were ever there.

Only the stream of running water and frogs croaking filled the air. She inhaled the refreshing damp air and exhaled hot cinnamon breath. She turned around, facing Mary's back. She had curled herself in a ball, her arms wrapped around her legs, and her chin resting on her knees.

She stood there, wondering. Did Mary want to be bothered? She was bugged. Should she ask what was on her mind? "Want to be alone?" Ayano managed to ask. She wasn't good at being Princess Counselor. She was usually the one in need of counsel.

Mary shook her head. Ayano moved to Mary's right side and took a seat. She placed her staff by her side and peered out. There was nothing but trees. Forest surrounded them along with woodland creatures and pine scents. The sun still raised but it was lower as the afternoon turned into evening.

How long had Kenta been gone? She hadn't looked at the time. Her only focus was the princesses and Aurora. It bothered Ayano greatly that she couldn't be by Kenta's side, fight with him, protect him, and ensure his victory. She had done so for over ten years. The fact that she couldn't do it now made her feel empty and even tense.

What if he was injured? What if he was on the brink of death and she couldn't even be there to hold his hand and try to help him? What if he died? The thought alone caused pain to stab at Ayano's chest. Her eyes watered. She shook her head, wanting the thoughts to leave. They left, but the worry was still there.

Kenta had been with her through so much. He was the first real friend she ever had. He brought her to life. He *gave* her a life after her caretaker had given birth to a girl with no hope. How could she live without him? It was simple. She couldn't.

"I'm scared," Mary admitted.

Ayano turned to her. Her legs bent to the side. Her hands supported her as she leaned back. "Scared? Of the battle? Of this new world?"

"For Kenta."

Ayano thought so. Every solution needed to be considered before speaking up personal thoughts you thought flowed through other's minds. She and Mary were thinking about the same thing.

"I wanted to go. I wanted to help him. I know I'm not as strong as he is, I'm not even as strong as you, but I didn't want him going into enemy territory without me by his side." Her shoulders shook. No tears fell. Her stilled hands, mumbling her words, covered her mouth. Even so, Ayano understood everything.

They were thinking the same. Their need to protect Kenta grew strong. Ayano knew, in the battlefield, they would be defending Kenta; no hesitations, no issues.

"Kenta's strong. He won't lose. He wouldn't allow it. If he did, he'd know he'd only return to an ass beating."

Mary sunk lower in her embrace but the sides of her lips quirked up, causing Ayano to grin as well. "You're right." Her eyes closed. "I just miss him."

Ayano turned her eyes away. Her focus went to the pond. The lily pads swerved as the water from the mini waterfall splashed down and entered the large space of water. She didn't even look into the murky pond. She knew she would see her reflection. The moment she saw herself, she knew she would see Kenta. His sharp cheekbones, his sun kissed skin, his shining eyes that matched hers, his maroon headband on his forehead and his short black hair that covered his face, creating a mysterious and inviting aura around him.

She didn't need her mind to tell her the obvious. She missed Kenta, too.

Story 12

Ties never *die*

How many years had it been since Damon stepped foot into this place? At least fourteen, he thought a moment later. Saki had assigned him a specialized team to invade the Demon Docks castle in secret and report possible attack and domination patterns so the Heavenly Beings could retaliate at the right time.

But the mission had failed. They were assigned to stay in the castle for three days.

They exposed in less than twenty-four hours.

One of Damon's team subordinates had formed an alliance with Lavida in advance, hoping for great power in the future. Forty Spirit Beings joined him on the mission, including Damon. Slaughtered, those men and women were. The traitor had been outsmarted. He was merely a tool to assist Lavida. She ended up decapitating him and fed his body to the lower level demons in the mansion.

Lavida had even managed to trap Damon in the process. Luckily, before she could torture him for kicks like she wanted to, Damon teleported out of harm's way, returning to the Mother Angel's throne room and automatically bowed his head apologetically. Mother Angel Saki had forgiven him, "There was nothing you could do." She said, her voice vibrating of love. "We have all of the information we need. You have done well, Damon."

Had he? Had he done well? If he had, he would have known an impostor was among them. He could have guarded them and protected them from deaths they did not deserve.

That event happened years ago. Damon never looked back into those vile memories. Then again, he never had a reason to, until now.

He was back in this shithole. Trying to find the ice princess. He'd seen her once before outside of little Yumiko's house. Yes, he knew the girls' names. Ever since Kenta had started his mission ten years ago, he'd known the names on the list thanks to a little sneaking here and there. He hadn't found out a thing, though. Saki had spotted him watching over her throne as she personally wrote the names down. She'd decided to tell him the names and he'd known then and there.

He never expected so many trial and errors though. Kenta was sloppy. The only princess he got right was Ayano, devious, ominous, yet sweet, Ayano. She was a keeper. Damon loved ominous girls, especially ones that kicked ass and always gave you that look of, "I'm going to kill you." So sexy.

That aside, after learning about Kenta's trial and errors, he'd finally got it right, finding the chosen princesses after twenty five times. Had to be hard killing so many teenagers. Oh, well. Not his problem.

He never expected the chosen girls to be so pretty, though. There was the fire girl, who had that, "I hate you," aura like Ayano did, but she was too hot to handle, literally. The girl was a walking furnace.

There was the water teen. She looked so decent it was scary. She was the one Damon had saved from Chikara's sudden attack. Damon had known by Kenta's reaction to her safety that he had feelings for her. It surprised him a bit, the fact that Kenta could love anyone, considering he was always Mr. Independent. Overall, Damon liked the girl. Mary was her name, right?

There was the redheaded girl, who must have been innocence walking. She had the biggest puppy eyes Damon had ever seen. She was cute, in a sisterly sort of way, but was a bit timid, which bothered him. Timid girls were hard to handle because of their constant fears and hesitation. Damon might not have known the girl personally. It was just an observation.

There was the blue streaked black-haired girl who Damon was currently coming to save. She was the rich girl, Damon knew. Surprisingly, she was tall with a perfect curvature. Any man would want her. They would kill to have her. Something told Damon the teen would appreciate the deaths of those who worshiped the land she walked on. That's also why Damon wasn't interested in her. Looks weren't everything; they were *mostly* everything. In this case, perfect looks and money weren't what he wanted. Besides, her voice was too high. Her attention span seemed to match an ADD rodent.

Little Yumiko is the one who shocked him, though. She was the youngest, ranging at eleven or twelve. How could Kenta allow a midget into a battle that's been raging for over hundreds of years? The kid might have died without even living. Regrettably, she was the destined light princess, so maybe Saki had plans for her, if she survived.

Then, there was his new blonde haired interest, Hiroko. Out of all of the girls, she was his favorite. She carried an orchid allure scent, mixing orchids with musk. One swish of her scent in Damon's nose and he wanted another. He still wanted another. He never imagined he'd find a young woman so addicting.

To him, she was a young woman, nothing more, nothing less. She wasn't a child. She wasn't a simple girl. In Damon's eyes, she was more than just a lady. Young woman suited her best. She really was lovely.

She had appeared in front of him, demanding for him to assist in the aid of her friend. Never in all of his years had someone demanded him of anything. Saki had always asked him to complete tasks. He followed because you didn't question the Mother Angel. That was just stupid! Aurora had forced him to do many things, ranging from changing hotel sheets on both of their beds to choosing their next destination.

Hiroko had been the first to demand anything. It had also been the first time Damon wanted to do something for someone else without feeling a shred of annoyance. He wanted to help her. He couldn't show her that. That would ruin the fun of their new partnership.

Aurora had almost ruined everything from the very beginning. She had pointed to Hiroko, claiming news Damon already knew. She said she was the one, the girl who he carried around in a photo. Aurora was right. She was the same girl in the photo he'd held for over ten years. Aurora was also right about her growing up. Hiroko had grown from the small child she once was.

He would have never known about her if he hadn't saved her father back in Cali.

He watched as the earthquake shook the bridge, shaking its structure and causing the people on the roads to panic. Aurora had been with him at least two weeks when the incident happened. She wanted to travel the world at the time and California seemed like a good place to start. He didn't know destruction would arrive. He didn't know there would be people who lost their lives thanks to others who were too busy trying to defend themselves.

Aurora had gasped, grabbing Damon's attention.

They watched as a silver Buick dropped down. Several other vans and cars ranging in color entered the seas below the bridge. Aurora stared in shock. Damon had paid it no mind back then. People lived, people died, people were murdered; life was cruel. Why should he care if . . .

A body rose from the water. A man, he realized. He wasn't breathing. Still, all of the others who entered the lake wouldn't rise up like he did. He didn't know what possessed him, but confidently, he said, "Let's go." Damon flashed to the man, picked him up without even stepping on the water and brought him to land, right under the broken bridge. By this time, the earthquake had ended but citizens still screamed. Damon ignored them, putting all of his focus on this one human. Why though?

Aurora appeared behind him soon after. She was learning to teleport. She could have been a little quicker though. She approached his left side, observing the human. He was dead, Damon thought. His skin was pale and his body was motionless.

To their revelation, the human opened his eyes, revealing pained crystalline. His body shook. He didn't move a limb. There was a gash wound on his forehead, his blood slid back and hid into his shaggy brown hair.

Aurora bent down and stuffed her hand into the man's white shirt pocket. She pulled out a brown leather wallet. Damon pushed on his knees as Aurora bent down further, revealing credit and insurance cards in some pockets and his family in the clear pocket.

A wife and a daughter, both blonde and so gorgeous.

The man opened his mouth, revealing a pool of blood. Damon shook his head and gently pushed the man's mouth shut, "Everything's going to be alright. I'll take care of your loved ones. Rest now. I'll guide you to heaven." In reassurance, he closed his eyes, entering his eternal sleep.

There was nothing Damon could do now. The man's soul would whither to Heaven. Saki or her husband would take care of the rest. Damon stood, not wanting to touch the human further. It wasn't that he found him disgusting. He just didn't want to bother his body anymore. Somewhat saddened, Damon asked, "What's his name?" He would fulfill his promise to the human. It was the least he could do for him.

Aurora searched his wallet and found his ID card. "Aki Kotani, age thirty-five. He's from Japan." She looked at the corpse. "He doesn't look very Japanese."

He might not have had narrowed eyes but he had the creamy skin. "Let me see the picture." She handed it to him. There might have only been two people in his family, but that was more than enough for Damon to handle. In the photo, his wife—blonde hair and brown eyes—was holding a little five year old blonde hair and blue eyes. He turned the picture over. There was cursive writing on the back. *"Kotare and Hiroko, 2000."* It read.

"His ID card has his address?"

"Yeah," Aurora answered, already knowing where their next destination was.

"Then, let's get this over with."

So they traveled to Japan, heading to a small town called Kayta Plains, where a big house welcomed them. Damon had shielded himself as he misted through the house's plaster walls. He told Aurora to stay outside. She did so, reluctantly.

Damon had entered the living room. It was huge with pale walls and turquoise furniture. A ruby antique rug laid center stage on the floor. A small child played her dolls on that rug as the black large box shaped television sat comfortably on a hardwood platform. It played the Backstreet Boys.

The girl held one Barbie doll on one hand-brunette-and another in the other hand-black haired. She flipped them one way and flipped them on the other. Damon hadn't entered the room several minutes when she noticed him and dropped her dolls. Children were more sensitive to the worlds they didn't understand. But did she have to find him so easily?

She waved with a bright smile. He wiggled his finger, signaling his hello, not wanting to say a word.

"Are you lost, Mr.?" she asked in the most innocent voice he ever heard.

He shook his head. He remained quiet. She didn't seem too bothered. Her short ponytail swung as she pushed to her feet and swayed with a smile. She then pointed to him with a pout. "You're bigger than me."

She was too cute. He didn't smile or grin. He hardened himself. He was here on a mission. There would be no distractions.

She took one mean bare footstep toward him. So demanding. "You want a piece of me, non-talker?"

Where did she get that assumption? He hadn't said a word. Was she always like this? If so, then her mother had a lot of hassle to deal with. Speaking of...

"Who are you talking to, Hiroko?" She had appeared from the pale archway leading to the enlarged beige painted kitchen. Kotare watched her daughter with a smile, facing the direction of the large beige framed windows.

She ignored her mother. "If you want me, you can't have me." She jumped, giving Damon a good view of her back. She stuck out her purple dress covered butt and shook it, shocking Damon completely. "Hiroko's too good for you," she sung, extending the "you."

Kotare wiped her hands on her white apron. She headed over and picked up her daughter with a chuckle. "Your imagination is too wild."

Hiroko pouted, losing her coolness. "But Mommy, I'm serious. There's a man standing right there and he's not saying a word."

"Of course, darling," she said. She didn't believe a word, Damon knew. Hiroko glared as her mother carried her into the kitchen. Out of sight, Damon decided to leave. Seeing this loving family was too much for him to handle. Later, he would ask Saki to do anything to fill in the dark void he knew Kotare would once have.

Two years later, Kotare's dark void diminished.

Looking back on it now, Damon didn't realize how one encounter would affect him in the present. All it took was ten years, one photo from the man he rescued and a spring of heavenly hope. Now Hiroko had entered his life. She knew his name, knew his face, yet, didn't recognize him. That was alright for him, actually. It would bring him great joy to remind her while teasing her at the same time.

All right, memories and thoughts of Hiroko had to wait. He had a mission to complete; a mission he looked forward to accomplish. If he found Reiko and personally brought her back to Hiroko, she'd be consumed with joy and thank him by pouncing on him and kissing him with passion she never thought she had.

Yeah, he'd get Reiko back.

He had to find her first, though.

Why did this mansion have to be so damn huge?

The place was too huge. A mansion? Please. More like castle. It stood twenty stories tall with stone as its structure. But inside, the walls were firm with either white or dark brown paints. Some hallways and rooms had solid ceilings, some were glass and others had none; which made it a pain for the room inhabitants when it rained.

At the moment, Damon hid in the shadows, watching for any suspicious movement. Every single person in this house was a Demon Docks member and each member possessed special abilities, whether they were the same or different from another's.

He peered over a dark coated corner. There were several foot soldiers coming down the hall. All four of them wore black suits. There was one woman standing in the somewhat middle. All three men, all brunettes, stared at the woman—blonde hair, black eyes—as if she was eye candy. They were probably going to hide her from the rest of the world and have their way with her. They were disgusting. All demons were that way, excluding a few Damon ran into over the years.

They approached, unknowing there was a Spirit Being ready to take them out. They would spot him, gang up on him, beat him down, tear him to the ground and eat is flesh to increase their own strength.

Damon chuckled. That shit didn't happen to him.

He was the spotter. The fighter. The killer. No, the murderer. Yeah, that was good.

Damon's only weapons were the daggers he strapped to his ankles. He couldn't lose, though. He refused to. The closest one was the shortest, with brunette hair and emeralds for eyes. A lot of demons had green eyes nowadays.

They advanced closer, closer still. They arrived. Damon struck, stabbing his dagger into the demon's temple. The other three pulled out their weapons; a sword, a knife and a gun. Damon pulled his dagger from his first victim and struck another brunette soldier, decapitating him on one swift stroke. He took care of the last man by stabbing him with both of his daggers to the soldier's temples.

As the bodies dropped all at once, the woman prepared to fire her gun. Damon kicked it out of her hands, grabbed it and slammed the woman against the wall. The gun's head was placed right on her closed left eye. "Reiko Takashima," he got in her face, "Where is she?"

She exhaled, "I don't know what you're—"

He gripped the trigger. "The Element Princess you mongrels stole. Where is she?"

"Like I'd tell you." Her opened eye spread wide as she stared closer at him. Realization must have kicked in because she froze altogether. "You're . . . you're . . ."

"Are you going to answer my question now?" he pressed the gun closer. If she wasn't what she was, he could have sworn her eyeball would have been pushed out and landed inside of her skull.

"Damon Sasaki," she continued anyway, gulping in absolute bewilderment. Rumors about Damon had rounded through the worlds for centuries. There was, *"The Stone Cold Killer,"* and, *"The Forever Spirit Being,"* but Damon's favorite was, *"The Silver Haired Menace."* That one made his spine tingle. He loved being praised. But he didn't want to be praised by himself. Hiroko would be the one praising him now. He would be sure of it.

"Reiko, where is she?"

"In Lord Riku's room," she tried to gulp, but the pressure Damon forced on her made the action difficult. "But why do you care? All you care about is . . ."

Damon stabbed her temple before she could finish. Interrogation was Damon's only strategy. Her gun helped with that of course. Using it would have made a scene. Besides, stabbing someone was much for fun.

She thwacked to the ground. The blood of all four soldiers scented the air, he knew. The action and interrogation had taken too long. Demons would sense the mess. Good thing it would be a random killing. They wouldn't be able to smell or sense him. They would think they committed suicide or another excuse they loved to come up with.

Damon now knew his destination. Reiko was with Riku Nakamura, one of the Demonic Princes. Did it *have* to be the prince with the attitude issue? He was such a human teenager, filled with attitude that wasn't even fun to be around.

Whatever, he had to move. Based on the blueprints from years ago, Riku's room was on the fifth floor, nearing the west. Damon stuck to the shadows once more, heading to the west.

Diamond knew Damon Sasaki had invaded the mansion with Kenta Shiroyama and one of the angels of heaven.

You had to be an idiot not to sense their pure presences.

Obviously, everyone in this castle was an idiot.

The scent of the sea swirled into Diamond's awaiting nose as she stood on the stone roof of the main section of the mansion. Other rooms and facilities surrounded her. Her focus wasn't those buildings; it was the fresh air that the sea brought. It welcomed her outside, enjoying her company.

Diamond enjoyed the sea very much. Considering Derek was being a prick, saying, "Stay in this castle at all times," she had a right to disobey his orders and travel to a place where she could really experience peace.

Who was she kidding? There was no peace here. There never would be. She was surrounded by idiotic demons that followed the orders of someone who was just as stupid as they were.

Just the thought of Derek made her blood boil. Her nails morphed into claws. Her hatred for him grew. Why did she have to be sold to him? Why did she have to spend her days in his bed? He wanted sex, she refused, he would get pissed, and thankfully, never touch her. That was a blessing. He drank her blood, calling it an addicting substance. The bite wasn't even passionate. It was a mere bite that drew blood and caused a pinch of pain. Nothing more.

There would never be more. Diamond didn't want anything more, and yet, how could this feeling of loneliness consume her so evidently? It was obvious it was there in plain sight yet everyone, even Derek, remained oblivious. No one could take this pain away. No one could, or would, fight her demons.

Her arms wrapped around her middle and her eyes squeezed shut. She shouldn't think about her ties to him. She shouldn't think about her eternal suffering all thanks to her *'loving'* parents. Still, she couldn't help it. The thoughts always came, always consumed.

Her hopes for peace were always diminished.

A familiar scent whiffed; sandalwood and a pinch of pine. She inhaled, deep and long. Oh, how she'd missed this fragrance. It had been so long; so devastatingly long. Unable to hold herself up, suddenly tired from a century's worth of holding herself together, her legs gave out, allowing her fall. She knew she wouldn't fall to the ground.

And she was right. Strong arms caught her before she fell. Her holder was welcomed. This wanted warmth was welcomed as well as the fragrance. One arm wrapped around her shoulders while the other placed below her knees.

Her eyes reached up, searching for . . . there he was. The gleam of the remaining sun shielded the moment he tilted his head to the side, clearing her vision to reveal the man she dearly missed. She loved everything about him, from his muscular build to his pale skin. From the three clawed scars on his right cheek to his inner personality. From his blood red hair to his silver eyes.

He was here. He was holding her . . . he was here.

"Kouta," she exhaled. She loved the sound of his name escape her lips. What was there not to love about it?

He grinned, both holding unexplained emotions and gloom. "Diamond," he exhaled back. That one release of breath proved that he missed her just as much as she missed him.

She pulled up her right hand and placed it on the hand on her shoulder. She shivered. He was always so warm despite his pale skin. "What are you doing here? You know the Docks don't want you here."

"They never want me here. There's nothing saying I've been banished. I can come and go as I please."

He always did find a way past a loophole.

She closed her eyes. His voice was deep and soothing, welcoming yet deadly if he was angry enough. How had she lived centuries without this, without him? "Derek suspected I had communications with you."

He rolled his eyes with a smirk, "You did."

Yeah, she did. They texted each other frequently. She had to stop because she feared Derek would take her phone. Yeah, he did that. He knew better than to take belongings of hers, but it would still be a pain if he found messages sent and received from Kouta.

The two Demon Lords hated each other since day one. This was thousands of years ago, a time when Diamond roamed free in the underworld and there were no fears. Long story short, Diamond's pack, she, Kouta and their other comrade, Ryosuke, had been interrupted of their good times of playing and hanging out and faced with the dilemma of life.

It sucked really, but it happened.

Now that she thought about it, she hadn't seen or spoken to Ryosuke in quite some time. Was he still a troublemaker? Probably. He was such a smartass and a teaser. Diamond loved the guy.

Thoughts of Ryo would have to wait. She was with Kouta now. That always came first.

She rubbed his knuckles with her thumb. "Do you plan to leave me again?"

His grip on her tightened. It wasn't painful in the slightest. "I'm not going anywhere. We've parted for too long. Far too long."

Far too long it had been. Diamond was starting to think she would never see Kouta again. He had always calmed her during her troubled times. He had always been the one to sooth her when she needed it most. In his eyes, she was not the youngest of the Three Death Daughters, she was not a Demonic Princess and most certainly, she was not Mrs. Southbound.

To him, she was Diamond.

She sunk into him. She couldn't help herself. He took her embrace as she pulled herself up and wrapped her arms around his neck. He wrapped his arms around her, meshing their chests together, bringing them as close as possible. "I've missed you," he admitted in her ear. His cool breath fanned her,

causing her to shiver.

She gripped him tighter, if possible, "I know." She said, joking him a bit. "I've missed you more."

This was the only time she could be herself. She wasn't the stone cold killer the Docks thought she was . . . okay she was at times, but she had a feminine side too. She was independent, curious, cautious, and loved a good fight, but she wanted affection, free life and even love. Yes, love. She wanted it. Kouta seemed the one to give it.

Diamond took his affections. She also gave him her own, creating a bond Derek would never know.

His embrace brought back so many memories. Kouta had morphed her from a chivalrous piece of rock to a hard, rough, and precious diamond. Ryosuke had helped in the process, of course. Except her feelings for Kouta is what helped her grow. Ryosuke was a brotherly figure who was taller, heartless and skinny as a twig. Kouta was the opposite body wise. Both men—not boys like most of these assholes—gave Diamond the optimism, companionship and self-esteem she required.

They pulled back, but remained in each other's arms. His silver eyes beamed as the setting sun bathed behind him. He was beautiful. Derek was nowhere near this good looking. Even Ryo looked better than he did. Derek was handsome, but to Diamond, knowing his personality, Derek was malicious.

"I made a friend," she announced, happier than she should have been.

Kouta's eyes widened in shock. His hands went down to her hips, hanging there. He grinned. "How did that miracle happen?"

"Respect," she answered, grinning herself. Was she not supposed to notice his movements? He knew better than to expect her not to. He was teasing again, she knew.

One hand came up her slender back. He pressed his nail through the fabric of her short sleeved brown shirt, creating random patterns. "Who's the friend?"

Diamond's eyes closed. She shivered again. She fought back a moan. *If only we were skin to skin.* "Nao Nakamura," she breathed. That wasn't supposed to come out.

Kouta's eyebrows shot up then fell back down. He nodded in approval, "The Powerless Demon, huh? I like him too. He's one of those rare demons who actually respect their elders."

Poor thing, Nao was. The unfortunate guy was nicknamed as *'The Powerless Demon'*. Unlike his fellow Demonic members, he was the only demon who held no supernatural abilities. All he had as a spiritual weapon was ... well nothing. Only his physical skills could protect him, and he couldn't even use those.

Still, Diamond liked the little fella. He hadn't betrayed her since their chat on the beach. He even still treated her like a higher up. They were equals now. Not power wise of course, but friendship wise.

Wow. Friendship. Other than Kouta and Ryosuke, she never thought she would have another friend. He could join the group; however, Kouta and Ryo had to agree first. Knowing Kouta, he would probably let him join their little posy. Ryosuke though—the bastard would get used to him.

Unexpectedly, Kouta threw his head back over his left shoulder, in the direction of Diamond's room a few steps away. She had the hovering room, the room with nothing but dark space underneath a stone floor. Honestly, she liked it. That's why it was *her* room. She came here when she wanted times away from Derek. You could only enter the room through the ceiling entrance, which made privacy so much better.

Diamond slid her hands onto his dark red shirt, feeling his rough chest expand as he sniffed the air. She sniffed, as well, wondering what he smelled. "Blood."

"Something happened," he said. He turned to her, eyes moving up and down, looking for something. What though, she didn't know. "You want to go check it out?"

The metallic tang smell swirled through the air daily, but this amount was a little questionable. She hadn't had much adventure lately so ... "Let's go."

Kouta stood to his feet a second later, bringing Diamond with him. He pulled her close, preparing to flash to the source of the blood. Diamond stopped him. "I'll fly you there. There's no need to waste your energy."

Kouta was a Vampire Demon, the lord of the Vampire Demons, actually, and vampires could only teleport ten times a year. He obviously flashed to get to Diamond's location. His appearance had been so sudden. She didn't know how many times he flashed before then so she wouldn't risk it. Vampires who teleported more than their limit suffered a world of pain as their punishment. Her own father, for the sheer fact that he didn't like vampires, placed this curse.

The bastard.

"It's alright. I only teleported once this month."

"Month?" She stared at him hard. Was that supposed to make her feel better?

He nodded. "Yes, this month."

She rolled her eyes this time. With a single mental command, Diamond's angelic jet black wings slipped from their slits, ripped past her T-shirt and expanded wide, bringing darkness upon the area.

Kouta gazed, observing every black feather and every vein pulsing through her wings. Her cheeks heated. "Beautiful," he said. His eyes reached hers. "Truly remarkable."

She cleared her throat. She couldn't appear into the castle like this. Kouta knew, once Diamond entered the castle, he would act as her second in command, standing behind her at all times like a trustworthy slave. He once admitted to liking the personality change. "I like a dominant woman," he'd said.

Such a teaser.

She flopped her wings. One flop, two, she was in the air. She grabbed under Kouta's arms as he gently but firmly grabbed her biceps. Together, the two headed off of the room and made their way to the source of the blood scented area.

Diamond only hoped Derek wasn't at the scene. If he was, an upcoming battle would be absolute.

Based on Jezebel's reading, Reiko was on the fifth floor. They were close, yet so far away.

Kenta and Jezebel had made their way through the mansion's underground facilities, past the main floor, dashed up a spiral stairway to the second floor, took care of several demons willing to rat them out, made their way to the third floor and now they were stuck. There was a staircase leading to the fourth floor on the other side of the hallway. Two large foot soldiers guarded the stairway, standing tall, heads high, eyes staring forward.

Jezebel described the men: chocolate skin, black spiky hair, muscled, and determined with swords. Not the best combination to have as enemies. As allies, they would be more than welcomed.

She pulled back from peering over the corner. They had a dark wall as an advantage. Because of Jezebel's white wardrobe, though, the shadows weren't their best friends. They had to move fast. "Fiddlesticks," she sighed, staring at the domed black ceiling.

"Can you take them out?" Kenta asked, willing to make the first move.

"I could, but I don't know if there are men at the top of the stairs, too. If the men at the bottom are mysteriously taken out, most likely they will contact their leader."

Lord knew, having Derek involved would mean a world of trouble. Kenta was surprised they weren't sensed already. Jezebel hid their scents and their presences, but because they were demons, their senses heightened. They might have been hiding the fact that they knew. Whether they knew or not though, Kenta still wanted to get out of here.

He hated this place. Almost all of the halls were painted in dark colors: some navy blue, violet, black, dark brown and even raspberry. It wasn't the colors that bothered him. It was the fact that there was a demon at every corner of this place. He knew something would pop out when he least expected it. He was on guard and cautious of every step.

He just prayed Derek and his Demonic members hadn't sensed them already. If so, then they were in trouble.

"Let's make a surprise attack. I'll go first, take them out and you dash up the stairs and look for the entrance to the fifth floor."

She stared. She just stared. Her face was so blank she looked like a completely different person. "Have you not been listening to a word I've said? We can't make reckless moves like that."

"Well we need to try something. Reiko's life is on the line."

He didn't want Reiko's life to end. That would be another family to enter a world of depression and questions Kenta couldn't-wouldn't-answer. Plus, he didn't want to return to his girls with news that he hadn't made it in time. To face them and inform them of such news would break their hearts and shatter whatever was left of Kenta's youthful soul. He'd given a piece of himself to every single group of princesses he brought together. Each death he had effected and ripped that piece he gave to shreds. He didn't have much left; on the other hand, he was willing to give what he had.

Returning with dreadful news would crumble everything else he had. He wasn't worried about himself as much as his girls. They had agreed to be a part of this fight. To break them with news like this, he wouldn't do. He wouldn't return to them that way. Never.

"We could mist past them," Jezebel suggested. By moving, they risked being scented but not physically sensed. By standing here, they weren't sensed at all.

Kenta bit on his bottom lip, debating the idea. He had to think fast though. The slightest second could mean salvation or damnation for Reiko.

He nodded, "Slow and steady."

Jezebel nodded. She led the way around the corner, Kenta right on her heels. The second she entered the hall, she stopped. Kenta bumped into her.

She didn't move on impact. He stepped to her left side, wondering what she was staring at. Because she was two inches taller than him, seeing above her was difficult.

The minute he stepped beside her, he saw why she froze so quickly.

Diamond stood in front of the guards with a tall man right behind her.

The guy was as tall of the foot soldiers, maybe even taller; standing well over six feet.

"How long have you been standing here?" Diamond asked. Her hands clutched to her hips in authority as her eyes pierced the two guards. Their knees shook.

"We just got here, Mrs. Southbound," the guard on the left reported.

Her eyes narrowed on him and her lips pulled back, revealing her canines. The blood red-haired man gripped her shoulder, instantly calming her down. She cleared her throat. The man pulled his hand away, placing it to his side. "Fine, good work. Now let me through."

The guards took two large steps to the side, giving her and the man more room than they needed. To Kenta's surprise, Diamond turned to their direction. She glared for several seconds then tilted her chin in the stairs direction.

Could she see them? Obviously, if she was instructing them to follow her. How long had she noticed them? Was this a trap?

She traveled up the stairs one by one. The man followed, of course. Together, Kenta and Jezebel zoomed forward and moved up the stairs before the guards could even move to their first spots. They were careful not to pound their way up the stairs. They were unnoticed, thank goodness.

They reached the fourth floor. This hallway was nothing like the previous ones. This hall was painted an icy blue, lighter than the sky but not quite white. It held no windows. Only large dark wood doors with crystal hexagon shaped doorknobs. Jezebel turned to her left, looking for Diamond. Kenta spotted her and the unknown man heading right. He tapped Jezebel's shoulder, signaling her to follow. She did so.

"Nice cloaking, but it didn't work on me," Diamond said. She continued her walk. It was more of fast steps than a walk. The man followed her with stride. "I expected someone to notice," Jezebel said. "I should have known it would be you." She didn't seem too bothered by the idea of being noticed by the one Demon Docks member that could blow you up without you even realizing what happened to yourself.

"Yeah you should have," Diamond chuckled with humor Kenta never realized she had.

He heard of Diamond, the youngest of the Three Death Daughters and Derek's Southbound's wife. She was a woman with no emotions, always ready to kill when needed, or in her case, wanted. He also heard that Diamond never took orders. The person who ordered her always ended up with their flesh and bones scattered around the area they once stood.

Diamond's one little chuckle with Jezebel had changed his perspective of her. Maybe she wasn't so bad after all.

"You're Kenta Shiroyama, right?" the man asked. He peered over his shoulder, glaring at Kenta with his stunning silver eyes. His voice was on the deeper side and his canines poked out as he spoke.

"Yes," Kenta answered, not knowing what else to say.

Diamond stopped in the middle of the hall, looking up to the man. "I didn't know you wanted introductions. You should have told me."

He shrugged with a grin, "I didn't want to bother you."

Was there a calming aura around these two? Surely not. They both screamed authority and power. Where was this gentleness coming from?

She looked both ways; left and right, then up and even down. They were alone.

She pointed from one to the other. "Kouta, this is Kenta and Jezebel."

Unable to help themselves, they froze. Maybe they both had the same thought here.

Kouta. As in the Kouta Vulturine.

"Lord Vulturine?" Jezebel asked, holding herself back from gawking.

The man nodded, apathetic by their frozen state. "Yeah, that's right."

"Oh sweet Saki," Jezebel exhaled, releasing a breath she didn't know she had. Her hands went to the heavens as she dropped to her knees. "Oh, sweet Saki, help me."

If "Oh, sweet Saki" was another statement for "Oh, sweet Jesus" then Kenta understood where this girl was coming from. Kouta Vulturine, the lord of the Vampire Demon clan, one of the most notorious warriors of the battlefield had joined the Demon Docks cause.

They were so dead.

Several foot soldiers entered the hall. Diamond and Kouta turned to each other, moving their mouths but whispering nothing. The soldiers acknowledged their presence with a nod then exited down the stairs. Their mouths stopped moving. "What's wrong with you?" Diamond asked.

Jezebel stood to her feet, eyeing Kouta. "Be straight up with me. Are you joining the rebellion?"

"No," he answered grinningly.

"Oh, sweet Saki save us from . . . wait, you said no?"

"That's right," he nodded.

Kenta opened his mouth but closed it again. What was he supposed to say? He should have been grateful. One of the most famous men in the underworld wasn't going to kill them.

That had to be a lie.

"I didn't come here to fight against your cause. I'm here for strict pleasure."

Pleasure? Not business?

When Diamond's cheeks headed to a rosy red, everything cleared. He was here for Diamond. No explanation required.

"That's your business, not mine," Jezebel said, hands up in allowance.

Kouta smirked.

Diamond cleared her throat. It must have been one of her uneasy gestures. "You want Reiko, right?"

Kenta nodded.

"Follow me." She continued her walk, turning to the left. There was another staircase in the center of the hall. They head up, ignoring the beings that passed them. The demons hadn't turned around in suspicion. They hadn't even tried to speak to Diamond or Kouta. That was good. That was very good.

They gratefully reached the fifth floor. These walls were painted the same as the previous floor but this hallway held large windows to the right. These windows had pieces of separate glasses of color, glued together and shining vibrantly as the setting sun casted its last shadows on the earth for that way.

Diamond's boots clicked on the hardwood as she headed down, ignoring all the rooms to her left until she reached her destination; a large dark wood door with a crystal knob. She twisted the knob. The door wouldn't budge.

"I'll unlock it," Jezebel said. She could maneuver her wind to slip through the lock and get the door open.

"No need," Diamond intertwined her hands and faced her palms to the door, stretching her fingers. Her hands dropped to her sides. Her leg lifted and her booted foot slammed against the door. It swung open, breaking the hinges and shocking the person in the room.

As Diamond stepped to the side, Kenta went past her. A huff of relieved breath exited him.

Reiko watched him. Her hands were handcuffed to the headboard. They rested to her sides. They wouldn't allow her to even shift to other sides of the bed. Her eyes were bloodshot. Her arms shook. Dried blood streaked her face and neck. "Ken . . . Kenta," She burst into tears.

Jezebel must have lowered her barrier against the outside world. She was able to see him. Now, they would be noticed. Kenta didn't care about something so trivial.

He rushed to her, searching the nightstand, the bed. Where was the key? Jezebel ran beside him and grabbed the cuff on her right wrist. She pointed to the lock hole and wiggled her finger. Reiko's wrist freed. Good thing Jezebel was here. Kenta would have sliced the bed to bits to get his friend free. She did the same action with her other wrist, freeing Reiko completely.

She jumped up, wrapped her arms around Kenta and clutched his shirt. She released her sobs and cries, not giving a care in the world about their audience.

What did they do to her? Kenta wondered as he embraced her back, thankful to have her safe and sound. In the time she'd been out of his sight, they could have tortured her. They could have abused her, seeking answers to their attack plan. Or worse . . .

Kenta brought one arm lower, sliding it under her knees, picking her up protectively. "I'm here princess. You're safe now."

He turned to Diamond and Kouta. She winked at him. Kouta nodded in acceptance.

"You're going to try and kill us now, huh?" Jezebel asked. Still had some doubts, huh?

They shook their heads. "We're not enemies."

"We're not allies either," Kouta said, all hint of kindness gone.

"But we wouldn't kill you unless *you* tried to kill *us*," Diamond added with a grin.

She was pretty when she showed emotion. Random thought gone. He needed to leave. He had to get Reiko to safety . . .

They needed to find Damon.

"We need to find Damon," Jezebel parroted his thoughts.

"He's close," Diamond said. She had sensed him and Jezebel. So finding Damon was no issue. "He should be here . . ."

Damon dashed into the room, observing the area, preparing to attack. He calmed the moment he saw the scene. "I'm the only Spirit Being who has been here before and I made it last?"

"Yup," Jezebel smiled.

"Whoa," Kouta grinned, shocking everyone. He took a step to Damon and outstretched his hand. "You're Damon Sasaki, right? 'The Silver—Haired Menace. Kouta Vulturine."

Damon gaped. "The Vampire Demon Lord." He grabbed his hand in a strong shake. "I've heard so much about you. You're kickass on the battleground. I would love to battle you one day."

"Same here. Clashing blades with you would be a real honor."

Kenta loved the collaboration and the promise to a good future, but they seriously needed to leave. Reiko's hold around his neck was loosening, signaling she needed help and fast.

"Talk later," Jezebel said, waving her hands, telling Damon to come closer. "We need to go."

The men separated. Diamond headed to the door, leaving the group while dismissively waving her hand. "You were never here."

"Nice to meet you," Kouta said then exited as well.

Without another moment's delay, the group teleported home.

☙

"It's getting dark," Ayano stated. It was more of a fact than a statement.

"Yeah," Mary answered, not really caring. She would wait all night if she had to. There was no way she was leaving this spot until she knew Kenta was alright. She kept thinking-believing-that Kenta would teleport back here with Reiko in hand. She didn't know why but she felt she needed to stay here. Was that so wrong?

The ladies rested on their backs, soaking up moist dirt. She didn't care. All Mary cared about now was Kenta and Reiko's safety. She wished the best for Damon and Jezebel too, of course.

They had waited there together, silent the entire time until now, when Ayano informed Mary of the upcoming darkness. Sazuma had called about an hour ago, asking if she was alright. Mary knew her sister cared about her. Leaving like that was a random spark of annoyance. Mary reported that she was fine and the call had ended there.

She didn't say when she was coming home. Sazuma understood, Mary guessed and allowed her to remain here.

Mary's mind wandered. It wasn't just from watching Kenta leave with his fellow Heavenly Beings that bothered her. It was the fact that they came to Damon for assistance. Kenta was strong. He could have saved Reiko with Ayano by his side, she was sure of it. Surprisingly, Jezebel had appeared out of nowhere; apparently Damon summoned her, knowing they would come to him for help, and changed Mary's game plan completely.

Plus, she wanted to go with them. She wanted to aid in the rescue of her friend, but Jezebel had denied that too. Mary wasn't weak. She could handle a few demons or two. *By what? Throwing water at them?* Her mind had repeated the questions every time the thought of assisting Kenta flew past her.

What was the point of having a Water Princess anyway? Water couldn't kill. It couldn't protect anyone. Demons could fly right past her water defenses and slash her on sight. She'd been shot once in Lune Park—today actually—so what was the problem with getting stabbed too?

She sighed. That was a terrible thought to have.

Meeting Damon. Yeah, she would think of that. Meeting Damon and actually getting a chance to meet him was interesting. One, she hadn't expected him to help. Two, she hadn't expected Kenta to work with him. And three, she was surprised Hiroko had demanded his help. He seemed to get a kick out of that and assisted them. If it wasn't for her, Damon wouldn't have helped, most likely.

And Aurora. She was a very beautiful woman. When it came to Damon, she was highly possessive. They had been together for over ten years so their relationship should have blossomed into something pleasant, tender and amazing.

Funny, that's the same amount of time Kenta and Ayano had been together.

Mary froze. My gosh, she was right. They *had* been together for over ten years. They should have been dating! What if they were and they had kept it a secret the entire time? Ayano had been depressed when Kenta decided to leave without her. Maybe that was a secret message saying she would miss him both partners and lovers wise.

Mary lolled her head, facing Ayano. She gazed at the midnight sky. The oranges and red had fallen over the horizon, leaving dark blues and violets and an approaching crescent moon. That moon shined on Ayano, causing her to glow. She was gorgeous! Her hair revivified a dark gray with a dash of silver instead of charcoal black. Her skin was the richest honey and her wardrobe hugged her body. She wore a blue short sleeved shirt that stopped at her belly button. Black jeans hugged her legs and flat black boots covered her feet. Her burgundy eyes were rubies now. The moonlight kissed her so lovingly.

It makes sense that Kenta picks her rather than you.

Yeah, that thought hurt. It killed her actually. Ayano was far more beautiful, far more talented and powerful than Mary would ever be. They knew each other, fought together, protected each other. They lived together. They were equals. He was a fine man while she was a decadent woman. How could Mary possibly compete?

Did a fine man and a feeble teenager sound like a smart match?

Mary didn't think so.

"You're staring," Ayano said. She didn't turn her head to face her.

Mary's eyes bore her down, watching her intently. "What's your relationship with Kenta?"

She blinked. "What do you mean?"

"You know what I mean."

"Relationships could mean anything. They could mean friendship, comrades, subordinates . . ."

She was stalling. "Are you two dating?" It was more rushed than she would have liked.

She faced her now. "Why does it matter?"

She wasn't answering the question! Cool it down girl, she thought next. She shrugged "Just curious."

Ayano smirked, "No, you want to make sure you have Kenta all to yourself." True . . . so? "Can you just answer the question?"

"I knew you liked him, since day one. He seemed to like you even before meeting you."

Mary hadn't always liked him. He used to be her and Sazuma's personal stalkers. There was no way she would . . . he liked her before they met? Curiosity rose furthermore. "For how long?"

She didn't pretend to not know what she meant. "We only found you for a day and a half, so I guess he liked you then."

A day and a half. He crushed on her for a week and a day . . . and a half. Mary couldn't stop her grin. It was ear to ear, threatening to spring into a full blown smile. He *did* like her too . . . now what?

Her sense of urgency and annoyance faded, "So . . . you two aren't dating."

She kept her smirk, "Not at all."

"Why not?" Yes, she was glad Kenta was single and had eyes for her . . . now why would he turn down or not even consider being with such a rare and prestigious woman.

"So many questions," she sighed, but kept smirking. "I should have known this was going to happen. You're too determined to know everything. Maybe you should loosen up on knowledge a bit."

"I refuse to be stupid."

"There's a different between being stupid and not knowing everything."

"Just tell me why you two have never dated." This girl was good at stalling. It almost worked, too.

"Who says we never dated in the past?"

So they had been together. Mary's eyes widened. "You were together before?" "No but who says we've never been?"

"Oh, my gosh Ayano!" Frustration was getting the best of her. Mary shot to a sitting position. Ayano chuckled, which still surprised her. She would have to get used to Ayano's released humor. That would come later. She needed details.

Ayano's hands disappeared behind her head, acting as a pillow. She watched Mary, holding back the rest of her laughter. "We never dated," she admitted. "We never wanted to date each other and we still don't. We're friends, nothing more."

"Friends for ten years?" Mary had never heard or seen such a thing.

"There is such a thing as a guy friend. Just because you know a guy, doesn't mean you have to date him."

Mary knew that. It was still strange. Kenta was so handsome. Ayano was so lovely. How could they resist reach other?

"I admit, I thought Kenta was handsome," Ayano said. Could she read Mary's mind? "I still think he is. As a child, he was my savior. He will always be my savior. He was like my knight in shining armor in a way, except he didn't wear armor and he was a Spirit Being."

Mary grinned. That was cute. The grin faded. Time to get serious. "He's lived many years. He must have had many girlfriends." And, those girls would pay dearly for being with him.

Ayano's smirk dulled, worrying Mary greatly. "Not many," she merely said.

Should she proceed? His past was none of her business. If she wanted the answers, she would have to ask Kenta. Knowing this, and coming to realization with the facts, she allowed the questions in her head to pass. "Oh," she said, turning back to the stars. "I bet they were lovely."

If all of his girlfriends had looked like Ayano, Mary was in for a good competition.

"They were okay," she spat with tedium.

They weren't gorgeous? Mary had a chance in the running to becoming Kenta's next top girlfriend?

"Don't get me wrong. They were cute, but he could do better."

Yes! Mary did have a chance. *Stop acting like a desperate schoolgirl.* Ignore the mind! Happy times waited.

"Why did he end the relationships?" Damn, there was the question. It slipped out without her permission. Oh well, no take backs.

Her eyes slowly closed, "You're going to have to ask him."

This was a dangerous road. Mary closed her mouth, not wanting anything else to come out. If she wanted answers, she would ask Kenta. Done and done.

"You guys are still here?"

Mary's sense of awareness sharpened. Lightning shot through her as she turned around to face the entrance of Valla Park. Kenta stood there, body relaxed, a gentle grin on his face.

He was here. He was really here!

Running on pure instinct, Mary leaped up and ran to him. He met her in the middle, wrapping his arms around her and squeezing her into him. She took it. She took it and loved every damn minute of it. She'd work on her language later.

She pulled back and grabbed his cheeks. She looked at him, recording every movement his features made. He did the same to her except kept his arms around her. God, how she missed him. She didn't realize how much she'd missed him until now. It had been too long. She wasn't leaving his side again.

"What are you doing out here?" He asked in a chuckle. "It's late, getting cold and the freaks come out at night."

She dared them to come. The weirdo's. "I wasn't leaving until I knew you were safe. If you returned here, then you might have needed help and I wanted to assist you the best way I—"

He pulled her in again. He hid in her black hair. One hand came up, pulling her head into him further while the other rested below her spine. He had hugged her like this before. He hadn't done this with anyone else. She thought she was special then. She knew she was special now. "All I need to know is that you're safe," he whispered.

She melted into him, allowing herself this pleasure. His warmth enveloped her. She hadn't realized she was as cold as she was. She intended to keep him close until she was warm again, of course.

Nah, she was keeping him anyway.

"Welcome back," Ayano approached. Her emotions were coming back. All of the dullness she held before dissipated. "How's Reiko?"

"She's with Yumiko. I might have surprised her teleporting into her living room, but Jezebel is teaching her how to heal quicker than usual. It's like a late training exercise."

"I'm sure it is," Ayano said. Mary didn't know if she was smiling. She was too busy liquefying in Kenta's tender hold.

"I'm guessing Damon's with her."

"No," Kenta answered. The hand on Mary's head slid down to her shoulder and slowly rubbed up and down. He was a really good hugger. "He went to Hiroko's house. He plans to stay there with Aurora."

"And what is Aurora doing?"

"Watching Sazuma. She told me you and Mary stayed here, acting as a lookout for me. Thanks for watching her."

"No prob," she said.

"Stella is with Yumiko if you want to pick her up."

"That information is appreciated."

Mary turned to her before she could teleport away. "Thanks Ayano, for everything."

She winked, then disappeared.

"Everything what?" Kenta asked.

Mary looked up at him. She was so close. If she rose on her toes, their lips would have touched. *Do it! Do it! Do it!* "Nothing," she answered. "Let's go home."

Kenta's grip on her tightened as they both flashed to the Kagami house.

Story 13

What *I* knew *then* and what *I* know *now*

Sazuma's cell phone vibrated, causing her to turn her attention from Aurora. The two had been discussing their favorite music and Sazuma even gave the girl permission to raid her closet. Other than five pairs of her school uniform, there was an assortment of clothes.

Sazuma was a fan of blacks, tights, and chains. There were T-shirts ranging on the darker colors with different fonts and statements on them. There were skinny jeans ranging of all colors of the rainbow and the same went for her converses racked on the shelves.

She lounged on the bed, caressing her violet bangs between her fingers. Her mind blanked. She couldn't think of anything to think about. Thinking about Mary would get her worked up, so there would be none of that. Thinking about how Kenta's mission was going would also rattle her up, so there would be none of that either. Thinking of Reiko's condition was also a rattle up in the brain.

She sighed. Was there nothing to think about?

"You have really nice clothes," Aurora praised, bringing a rainbow striped T-shirt up to her chest, seeing how it suited her. Honestly, Sazuma had no idea how a shirt like that got in her closet. Must have been a random sale, she thought.

Well, look at that. She was thinking again.

"Thanks," she said, not giving a care in the world.

"I wonder how Damon is doing."

Aurora clearly wanted to talk. Wouldn't this talk be pointless though? They could talk to themselves in the security of their minds. Why must voice boxes be used in conversation so casual? "They're fine." Sazuma said. Other than telling, "I hopes," and, "I knows," and even, "I believes," are not going to bring him, Kenta, and Jezebel back any sooner.

Aurora hung up the rainbow shirt and brought another one to her chest. This one was black studded with crushed diamonds; giving it a starry night look. That had been a gift from her mother. The shirt had originally been for Mary. Being as kind as she was, and oblivious to Sazuma's side turmoil, she had given it to Sazuma as a random gift of love. Sazuma never wore the thing. It was too shiny.

"If you didn't want to talk, you should have said so," Aurora pouted, placing her chosen shirt on the rack and peering through the others in the small space.

"If you want to talk then find something interesting to talk about." *Please don't find anything interesting to think about.*

Aurora rushed out of the closet. She plopped onto the bed, landing on her knees. Sazuma, who had been laid out toying with her hair, brought her chin to her sternum. She glared. Aurora grinned. "I have something to talk about alright."

Sazuma rushed up. Her hair was forgotten. What did she have to speak about? Angels? Demons? Other supernatural creatures like the Loch Ness Monster and Sasquatch?

"Damon had a lot of adventures of his time," she started. Sazuma's interest dropped, leaving nothing but uncaring. Did it look like she wanted to know more about Damon?

He was a good looking dude who must have had a thing for Hiroko. He kept smirking at her when she wasn't looking. He and Kenta had a past and she couldn't care, even if she tried. That was their business, not hers. Sazuma could tell Damon was powerful. It seemed to radiate from the guy, as if he had an infinite supply.

He *was* a Spirit Being. How long had he lived for?

"Damon doesn't tell me a lot about his past. Even though we've been together for years, he hasn't told me much of anything. But to shut me up, he did tell me a few things." Sazuma quirked a smirk. *Just to shut her up, huh? Nice.* "He told me he was involved in some battles here and there, he watched history evolve from bad, to better, to bad again. He even met a lot of people along the way."

Aurora paused, waiting for Sazuma to ask, "Who did he meet?" Once she asked with a sigh of callous, Aurora continued, "Well, the people Damon met were humans and all kinds of beings. Only certain people caught his attention, which I am not at all surprised about. Damon's picky about the people he hangs around." She put up her fingers. "He met the Mother Angel Saki, some other angels, and even some demons. He met the Three Death Daughters, some demon ninjas before they were assassinated, Bat Demons, and Ryosuke, but he always wanted to meet Kouta Vulturine."

Sazuma praised her palm up, stopping the girl. Shock zapped at her like a lightning bolt. "Ryosuke, the Gate Keeper of Hell?" Was she serious? Damon couldn't have met someone so powerful.

When she nodded, Aurora proved Sazuma wrong. "Yeah, the Gate Keeper. I never met him, but Damon says he's a nice guy if you don't piss him off."

The supernatural world just got a whole lot realer. Sazuma thought she could handle the occasional demon and even a horde coming at her out of nowhere—A.K.A. Lune Park—but she couldn't believe that Demon Lords were a part of this fight now. This went far more than just seven teens and Spirit Beings defending this area like the Princess Squad that they were.

These were actual Demon Lords. Sazuma had researched them while having her obsessed moments some year or two ago. Demon Lords were rulers of the separate sections of Hell. Okay, yeah, that was obvious. But then again, Demon Lords couldn't travel above ground without a soul to conquer. Yeah that was a given too, but the sons and daughters of those demons could rise up and act in place of their parents.

Ryosuke was one of the names she found. He was the son of Hades; one of the main lords. Because of a sin he committed, he was punished by forever guarding, opening and closing the gates of Hell. That was strange to her. If he committed a sin, shouldn't he have been praised? He was a demon. They lived for committing sins.

She sighed. Whatever. The fact that Damon had met Ryosuke was unbelievable. How had the two met? Had they dueled in the past? Most importantly, why was Sazuma caring about this so much?

Because your life just became a thousand times more precious, her mind answered for her. She spoke the truth though. No wonder the past princesses wanted to bail.

"Who else had he met?" Sazuma asked, wanting to know more about the silver haired Spirit Being. What brought the sudden wonder, Sazuma didn't know.

Aurora shrugged. "He met Akira, Kenta and Ayano before he resurrected me. I don't know much about him other than what I told you."

"Resurrected?" Sazuma's head tilted. She didn't know about Aurora's past, neither did she care, but the urge to know was rising. "Damon has that ability?"

Her eyes turned away, facing the floor, and leaving Sazuma in a slight state of surprise. "Nevermind. I told you too much. If Damon finds out I told you anything, he might leave me."

Leave her? Was that why she was so possessive? Sazuma had thought she just wanted Damon for herself. She didn't want seven teens flirting with her man. Maybe Sazuma thought wrong.

"You don't have to tell me about you and him in general. I don't care about that. I just want to know more about the demons he met." What other demons had he met? How extreme was this fight going to be?

"You're going to have to ask him," she said. The amusement and excitement from speaking of Damon was gone, as if it was never there. Either she switched emotions too swiftly or the topic was painful enough to discard the exciting emotions.

"But," Aurora said, the mood brightening a tad, "I would like to know about you."

There wasn't much to know, she wanted to say but didn't. Aurora had admitted some things, so Sazuma knew she had to do the same. "I'm sixteen with black hair, black eyes and I hate most people." Those were basic facts but it was something.

Aurora grinned again. It still held sadness. "I know that Fire Princess," she said, knowing Sazuma might say she was the princess of the flame, "but I want to know something your friends might know about you; something I don't know, but your closest friends would know."

Why confess something so personal if info like that remained a secret? She shrugged, "I like black, I'm a loner, and I'm interested in nominal things."

She giggled. Okay, what was so funny? Sazuma didn't pop a joke. Why the laughing?

"What's so funny?" She glared, contemplating whether to stop confession time or not.

"You say you're a loner and, yet, you're with a group of your friends. The fact that you have friends shows you're not a loner."

Okay, yeah . . . she might have been right, but loners had friends too. There was a group of loner people in the world . . . right? "I barely depend on them." She hoped Aurora hadn't heard the defiance in her voice. She must have because she giggled again.

"You're not a loner. You just have issues when it comes to people."

Sazuma might have viewed people as idiots until they revealed their smarts. That didn't mean she had problems with people. She was just a loner. "Say what you want, but that's what I am."

"Uh huh," Aurora crossed her arms. "I warn you, someone will appear into your life and show you that you're not alone or a loner. Just you wait."

Sazuma would say she was scared, but she wasn't. Bring it on.

"So about Damon's connections," She scratched her head, "You have to know something, anything. Any form of information would be—"

All words and movements froze. Kenta and Mary arrived into the room, not here one moment, randomly popping out of nowhere in the next. Aurora leaped from the bed, landing on the floor.

Sazuma's mini heart attack died down. She fluttered her hand over her heart, making sure she was well enough to move, or do anything. "You damn Spirit Beings. Causing heart attacks and shit." This was an experience Sazuma never wanted to feel again.

Mary, who had been tucked in Kenta's arms, pulled out of his embrace with a grin. "Sorry. It was the easiest way to get home."

"You shouldn't have stayed in that damn park!" Sazuma's hand continued to flutter. She had to calm down. Her voice squeaked. She only did that when she was utterly angry. How she got her squeaker, she'll never know.

"Reiko's returned," Kenta reported. "Yumiko is tending to her injuries. She's taking care of her parents as well."

Sazuma was beyond relieved about her friend's safe return. She had injuries, Sazuma expected that, but she was here and well. In one piece, she hoped. Her fear calmed. Her fluttering hand died down.

Aurora rose from the ground. Her hands flattened on the bed. She panted, slowly calming. That Spirit Being teleporting crap must have been a shocker for her too. She was a Spirit Being too. She shouldn't have been so startled. Oh well. At least she wasn't alone.

"So where's Damon?" She asked, clearing her throat, acting like she hadn't just fallen on her ass from fear.

"He's with Hiroko." Kenta answered.

That was all it took for Aurora to disappear. She teleported away, heading to Hiroko's house, leaving the Kagami's for a night to themselves. Scratch that. She left the Kagami's alone with Kenta. Her mother wasn't home yet, so they truly were alone. Didn't scare Sazuma one bit. Mary, on the other hand, wasn't a fan of loneliness.

But why? She was the one everyone loved. Appreciation, adoration and want were her allies. How could someone so loved, hate aloneness?

Mary made her way to the bed. She plopped onto her azure sheets and slipped off her black sneakers.

"I'll be on the roof," Kenta said. He turned to the window, preparing to teleport, Sazuma guessed.

"No, wait!" Mary shot to her feet. Kenta peered over his shoulder, looking at her in concern. Realizing how desperate she looked and sounded; her cheeks shaded a rosy red. "I mean, stay safe."

He grinned, "I should be saying that to you." He disappeared. There were thuds on the roof, signaling Kenta was there. He must have sat down, because there were no other noises after that.

Mary placed herself on the bed again. She covered her face, hiding in shame.

This was the perfect opportunity for teasing. "Mrs. Desperate misses her man."

Her arms came down, circling around her middle. "He's not my man." Without a doubt, she held gloom, as if Kenta would never be hers. Secretly, Sazuma knew her sister liked the dude, but not to the extent of considering him as a boyfriend. She couldn't date a Spirit Being. They were from two different worlds, never meant to unite as one unit, never meant to be together.

Why was *The Little Mermaid* coming to mind?

"He might not be mine," Mary inhaled. She exhaled with a grin, "Not yet."

Yet? There was a yet? "Whatever you're thinking, I don't approve. You can't date him."

Her mouth dropped. She couldn't believe she had heard those words. Sazuma couldn't believe she had said it. "Why not?"

"Because you can't be together," she answered, not hating herself in the slightest. "You barely know this guy and you're willing to date him?"

"I'll get to know him," she murmured.

"I don't care. You can't date him and that's final."

Mary stuck out her tongue. Sazuma rolled her eyes. If this was going to be an argument, Mary could have at least cussed at her. She could have done more than just stick out her tongue. She could have thrown a pillow, stood with anger, or even shout at her. But stick out her tongue? She was so innocent.

She twisted around and plopped her head onto her pillow. Her back was in Sazuma's full view.

"I stick by my decision."

"We're not talking about this anymore," Mary shouted with authority, as if she won the conversation.

Sazuma's eyes rolled. She got off her bed and took this chance to get ready for her evening of rest. She sighed, not knowing what else to do but change her clothes to nightwear.

Why can't she date Kenta? she wondered. Why indeed though. He was a nice guy—respectful, charming and powerful. He even brought Reiko back, returning her to her rightful place among their group.

So why not let her have him? Did she want him all to herself? Sazuma shook her head as she brushed her teeth. She didn't want Kenta.

She didn't . . . did she?

Derek had summoned the Demonic Princesses and Princes to tonight's dinner in the main dining hall. He found out about the Spirit Beings and the angel Jezebel infiltrating the castle and taking their princess back.

Riku had heard about it, as well.

But, he was too late.

After sensing not one, but two Spirit Beings and an angel in the castle, he rushed to his room, knowing exactly why they were there in the first place. Riku had been in one of Derek's many 'relaxation' rooms, where humanoid demon women danced and bathed themselves with the wine that humans called 'fine'. Once the feelings of his enemies emerged, he dashed out of the room, forgetting the women he found somewhat pleasure in watching. Too bad the location of that room was on the other side of the mansion, nowhere near his room.

If only he hadn't been so far away. He could have made it to his room and challenged the beings then and there for custody of Reiko.

Damn it! He couldn't even face them. His door has been kicked in. A heavy boot had caused the damaged based on the imprint left on the door. The scent of sandalwood whiffed the air and Reiko was gone. Droplets on Riku's tan sheets were the only evidence left that she was even there.

He had raged. He'd raged more viciously than he ever had. He ripped his sheets, punched holes in his walls and shouted to the top of his lungs. His gray cat ears pointed on his head and his matching tail swished angrily. His fangs stretched, poking his bottom lip when his mouth closed. His furious emeralds glazed.

How dare they? She was his property. He didn't even have time to play with her. Mayu had had all of the fun. Now what? What was he supposed to do? He couldn't leave. Derek had denied his request to search for her. He couldn't even go get his toy back from his enemy.

She was no toy, he thought. She was a toy. She belonged to him for his entertainment and joy. She meant nothing else. *Then why did you leave her unconscious on your bed and allow her to rest?*

He paused on that one. He had left her, hadn't he? He hadn't had his way with her like he wanted. He only left so he could wait for her to recover so he could mess her up again. It's not as if he cared for her wellbeing and left her alone.

Lying to yourself leads to future care.
Oh shut up.

He exited his thoughts as Derek entered the dining room. He was alone, which was a first. Scratch that. Lavida was close behind him. Riku had been the first to enter the room. He took a seat in one of the many black-ironed chairs around this long rectangular glass table with black iron legs. The walls were pale and two golden chandeliers with crystal hanging around the light bulbs were overhead.

Derek sat at one end of the table, nearest to the single large window, overlooking the shore. The sun had disappeared behind the horizon, leaving dark tones in the sky. Azure waves splashed onto the shore. The singing of the sea and the beach could be heard through the room's thick walls.

Lavida took her seat to Derek's left. Riku was in the center, about three seats away from them. She wore a long sleeved black dress that V-ed down below her breasts, exposing a good amount to make any man's head turn.

Any man, except Derek, apparently.

The Demon Docks leader rested his chin on the top of his intertwined hands. His elbows took on his weight as his attention went to Riku. "How are you this evening, Mr. Nakamura?"

Other than losing my woman in one day, I'm good. And yes, Reiko was his woman. The moment she touched his sheets, she was his. This applied to any woman who touched his bed, of course. Except for Mayu. He could live without her. "Fine," was all he could say. He didn't want to lie. Lying to Derek was a crime all in itself.

"You don't seem fine, dear boy. Does the loss of a princess mean that much to you?"

Hell yeah, it did. "It doesn't bother you?" He and Riku wanted Reiko for separate reasons.

Derek nodded, "Indeed. It's a shame we lost such a beautiful woman. I should have expected a sneak rescue. I guess the thought just slipped."

Slipped? Yeah right. Derek is a Demon Lord for a reason. Nothing slipped by him. Either he was distracted by Diamond . . . or he was distracted with Diamond.

Speaking of, Diamond entered the room with . . . oh, Lucifer . . . it couldn't be.

Increasing tension busted into the room the moment Lord Kouta Vulturine entered the room on Diamond's heels. Derek growled low in his throat, creating a deadly sound. Lavida sucked her teeth as she stared in loath. Riku was just shocked the Vampire Lord was even here. What business did he have here? He and Derek hate each other. Despised each other, based on the stories he heard around the mansion.

He'd heard from foot soldiers that Derek had stolen Diamond right out of Kouta's grip. The Docks lord had bought her from her father and Diamond's own flesh and blood had given her to him, defying Kouta's request not to sell her. He hadn't seen her since then and that was hundreds of years ago.

Now, he was here, back—and apparently bad. His hair was blood red and awesome!—in person. He intended to be by Diamond's side. He was doing a good job at it. Diamond sat at the other end of the table. Kouta sat to her left.

Derek glared. He hid his chin behind his hands. He glared with fury.

Diamond stared emotionless. Riku couldn't help but wonder, what was going on through her mind.

"Explain this," Derek commanded with a growl.

Diamond blinked, tilted her head and pointed to herself, all innocence. "I'm sorry. Are you talking to me?"

He clutched his hands so tight, they were becoming white. "Diamond, I demand an explanation. Why is this vampire here?"

She looked around, looking anywhere but in Kouta's direction. "I don't see a vampire demon anywhere." She then turned to Kouta. "Oh, you mean the *Vampire Lord*. You should have said so." She smiled wickedly. She held a schoolgirl tone, unduly animated and completely guiltless.

The shocker was, Lord Kouta was grinning at her. His silver eyes locked on her, watching her every move and he grinned the moment she looked in his direction. The intensity in the room increased dramatically. There was a mounting pressure Riku could barely keep away from him. It was getting difficult to breathe.

"You have a lot of nerve looking at my lord's wife so decadently, demon," Lavida spat.

Calmly, assertively, Kouta moved his head to her. "Where my eyes land isn't my fault." He licked his lips, sheeting a coat of moisture on them. "But so far, when I look at her, I like what I see."

Derek's growl no longer hid. Kouta didn't even turn to him to have their harsh stare off. He merely turned back to Diamond and winked at her. She leaned back in her chair, placing her back on the black cushions. She quirked a smirk and wiggled her eyebrows.

And Riku thought the room was harsh before. That was nothing. This feeling was entirely different. The air thickened. The room seemed to be less bright. Derek's shoulders shook as he held back his rage, shaking the table with him.

Lavida, who usually calmed Derek down during stages of annoyance, hadn't made a move. She knew she couldn't stop him. Not this time. Not only had Kouta made a move, but Diamond, his own wife had flirted with his nemesis.

For some reason, Riku couldn't change the channel. He liked this drama show.

The Yamada sisters entered the room next. Their injuries from their battle with the Silver-Haired Menace, Damon Sasaki, healed. Chikara's clothes for the evening were simple. She wore a lavender long sleeve with jeans and black flip flops. Her long hair held high in a ponytail. Her eyes were bloodshot. She must have been sleeping and was interrupted.

She was smart. She wouldn't turn down Derek's dinner request just because she wanted to sleep. Derek would have hunted her down personally. He was just that kind of person.

Emiko entered behind her, wearing a short sleeved black shirt with a turtleneck, a long zebra skirt reaching her ankles and white flip flops. Her jet black hair hung over her shoulders, reaching midway on her back. The sisters sat in front of each other. Emiko sat beside Lavida. Chikara was in front of Emiko, leaving a space between her and Derek.

Why leave the space?

Mayu entered next, wearing the same olive green shirt, matching heels and white skinny jeans she had once before, earlier in the day, actually. "Sorry I'm late everyone, please excuse my rudeness." Her hands waved up and down as she made her way to the seat between Derek and Chikara.

No one cared how late she was. No one cared for her, period. She was such an annoyance. Her voice, her movements, her self-care. Even looking at her pissed Riku off.

You're just mad because she marked your woman.

That might have been a part of his anger, but that wasn't all of it . . . was it? Nao entered now. Late, as always. Good. Now that he was here, Riku could put all of his frustrations on his little brother . . . at least that's what he thought until he placed himself on Diamond's right side. He pulled the chair up and scooted in her direction; far enough to leave space but close enough for personal comfort.

And, Diamond didn't mind at all! She allowed him to come closer. She entered him into her personal bubble. When the hell had this happened?!

"You got a problem with the demon, boy?" Diamond asked, glaring at Riku now. He hadn't even realized he was staring his brother down.

He shook his head. "Not at all."

"Acknowledge her properly," Derek said. The words *'Or else'* echoed in the air. They didn't need to be said for Riku to catch the message loud and clear.

"Excuse my rudeness, Mrs. Southbound."

"Don't call me that," Diamond's eyes narrowed. Riku could have sworn some part of his body was going to explode any second. Speaking of, he wondered how Mayu's little injury was doing. Her own daughter exploded her mother's stomach. How was that healing coming along? She must have been fine. She walked without a single limp.

"It's a fitting name for you." Lavida said. "You should be grateful to have Derek's last name."

"Last time I checked, I didn't ask for it," she snapped. Derek and Kouta's eyes stayed on her. The others looked down, hoping their bodies wouldn't explode if Diamond's vicious stare went in their direction. Riku joined them.

The thickness got stronger. Riku's inhales were sharper.

"I hope we're not interrupting," a feminine voice eased bits of the thickness. Riku raised his head. Three foot soldiers, all of them women, stood at the doorway, standing shoulder to shoulder. Each wore ankle long capes that wrapped around, hiding their entire body but the material rose in an arch, hiding the back of their necks.

A black-haired woman stood in the center. She had teal eyes, a button nose and lush red lips. She was the one who spoke. Her cape was rosewood. It shimmered with the light in the room.

To her right was a woman with blonde hair locked tight in a bun. There wasn't a single strand out of place. She had lime green eyes, a sloped nose and small lips. Her cape was red.

The last was a shorter woman, who actually looked more like a child. She had large brown eyes and long black hair that traveled down her cape, shielding its true length. Her cape was wisteria violet.

Each of the capes held random designs and patterns that were glittered silver. The women each had pale skin and their focus rested on Kouta.

"You haven't interrupted anything," the Vampire Lord said. He urged them inside. They followed, taking their seats beside their lord. The black-haired one sat to Kouta's left. The blonde and the brown-haired one sat to her left, leaving two empty chairs on Derek's right side.

"You've got to be kidding me," Lavida sighed, wiping her hand down her frustrated face. "Why are you demons here?"

They didn't answer. Their eyes touched the table.

Derek straightened in his chair and grinned, or tried to grin. He was still irritated with Diamond. "Good to see you girls again."

Not really, Riku thought. He had no idea who they were. They were hot, though.

The brown haired one, the one sitting two seats from Chikara, pointed her finger to Derek. "Fuck you, good sir."

Now Derek grinned. "What time and place."

The blonde *tsk*ed. "Your wife is in the room and you want to flirt with another woman."

The black-haired one shook her head in shame, "Disgusting."

"You girls are the ones who made the first move."

"That doesn't mean you had to take it," Kouta said. He leaned back in his chair, placing his head on the back cushion. "And where's the food? I'm starving."

"No food for you," Derek's eyes narrowed. "You weren't even invited. And, neither were your girls." He turned to the three newcomers.

"Who are you?" Nao asked curiously. It was more of a mutter. He didn't want to be rude apparently, so he'd asked so pitifully.

Riku was ashamed to have the same face with such a timid child.

"Introduction time," Kouta said, answering Nao's question, "These are three of the vampire ranks." He pointed to each woman. "This is my second in command, Aiko. Beside her is my third seat, Adriane, and beside her in the fourth seat, Bonnie." All three bowed their head in unison.

Adriane spoke, "You're Nao Nakamura, the Powerless Demon?"

It was a damn shame to have a nickname like that. Nao had no one to blame but himself for being born without any abilities.

He lowered his head, feeling the shame he deserved to feel. "Yes."

"Pleased to meet you," Bonnie smiled. With a smile so wide, revealing shining whites, she really was a child. "Lord Vulturine told us about you. Adriane thought you were a cute little *thang*."

Adriane sat straight in her chair. Her eyes darted to Bonnie. "I said no such thing." So casual, her reaction was.

Nao scratched the back of his head, nervous as all get out. Come on now! That was a nervous gesture. Demons didn't have nervous gestures. They were never nervous to even gain such gestures. What the fuck was wrong with him?

Riku sighed in irritation. He slouched in his chair, not wanting attention from Nao's new friends, who seemed to love his presence more than Riku ever would.

Adriane turned to him. "And you're Riku Nakamura, The Canceller."

Unlike Nao, Riku did have abilities. He had the ability to take other people's powers and use it against them. But his powers were limited. He could take a good amount of power, but he would soon need some more. If he took more than the holder could handle, and that person died, then Riku would lose the powers he tried to gain. He couldn't kill the person he stole the power from, which caused him to use his powers with caution. Caution sucked.

"Yes, I am," he said, not knowing why she asked.

Aiko shook her head, "Such a jackass." Her French accent made the insult sexier than it should have been.

Riku shot up straight in his chair. "You have no business calling me that." He might have been an asshole, a pedobear, and even an executioner, but he was no jackass.

"You are a jackass, good sir." Bonnie pointed. Who was she? The pointer?

"Don't call him a jackass on the spot," Kouta said.

The girls sat straight, heads high, noses up. "Sorry, my lord. It won't happen again."

Surely, they were Kouta's robot squad. They were in sync so much it was scary.

Kouta's black eyebrow rose, "I'm not saying don't do it at all. I mean call him a jackass, a dumbass, good for nothing son of a bitch."

They nodded. "Oh, good idea."

Bonnie pointed. "You are a jackass, dumbass, good for nothing son of a bitch."

Dude . . . really?

Nao covered his mouth as he chuckled. The brothers stared down. Nao kept chuckling. Things wouldn't be so funny once Riku punched his face. But he held himself back. Diamond's deadly gaze at him was more than enough to stop his wanted actions.

Destiny entered the room, wearing a black and white Lolita outfit with ruffles on the hem of her skirt. She hadn't said a word and the thickness of the room didn't bother her, at least, it didn't seem like it did. She made her way to the seat beside Emiko, two seats down from Riku.

He tensed. The spaces were getting filled.

Next came two men, both tall and both with indigo hair. Both men stood at the same height, six-foot-three-both taller than Riku-and wore black clothes. The first man to enter had brown eyes. He wore a violet cape; nothing like Kouta's ranked officers. He wore a short sleeved black shirt, dress pants and shoes. His long hair was kept in a low ponytail.

The other wore a black coat that stopped on his hips. Faded black pants and boots covered below his waist. His indigo hair hung freely, flowing as he entered. Both men also carried brown books tucked under their arms. It was a Kung fu grip under their armpit.

Riku realized exactly who the men were once he found those books.

Derek sighed in relief. "Good, you're here."

"We wouldn't miss this meeting for the world, Lord Southbound." The first man to enter said. They took the two empty chairs between Bonnie and Chikara, completely filling Derek's right side.

"This just got interesting," Diamond murmured. She was still leaned back in her chair.

Derek turned to her, preparing to speak, but he stopped when another pair of men entered.

How many people were coming?

Riku turned to them. There was no need for confusion. Riku knew exactly who these men were. Kaito and Jun, the past angels. Past angels were pretty much fallen angels, but these guys were special. Kaito, the black-haired menace, slaughtered thousands in combat; those slaughtered thousands had been innocent humans. His brother Jun, who reminded Riku of Nao, had fought alongside him but hadn't killed nearly as much as his brother. Both men were claimed as Tainted and banished from the Heavens, only to become demon allies the night they had fallen.

Kaito is notorious for his skills in battle. Jun is just as good, but he didn't praise the kill like his brother did.

The men entered, Kaito leading the way, of course. They were pretty much more muscled versions of him and Nao. It was sad really.

Kaito's spiky edged hair caressed his forehead as he stomped inside. A mahogany jacket layered a white shirt. Jeans hugged his tight legs and steel toed black boots covered his feet. Daggers and throwing stars were strapped to his black leather belt.

Jun followed his brother's trail. He wore a long sleeved white shirt that V-ed down, giving off a little bit of muscled chest. He too wore jeans and steel-toed boots. Fingerless gray gloves shielded his palms. Blonde hair tapped his temples and his forehead as he plopped in his chair. Kaito sat directly to Riku's right side.

Derek sat straight, leaning his back against his chair. "Good, the gang is all here."

Finally, Riku mentally sighed.

He snapped his fingers. Female servants wearing short violet, navy blue and black dresses with matching high heeled boots entered, carrying trays of food. Several came inside and placed down pale, gold-rimmed plates with matching silverware and napkins. The table was covered in a matter of seconds.

Silver lids were thrown off and varieties of scents consumed the room.

Riku's mouth watered. There was so much to choose from. There was turkey, grilled spiders, and boiled frog legs. There were also pork chops, raw steaks, chicken breasts, and much more. There were other dishes with baked ogre skins, fried bat wings, and perfectly seasoned dragon legs.

Pitched forks were grabbed, regular forks were positioned to strike and knees bent as everyone prepared to dash to their desired foods. Riku joined them. this was going to end up messy and someone might end up stabbed, but this was survival of the fittest ... Riku just hoped he wasn't the one to get stabbed.

"Go," Derek whispered, but everyone lashed out anyway, stabbing the steaming tanned turkey, pork chops, and steaks. Ogre skins were snatched, the grilled spiders were there one moment, gone the next; Riku hadn't gotten a single one, and the fried bat wings were heading to extinction. Riku snatched one before Mayu could get her hands on one.

He went for the chicken breasts. One, two, he threw them on his plate. He went for another, but Diamond had landed overhead, stealing the rest of the chicken. She even took the bat wings and dragon legs. She disappeared. Riku continued to snatch until there was nothing left.

All demons went back to their seats, plates full, and eyes glaring at the other. Some had got their desired food, others didn't. They would eat their platefuls anyway. Food is food.

They took their utensils and dug in. Riku held back his grin. Aiko's hand was bleeding. He knew someone would end up stabbed. He was thankful it wasn't him.

Two maids, a blonde wearing red and a black-haired wearing black, entered the room with a tray of wine glasses in one hand and chilled bottles of wine with the other. They placed the tray down and gave each dinner member a glass.

"Red or white?" the blonde asked. The reds gave their orders and the black haired moved into action, giving them their desired substance. The blonde popped the other bottle and poured the remaining members their drink. With that, they exited.

Bonnie was the first to sip. Was she even allowed to drink?

She shook her head while pressing her lips together. Her eyes squinted shut. She made the perfect sour face. "Whoa that's good!" She smiled, getting over her moment.

"Aren't you a little too young to be drinking?" Nao asked, curious about her in every way.

She shook her head. She stuck up her nose proudly, "I'll have you know, I am over two hundred years old."

"You're an infant," Kaito said, ripping the skin off of a green-skinned dragon leg. His black eyes went from her then back to his dish.

She pointed, "I'm not talking to you, Kaito!"

Yeah, she was the pointer.

He paid her no mind. Jun held back a grin and forked a piece of fried spider into his mouth.

"I must say, I'm surprised Lord Vulturine is in the premises," Eric said, facing Derek. The Vampire Lord continued his meal. He even sipped his white wine.

"I did not invite the insolent being but Diamond prefers to have him here. All I want is for my wife to be happy."

"Ick," Diamond said. Her elbow rested on the table as her hand held up her head. She forked an ogre skin and slid it into her mouth. It squished as she chewed. Ogre skins were the chewiest substance in the underworld. Funny, they weren't impossible to eat.

Derek faced her. "You should be grateful that I allowed that thing beside you to remain in the castle. I can have him killed." He sipped his red wine.

Diamond leaned to Nao. "You are no thing, little Nao. You're a demon and Derek knows it."

She knew full well Derek was talking about Lord Kouta. Nao slid his index finger from below his eye to down his cheek, acting it as a tear. For such a movement, Riku would have slapped him upside the head. However, one, the action would piss off Diamond. And, two, he would have to stretch past a chair in order to do so. That was too much effort.

There was only one empty chair at this entire table. Derek had said this was everyone. Too many seats maybe.

"Is there someone missing?" Chikara asked after sipping her red wine. She and Riku must have been thinking the same thing, or the random chair was just something they couldn't ignore.

Derek sighed, trying to calm from Diamond's little game. "No, this is everyone. The chair is just there." He snapped his fingers. "Ladies, please remove the chair."

"Lazy as always, huh, Derek," a seductive voice sang, causing everyone, even Derek, to freeze. Heels clicked around the corner. These steps were leisurely; nothing like the heels of Derek's house cleaners.

The steps approached. One click, then two. All forks and foods dropped to their plates. Finally, the owner of those heels entered the room. Jaws dropped.

Oh no . . . oh no. This was not good. Why was she here? How many unexpected people were going to arrive in Riku's life?

The tall woman's eyes scanned the area. Her verdant apple red lips pulled back into a grin. "Miss me that much, did you?"

Riku's eyes closed in ecstasy. That voice. That slurred and seductive voice. Riku only knew of one woman with such delicious vocal cords.

"Casella," Derek groaned. He slouched in his chair, surrendering to the events of this night.

The golden-eyed, short strawberry-haired woman moved her black jeaned hips to her left, bringing all of her weight over there. Her matching gloved hands gripped her hips. "Derek," she said, looking at him with her continual smirk.

Casella was a work of deadly art. She had hair that gleamed pink in the sunlight, the creamiest skin, wide hips, tight and thick thighs, and a slender frame. However, she was only slender with clothing on. Behind that was a built woman with muscle at every place you looked. Riku had only seen Casella in her underwear and that was once when she was jogging on the beach.

Thank goodness, he wasn't sleepy that night because he saw her without clothes hiding her skin. She had worn a sports bra and short shorts. He had never seen her like that again. She was every man's wet dream. Except for Derek, of course.

It would definitely be weird if you had wet dreams about your older half-sister.

"What are you doing here?" Diamond turned in her chair and looked with amusement. Riku should have known the two knew each other, and were actually acquaintances.

Casella's knee high black boots clicked as she took two steps to Diamond's chair and patted her hands on Diamond's gray shirted shoulders. "I heard Kouta was up here so I figured I'd come visit too."

"You're always following me. Can't I have a break?"

"You should know better than to ask me stupid questions," She spoke to Kouta and patted Diamond's shoulders. "I should have known you'd come to visit your little friend. You two are so inseparable."

"Please leave," Derek shot to a stand, shocking everyone, including Riku. Casella hadn't reacted at all.

Her visit must have drastically affected him if Derek was lowering himself to such a low level. The Demon Docks leader never said, *'Please.'*

"You certainly know better than to command me to do anything," Casella stood to her full height-six foot five, by the way. Challenging her was like challenging Diamond. Casella might have even been worse than Diamond.

Nah, he thought next. There was nothing scarier than coming into contact with a woman who could blow you up with only a thought.

"I'm not commanding anything. I just insist that you leave."

"I insist that you stay," Bonnie pointed with the upmost respect.

"I second this," Adriane said.

Aiko nodded, "Ditto."

"How about you, little fella? Should I stay?"

All eyes turned to Nao. He was too busy looking at Casella to notice everyone's, even Derek's, death glares. "Most definitely," he responded.

Derek's nails, scratch that, claws, pierced the table, cracking the glass around his, Lavida's and Mayu's areas. The ladies picked up their plates, not wanting their food ruined.

Casella ruffled Nao's head.

When did he get so popular?

"I'll make myself at home then. Thanks Derek." Casella turned on her heel and exited. She clicked and clocked as she moved from one location to the other with a leisurely stride.

Silence engulfed. The thickened aura was getting hard again. Riku inhaled deeply. Derek's head lowered, lowered, contemplating something. He was too terrified to find out what. Riku had never seen Derek explode. He hoped he would never have to see it.

Not even Lavida was calming him down. She wasn't even attempting. She was too busy eating her pork chops. What the hell?

"So," Diamond said, all innocence, yet again. "I guess dinner's over huh." She grinned sweetly as she crossed one jeaned leg over the other.

Derek raised his head, eyes shining red. He growled.

Dinner was definitely over.

※

Most people would have thought this was weird. To Kenta, he didn't care. He couldn't help himself. He couldn't bring himself to care. His current interest slept soundly in her azure sheeted bed. A white hair band held her black hair together. She inhaled slowly and exhaled dreamily. He was no stalker when she slept, but she was a beautiful sleeper.

Kenta leaned against the wall beside Mary's bed. She faced him; eyes closed, both hands placed beside her head with curled fingers, and a blanket covered chest that moved up and down from time to time.

Because Spirit Beings couldn't sleep, he was wide awake, protecting the Kagami twins. He entered the house after smelling the fresh scent of upcoming rain, witnessing approaching storm clouds and even feeling cool raindrops on his nose and forehead. That had been at least hours ago.

Now it was a downpour. Streams of rain slid outside the window and pattered on the roof. Only that and Sazuma's light snores sounded through the room. Overall, the night was peaceful. It was a night Kenta had come to like. Protecting these girls was an easy job, if they were asleep. During the daylight hours was a completely different story. There was the chasing, the warning, and the demands to run during enemy attack. The scuffle at Lune Park had taught them the randomness of demonic attack. It had also caused Kenta's heart to pulse into overdrive. If he were human, he would have died of a heart attack, for sure.

Leaving the girls to rescue Reiko had also been difficult. He knew the ladies would be fine with Ayano watching over them; however, the need to stay with them and protect with his hands and watch them with his own eyes grew stronger with every step away from them.

The emotion that struck Kenta the most during today was his guilt. When finally finding Reiko, Jezebel had released her wrists from their bondage, allowing her to move. The moment she did, she went straight into Kenta's hold, letting out tears that she refused to fall. She released everything then and there, overflowing with gratefulness.

Kenta had hated himself immediately. She was a victim. He could have prevented it. She'd been stolen from him and he hadn't made it in time to bring her home before any demon touched her. But, no. He'd been too late. Her neck was punctured and her blood had been spilled.

Guilt ate him good. He didn't deserve to be called a Spirit Being. He didn't deserve the honor of meeting his girls . . . he didn't deserve Mary's worry.

He sighed, eyes peering to the sleeping Kagami with tenderness. She was such a sweetheart. He'd even called her that when she'd been shot. The Docks would pay for every bullet they shot and every weapon they threw, by the way. After dropping off Reiko at Yumiko's house-which shocked the twelve year old so much she literally jumped from her living room couch when he teleported right in front of the TV screen, he had gone to the Kagami house,

finding a cheerful Aurora going through Sazuma's closet.

He had teleported near the window. Sazuma had been listening to her music, her headphones blasting rock metal through her ears. She hadn't noticed a thing as she played with her violet bangs. Aurora noticed though. She looked around the corner with a smile. "Well, hi."

He searched the room, immediately knowing who was missing. "Where's Mary?"

"Valla Park with Ayano. She refused to leave without knowing you got back safe."

Back then, Kenta thought it was smarter to travel home, but he saw her reasoning right away. "Alright, I'll be back."

Aurora waved then shouted at Sazuma to pull out the earplugs. She complied with a roll of her eyes just as Kenta teleported to the park. His energy was wearing thin. Trees surrounded him. The sound of rushing water and voices pooled his ears. He must have barely missed his destination.

With several steps, Kenta made it to the Valla Park entrance, an arch of trees with moist dirt as the pathway. The female voices guided him. It was Ayano and Mary. He grinned, unable to wait to see his Darkness and Water princesses but he paused just as he opened his mouth to speak. He hid behind the trees, hiding his presence in the already ominous area.

He leaned in, listened in. This might have been eavesdropping, but the conversation they had made these actions necessary.

"He's lived many years. He must have had many girlfriends," Mary was saying. She sounded curious. But for who? For Damon? Irritation had boiled his blood. Why was she curious about Damon's love life?

Unexpectedly, it wasn't Damon she wanted to know about. It was him. She wanted to know about Kenta. He would have been happy about that except the conversation had continued with Ayano saying, "Not many." That's how he knew the conversation was about him and his love life.

Had Ayano told Mary about Hiroko; his love from the past? It was a love Kenta held deep and admitted to no one. Of course, Ayano knew about it. Only Saki probably knew about it. That was it. If Mary found out, Kenta wouldn't mind. Eventually, Mary and the others would find out about her. When? Now, that was the real question.

"Why did he end the relationships?" Mary asked. Kenta gulped.

He exhaled a breath he didn't realize he held when Ayano said, "You're going to have to ask him."

He figured then and there was the perfect time to make his appearance. He brought himself out, grin in place with looking eyes. The girls had been on the ground chatting. Mary was the first to notice him. Kenta could pretty much feel *her* happiness build up as she stood and made her way to him. His arms wrapped around her so perfectly. Her jasmine and moon flower scent struck his nose deliciously. Kenta inhaled deeper, receiving and loving more of her.

After having Reiko kidnapped, he didn't deserve such bliss. He was a Spirit Being who wasn't even powerful enough to rescue an unharmed princess he was told to find and protect. He didn't even deserve to be a Spirit Being, a warrior of the Heavens.

A whisper got his attention, "It's not right to stare."

The strong scent of holly berry drifted into his nose. He didn't even look to see who appeared right beside him. "Where have you been?"

Jezebel made a HeHe, "I was doing my rounds. I checked on everyone before coming here. I also went to Heaven to check on the Mother Angel. She says now that Reiko's safe, she's calm again."

So, Saki had seen his failure too. He should have figured. You could hide nothing from the Mother Angel. "I won't let it happen again." And that was a vow.

"Don't make vows you can't keep," she wagged her finger.

"I know that." Kenta crossed his arms. "How long are you staying?"

Jezebel leaned back with him, parroting his gesture. "I'll be here, there, and everywhere if I want to. I have the authority and power to do that."

As the Element Angel of the wind, of course she could.

"Well as long as you can hear me summon you, then feel free to roam."

She made a Haha, "You couldn't stop me even if you didn't want me to leave."

That was also true. Plus, Kenta wasn't dumb enough to stop Jezebel. One, she was his mentor. Two, she was his friend, so she knew more about Kenta than he knew about himself. And three, he just wasn't that stupid.

"Thanks for coming Jezebel," he said. She had done so much, and arrived so suddenly. Why had she come all of a sudden?

"Damon sent me. I came to assist him. I just happened to run into you in the process," she was filled with glee.

Damon *had* summoned her, hadn't he? He knew Kenta and the others would come for Reiko. He also knew the demons had been at Lune Park and could have helped take care of them like he'd done when Chikara had kidnapped Stella.

Damon was such an ass sometimes—for good reason, Kenta supposed, but didn't seem to care. "Thanks anyway," he said. "I owe you one."

She nodded. Kenta should have expected that too. Jezebel took any appreciation she could get. Not for the good or guts, but for the glory. "You can owe me by doing me one simple favor."

He turned to her, curious, "What's that?"

She smirked, "Admit your feelings to the water girl."

His eyes widened. His cheeks heated. Admit his feelings for Mary? So quickly? It's only been a week since they met. He could never do something like that. It was far too soon.

Jezebel giggled and poked his cheek with her square nail. "You're so cute when you blush." She pulled back and waved, "Bye."

She disappeared, teleporting to Saki knows where. Slowly, Kenta turned back to the sisters. They were still sleep. His eyes lingered to Mary, watching her yet again as she rested so peacefully.

He couldn't confess. He wouldn't.

Story 14

Should have *known* better

A cell phone ringer echoed through the Kagami house. It was an upbeat tone, causing the twins to jump in their beds, scanning the area for the sound. It was Sazuma's phone. It rested on the nightstand in the center of their beds, both releasing the loud ringtone and vibrating to the side.

In a slugged hurry, Sazuma slid to the left side of her bed and reached out, grabbing the phone and sliding it open. She didn't even have a nerve to check the caller ID. "Yeah," she yawned, not even trying to sound refined.

"Hey Sazuma," It was Kenta. Why was he calling now? He was on the roof. He could have come in without having to wake her up completely. There was no way she was going back to sleep after this. "Tell Mary I'll be at Ayano's place for a while. If you plan to leave, inform me before leaving the house."

She glared, not really glaring at anyone. She imagined Kenta standing in front of her, saying the words he wanted her to share with Mary. Sazuma scowled. "You could have called your girlfriend."

"I didn't want to wake her."

He didn't deny Mary was his girlfriend.

She frowned now, gripping the chestnut sheets. Her irritation rose. "Yeah, whatever. I'll let her know. Can I go?"

"As long as you pass the information down, then sure thing."

Sazuma hung up. She dropped her phone onto the bed without a care. Mary brought herself to a sitting position. "Who was it?"

"Your boyfriend," she responded with an agitated grunt. She gave Mary Kenta's message as she plopped her head on her pillow.

Mary nodded. "But just to be safe, I think we should go. There might be an important matter to . . ."

"No!" Sazuma flopped to her right side and hid herself underneath her sheets. There was no way, no flipping way, she was going outside. She didn't have to look out the window to know it was raining. She didn't have to know there would be more rain on the way and that the streets were soaked with raindrops that had continued for hours. "I'm staying here," she grunted.

"Better safe than sorry," she said, hoping Sazuma would change her mind.

She didn't. "You go. Have fun. Get wet." And that was it from her end. Whatever Mary did was completely her decision.

To Sazuma's surprise, Mary leaned back into her bed and turned to her left side. The sisters' backs faced each other. "Not going?" Sazuma asked, pulling the sheets off her body. It was getting hot under there anyway.

"I thought you coming with me would persuade me to leave the bed." She sighed as she cuddled up to her pillow. "But after the long day yesterday, I just can't find myself wanting to leave my bed."

A lot had happened yesterday. There was the training, being shot, Reiko being kidnapped,—and in Mary's case—waiting for the Spirit Beings and single angel to save their friend. Sazuma would have said her life was fun . . . but it wasn't.

It didn't take long for Mary to drift off to sleep. She obviously didn't want to go to Ayano's house. Her apartment was on the other side of town. They couldn't teleport or drive. They didn't even have a bike. Their only option was walking, and Sazuma knew without a doubt she was not walking across town for a meeting Kenta could inform them about later.

Sazuma exhaled, also snuggling to her pillow. She drifted off without a care. Sleep was her only concern.

✥

"Ken-Ken!" Akira shouted with glee as she pounced on Kenta and rubbed her knuckles on his head, ducked right under her arm.

That had been a shock. Akira, his friend for many years, had arrived. It had been a few years since they saw each other. They hadn't even communicated. She was here, in the flesh, gleeful as ever, and rubbing her muscled knuckles on his sensitive head.

"Alright Akira. It's good to see you, too," he pushed out of her tight hold. He stood to his full height, five inches shorter than Akira. Why were all of his female friends tall?

"Thanks for coming," Ayano said, sitting on the couch further from the window. Stella sat on her right side.

"It was necessary," he answered. Under five minutes ago, Kenta had gotten a message from Ayano asking him to come to her apartment for an informational update. Jezebel had visited her last night and Akira had warned her about incoming forces from Hell. This meeting was very necessary.

Jezebel hovered a foot in the air. Both of her knees bent up, her ankles touching her butt. Her arms were outstretched, as if balancing her. Her eyes focused in, acting as her ears as the conversations went on.

"What's new?" He asked, turning to his white haired friend.

Jezebel blinked, signaling she was listening with her ears now. "I think you should ask Ms. Wolf what info she has first."

All eyes went to Akira, standing on Kenta's left.

She crossed her arms and started off saying, "Shit just got real."

Kenta guessed all staid sentences started like that. "How do you mean?"

She turned to him, shrugging her shoulders and nodding her head. "Like I said. Shit just got real. I received a gust of hellfire and demons last night. I thought I was just going nuts or something, but these scents are not wrong. The Demon Docks have heightened their A-game."

The scent of hellfire? Had Hell's gates been opened, releasing more devious demons from the bottomless pit? "What scents did you receive?"

Her navy blues turned away from him. Her lips pressed into a grim line. "The son of Hades."

His eyes widened. Panic swam through his veins as realization sunk in. Ryosuke was here. If he was siding with the Demon Docks, and most likely, he would be, the girls had another thing coming to them. No one could beat Ryosuke . . . no one.

"That's not all," Akira continued, "I got the scent of The Dark Panther, the Vampire Demon Lord and even Mayu the Demon Queen. There are Lucifer's sorcerers here as well along with several high-ranking vampire demons. They're increasing, as if Derek called in some backup."

Kenta pushed his hand through his hair, contemplating what to do. He couldn't panic. Warriors never panicked, especially in battle. He had to think clearly and fluently. The best strategy for this situation swirled somewhere in his mind. He just had to find it.

"Alright," he exhaled, calming himself down from a panic attack, "How long have they been here?"

"Since around nine last night. Ryosuke appeared this morning around three a.m."

Ironic. "What else do you know?"

"Nothing so far," Akira answered.

"That's where I come in," Jezebel smiled. She brought herself to the ground. Her heels clicked as she landed. Her hands went to her hips. "Before leaving for home, I visited Ayano's apartment and Akira told me the whole story. Therefore, I went back to Heaven and asked Saki what she knew about the approaching demons. She said she couldn't report anything. She was too busy assisting her husband with other matters, so I visited one of my fellow angels, Daisuke."

Daisuke; the healing angel. He was also the light Element Angel. As the Light Angel, he had the ability to find anyone around the world, no matter the distance or time. How he managed to find them, Kenta didn't know. However, he had met Daisuke several times during his times in Heaven. He was a rarity, Daisuke was.

"He informed me of the demon's wants and needs," Jezebel went on. "Some are here for pain, others for pleasure."

The basic demon needs, Kenta thought. "Any of them on the move?" If they were, he needed to advance his strategy skills.

"Not so far. I asked Daisuke to keep an eye on their movements. He said he'd informed me if any of them thought to invade."

Ayano sighed. She jabbed her elbows into her knees as she slid her fingers through her thick black hair. "Out of all things to come up, it had to be the worst circumstance."

"There's no way we can win, is there?" Stella asked, rubbing her friend's back up and down. Her expression filled with gloom.

She had every right to worry about their victory. These high classed demons were just as strong as Demon Lords. The princesses, except Ayano, of course, couldn't even handle minions and Foot Soldiers. They didn't have a chance. Moreover, if Kenta was the one saying that, they truly were damned.

Even so, Kenta shook his head. He wouldn't surrender this fight. He hadn't met one of those demons a day of his life. That did not mean he was going to throw in the towel and give the world to the Demon Docks. It was his and the princess' jobs to defend the Earth with their elements.

They were going to do this. They were going to win.

"We have a chance. We will have to fight harder and fight back with everything we have. We will win. You girls might be small and fragile compared to those demons. But, prove to them that they're wrong."

Ayano peered through her fingers. Her large hands hid her face, but Kenta could clearly see spheres of glistening burgundies beyond her skinny fingers.

Kenta turned to Jezebel. "Thanks for the assistance. Keep it up."

She nodded with an ear-to-ear grin.

He then turned to Ayano. "Call if anything else happens. Updates are mandatory."

"You sound as if you're going somewhere," Akira said, placing herself next to Stella on the couch.

It should have been obvious where he was going. Akira apparently hadn't registered the way things worked around here. "I'm going back to the Kagami house," he grinned, unable to wait to arrive back to his lethargic Fire Princess and charming Water Princess. He teleported out of the apartment as Akira opened her mouth to speak.

※

Demonic Ninja Chikara Yamada strapped herself down with weapons ranging from throwing stars to the sword hanging on her right side. Her motions were swift and her eyes darted from one weapon to the other.

She was already annoyed about the little dinner party last night. Today's encounter with Derek's older stepsister had not made her day any better.

After working out in the closest weight room near her corridor-and having all male soldiers stare down her every move-she had exited and made her way to her room. To her expense, Casella had been leaning against the wall, having conductive conversation with Emiko and Nao.

They were grinning, smiling even, and that pissed Chikara off greatly. Emiko had to increase her hostility skills. She did not have time for conversation filled with humor and certainty.

Everyone went around the group, not wanting to encounter the short strawberry-haired woman. Chikara approached anyway, acting with more irritation than anticipated.

They faced her. Emiko and Nao's grins vanished. Their eyes touched the hardwood floor. Good.

Casella turned to her, golden eyes shining bright. "Can we help you?"

Chikara's fists jabbed into her hips. "I want my sister back." Authority was key to confrontations like this. They showed discipline, influence, and fortitude.

Unsurprisingly, she was unaffected. "I want her for a while. You can have her back later."

Before Chikara could stare her down, she would be staring up in this case. Casella was much taller than her, Emiko spoke. Her hands went up in panic and certainty. "It's alright, Ms. Casella. I will go with my sister. We can chat later."

Casella shook her head. The small curls at the edges of her hair swung. "No, no, dear. You're staying with us. Little Ninja can wait her turn with you. Let's go." She pushed on Nao and Emiko's backs, urging them down the hallway.

"Emiko, come." There was no way this little tramp of a sister was going to ignore her.

Emiko turned to Chikara, preparing to follow, but Casella grabbed her shoulder and spun her around. "You're not a dog. You don't have to obey like that." So Emiko went on, turning down the hall, disappearing out of sight.

But that measly encounter wasn't why Chikara was strapping weapons to her body right now. That encounter with Casella had only ignited the irritation spark growing within the lavender-haired princess. What really got to her was the run in with the Takahashi brothers.

Eric and David were a part of a clan of sorcerers—male witches, Chikara liked to call them. They were members of the Takahashi Clan, a clan of thrill seeker witches that claimed the lands of high-ranking families. Their clan hadn't gotten far on the popularity list, though. They were located on the outskirts of Hell, close to where one of the lava valleys was located.

There were rumors saying that the clan had been overrun by rebellious foot soldiers seeking blood and damage. However, there were also rumors that some of the members had survived and concealed themselves in any dimension they could inhabit.

That rumor must have been true because Eric and David were living proof that some members had survived.

At the time, Chikara wished none of the clan members had survived. These people were so irritating.

They had crossed paths on Chikara's room floor. As it turns out, the brothers were going to be occupying the two rooms on either side of Chikara's, which pissed her off even more. They were conducting conversation right in front of her wooden door, arms crossed and heads close, whispering as they spoke.

The hallway was empty so it was easy to hear the lavender-haired ninja make her way to her room. Her stomping feet made her an easy target for peering eyes. Those eyes would include the Takahashi brothers.

She grumbled as she reached for her golden round doorknob, but David stepped in the way. "Move."

"Say please," the youngest brother grinned playfully. He was so naïve. He obviously couldn't read Chikara's "I'm going to kill you" expression.

She glared at him. The thought of using the sweat soaked towel around her neck to strangle him sounded really good right now. "Move," she repeated, knowing next time he would end up strangled.

Eric must have sensed it too, because he pushed his brother aside, creating the path to the doorknob again. She reached out again. Eric stepped in the way this time. His indigo side bangs swung as he stepped to his left.

Her eyes darted to his. He was a few inches taller than she was. He didn't tower her but he was tall enough to make a connote impression. A peculiar scent drifted up her nose. Pomegranates and grapes? Strange combination, surely. "You're being rude."

He was one to talk. "You're standing in my doorway and you have the nerve to tell me I was being rude?"

"Yes," he said, raising his head with a smirk.

Her eyes narrowed. He thought he was better than she was. He thought he was faster, stronger and better than her. He was a fool. He was a damned fool! She's a Demonic Princess. She was born with the ability to travel into the minds of anyone she wished and feed on their feelings. She could sense those emotions and used them against her enemies.

In this case, Chikara could deny Eric of his self-proclaimed authority and feed on his inner misery. Yeah, that plan sounded good. "You think you're better than me."

He shrugged with crossed arms. His button up white T-shirt stretched with his movements. "I never said that."

But you were thinking it. "You are nothing more than a member of a clan who became extinct in one day."

His smirk grew into an amused grin, causing Chikara's already simmering blood to boil. "So are you."

That hurt. Chikara froze. Her chest pinged with pain, as if she was stabbed with a kitchen knife. He was right. She was also a part of a clan that was annihilated in one day. The demonic attack on her family had lasted less than an hour and the entire Yamada clan had been number one of the endangered species list. Only she and Emiko remained. They were the last members of the Ninja family ever.

"Do not bring the Yamada's into this." He was ruining her plans. Instead of damaging his emotions, *he* was damaging *hers*. "You have no right to speak of them."

"The same applies to you. You did not know the Takahashi clan so you do not speak of us. If you have business then you address David and I. If you intend to bring the past into this, then don't. You are stepping on a line that no one should ever cross."

The line of relations. Chikara knew that line very well, and she almost crossed the brothers' line. She should have known better. Too bad she didn't care. Key word: *didn't*.

She scratched her head, wanting this whole event to stop. "Just move." She lowered her head with a shake. She was growing tired of this. Images of the past were returning, no thanks to her.

She thought this was all over. She thought the brothers had had their fun, but she was wrong. David spoke first, "I heard about the battle between you and Damon Sasaki. You got your ass kicked. It's pitiful, actually."

Out of all of the things to discuss, it had to be that. Yes, Chikara remembered it well. Her hands were almost on the water princess, but Damon Sasaki, sometimes called the *Silver-Haired Menace*, had literally appeared out of nowhere and dashed Chikara back, causing her to slam through an entire tree and get stabbed by sticks and thorns.

When Emiko returned after trying to steal one of the princesses, she had said she and Damon had a battle of their own. Blades sparked and growls escaped. In the end, Damon had won, throwing, stabbing, beating, showing no mercy to a mere girl, she might have been a demon, but she was still a girl.

"Don't touch my girls," he had told her before breaking her ribs with one sharp kick and teleporting away.

The Yamada's encounter with the esteemed Spirit Being had been rough and the brothers might have known about the attacks, but they didn't have to know about Emiko. She hoped they didn't know. One Yamada getting her ass kicked was embarrassing enough.

"You know how powerful Damon is," Chikara said with a sigh. She stood tall, not faltering with the brothers' intrigued eyes. "He has over thousands of years of experience. It makes sense to lose the first time. I won't lose again."

"You sure about that?" Eric asked. His right eyebrow rose. "You haven't exactly proved yourself worthy of victory. You can't even beat a simple Spirit Being."

"I could too." She responded like a human, child-disgusting and unforgiveable on her part. She refused to back down.

"Let's have a bet then, Ms. Yamada." Eric leaned his back against the door. "Successfully destroy Kenta Shiroyama and we'll see if you're capable of victory."

She cocked a chuckle, "I have nothing to prove to you."

"Don't prove your skills to us. Prove them to Derek." David leaned in and whispered in her ear. "That's if you can."

"She can't do it." Eric brought himself up and made his way down the hall. "She's a Yamada. She's feeble, superfluous and nothing but a beautiful slave." David followed his brother with a mocking laugh.

That had set Chikara's adrenaline on overdrive. Her blood boiled over. Her teeth gritted together as her breathing became a vicious heave.

Now, her weapons were strapped and her urge to destroy elevated. Her mind kicked in, wondering and strategizing the best place to travel to first. She could search Kenta's location and demand a final battle then and there . . .

Or, she could destroy the girls he so much loved.

Chikara grinned devilishly. Back in Valla Park—was that the name of the place?—before teleporting to the safety of the mansion, she had seen Kenta rush over to the black-haired water princess with as much worry as a new mother had for her newborn babe.

Yes, the Water Princess would be the target. Kenta would watch it all. He would watch as multiple weapons pierce her body. He would watch as her blood eased out of body as easily as a stream entering a river.

It was a good plan, a devious plan, and Chikara loved everything about it. She teleported out, ready for anything. She was going to destroy her enemies for herself, and not because of the brother's claim of her weak state, she hoped.

✥

"How long has she been asleep?"

"Most of the morning. I warn you, this is a sleep she's needed. She's been here, there everywhere and not to mention, she waited for you in Valla Park all those hours while you were at the Docks headquarters. She might have a cold."

"I'll nurse her back to health if that's the case."

"You aren't touching a single hair on her pretty little head."

"If you wanted the honor of taking care of her Sazuma, then you should have said so."

"The honor of taking care of her? Dude you are so cutesy it's sickening."

"I see nothing sickening about nurturing someone back to health."

"Shut up. Just shut up."

Mary's eyes squinted open. Shining gray light blinded her for mere seconds. It cleared, revealing Kenta peering down at her with a beautiful grin. "Good morning, princess."

Her heart skipped a beat in that second. She couldn't fight her own grin. *He called me princess.*

"Gag," Sazuma shot her mouth open, inserting her finger in its direction. Mary rolled her head to her. "That's not lady like, Sazuma."

Sazuma's eyes rolled. "You've known me for sixteen years. You know I don't give a damn." She stood to her five-foot-eight height and pulled down the hem of her shirt, causing it to touch her skinny white belt.

Mary blinked, clearing her vision further. To her surprise, Sazuma was completely dressed. She wore a white shirt with *Pirates of the Caribbean* logos and brown skulls covering most of the white. Black skinny jeans hugged her legs and knee high, gothic boots with white laces covered the jeans below the knee. Her black twin braids hung over her shoulders. Her lips were glossy. She must have slid on some chap stick. "Where are you headed?"

"Out of the house." She threw a twilight colored carrier over her shoulder.

"She's only leaving because I requested she not leave the house."

"You just so happened to ask me not to leave on the day I desperately want to leave." She bent down and double tied her bootlaces. "I've had a week filled with demons, princesses, and other crap I sadly signed up for. All I want is a day of being human. Is that too much to ask?"

"Of course," Kenta pushed his fingers tiredly through his hair. "I told you that Demon High Lords are now in the mix of things and they most likely seek your heads on a silver platter. You really want to have a "Human Day" at the time like this?"

"Yes," Sazuma's arms crossed with determination. Mary would have scolded her for the attitude, but she was too tired to speak. "I'll be fine. I'll even ask Hiroko to accompany me. Will that help Mr. WorryPants feel better?" Sazuma's lip poked out, as if she was showing sympathy for a child that scraped his knee.

"Give me a break. I'm tired too."

"Then sleep."

"Spirit beings don't sleep."

"That sounds like a personal problem."

"Enough," Mary rasped out. Her throat was dry and her body felt like a rock; dull and heavy. She rolled her head to Kenta. His expression gentled with concern. "Kenta, please accompany her to her destination."

"I don't need him coming with me," Sazuma protested. She was ignored.

Kenta bent down. He brought up the covers to Mary's shoulders and pushed a strand of hair behind her ear. He was so tender. As he brushed his fingers against her skin, his warmth seeped through her pores, causing her to lean into him; seeking further warmth.

"I can't leave you. I'll have Damon and Hiroko join her."

"I don't need anyone coming with me," Sazuma shouted, exiting the room door. Kenta never turned away. He only focused on Mary, which caused her cheeks to heat.

"No, no, I'm just going to sleep in. I'll call you if there's anything wrong."

The slam of the front door closing got Kenta's attention. He looked up then turned back to her again. His knuckles slid down her cheek, creating a line of affection. "If you need me for anything, and I mean anything . . ."

"Go," she brought her hand up and pushed his black hair back, revealing more of his maroon headband. "Watch my sister for me."

He hesitated, but he nodded. He teleported a second later, leaving Mary alone with the house. There were no sounds for a while. Her mother must have gone to work. She truly was alone. She was free to roam around the house she knew so fondly. She was free to eat the snacks Sazuma always got to first. She was free to sleep, which had been her reason for staying in the first place.

Sadly, she wasn't tired anymore. Her body remained heavy but her eyes refused to shut and her mind refused to slow to a settling speed.

Her mind wandered. This was an eventful week. It all started on a Monday in September. Mary thought it would be a regular Monday filled with learning, smiles, and homework. She had had that day, but the afternoon was completely not expected.

She had become an Element Princess; a human with extraordinary abilities who assisted the Heavenly Beings in a battle that's raged for hundreds of years. She had heard about Element Princesses in books, websites, and rumors, but never in her wildest dreams did she believe she would become the supernatural being she'd done a research project on in the seventh grade.

However, that wasn't it. The supernatural world existed. There were demons, angels, angelic warriors of the Heavens, dark warlords of the Underworld. She even had proof of this. She met Jezebel, an angel of Heaven. There was the newcomer, Akira, the Wolf Demon. There were demons, such as Chikara, Emiko and those other members of the Demon Docks. In addition, Mary could never forget her memorable Spirit Beings, Kenta, Damon and Aurora.

This was a world that was always there; always had been, always will be. She was grateful to be a part of this world, this battle and this eternal friendship. She couldn't have asked for a better life.

As her mind traveled to the possibilities of a better future, her eyes closed. Rest was approaching. Sleep dawned. It felt good to lean back in the mattress and prepare for another eventful slumber. This was a sleep Mary desperately needed. It was like the events of the entire week ganged on her in a fierce assault, draining Mary's energy like liquid escaping through the drain.

The scent of carnations drifted in a random wind. Mary sniffed, recognizing the smell. It was sweet and feminine, but it was hefty, getting stronger with every passing second. Heavy stomps bounced the room as a frustrated yell sounded.

Mary's eyes shot open. A dagger flew toward her head. Tiredness dropped. Alert and instinct kicked in. She rolled out of bed just as a dagger stabbed her pillow. Lavender-hair blurred in Mary's vision. Her back pushed against a wall as her vision adjusted.

Another cry sounded. This time a small weapon flew through the air. Mary ducked, blocking as the throwing star hit the wall. Now, her vision cleared. Chikara faced her. Her lips pulled back from her lips, revealing daggers for teeth. Her eyes, usually a sharp amethyst, were now bright red, filled with anger and increasing rage. Both hands held dagger and a belt filled with weapons were collected and strapped to her hips. Her face scrunched up, terrifying Mary even further.

"You're mine." Her voice alone forced Mary to jump out of her skin. She wanted out of this room, and she wanted out now.

But how? Chikara blocked the doorway. The window was only an arm stretch away. She could do this. All she needed to do was push it up and she was home free. She knew it wasn't that easy. Chikara had weapons that flew at her faster than the speed of light. One move and Mary might have lost her fingers, or worse, her hand.

"You can't get away from me, child." She put her hand to her belt and pulled out another black metal throwing star. She positioned it between her index and middle fingers, preparing to throw.

Think smart, she thought. One move and she would be hit. How to move, though? Where to go? Those were the things she needed to think about in the short amount of time she had. Chikara would strike again. Mary had to choose her next move or . . .

The throwing star jabbed into her thigh.

How many injuries had she received this week? She lost track at one.

She pressed her lips together and bit on her bottom lip, silencing the sharp pain coursing through her right leg and entering her hips. She exhaled harshly and inhaled painfully. Tears threatened to fall as blood gushed from her wound.

Another came flying, aiming for Mary's left shoulder. She dodged, only to run into another one, this one hitting her right shoulder.

Chikara chuckled devilishly. Mary slid to the floor. She pulled out the star from her shoulder with a grunt and pulled out the one in her thigh with a holler. *Stand up,* she yelled to herself. *Stand up and fight.* She had martial arts skills. She could use them.

The beautiful attacker strolled around the bed, her metal-toed boots clocking as she neared her. She licked her dagger blade. "Someone's going to die today," she sang with a tease.

Mary pushed up, throwing her weight to her hands, trying to stand. It failed. She collapsed, falling on her injured leg. This time, her shouts of pain released. She fought the urge to scream. Her mouth closed as a grunt threatened to break from her lips.

"Oh princess, I'm so sorry you got hurt." Based on her tone, this demon wasn't sorry at all. Her hands slapped on her knees as she peered down at Mary. The tired Kagami fought on, trying to fight her pain and stand bravely. She had to defend herself. There were no excuses.

Chikara *tsk*ed. "Pathetic, truly pathetic." Chikara kicked. Her toed-boot met Mary's delicate ribs. She was thrown back, slamming into the wall. Her breath rushed out in a violent wave. Her mind dazed. Dizziness came. Stars cleared her vision along with spots of darkness.

There was no point in trying to move now. Whatever energy Mary had left was gone.

Chikara grabbed her sky blue, spaghetti strapped nightshirt, stretching the material as she brought the weakening Mary. Streams of blood came down, staining Mary's clothes. Chikara licked her lips, loving the very sight of her falling enemy. "I would give anything to see Kenta watch you die."

This was about Kenta? She wasn't here to end her enemy once and for all?

"It's a shame," she pouted. She smiled a second later, "I guess watching him find you dead would be even better."

Shock coursed through Mary's veins. Fear joined in the mix as Chikara grabbed Mary's neck and pinned her to the wall. Her blood spattered as her injuries ripped further. Her body cried for her to stop the abuse. Her blood screamed in disapproval as it forcefully slid down her body. Her eyes threatened to close, allowing Chikara to do anything she wished.

She didn't falter. Her eyes didn't close. She brought her hand to her enemy's wrist, squeezing tight. With strength she didn't know she possessed, Mary brought her knee up, making contact with Chikara's stomach. She doubled over but her grip on Mary's neck only tightened. She choked on dry air. Her face heated. Energy was seeping . . . seeping further.

"Damn human," she gritted. She brought up the black hilted dagger in her left hand, gripping the hilt as if her life depended on it. Mary's eyes narrowed on it, preparing for a move—any move.

Call Kenta! her thoughts cried.

Time slowed. Her pain faded. Her thought process remained the same. Even Chikara's actions slowed. Her arm was falling back in a striking position that would have arrived at quick speeds if this time hadn't slowed.

Call him. Call Kenta, Mary. Please!

If you need me for anything and I mean anything . . . He had said such words moments ago. Not that much time had passed and already she was on the verge of death. Time flied when you were dying, huh.

Mary please, her thoughts whimpered and shouted with fear. *Kenta can save you. He's done so before. Let him save you again. Call him!*

He had saved her. He'd always been there for her. In this short week, he had done more than her father ever had. He had done more than anyone ever had. Sazuma had saved her from perverts at school, but nothing compared to the protection and reassurance Kenta gave.

He was a black-haired angelic warrior.

He was Mary's warrior.

Call him. Her mind whimpered. Chikara's hand was coming forward, aiming somewhere near Mary's neck. It was the final blow, she knew. Nevertheless, should she call Kenta? Would she stoop so low as to shout out the name of someone she knew would save her?

Yes, she sure would.

Time sped back up. Chikara's dagger came flying down.

Mary's tears broke out as she inhaled, grabbed whatever air she could and screamed to the top of her lungs. "Kenta!"

In that moment, a growl sounded. Chikara flew back. Her dagger dropped as she landed smack down on the floor. Mary's vision fogged again. A figure darted to Chikara with a vicious snarl. Lavender hair flew, signaling Chikara had stood to her feet. The sound of clashing swords sounded. But another figure blocked Mary from seeing the fighting.

"Mary. Mary!"

Whose voice was that? Mary couldn't decipher it.

"Mary, come on. Say something." Her head swung back and forth, as if someone grabbed her cheeks and shook her head. "Speak to me. Come on!"

The figure had black hair. Were those braids on her shoulders? There was a white shirt too. Heat radiated onto Mary's cheek.

Braids . . . white shirt . . . heat. "Sa-Sazuma?" She gorged out. Her mouth tasted tangy and metallic.

"I'm going to help you, okay. Just hang on."

Something wet touched her cheeks and landed on her hands. The contact brought welts to her skin. Usually, she would have thrown her hand in pain, but this time, she did nothing. "Don't . . . don't cry."

"Shh. Don't say anything. Big sis is right here." More tears dropped. More welts formed.

An agonized yell sounded. A blade pushed through flesh. The scent of blood filled the air. Sazuma was no longer the blocker. She witnessed everything, or at least everything she could see. Lavender hair swung back as a head flew back. A crimson blade pulled out from the lavender-haired woman's stomach. As the stabber prepared for another strike, she teleported away, retreating with her injury.

"Kenta," Sazuma wept.

The large figure came forward. The swerved crimson blade was forgotten. The scent was sandalwood rushed into Mary's nose. She grinned. This was Kenta. He was here, with her now.

Moments with him would always be like this, huh? Either she was injured or they were stuck together, saying nothing. Pretty sad relationship. *What relationship?*

"Hold on, sweetheart. I've got you." The next thing she knew, Mary was lifted up; one arm was under her knees while the other grasped her shoulder. A whoosh of air startled her as one fogged location changed to another. She wasn't in her bedroom, she realized. This location exposed nothing but white with beige furniture.

The scent of lemons drifted, calming Mary down just a bit.

"Yumiko," Kenta said, louder than he probably wanted. His voice boomed in her ears, louder than she expected it to be. The anxiety and downright panic in his voice heated Mary's cheeks. He was concerned for her. Hiding her grin was pointless.

"Oh, dear lord. What happened?"

"Chikara . . . attack . . . please help her." She was placed on a sofa cushion; a sofa, she knew. She blinked several times, trying to clear her vision. It was useless. She was losing consciousness. The dark spots that dotted her vision were expanding. Her temperature was decreasing and her breathing slowed.

Was this what death felt like? She hoped not. She couldn't die now. She should slap herself for even thinking of that idea. There was no way she was dying now. This was just a loss of energy and blood. She would wake up from this . . . wouldn't she?

Warmth enveloped around her entire body. Auburn light cascaded over her eyes. Slowly, her fogginess cleared into the vision she once had, vivid and firm. She blinked. This wasn't a lie. Her vision truly had cleared. Her attention focused on the auburn shape hovering over her. It was wobbling, similar to jello. It was unsteady, as if with a single touch, it would collapse. Without a doubt, this shape had given her the warmth she craved. But how?

Her head rolled to her left side. Yumiko and Kenta stood side by side. Yumiko's hands hovered over the shape. A single drop of sweat slid down her temple and disappeared in the shadows of her neck. Mary looked around the best way she could. She was on Yumiko's long couch, encased on a wobbling rectangle.

Mary had forgotten the Light Princess had the ability to heal. Thank goodness, too. Having a healer in the group saved their lives immensely.

Her attention went back to the two people standing next to her. "Don't worry," Yumiko said, desperately maintaining her powers. Her focus was tough, "You're going to be fine."

"Thanks," Mary said. Her voice never sounded so clearer. She worked wonders, little Yumiko.

Mary brought her eyes to Kenta. Onyx locked with burgundy. His lips pressed into a thin line. His face was taut and strained, as if he was fighting back his inner self. "Yumiko," he rasped. He sounded as if he was fighting tears. His tone deepened. His eyes squeezed shut. Looking at him like this broke Mary's delicate heart. She found tears of her own, tears for him. "Can you sense the exact areas she'd been hit?"

The tense girl nodded. Her focus remained on Mary's aid.

"Tell me everywhere she's been hit."

Every single detail? Why? She was fine. Yumiko was healing her. She turned at her leg and saw her thigh injury healed. Her shoulder no longer throbbed. Her breath returned to normal. Her vision cleared to levels Mary never even imagined she would see in. Why would he care about . . . ?

Realization dawned. He was going to give Chikara the same treatment she gave Mary.

"Kenta, I'm fine," she sat up, feeling the slightest twinge of pain in her ribs. She forgot she had been kicked. That was ignored. "You don't have to know my exact injuries."

"Yumiko," Kenta said again with such demand the youngest member of the Element Princess team was too afraid not to answer.

"There were two stab wounds, one to her shoulder and the other to her thigh. Her shoulder veins were scraped; one was cut, causing massive bleeding. She should recover after a few more minutes of . . ."

"What about her ribs?"

Yumiko's body stiffened. Mary's did as well. He knew about her broken ribs. He wanted to hear the words, she knew. He wanted to hear everything that happened to her. Maybe he even wanted Mary to hear, so she knew why he was going after the demon Ninja.

"Her ribs were broken," Yumiko strained to say.

Kenta gritted his teeth, "How many."

She gulped hard. "Three."

Kenta eyes opened, revealing fierce burgundies she'd never seen. She shot up, arms outstretched, hoping to grab onto Kenta before he made any movements. Mary zoomed by Yumiko's healing barrier, ignoring the startled child and her sore ribs.

She reached him, grabbing his short-sleeved black shirt and stood in shaking legs. "Kenta, don't."

He didn't pretend to misinterpret. "I must."

"You mustn't." She shook his shirt. He didn't move at all. "Listen to me. Do not do something you will regret later. Don't attack Chikara, please." "She's hurt you too many times. She has to pay."

"The injury you inflicted on her was enough."

"That's never enough. Any injury inflicted on you leads to the causer's demise." His words were sharp. His rising anger intensified. She had to calm him down. Somehow, she had to calm him before he teleported to his death.

Not knowing what else to do, Mary pushed herself up, gripped Kenta's shoulders and pressed her lips onto his. Would this calm him? She hoped so. At this point, she needed to do something. Allowing his anger to rise would bring harm to both teams in this fight.

To her amazement, he calmed. His stiffness faded, she could sense it. His shoulders, once squared with determination, now slouched down. Mary brought herself back down to her feet. She wrapped her arms around him, giving him the love and tenderness he gave her every time they embraced.

"I'm right here Kenta. I'm safe. I'm alive." She squeezed him tighter. "Don't leave."

He answered her by embracing her back, pulling her closer. She hid in the hollow of his neck, receiving more of his addictive scent. "I'm not going anywhere."

That was sure a blessing on Mary's part. He was ready to teleport to the Demon Docks castle and give Chikara more damage than he already gifted her. What he was not thinking about was the sheer fact that his assault would have ended in an ambush and he would have died in that hellhole. If this kiss hadn't calmed Kenta down, Mary knew there would have been no hope to stopping him.

A strict cough sounded, getting their attention. A woman stood at Yumiko's closed front door. Her apple red leather boots tapped impatiently. Her fists clutched her hips. Her supple glossy pink lips puffed out as her eyes of ruby stared them down. Violet hair hung high in a ponytail. A short dressed nun outfit covered her creamy skin.

Jezebel stood on the woman's left side. Her hands held behind her back as she moved her shoulders nervously from side to side. "Heeey," she smiled long, as if anxious.

Kenta's hold on Mary never wavered. Yumiko turned to her front door puzzled. "What is this about?" Kenta asked.

"We have some business to discuss." Jezebel pushed up on her toes and landed back on her heels. She repeated the process. Nervousness was palpable.

"What business?" Yumiko asked, knowing she was in on this too.

The unknown woman's arms crossed, stretching her outfit. She brought her weight to her right side. Attitude radiated from her. "Where's my princess?" She asked, clearly impatient. "I want to see my Fire Princess, now."

Story 15

The *Flame* of equation

"Are you alright?"

"Yeah," Mary answered Hiroko.

After teleporting home, Sazuma grabbed Mary tight, thankful for her return and well-being. Those welcoming times didn't last long, though. Sazuma's angel, Haru, flashed into the bedroom with Jezebel at her side. Haru had spat out profanities while stomping to Sazuma. She grabbed her collar and flashed away, gone so suddenly. It was as if Sazuma had never even been in the room. Where they had gone, Mary wondered.

Jezebel had stayed behind, sitting on the edge of Sazuma's bed.

Kenta and Mary pressed on azure sheets, sitting side by side, attention focused on the angel in the room. Jezebel sighed long and hard, relieved that Haru was out of her care. "So tired."

"Why is she here?" Kenta asked, just as surprised as Mary felt.

"See . . . I didn't see this coming."

"That doesn't explain anything. Why is she here? No one summoned her. Aren't angels supposed to arrive to places where they are summoned?"

"Angels have free will, dear boy. Take me for example. I can travel anywhere."

"But you're special."

"Haru is special too. Don't forget that. She's in the same high level rank as I am."

"Is Haru some kind of special angel?" Mary asked. She had no idea what was going on and the reasoning why Haru arrived wasn't announced as clearly as she would have liked. Was the question even answered?

"Haru is an Element Angel. She controls fire."

"Whoa." Mary couldn't find words to say. She should have known as much. Haru has a beautiful face. Her fashion sense was interesting. Her expression was tempered. The urge to find Sazuma must have been a strong one. Still, she should have known Haru was no ordinary being.

Jezebel nodded with a grin. "Don't be afraid of her though. Haru is made of steel. Her heart is locked away in a solid gold box with a single iron lock. That box is surrounded by stonewalls, surveillance cameras, electric fences, and barbed wire. Around that area are mad-hungry pit bulls, a circular tank filled with man-eating sharks and bloodthirsty wolves, and all of this is trapped within an iceberg made of fire."

That was Haru's heart. An angel's heart was protected that much, or was Haru just that special?

"Why is she here?" Kenta repeated, losing his patience. He still wasn't calm. Mary's kiss had lowered his anger levels. They still were not low enough.

She grabbed his hand, intertwining their fingers. She expected Kenta to pull away, not wanting to touch her in anyway. She was wrong. Kenta had tightened the hold. His focus stayed on Jezebel. He calmed leisurely. Mary grinned, rubbing his knuckles with her thumb.

"I went to Heaven to check on Saki," Jezebel began. Mary reminded herself that Saki was the Mother Angel of Heaven. She nodded, hoping she could understand the rest of her story. "She informed me that high ranking demons were here, yadda, yadda, yadda. I told her I understand, blah, blah, blah, and then she informed me that humans are getting affected. Some of the lower level Demon Docks members were messing with humans. She sent other Spirit Beings to protect the town, all of Japan and other parts of the world."

"What else?" Kenta urged on.

Jezebel continued, "Saki said as long as we can keep things under control then we should be fine. She doesn't want to get involved with this battle. If she ends up leaving the Heavens or possibly killed, then the balance of the world would be affected and we'd pretty much end up screwed."

Kenta nodded. "Saki doesn't need to be involved with this anyway. She'd too delicate to get involved."

"That's what I thought as well." Jezebel leaned back, putting her weight on her hands. "So, I was about to leave and return to you guys for kicks, buuuut I was stopped by Angel GrumpyPants."

"She came here for Sazuma," Mary said.

"Pretty much," Jezebel nodded. "She kept going on about seeing Sazuma freak out the moment Kenta teleported you to Yumiko's house. Sazuma had been on her knees, praying for your safe return. She didn't know what else to do, so she believed praying would work. It did of course," she smiled this time, "and now everything's okay. Haru's mad, though. She says Sazuma was a," she bent her index and middle fingers, quoting her words, "Lame-O" and "A pansy." But, oh well, that's Haru for you."

Mary knew Sazuma only cared. Was it so wrong to care for the safety of someone you loved?

"How long does she plan on staying?" Kenta sound agitated, as if the thought of Haru alone made him upset.

"Not a friend of yours?"

Kenta shook his head. He turned to Mary startled, "No, no, that's not it. Haru and I were close friends, allies in the battlefield even, but her attitudes were... inhospitable."

"Inhospitable, Haru," Jezebel smiled. She swung left and right, loving the movement of the mattress.

After several more minutes of discussing Haru's hostility, Jezebel left the scene, leaving Kenta and Mary alone once again. The moment Jezebel left, Hiroko called, freaked out of her mind. That's where their conversation had started.

Hiroko was informed about Haru's appearance and Sazuma's swift kidnapping by the said angel. Hiroko had understood that, but she was still shocked by the zapped sensation she felt. A bolt of worry coursed through her spine, causing Hiroko to dash from her kitchen to her bedroom for her cell phone and call Mary ASAP.

"I'm fine, really. Yumiko healed me. I'm alright."

"That doesn't make this situation any better," the terrified blonde said. It was rare for Hiroko to expose emotions like distress, anxiety, and even panic. The fact that she allowed Mary to see her concerned side made her smile.

"Kenta's with me, so everything's alright."

That was no mere saying either. Mary laid in bed now. Her back squished her pillows between her and the white arched headboard. Kenta was on the other edge of the bed beside Mary, watching her as she spoke to her friend. His sword leaned against the wall and his boots were off his narrow square nailed feet.

Hiroko breathed into the receiver, trying to calm herself down. "Man I hate these random attacks. There's nothing to accomplish on them." *No kidding,* Mary thought. Hiroko continued, "Do you need me to come over. You know I'll move in if you're scared or anything."

Mary had never had a friend 'move in' here before. However, out of all of her friends, she rather have Yumiko move in. Unlike Yumiko, Hiroko brought unneeded supplies to the locations she traveled, too. She ate what she wanted, explored what she wanted and slept wherever she wanted. She was a single child blessed with wealth. She was also spoiled. Yumiko was a better choice for a move in. The reasons why she was better suited? Mary wasn't going to think about those now.

"No need to move in. I'll be even better if I know you're safe."

Hiroko popped a chuckle. "Safe? Here with Damon? Not a chance. This dude is so irritating its crazy. He thinks he's better than I am, smarter than I am, more powerful than I am . . . the powerful part might be true but I don't want to hear those words coming from him. You have no idea how mad he makes me. Just this morning . . ."

Mary's eyes rolled. Hiroko's complaints and rants went on for over ten minutes. The name 'Damon' had occurred repeatedly. It was almost mentioned in every sentence. Mary had no idea Damon made her so angry.

"Anyway, my mother just pulled into the garage. Give Sazuma my love for me."

"Sure." The girls hung up. She placed her phone on the nightstand.

"I received a telepathic message from Ayano," Kenta informed. Mary turned to him.

"She told me she felt you in danger. She tried to contact me before but she couldn't connect with me. I told her you were alright and Haru grabbed Sazuma. She suggested I stay here with you." He grinned, "I planned on doing that away."

She nodded. He might have grinned, but Mary didn't believe it. He had been in a state of rage just minutes before. He had stabbed an enemy to the point where she had to retreat to regain herself. At this very moment, blood soaked into her floor and stained her wall, leaving memories of a recent battle.

The blood was going to be cleaned up soon, right?

"I should clean the blood for you," he said, as if reading her mind. He hadn't moved though. He hadn't moved an inch. He just stared at her. His eyes locked with hers. Mary's breath caught. She wondered, what was he thinking?

She gulped. *What am I supposed to say?*

"I'm sorry if I always act overprotective," he admitted. His head lowered. His black locks shadowed his eyes. "I guess it's a trait I've gained over the years."

It made sense. With Demon Docks members on the prowl, seeking the lives of those he cared for, being overprotective was comprehensible.

She shook her head. "It's fine. You're kind of like a father to us."

Lies, her mind echoed. Mary was lying to herself. She knew it well. Kenta turned away all together. "I guess I am a father to you guys, huh?" *You are much more than that to me.* "Well," Mary shrugged nervously, as if Kenta could see her, "I wouldn't say 'Father.' You're more like a forever protector who wants nothing but the best for his girls."

He turned back to her, full grin. Her heart skipped a beat. "So, a father, pretty much."

Her head lowered this time. "I guess." She screwed up, she knew she screwed up, and she couldn't think of a way to make this situation less awkward. She was better with smarts, not wording.

Kenta was no father to her. He should have been, but he wasn't. He was more than that. He was a warrior of Heaven who lived lives humans could never handle. He was brave, willing and a true strategist. He was handsome, cunning, charming and his protectiveness made Mary feel special, as if he was only saving her, even though that was far from true. Kenta protected Mary's fellow princesses. She was no one special.

Yet, he hugged her so tenderly. One hand went to the back of her head while the other rested on the curve of her back. He embraced no one else like that. He wasn't even seen embracing anyone else, not even Ayano. Still, Mary wasn't special.

Wait, if she wasn't special, then why had he called her 'sweetheart'? Dawning arose. He gave none of the other girls endearments. He hadn't called Sazuma 'Fire Bearer'. He hadn't named Yumiko 'The Healer' and he hadn't even called Reiko a 'Drama Queen.' None of the other girls had endearments; at least that's what she thought.

She *was* special.

"What are you thinking?" Kenta asked.

Mary escaped her increasingly happy mind. Kenta was watching her curiously. How long had he been watching her?

"Nothing."

"It must be something. You went from a blank look to an excited grin. What's on your mind?"

You. "Our journey so far."

He nodded, "It has been a long one hasn't it. This must have been the longest week of your life."

He was right about that. This had been a long week, but he missed Mary's meaning completely.

"As a group, this week has been troublesome, but that wasn't what I meant. I was thinking about *our* journey so far."

His head tilted up, understanding dawned. "You and I."

With heated cheeks, Mary nodded. "It was just a random thought." She didn't want him thinking she wanted to move to the next step in their relationship. *You already did.*

The kiss at Yumiko's house popped into her mind. Her cheeks heated further. Just one brush of his lips and Mary wanted more. Was it bad that she wanted to wrap her arms around his neck and take more of him?

Do you really consider him as your father now?

No, she did not.

"What about us?"

Mary turned away. Deep breath in, deep breath out. Anxiousness was rising. Be cool. "I was just thinking if you ever gave endearments and kissed other girls." She shut her mouth. That was not supposed to come out. *Real smooth, girl.*

Kenta chuckled, surprising Mary completely. "Yeah, I gave endearments." She turned back to him casually. She had to keep her cool demeanor. Inside, those girls were going down, even if she didn't know them. "I used to call Ayano 'Chubby Cheeks' because she had the chubbiest and roundest cheeks I'd ever seen."

Mary calmed. He only nicknamed Ayano. Good. "Anyone else?"

"I called Akira 'Kira' sometimes just as she calls me 'Ken-Ken.' That is a stupid name by the way," Mary smiled. He knew it was cute. "I call Jezebel 'Jezzy,' even though she hates the name and I call Damon 'The Jackass'." Mary didn't even have to wonder why he called him that.

"Have you ever named anyone 'sweetheart'?" His entertained expression faded, worrying Mary. His bangs casted shadows around his eyes again. "Once or twice. They never caught on."

Never caught on? Mary's mind wandered. He had tried giving other's this endearment and they hadn't worked. There had been others?

"You've named your girlfriends this?"

"Not all of them." He leaned back against the headboard, staring at the white ceiling. "Just one."

Should she ask? Dare she ask? "Which one would that be?" What nerve she had.

"I heard you two talking, you and Ayano."

Confusion misted Mary's mind. It soon cleared, bringing back the memories of her and Ayano at Valla Park. They had discussed Kenta's relationships and why he had ended them. Ayano had told her to ask Kenta about it, not wanting to give away information he might not want her to know.

Mary was glad Ayano hadn't said anything. Hearing this info in Kenta's words made a stronger difference. What surprised her was that he heard everything. He had appeared at the entrance, now that Mary thought about it. He hadn't shown up randomly near the pond like she thought he would. He came from the shadows of the scenery.

All right, he had heard. This should make the conversation easier. "Does it bother you that we discussed you?"

"Not really. You have questions. I do not mind answering them."

He didn't look too bothered by answering. Was he telling the truth or was he forcing himself to speak? Well, if he were willing to answer her questions, she would start this off easy. "How many girlfriends have you had?"

When he answered "Two", Mary was stunned. He was so handsome. Guys with his looks wouldn't waste their time in one place. They would go here and there, seeking the attention of any girl they could grab. Then the term "Human" came to mind. Only humans would do such thoughtless and egocentric things.

What also stunned her wasn't the fact that he had girlfriends at all; he was a young man with good looks. Of course, he had girlfriends, but it was the fact that he had a low amount. Why only two? Did he not focus on romance?

"They must have been beautiful." It was all Mary could say. She didn't want to ask questions that were too personal. That would turn Kenta away and Mary had no intention of him leaving.

"They were gorgeous." He wasn't grinning. He didn't hold pride like most old boyfriends did. Was it a bad break up? "In all honestly, I lost them too quickly."

"Lost them" could mean many things. They could have moved. The parents of the girl might have forced her to leave him; but that was only if his girlfriend was a teenager. By the way . . . "How old were they?"

"Haley was twenty-two and Hiroko was seventeen."

Haley. It was a pretty name. Hiroko, though. Mary wondered again. She knew he wasn't talking about this Hiroko, the present wind princess. So he had . . . "You dated a princess from the past."

He nodded. "The wind princess."

She leaned back as well, eyes directed on him. He hadn't moved. He must have not minded. Pinches poked Mary's chest. She didn't want to stop this conversation. She wanted to continue, to ask more questions, to know more about Kenta's love life. It was none of her business, she knew . . . still. "You don't have to tell me about them if it's too personal."

He shook his head, still not facing her. "Just ask me a question. I'll answer it for you."

So ask questions she had. They discussed Haley, the brown-haired, hazel-eyed, twenty-two year old. Their relationship hadn't been long, lasting a week or two. Their romance hadn't even begun. They had no chance. It was sad to say, but true all the same.

Their talk of Haley did not last long. Their talk of Hiroko caught her attention. Kenta told her about their meeting. He told her how bright Hiroko's smile was, how lovely she looked in the multicolored dresses and skirts she always wore, even in the winter, just like the current Hiroko. He told her how she was the top student of her class, how she was the president of the Science and Psychology club and how she loved to participate in Lacrosse and Soccer matches . . . of course, this was all before she became a princess. Afterward, her school life ended there. Only the Demon Docks and her core classes were her focuses.

He'd even told her about the times they were alone. Their love was secret for a while until Ayano informed him that she knew about their make-out sessions. However, they hadn't spent their time sucking on each other's faces. After school, he would walk her home; not to her doorstep but just down the street, close enough to the house where she could make a safe entrance. He would sneak into her room and play board games, discuss the happenings of the day and even tell stories of their past. During weekends, they even went on silent dates. Kenta would reveal himself to the world for a certain amount of time and travel to the park with her, take her to the bookstore and even go to local fairs and conventions.

All of this happened in the course of four months.

Kenta had also told her about the Nagoya attack. His princesses had died—Ayano the only survivor. Hiroko had been injured but her life was slowing dimming, causing her to experience a steady, agonizing death. Kenta had shown her mercy and took away her orb, ending her completely, allowing her to enter Heaven without a stroke of pain or thought. Every year, on October 1, he would visit Hiroko's grave in Nagoya, giving her and his fallen princesses the respect they deserved.

"There's nothing worse," Mary exhaled sharply. The pokes in her chest turned into stabs. Her throat dried and her eyes stung, signaling tears were arriving. She wanted to console him but he probably had enough of that from Ayano. There was no greater pain than losing the one you loved. No other pain compared.

"It's fine." Based on the harshness of his tone, he was far from fine. Unwanted memories were most likely returning and it was all Mary's fault. Curiosity was an enemy in this case and she hadn't seen it. She should have. Kenta didn't need further pain. He didn't earn it. "Mary, can I ask something."

At this point, anything. "Sure."

"Let me borrow your warmth . . . just for now."

She reached out, grabbing the shirt's material at the shoulders and pulling him down. His head landed restfully on her shoulder. She stroked her fingers through his cotton soft hair in a slow rhythm while sliding her thumb on his knuckles in the same motion with her other hand. "I'll give you my warmth if you let me borrow yours."

He leaned in closer. His sandalwood scent consumed her nose. She leaned her head on his, closed her eyes and continued the motion. "Thank you," he exhaled, slouching his body, giving Mary his weight.

She took it. She took him. And she loved every bit of it.

※

Yet, another failure. He should have expected that from Chikara. The girl was slipping. She used to be swift, stealthy and exposed no mercy to her enemies. Now, she had given more failures than wanted. Chikara never failed anything in the first place. The first slip up should have been a warning to Derek's senses. The second mess up should have been Chikara's end.

Sadly, he couldn't get rid of her. She was one of the Demonic Princesses. She was a vital piece to his army. He couldn't replace her. He wanted to but he couldn't. There were no other Ninjas in the entire underworld and there were no other demons with the ability to use the true emotions of their enemies against them—at least, no one Derek knew of.

It was appalling really. How could a member of the Demon Docks lose to a Spirit Being and his seven teenage girls? Diamond wouldn't have failed. She never failed. Her abilities were straight forward, taking care of business with a single blow. She and Chikara might have been the same species wise, but that and the fact that they were Demonic Princesses was all they had in common. The thought of his cherry blooded, and recently anger stricken-wife, caused him to grin. Diamond would complete any mission. Unlike Chikara, her powers were absolute and single goaled. The power to explode anything with only a thought both inside and outside someone's body as astonishing and it was so rare that no other being had ever seen something so extraordinary.

And, she was his wife. Based on her attitude toward him recently, she didn't like that idea. Alternatively, maybe Derek was paranoid. Kouta Vulturine had arrived, poisoning Diamond's mind. She will soon be cleansed. Derek would make sure of it.

He shook his head. He had other imperative matters to think about. Diamond's attitude would have to wait. Right now, The Docks would have to regroup and create another and more affective strategy.

Chikara was down for the count. She had been stabbed in the stomach. Kenta's swerved sword had pierced through her, hitting and cracking her spine. Her sister Emiko was nurturing her now, giving her sister anything she desired.

Lavida and Destiny isolated themselves in their rooms for reasons Derek didn't know, and actually didn't care. Diamond's location? Derek sniffed. The sea's scent mixed with the hundreds of scents on the island until . . . her scent was detected. Cherry with a mix of . . . vampire. She was with Kouta again. Derek would have been pissed but there had been so many reasons for it that Derek was tired at this point. He would allow her to play with her pet, for now.

His older sister Casella, who had caused him an overwhelming sensation of annoyance and irritation since her arrival at dinner, resided with Nao Nakamura. Their scents collided together in one location. Most likely, Nao was Casella's pet, her personal property. They would play for a while, and soon, Casella would dump him. She always threw away her favorite toys after overusing them.

The Takahashi sorcerers, who were loyal to Derek and his cause long before the clan was attacked by foot soldiers, too resided to themselves, locking themselves away to conduct spells, most likely. They had very bad people skills and trusted no one. However, they loved to tease those with perturbed emotions. The Takahashis were skilled with mental mayhem. Derek appreciated that they were here now.

The Past Angels, Kaito and Jun, conducted their business around the mansion. Jun was probably drawing a mental map of the mansion while Kaito exercised in the workout room. One brother focused on strength while the other focused on location and precision. Smart duo, those brothers.

The winter mint, spearmint and citrus scents of Kouta's three vampire ranks drifted through the air. Their scents mixed with their leader's and Diamond's. He hadn't noticed them before. At least they were together and not prowling around the mansion, strapping bombs for a haphazard invasion . . . he would have to ask Eric to inspect the mansion later.

Derek's back length chocolate brown hair swayed to the left, striking his forehead from time to time. He curled his feet back into the warm sand of his island. And yes, this was his island. He had spent months battling for it and he sure as hell was going to call it 'His Island.'

Personally, he needed a break. After the failures, the holdbacks and the unexpected visits from uninvited guests, Derek had had enough. This was his time for peace. He hadn't had peace in a while. This was his only time to be alone, to leave the troubles behind and take in the gifts of the earth . . . the earth he would soon dominate, of course.

"So what now Derek?" A feminine voice broke Derek's calm. The annoyance didn't return, though. He peered over his white short-sleeved shirt. Mayu stood behind him, so close he could feel her cool breath on his shoulder. How she had cool breath, Derek didn't know. He didn't care. He seemed to be doing that a lot lately.

"Not sure," he answered, "But I don't expect any failures anytime soon."

"The only reason you have failures is because you choose the wrong people for the jobs. You need to use another chess piece."

She was right. Derek had many knights, bishops, and most certainly, pawns. He would send in a knight for this next move. There was no way his queen was getting involved in this.

"Fine," he said. "No moves, as of yet. I want a break."

Mayu nodded. She pressed her body against his back. She must have been wearing a swimming suit because Derek barely felt clothes on her body. There was just enough to cover her chest and lower areas. "A break, you deserve."

Damn right, he deserved one and he would have it too. He allowed Mayu's arms to wrap around him and stroke his shirt-covered abs. This action didn't affect him the slightest. He harbored no feelings for Mayu. She was the mother of his wife. Considering being with her was just sick . . . but she was a sexy demon. There was no doubt about that.

Derek sighed. There was so much to think about. A nap sounded nice right now. Naps didn't make you think. Naps cleared your mind. His bed called to him. It was only a small walk away. He could take it. He could nap and rethink his strategy to getting rid of the princesses and their comrades.

Once the angel Haru's presence was detected, Derek knew all odds were off. They had an advantage. Two Element Angels were in this game. There would be no holdbacks-even though there never were. And even now, Ryosuke was in town. He was a player and loved to tease Derek at any chance he got. He might even side with the Element Princesses just to get off Derek's nerves. If that happened, the Docks were screwed. Not goners but, ultimately, screwed.

Derek would win this game. No way were those teenagers and their feeble Spirit Being winning this hundred-year war. There was no way indeed.

Haru was an intimidating woman. Nevertheless, she was a fighter to her core. Sazuma liked that about her.

If you looked beyond the aggravation of her expression and the harshness of her foul language, you could see the supple side of the angel; the fire angel, Sazuma had learned.

Haru had appeared with a mission. She intended to assist Sazuma with her emotional skills. "I'm ashamed to call you my Element Princess," she had said, just as they teleported to Lune Park, a good distance away from town. The evenly trimmed grass shined as the rain poured down, watering the amount it truly needed.

Sazuma's clothes soaked in less than a minute. Her eyes went to Haru, who stood in front of her with narrowed eyes. "You think you're strong? You think you can handle the Demon Docks?" Sazuma knew she couldn't handle those demons. She could barely comprehend that her sister was in danger.

A zap had traveled through Sazuma's spine. It was a familiar zap yet she had not been able to tell what it was. It was no cold chill. It was no random spaz attack. Worry flowed through her veins, yet, she hadn't known her sister's danger until that zap accelerated, coursing through her spine, to her brain and the rest of her body.

She knew Mary was in danger then and there. There was nothing to hold those thoughts back. Kenta felt it too because he grabbed Sazuma's arm and teleported back to the house. They had made it down the street but the house was too far to run. Teleporting was the only solution. Sazuma was thankful Kenta took that route. If they were any later, Mary would have died.

Haru had told Sazuma she'd seen the whole event. She watched as Kenta took her sister into his arms and teleported away. Haru had seen Sazuma drop to her knees and pray to the gods she now respected with every atom of her being.

Haru had also said her actions were deplorable. "Never pray, even in the worst of times."

She was an angel. Wasn't praying encouraged? Sazuma interjected, "I wanted my sister safe." She had to raise her voice. She wanted to make sure Haru heard her words through the heavy rain. "I could do nothing but pray."

The atmosphere around Haru filled with steam. Her clothes and body dried as rain continued to fall on her. Honestly, her radiance grew in that moment. It was amazing how rain could land on her yet she remains dry, as if she had dealt with days of sunshine. "Never pray," she repeated. "You might not have the gift of teleportation and you might not have the gift of advanced speed, but even so, you never pray. You will never again bring yourself to such a shabby level."

Sazuma's head lowered. Her nails dug into the drenched grass and dirt. Streaks of water slid down her cheeks and down the slope of her nose, merging with the streak on her left cheek. "What am I supposed to do then?" She never felt so frail, so vulnerable. She had almost lost her sister. Without her, Sazuma wouldn't be able to function. A sense of loss would befall her; bring her to a state of depression that nothing could solve.

"You find a way to fight back," Haru answered in the most sensitive of voices. Her expression had not changed. She was still narrow eyed, but her expression was one of understanding and modestly. She wanted to assist her, even if it meant doing it in a harsh way.

Maybe that harshness was what Sazuma needed. She was used to the harshness of life. She was used to the threats, the pushes and pains of others. Subtlety was never given, so Sazuma knew no better. Maybe Haru arrived at the perfect time. Maybe Haru could give Sazuma that push she so desperately needed.

"Now stand princess of the flame. It's time to strengthen up."

She swallowed her fears. She shook out her weaknesses. She gulped down her pride, sending readying strength through her body. Haru's head rose with conceit.

Sazuma rose.

My book name is Jenaia Williams. I grew up in Georgia with my grandmother, my mother, and five dogs. I am on the way to college and plan to graduate high school in May. I love writing, plan to become a Creative Writing major, and I love the Japanese culture. In my free time, I'm writing, doing homework, reading books like *Vampire Academy* by Richelle Mead and *Lords of the Underworld* by Gena Showalter. I always find an opportunity to write and take it willingly.

My upcoming projects are more *Element Princess* books, separate stories with the same Element Princess world and maybe other stories not related to the princesses.